PEOPLE
ARE
TALKING

PEOPLE
ARE
TALKING

A NOVEL

AMANDA EISENBERG

THREE ROOMS PRESS
New York, NY

People Are Talking
A Novel by Amanda Eisenberg

© 2025 by Amanda Eisenberg

ISBN 978-1-953103-59-8 (trade paperback)
ISBN 978-1-953103-60-4 (Epub)
Library of Congress Control Number: xxxxxxxx

TRP-118

Pub Date: April 22, 2025
First Edition

BISAC category code
FIC076000 FICTION / Feminist
FIC044000 FICTION / Women
FIC071000 FICTION / Friendship

COVER AND INTERIOR DESIGN:
KG Design International: www.katgeorges.com

DISTRIBUTED IN THE U.S. AND INTERNATIONALLY BY:
Ingram/Publishers Group West: www.pgw.com

Three Rooms Press
New York, NY
www.threeroomspress.com
info@threeroomspress.com

To my friends: past, present and future.
I burn for you.

PEOPLE
ARE
TALKING

CHAPTER ONE

MAL
THE 101, LOS ANGELES
APRIL 17, 2024 — AFTER

MAL THINKS THERE'S A GHOST IN her stomach.

If she had money, which she doesn't anymore, she'd see a doctor. Instead, she's doing everything she can to cleanse her spirit, her stomach, her soul, and her home, and that involves checking her mailbox—a task she's ignored since her girlfriend moved out.

Amid the stack of eviction notices, debt-consolidation offers, and other junk mail, the crisp white envelope stands out. The black ink, which bears her name incorrectly, swirls across the weighted paper. Mal's first instinct is to set the unopened envelope, a blatant money grab, ablaze. She's not wanted at this wedding, but a check and an RSVP with her regretful absence is surely what they're looking for. She wants to watch the invitation curdle from the flames and turn to ash—a fate she wishes would befall her college memories.

Her stomach gurgles. Ghosts conjuring ghosts. What a concept.

As she heads to a last-minute meeting with her literary agent, the idea continues to haunt Mal. How did Marcus and

Tamar even find her? None of her college friends know where she lives, and she's made sure it's stayed that way. Mal begged Cara to leave her name off the lease, but now that's come back to bite her in the butt. The landlord is well within his rights to evict Mal, even if she *were* paying the rent. Still, the sheer presence of the invitation in her mailbox—it doesn't matter if it's been in there for a few hours or a few weeks—makes her feel as if someone planted a bomb.

The traffic is slower than usual, prompting Mal to slam the car horn while shoveling the last of an In-N-Out cheeseburger into her mouth. She crinkles the wrapper and forcefully throws it at the passenger's seat, but the paper lazily floats to the floor, infuriating her even more than the density of cars, each one costing more than her college education. The wrapper is just another example of how Mal's efforts are always futile, no matter how much energy she throws into her endeavors—or her friendships.

"Can we get a move on?" Mal yells over the music blaring from her car, adding in a few expletives. As if to punish her for using profanity, Chappell Roan cuts out and is replaced with an incoming call.

"Bubela, I can't wait on you all day," Joan's thick Brooklyn accent booms from the speakers of the beat-up Camry. "I'm only in town for so long."

Mal lowers the volume to complain about LA drivers, but her agent cuts her off.

"Listen, we need to submit something by the time Meredith gets back from the Hamptons," Joan says. "I understand inspiration hasn't struck, but I don't want to keep reminding you that they're expecting something. We were supposed to strike when the iron's hot, but now it's gonna be a harder to get another deal as good as your first—"

2

"Joan, I gave them two other book ideas in the past year with sample chapters," Mal reminds her, her tone dripping with frustration. Uncharitable people may call it condescension. "I'm being punished for having a successful breakout."

"Those ideas were half-baked, and you know it." Joan's voice is stern but not unkind. "Don't bullshit me, Mallory. I've been in the business longer than you've been alive."

"If I'm such dead weight, then why don't you drop me?" Mal asks. Joan brings out Mal's inner brat, an honor that once belonged to an ex. His face, with those appraising green eyes, flood her mind in such vivid detail that she can see his features form in the sun's glare. Mal smacks the visor down to block it out.

"Sweetheart, that's what the meeting was about if you could have been here on time," Joan says. "I don't think this is going to work out if you can't meet deadlines. I've been patient because taking you on was a personal favor—"

"It's served you well, though," Mal says, signaling to get off at the nearest exit. She needs a cocktail, and if it's not on her agent's dime—funded largely in part by her own work!—she'll have to make do with Serena.

"You have another novel in you," Joan says. "I'm letting you know what the reality is. When I signed you, I promised I'd tell you the truth, always. I need something—a real something. It could be the first three chapters, but it has to be better than the other attempts."

Joan pauses.

"This is not a threat. I went back and forth on whether to tell you, but I want you to understand the severity of what they're telling me in New York. Meredith has threatened to blacklist you. You won't be able to sell to any publisher beyond the indies if she makes good on her promise. I don't know what you did to piss her off so badly, Mallory. I really don't."

Indignation shoots through Mal's body. She knew this was a possibility when she signed with Meredith, but she thought the accolades, the Hulu adaptation, and the money—God, she made them so much money—would have insulated her from this. She was right to have told them to fuck all the way off, but she isn't willing to lose. Not like this.

"What's my deadline?" Mal musters through a clenched jaw.

"I told you." Joan no longer tries to hide her exasperation. "End of summer. Labor Day."

"You want a whole book by then," Mal says flatly. It's not a question.

"I'll check back next month," Joan says. "I have the utmost faith in you."

The music seamlessly resumes after Joan hangs up, but Mal jabs at the power button. She hasn't been writing much, or sleeping, for that matter. Whenever she gets into bed, regardless of if she's done yoga or listened to some meditation the Alfred barista absolutely swears by, the voices flood her brain. No, not like that.

It's like the villains of her life appear and start arguments with her. Most times, Mal will play out these fights, often iterating on previous imaginations, and escalate them to see how far she can push people in her head. At what point can she make them swear her off for good? Other times, she reenacts the conversations as they were. For those, she knows every line. Sometimes, the sparring goes on for hours, all that pent-up rage free flowing but still contained within her brain. And then Mal will turn her head and see daylight peeking out from behind the blinds.

While the sleep deprivation is bad, her failed attempts at writing are even worse. It's like the second she touches a pen or her notes app, the voices go silent. She just wants to lasso the grievances but finds that they've slipped away. Worse, the retreats are short lived. The voices merely slink back below the surface, ready to terrorize Mal the next time she lets her guard down. So, she drinks, which quiets the voices altogether, to get some semblance of words on the page. Mal doesn't know if she'll be able to pull off another book without the fervor of youth or the joy that once came so easily when writing for pleasure's sake. Worse, maybe his presence fanned her literary flames. In isolation, perhaps she's no one worth knowing.

Mal slumps against the steering wheel as she pulls into the parking lot of a strip mall, sliding into a spot designated for families with young children. Why should the government assume the only aggrieved people are those with kids? She paws at her bag, slouched in the passenger's seat, and extracts the envelope. The effort dislodges her tattered paperback copy of *The Secret History*, a green Juul, and a bevy of unpaid parking tickets.

She ignores the spill and repeatedly flicks at the red seal on the back of the invitation, wondering if it's better to open it before setting it on fire. She glares at her Juul. If she were cooler, she'd have a pack of Marlboro Lights and a lighter, which would allow her to burn the envelope and really be done with it. Mal stuffs the invitation back into her bag and glances at the clock. It's 12:20 p.m., which means it's 3:20 p.m. in New York—almost happy hour.

Mal barely settles into her seat at the Bar That Knew Too Much before Serena plops a freshly made mojito in front of her.

"You're in luck, someone else ordered it before you got here," her best friend says.

"He changed his mind?"

"No, I'm just letting you skip the line," Serena grins. "Bartender's choice. He can wait."

Mal smiles for the first time that day once the fizz hits her tongue.

"You're in a good mood," Serena says.

"I'm really not," Mal replies, and then wonders about all the other folks who are drinking at this hour. She swivels in her chair to eye the crowd and the chintzy decor. A few men meander about, and Serena points out the regulars with a little wave. It's a whopping 180 from where they both started: waitressing at Theo's in Los Feliz. Mal left after her confrontation with Creepy Harrison. Serena, on the other hand, endured his harassment for much longer—until she couldn't. Still, there are some redeemable qualities to this trashy tiki bar: One, Mal drinks for free, and two, it is notably un-Hollywood. No one who is anyone would be caught dead here.

The Bar That Knew Too Much has become the unofficial headquarters for Mal's other area of expertise: revenge. She knows that makes her sound like a daytime soap villain, but it's where they strategized against Creepy Harrison—though Serena decided not to go through with it. Mal's also brainstormed acts of revenge against a variety of people, from those in her professional sphere to her own family, who may have wronged her on any given day. Joan's warning rings in Mal's ears—often, her enemies started out as friends—as she slurps the last of her drink and fills Serena in.

"She's not going to drop you," Serena says before turning her attention to a customer approaching the bar. His overgrown mullet doesn't hide his gaze, which is lingering on Serena's low-cut tank top, even as he orders.

"Blue Moon? You got it," she tells the guy, smiling brightly.

Turning to Mal: "Didn't Hulu tell you to pitch them with your next idea?"

Mal glares at Mullet Man until he sheepishly puts cash down and stalks back to his table, beer in hand. She toggles between the belief that *Variety* or another magazine would send a putz like him to trail her and publish her drunken musings, and that no one cared enough about her to do that in the first place. His haircut doesn't seem hip enough for a journalist, anyway.

"Maybe I'm a one-hit wonder, bound to live off my novel until the day I die," Mal says, banging the empty cup on the bar. Serena swipes it and starts on Mal's second drink.

"You're not a one-hit wonder," Serena assures her, muddling fresh mint. "You've got at least one more book in you. Two, if you're lucky."

"What about three?"

"Slow down, you're not Sally Rooney."

"This is why I keep you around," Mal says. "To keep my ego in check."

Serena swipes the cash from the bar and counts it, making a face to indicate that his tip wasn't worth the ogling.

"You say that now, but I know you'll get your revenge by casting me as the aging mother in your next TV show." Serena puckers her lips as Mal takes a swig from her glass.

"Don't do that. You paid good money to stop wrinkles from forming in the first place," Mal reminds her, swatting a hand at Serena's long blonde ponytail. "You'd play a mid-level magazine editor. I would never cast you as a mother. How dare you accuse me of such an unspeakable act of violence?"

"It'll be my best role," she bemoans before killing their bit. "I keep giving myself five years to break in, but nothing is sticking. I'll be a bartender forever at this point."

"You said you were going to be a waitress forever, and look at you now."

Serena wields the soda hose at Mal before spraying seltzer into a draft mug.

"You need to drink three of these before you're served another adult beverage," Serena says, pushing the drink in front of Mal.

"Maybe I'm wrong, you'd be a great TV mother," Mal grumbles as she sips her seltzer. It's not enough to water down the rum, though, which is coursing through her veins in the way she loves. It's like wearing a weighted blanket, but inside your body. She puts down the glass with sudden frustration.

"I hate that Harrison is the reason you work here. You should be running Theo's instead."

"Assuming my acting career doesn't take off," Serena says pointedly, causing Mal to blush. She still says the quiet part aloud, but Serena must know by now it's not going to happen for her. "Still, his family has run Theo's for generations. And even if that weren't the case, there was no one to complain to."

"We could have done a whole #MeToo thing in the trades," Mal says. The memory comes to the surface like bubbles. "You know, I was doing that kind of stuff even before Harvey."

Serena cocks her head and takes a pen from her apron.

"What kind of stuff?" she asks.

Mal wiggles a finger.

"One rum and Coke, please."

"High cost of entry." Serena nods and follows Mal's orders.

It's not long before Mal snatches the well drink from Serena's hands and downs it in three gulps. She picked up a few helpful things from college, but nothing quite like binge drinking.

"I was part of a vigilante group," Mal says, dropping her voice to a whisper. Now, she really hopes Mullet Man isn't a reporter. Serena scribbles on a bar napkin as Mal explains how she was tapped for the Newts, a campus club that uplifted women—or at least purported to.

"And then it...evolved," Mal says, surprised that she can still revel in the drama of it all, "into something more organized. We created a whisper network for predators at our college and tracked them as they entered the 'real world.'"

Mal casts her gaze up at Serena, who is writing big, blocky words onto a napkin, the ink bleeding through. She flips it around for Mal to read.

"It happens every night?" Mal asks. She looks up and gestures for another drink, a request Serena ignores.

"Your next novel. A secret society run by angry feminists? Writes itself," Serena says. "Though I'm pretty surprised you've kept this to yourself for so long. No offense, but I thought I knew everything about you."

Mal pushes herself off the barstool, just the teensiest bit tipsy.

"I try not to think about it too much," she says, though that's not true. Mal's always thinking about the wrongs she could have righted, had she picked better people to help her achieve those goals. "But speaking of, you won't believe what I got today."

Mal extracts the invitation from her bag and smacks it down on the bar top. Serena carefully opens the envelope, an act of kindness on her end. Mal would never describe herself as a coward, but today she needs a little help facing the people she's tried to keep in the past.

"Marcus' wedding? I thought you said no," Serena says, and then hands Mal the thick cardstock. Mal skims the invitation to see that the parents of Tamar Cohen and LeMarcus J. Nelson would be "deeply honored" if she attended.

"How could anyone buy into this patriarchal bullshit?" Mal asks.

"Wait, were any of them in the secret society with you?" Serena asks.

"It was an extracurricular activity," Mal drawls. "But yeah, one of them. We don't talk."

"So you have an opportunity to attend a college reunion—essentially—and all your ex-friends will be there, including one of them from your 'secret society.'" She makes air quotes. "I'm not a writer, but even I know this is gold, Mal. You need to go."

Serena's eyes are wide with sincerity. A rush of affection floods Mal that's so strong she doesn't even bother making a crack about not getting a plus-one. Serena extracts a pen from her apron and hands it over.

"Fill it out," she says, pushing the RSVP card in front of Mal. "I'll mail it out tomorrow."

Mal considers it once more. At least Marcus and Tamar's parents aren't tacky enough to ask ahead of time whether she wants the chicken or the fish. Mal scribbles out her commitment before she can change her mind.

"I don't think it's going to be as fruitful as you think. They're all boring now," Mal says. "Boring and lacking ethics."

Serena starts grinding beans near the espresso machine.

"You're taking a shot before you drive home. Not the fun kind," she adds, but then her expression softens. "You know you don't have to hold yourself to higher standards than everyone else, right? It's okay to be selfish."

"Cara would disagree with your assessment," Mal says. It's easier to blame Cara then consider how she squandered her own personal and professional opportunities. Easier to drink and bemoan a breakup that didn't affect her too much in the first place.

"Well, Cara's opinion doesn't matter anymore," Serena replies. "And I think this will be good for you. You'll get some dirt and closure, which is ideal."

Mal wants to be annoyed, but Serena's right: Talking about the Newts for the first time is giving her that tingly feeling she got writing her first novel. And, if her intrusive thoughts about Andrew Rosen are correct, she's willing to sacrifice her comfort for her art. The thought fortifies her. It'll be a way to win those arguments that have plagued her mind for years, for history to be rewritten by the loser.

For a split second, Mal wonders how they'd feel if she commodified the best four years of their lives. But then, with sobering clarity, she remembers: Her college friends are assholes.

* * *

Back at her apartment and too sober for her liking, Mal crumbles up the third notice from her landlord about unpaid rent. He's resorted to slipping the notices under her door since the mailed notices have done little to get her out. The apartment was barely affordable when she split rent with her girlfriend, and now her savings are decimated from just two months of living alone.

Mal surveys the space she's called home for the past year, assessing a Persian rug from a Moroccan bazaar and art Cara left behind before doing some *Eat, Pray, Love* bullshit throughout Southeast Asia. That, and dumping her.

No one would look at Mal's apartment and assume she's absolutely broke. If the credit card company tries to recoup the money she owes, they'll have to bring in a repo man to pawn off her material objects—which Mal would prefer rather than ask her parents for money. She doesn't want to owe anyone anything—a fact Cara unhelpfully pointed out during one of their many fights as they hurtled toward a breakup. Look where owing somebody got her.

Still, Serena's words ping-pong through her brain.

Mal checks her bank account. Although she's joked about living off her advance, royalties, and the TV money, Mal has burned through it faster than expected. Part of her logic was that she'd make more money with the advance from her second book, despite the overwhelming evidence that her writer's block has become debilitating. And the weight of not writing has gotten so heavy that it feels almost impossible to return to the blank page.

Wells Fargo informs her that she has just enough money to cover the flight and a gift, but maybe only if she flies four different Spirit flights. At least everything else will be covered; there's no easier bet for a free ride than a Jewish woman taking care of her guests.

Mal reasons that if—when, she reminds herself—she sells her book, Mal can also write the trip off her taxes. Research. And she needs to come up with some money to store her belongings in anticipation of her forthcoming eviction. Maybe she should just sell everything, a tabula rasa in the most literal sense. After all, every item in her apartment reminds her of all that she's lost. Her twenties should have borne fruit; instead, the decade left her with hollowed-out shells of what could have been, had she tried harder to get along.

Her gaze flits to the hallway closet, which she treats as a walk-in junk drawer. It's also where she's stashed the time capsule, which has stayed with her since their freshmen year. Almost always true to her word, Mal hasn't opened it, even as she's moved dorms and then cities. At first, the box went untouched out of loyalty, then pain, and finally anger. Now, curiosity overtakes her. It could be a gold mine.

Mal gets onto her knees and nearly dives into her closet to wrestle out the large cardboard box. Dani meticulously wrapped the box and its corresponding lid in Weston-crested wrapping paper, taking great care to make sharp creases and expertly tape the thick paper in place. They planned to open it 10 years after graduation, in 2027, a time when Dani and Peter would be expecting their first child and Mal was a national bestselling author a few times over. How hopeful they had all been.

Grabbing a box cutter, Mal carefully slices the lid off to reveal stacks of documents: letters to each other, CVS envelopes filled with vintage point-and-shoot shots, and other mementos from their college years. Mal finds the letter toward the bottom of the box. Her breath catches as she carefully unfolds the paper, taking in Andrew's small and serious handwriting. It's the letter that changed everything, or at least was the start of what came next. She puts the letter aside, feeling like she just prodded a seemingly healed scab, only to find it still bleeds.

She continues parsing through the artifacts of her college years, the memories no longer bright and shiny, until she finds a photo that was once her iPhone background.

The photo is overexposed. That Labor Day weekend was stunningly hot, and it was the summer that separated the Before from the After. The two girls were on the front lawn of Dani's Hamptons house. Mal still thinks of them as girls back then, even though they had both recently turned 21. Their hair is wet, and Dani wears Peter's Weston sweatshirt, which hangs to her knees like a dress. Mal has on a ratty T-shirt with "Brickwood Lacrosse" emblazoned across the front. The two hold each other close, their faces smashed against each other mid-laugh, squinting in the hot sun.

Mal's cheeks flush with anger as she reflects on their friendship, and all the tiny turns they made to wind up somewhere completely unrecognizable. Sitting alone, surrounded by the artifacts of their youth, Mal decides she's going to prime them like a pump: All their dark, twisted secrets and fuckups are going on the record.

Vindication for Mal, at long last.

CHAPTER TWO

DANI
FLATIRON, NEW YORK CITY
APRIL 25, 2024 — AFTER

IT'S LONG BEEN DARK BY THE time Dani gets home from work, and she knows for certain that she spent every hour of sunlight on the phone talking to people. Her team. Her wedding planner and travel agent. Various advocacy groups and reporters who have her cell phone from when she desperately handed it out. She wanted to be reachable. She wanted to be accessible. She wanted to be their Assembly member.

Now, her phone is a constant source of stress—a vessel of promises that they'll wind up spinning into "lies" if she doesn't deliver. The delineation of true or false drives her mad. Most things fall in the middle, and a strong grasp of that theory can make the difference between a good politician and a great one. For most people, the ease of slipping into a lie probably stems from childhood, when kids fib with abandon. Dani's no different. She remembers a particularly frigid recess during elementary school, when her teachers insisted the kids run around to burn off their energy. Dani approached an aide and insisted that the cold would exacerbate her asthma.

She didn't want to use her inhaler—or God forbid, require a nebulizer—later that night. She had seen her asthmatic cousin use the device a few times—the squishy mask dispensing a sweet, medicinal stream of air for the entirety of two *Spongebob Squarepants* episodes—and her medical knowledge was the secret key. The aide quickly ushered her inside, where she could play her Tamagotchi in the warmth of the unoccupied music room. Dani learned an important lesson early: It didn't matter whether she personally had asthma, but that she found the truth in the lie, and it had prompted people to work in her best interest.

And really, what was the harm in that?

On the 34th floor of a luxury Manhattan high-rise, Dani fumbles with her key as she tries to balance a phone and drycleaning bag in each hand, accompanied by a bulging tote falling down her shoulder. Dani regrets giving Carly, her chief of staff, time off to go on an African safari for her 30th birthday, but the optics would have been terrible if Dani said no. The lights from nearby skyscrapers send long shadows throughout the apartment, illuminating the foyer.

She tosses her keys into the L'Objet catchall by the door. But, before she can flip on the light switch, a shadowy figure catches Dani's eye. It stares her down—eyes gleaming—from the other end of the apartment before barreling toward her. Dani braces for impact and thrusts a palm forward with such force that her dry cleaning swings wildly.

"Don't touch me," she says forcefully, though her legs feel like water wiggles. The charging figure pauses in front of Dani and cocks its head to the side.

Ziti thumps his tail against the tile floor and looks at her expectantly. Dani blows out a sigh of relief that he hasn't jumped on the plastic sheath covering her gown and her fiancé's tuxedo. The eight-month-old goldendoodle tends to tear at anything he can get his little paws on. It's overwhelming on most days, but today it's just too much. A thought interrupts her resentment: At least he understands consent.

The sound of her phone ringing sends Dani's anxiety level from "on edge" to "threat level 5: full-blown meltdown." With Carly out, Dani's been on her own, meaning she needs to pick up her dry cleaning, schedule her next volunteering shift at the domestic violence shelter in her district, and go as far as answering her own phone. Her mom, had she lived long enough to see her take office, would have chastised Dani for not having an executive assistant so she'd never be stuck performing such menial tasks like running errands. The reminder that her parents are dead prompts a tinnitus of sorts that rushes through her head just before she's about to have a panic attack. Ziti watches Dani's hand sink into the pocket of her Veronica Beard trousers and jumps up, ready for a treat, but Dani's too quick. He smacks his snout on the door just after Dani locks herself in the bathroom. With her back against the door, Dani squeezes her eyes shut and tries to modulate her breathing.

Before the call goes to voicemail, Dani fixes a smile on her face. Rule #2: A smile can make you sound pleasant, even when the things you're saying are anything but.

"You caught me just as I nearly got clobbered by my dog," Dani says as she drapes the dry cleaning on the tub's edge and struggles to get comfortable on the bathmat. Her trousers push against her stomach, so she unbuttons her pants for extra relief. Dani silently curses the brand for only going up to a size 16. "I'm surprised you can't hear him scratching at the door."

"Wait until you have kids," Alexia coos, her buttery voice bouncing across the high ceiling from Dani's speakerphone. "I'm lucky if I can take a shower without one of them screaming for me."

Dani considers Alexia's nanny, unseen on her social media but very present everywhere else, and says nothing. An intrusive thought blossoms as she wonders whether her own mother, who had hired three au pairs throughout Dani's childhood, ever spoke to her friends like that. Dani's childhood was punctuated by memories of unmet needs. She had learned to repress those urges, but they've since roared back in the years since the helicopter crash. It often feels like she is holding a vase with wanting overflowing from it, and there's no place to deposit it. No one to whom she can unburden herself.

Dani's eye twitches. She needs to focus on why Alexia is calling her twice in one week but pretending like it's business as usual—as if they didn't speak days earlier about how the tests were progressing for the serum. Dani waits for the silence to settle on the line, a tactic she learned from one journalist at the *Sentinel* who was profoundly good at letting politicians squirm.

"I know it's late, but do you mind if I come over?" Alexia asks. Dani glances at the heirloom Cartier watch on her wrist. Ben is meeting with Hong Kong, so she's confident he won't return to their apartment anytime soon. "I promise it won't be long."

Dani sighs and agrees. She's known Alexia for long enough to know a house visit doesn't involve gossiping or braiding each other's hair, but the thought saddens her. At this point in her life, Alexia is Dani's closest friend, the only person left who's truly a confidante. Yet Dani's wondering whether she should continue hiding in the bathroom until Alexia arrives, unsure how to prepare for the surprise visit.

Frozen with indecision, Dani eventually changes into a matching black pajama set trimmed with feathers and layers on some gold necklaces. The doorbell rings just as Dani reapplies her signature brick red lipstick, sending Ziti into a barking frenzy. She fixes another smile on her face as she leisurely moves to answer the door, like she's never had an unpleasant thought float through her head. Ziti's already forced his way into the hallway and up Alexia's leg. Alexia hands Dani a bottle of Cabernet and scoops Ziti up into her arms. He fans out on his back so Alexia can rub his belly, prompting Dani to roll her eyes and pull out two wine glasses. He's so needy.

They settle into the leather bar stools stationed around the kitchen island while Dani smiles politely, waiting for Alexia to get to it. Her takeout from Carbone is coming in 40 minutes, so Dani wants Alexia out before her veal marsala arrives. To Alexia's credit, she looks nervous as she takes a big gulp of wine and smoothes her blunt bob.

"We have a problem," she blurts out.

"The wine didn't have time to breathe?" Dani mutters.

Alexia eyes her, like she used to when their power dynamic was flipped and Dani was the subordinate one. Though, back then, it wasn't Dani who was the out-of-pocket freshman.

"The Newts are in trouble," Alexia says.

"You came all this way for a check?" Dani asks, angry about wearing makeup past 8 p.m. on a weeknight. This could have been a text message.

"No, our books are very healthy," Alexia says. "It's an existential threat. Gen Z thinks we're out of touch because the bylaws only allow women to join and also because we only track and report men."

"So, we're not woke enough for female college students to join the cause." Dani presses her fingers to her eyelids in a lame attempt to stanch the tension headache that'll surely come on shortly. Her gaze returns to Alexia after a few moments. "Do you have a plan?"

Alexia looks gobsmacked.

"I'm a scientist," she says, shaking her head. "You're the politician representing that generation. You understand them. And you've done it before."

"Done what?"

"Saved the Newts from obsolescence," Alexia says.

The wine tannins suck the moisture from Dani's mouth. She says nothing as Alexia gazes at her with big brown eyes filled with desperation.

"You know how much the Newts mean to me," Alexia starts. "It's my family's legacy. I can't let it fall apart. And I don't think either of us could have imagined back when we were in college what it would've turned into. We can't let the source of our network die with the times. Especially with your next steps and the serum—"

"Let me sleep on it." Dani feels panic rise in her chest. She needs Alexia to leave. She needs to think. Thankfully, Alexia gets the memo and rises.

"Are we still on for Sunday?" Alexia collects her belongings and gives Ziti one last pat.

"Let's skip it. I'll call you between now and next Sunday if anything changes."

Dani narrowly avoids hitting Alexia with the door on the way out before locking herself back in the bathroom to start her breathing exercises for panic attacks. She can't lose the Newts, especially not now. She meticulously planned every meeting and interaction with the Democratic National Committee knowing the Newts could support her. Without it, she's just like all the other no-name Assembly members who will quickly be forgotten when they don't advance their careers. She will not wind up like one of them. She will make her parents proud.

A text message pings on her personal cell phone, interrupting the Calm-app-aided meditation. Dani's annoyed she didn't set her phone on "do not disturb," but is intrigued when Seb's name pops up.

Mal's coming to the wedding!! Gang's officially getting back together.

The words bear into Dani's soul, and for the first time in probably years, excitement—and maybe hope, or is it joy?—ripples through her, and a plan forms in her mind. First, she texts Seb back with a celebratory emoji and suggests the group rent a house in Austin for the weekend—for old time's sake.

Think everyone will be up for it? Dani writes.

Mal will only go if ur paying. That gurl is deadass broke lol. If you want Rosen to show, Peter will need to come. You OK with that?? Seb replies.

No worries to all those things. I can also reserve the chalets for the night of. I think the wedding is in Austin's wine country Dani writes.

Kind of you to call it wine country but go off queen. Im in Seb texts back.

Mal being broke is nothing new, though Dani's a bit disappointed Mal didn't manage that million dollar check properly. The book deal alone cost Dani a lot of promises to Meredith, considering Mal's post-college status as a pariah. At least that'll help Dani get the ball rolling.

Within 10 minutes, Dani's booked a charming rental house in downtown Austin, reserved everyone their own chalet at the wedding venue in Texas Hill Country, and sent an email to her college friend group with the itinerary. Finally, Dani calls Alexia and fills her in on the plan, finding the tenor in her voice that galvanized voters to make Dani's victory one of the biggest upsets last year. She's about to get her life back on track.

CHAPTER THREE

MAL
THE RENTAL IN AUSTIN, TEXAS
MAY 23, 2024 — AFTER

MAL'S KNEE NERVOUSLY BANGS AGAINST THE back of the driver's seat, and it's happened enough times on the short ride from the airport that it'll probably ding her rating. The seatbelt, taut against her clavicle, digs into her skin and seems to tighten as she gets closer to the house. She flips to the bookmarked page of her Moleskine for the umpteenth time as the car turns onto a pretty, tree-lined street. Her handwriting stares back, grounding Mal to her mission. The goals are simple:

1) Get a full account of The Incident from each person present, including what happened during and after, and understand why that person made those decisions.

2) Don't fall back into old habits.

She knows the second one will be harder. Mal uncaps a pen with her teeth and tries to map out her best course of action: goad the boys and buddy up to Dani. Hold her tongue. Let them talk.

As the car slows to a sage green house with a large tree shading the front lawn, a shiver runs up Mal's spine. She's not sure how easily she'll be able to slip on her college skin, or if she'll be successful at all. The voice of her writing professor, Patricia Peterson, rings through her head—a sound she hasn't heard since she was in school.

"It's all about doing the work," Peterson told Mal, Andrew, and Seb on their first day of their four-year writing seminar. "It doesn't magically appear unless you work at it, a little every day, until you run out of time or can't go farther. You'll know when it happens. And remember: It's always a good day to show yourself how far you can go."

Stepping out of the car, Mal slings her duffel bag over her shoulder to face the house. Through the large window she can see people moving around inside, and birds are chirping loudly. They're nearly loud enough to mask the sound of her heartbeat, which pounds more quickly as she walks up the steps. The wooden door is propped open, though the screen door is shut. The plastic door screeches as she enters, following the laughter into the living room.

"Miss Hollywood made it."

Seb rushes toward her, his body cool against her sweaty, airport-reeking clothes, and gives her a tight hug before pulling away and assessing her.

"Your hair looks incredible," he says, pulling on a curl, which bounces back into formation just under her chin. It's the shortest she's ever had it. "It suits you."

Mal releases the breath she's holding and thanks him. Seb always has had the ability to make her relax. Maybe she should have made more of an effort to stay close after they graduated, though Mal felt then he was lucky she even spoke to him at all. No one else deserved that luxury. Plus, it wasn't like she lived in New York and could see him regularly, beyond the few trips she took out there for book publicity and meetings with her agent and publisher. What she didn't want to admit was how much it hurt to see all of them living in New York City together, spending their post-grad years doing the stuff they all talked about, only without Mal—in the city she always wanted to live in. All because she stuck to her morals.

The memory reminds Mal they're traitors, and she reassesses Seb's caring nature. Now she's not sure if it'll be an asset or a liability this weekend.

Mal surveys the pile of luggage in the corner of the living room to determine if she's the last one here. She dumps her bag—an ancient, quilted Vera Bradley that some teen tried to buy off her for $20 at LAX—near Seb's well-worn suitcase from his constant travels and Dani's pristine set. But there's only one backpack where there should be three.

"Who's missing?" Mal asks.

"Peter's on his way, and Rosen's coming tomorrow," Seb says, a flicker of concern shading his eyes.

"We were waiting on you to divvy up the rooms," a voice calls out from the kitchen.

Dani shyly pokes her head out, and Mal is startled by how familiar and foreign Dani is to her. Even from LA, Mal saw the New York political coverage of Dani ousting one of the longest-serving state legislators. Mal can't say how a bill gets passed in the state, but she knows that Dani has been crowned by the toughest press corps in the country as one to watch. Yet, standing in front of her, there's no deep red lipstick or glossy brown hair. Her face looks a little red, like it's been freshly washed, and her hair is held up in an expensive-looking claw clip. Dani looks good, except her face has a strained quality to it, like she's trying extra hard to be peppy.

When Mal locks eyes with Dani, she can see that mask slip off, even if it's just for a split second. Good. Maybe they can finally be real about what happened junior year.

"That was your favorite Hamptons ritual," Dani says.

"Yeah, not where we ate or who drove or where we were going, just whether you could have the room with the seashell wallpaper." Marcus emerges from upstairs and leans on the banister, keeping a safe distance from Mal. He eyes her suspiciously, like a timid kid approaching a prickly dog. One who bites.

"I cared that Rosen didn't drive," Mal offers, her gaze sweeping over the group. She doesn't like how everyone is fanned out around her. She's surrounded.

But the mention of his name seemingly does the trick, snapping them out of their memories and back to the task at hand: sleeping arrangements.

"The listing said there were six beds, but it's really four rooms and a pull-out couch," Dani says. "So, with Marcus here just one night and Rosen staying for the others, that means two people need to share."

"I figured you and Dani could sleep together so the guys could have their own rooms," Marcus shrugs, which forces Mal to bite the inside of her cheek.

It's the most infuriating gesture, a shrug. She would kill to give so little shits about anything, and to be allowed to. Oh, so you were hired as a waitress at $2 less an hour than a waiter at the same restaurant, even though he gets the specials wrong every night? Shrug. Your big-time book review refers to your writing as "chick-lit," even though what's-his-face got a bigger advance, better coverage, and still sold fewer books than you did? Shrug. Shrug, shrug, shrug.

Marcus is still talking.

"You two probably haven't had a sleepover since college," he says.

"Yeah, and for good reason," Mal snaps, picking her duffel bag up from the floor and hiking it over her shoulder like it's her security blanket. "Dani, you're right. I love picking out my room. I'm going to do that right now."

Mal flashes a giant, fuck-you smile to the room and takes the stairs two at a time, brushing past Marcus and trying to tamp down the voices in her head screaming to behave.

She's off to a bad start.

DANI
THE RENTAL IN AUSTIN, TEXAS
MAY 23, 2024 — AFTER

Dani's smile crumbles as Mal nearly sprints up the stairs to get away from her. It's embarrassing that she thought Mal would be a little bit more gracious about the whole thing, especially in front of the boys. Why can't she just smile and fake air kiss and be civil for a weekend? But Dani knows the answer. It's the reason they bonded in the first place, why everyone is here this weekend. Without Mal being Mal, everything would be different.

"Don't let it get to you," Seb says, rubbing her shoulders gently. "She's just cranky, but you know how she is. One hot shower later and she's fine."

Dani's shoulders droop but she puts on a strong face and flashes a smile.

"I would love a sleepover if you're up for it," she says to Seb, who plants a kiss on her forehead.

Dani leans into Seb as he does this, reveling in the tenderness he so easily doles out. And even though he's gay, that small gesture is enough to send tears to her eyes from the sheer intimacy of it—something Ben hasn't given her in a long time. She and Ben often act like business partners, showing up to each other's work functions (often political events and charity galas for her, and end-of-year work parties at his venture fund for him) and playing the part of doting partner—a shiny counterpart who will ultimately reflect well on the other. But then they always get back into the car with their phones in hand and attention spans miles apart. Two parallel train tracks, never to touch. Dani wasn't sure if this was included in her mom's vision of the right kind of the guy, the person who would presumably navigate the world beside her.

"Let's pick the room next to Mal's to mess with her," Seb says.

"Finally, a prank that doesn't involve grand theft or severe mental distress," Dani says, relieved to get out of her funk and the doubts about Ben that rear their ugly heads with every wedding leading up to her own. Ever since the engagement, Ben's parents have needled them to set a date. To his credit, Ben held them off for as long as he could, understanding that Dani didn't want to face walking down the aisle alone—or at least that's the reason she gave him. The truth, again, is much more complicated. But now they're getting antsy, and she can't push her wedding off much longer.

"Why poke the bear?" Marcus groans as he settles onto the couch and props his feet up. "We could be having a lot more fun without her."

"Take it up with your wife," Seb says, grabbing their luggage to take upstairs. The owl tattoo on his bicep flexes from the effort. "Tamar is classy. It was the right thing to do."

"Not that it matters. All the rooms look the same. There's absolutely no character," Dani whines. It didn't occur to her to click through every single photo when she booked the rental, considering Carly does all her planning. "The place looks like it was gutted and redesigned to appeal to tourists. There's not even a key for the house, just a soulless smart lock. It's disappointing to see how these companies have contributed to the gentrification of Austin. That's why I was proud to co-sponsor a bill that bans—"

"Assemblywoman, please," Peter's voice booms from the foyer. "We're off the clock."

29

Peter enters the living room, and Dani's body begins pulsating. The thrum of energy vibrates around them, and she can hear her heartbeat in her ears when they lock eyes. She surveys him: buzzcut (new), bloodshot eyes (old), scratchy beard (old), a rumpled black T-shirt and jeans, scuffed white sneakers (old, old, and old). Her gaze shoots to his left hand; no gold ring on his finger. He seems happy to see her, which is markedly different from the last time they were at her parents' funeral six years ago. The event, and Dani is disgusted that a lot of people in New York would consider it an event, took place in the ornate synagogue in midtown Manhattan where she was bat mitzvahed and her parents had wed 15 years before that. Dani was forced to greet other billionaires and accept their warmest condolences that her entire life had been blown apart by a mechanical error. Even after the pandemic, 2018 was still the worst year of her life.

In the front row of the temple, Dani clamped her eyes shut to stop another wave of tears and the corresponding panic that rose through her chest. Peter took Dani into his burly arms, which bulked up in the one year he had stopped playing college lacrosse. The smell of his cologne—the same one she bought him their freshman year—and the familiar scratch of his beard on her head sent Dani into another round of sobs. Peter's large hand smoothed the back of her blowout as he whispered sweet nothings into her ear. They could barely focus on the ritual because she was overcome with emotion, and he was too focused on tending to her.

At one point in the service, Dani darted out of her seat and moved down the aisle that connected the synagogue's main room to the lobby. She heaved open the heavy wooden doors, and the smell of apple juice overwhelmed her senses. It used to be a comfort, but, under these circumstances, it churned her stomach. Dani barreled toward the bathrooms, cognizant of Peter's footsteps, heavy and sure, behind her. She threw herself in front of the toilet, waiting for sickness to come. Peter's hands clumsily moved through her thick hair and held it up as she dry heaved into the toilet.

"I need some space," Dani managed, and Peter backed out of the stall.

She wiped her mouth and stood up, rummaging in her bag for some Big Red gum and a travel vial of her perfume, Baccarat Rouge 540. She wanted to mask the scent of death and nausea with cinnamon and saffron. Dani felt Peter's eyes on her, but, when she turned to face him, he was at a respectable distance. He leaned against the granite countertop where women normally reapplied their lipstick. She saw her reflection in the mirror, a woman brimming with sexual urgency and grief and the wild look in her eyes, like she was just about to blow up her life.

"You smell good," he said.

The words scratching the back of his throat reminded Dani of the brambles at Weston where they would sometimes sneak away to. Her desire for destruction intensified as she stepped forward, each click of her heels on the tiles a warning to stop. Dani's perfume wasn't dissimilar to his cologne, a swirl of amber, cedar and tobacco mingling like the smell of the ocean air right before a storm hits. The combination was potent and dangerous, like a riptide, and she was about to drag Peter under. Dani stopped just in front of him, electricity closing the physical distance between them. Peter looked at her with a hunger she had never felt the entire time they dated, or even in the weeks before they got together. It was urgent, carnal.

Peter pushed past her, locked the door and stood still, his hand hovering over the brass doorknob. He turned around quickly and charged at Dani, picking her up and placing her on the countertop so they were eye level. Then, he went for her neck. Dani's back arched the moment Peter's teeth dragged upward and onto her ear, his hands grabbing her boobs and waist. She grabbed his face and started kissing him, and Peter pushed her back farther on the countertop so she was prone against the mirror. He pawed at her dress so it pooled at her waist and fumbled to roll down her tights.

"Just rip them off," Dani mumbled, exhilaration coursing through her body. She wanted to be drilled until her brain went numb. Until she felt absolutely nothing, except this, because only she knew what was coming next.

The nylon ripped as Peter yanked them down toward her ankles, and he moved her body closer to the edge so he could go down on her. Dani wrapped her legs around him as Peter confidently navigated around every inch of her vagina, his tongue sending shockwaves through her body. Dani let herself come before she thought about the implications of what she'd done: let her longtime boyfriend, the man she now needed to dump, eat her out in her Hebrew School bathroom during her parents' funeral.

The sound of people exiting the service caused them to jump.

"Are you good?" Dani jutted her chin toward Peter's erection.

"Yeah, yeah, it's fine," Peter said, his hand brushing his pants.

Dani slipped out of her heels to remove her ripped tights and tossed them in the garbage.

"I don't think it's a good idea for you to come back with me." She smoothed her dress down so she could avoid looking at him.

"I can come over after shiva," Peter offered after an awkward pause.

"I need to be alone," Dani said, finally looking up at him. "For a while."

The look on Peter's face broke her. The mix of pain and confusion and anger, all tamped down by his knowing that her needs trumped his own. After all, he still had a family. For Dani, there were no bodies to recover, so there wouldn't be a burial, just a week of shiva at various friends' homes—all of whom knew Dani as a disaster, a problem child, from her time in high school. She wondered if they would smell him on her, if they'd know what she had done. Shame spread through her chest.

"Please," Dani whispered. "I can't do this anymore."

Peter's lips parted, and his cheeks flushed an angry red before saying a bunch of things to her that Dani, to this day, cannot remember. Her memory of that time ends with him staring at her, dumbfounded, before it disappears completely.

Now she's staring at him again, but this time it's in the fading Texas sun. Dani's heart thumps wildly in her chest. Peter looks even more grown up than before, and his gaze is heavy and intense as he takes her in. She basks in his observance. It never occurred to Dani that Peter could still look at her like this, especially after how she treated him. The answers she refused to give him. Peter closes the gap between them and brings her in for a bear hug, lingering so much that she knows the others are watching intently, but she can't find it in herself to let go first. He finally does and swipes a thumb across her cheek.

"Let me get a better look at you," he says, and then lowers his voice just so she can hear him. "I'm so happy you emailed and set this up. This was worth the wait."

He holds her at an arm's length, his hands slowly running down her arms before letting go. She knew Peter would be a wild card going into the weekend, but she didn't account for her own feelings resurfacing, never having disappeared in the first place. Dani goes to twist her engagement ring, a repetitive motion that comforts her, and realizes she never put it back on after the flight. Her hands always swell for at least 24 hours after flying.

"You look exactly the same," he says at a normal volume.

She scoffs but feels gratitude for the mean Russian woman who administers her Botox and her parents for their good genes. Not that it matters. She's not going to pass along any of those genes because Ben does not want kids. Neither does she, but seeing Peter reminds her that she wanted kids, once, with him.

"I mean that as a good thing!" Peter says, mistaking her whirring brain as taking offense.

He touches her back gently before turning to Seb and Marcus to greet them with equal levels of enthusiasm. Maybe she just imagined electricity.

Dani's not sure how long she's been standing awkwardly in the living room until someone grabs her arm. She blinks to stare into Marcus' kind eyes, feeling lightheaded. Everyone has dispersed, so it's just the two of them.

"Hey, are you good?" he asks. "You seem to not be here."

"What do you mean?" Dani asks, though it's futile to lie to Marcus. He was her first real friend at Weston, bonded by their otherness—his early toe-dipping into respectability politics at their very-white school coincided with Dani trying to hide her Israeli name and immense wealth. Marcus could often gauge her temperature on something faster than Dani herself could.

"You know, really in your head. Not present." His dark eyes scan her face. "I need you here this weekend."

"I'm sorry. You're the only one here who knows what's going on with work," Dani says.

"I wish we could spend more time together. It was a battle getting Tamar to agree to it." Marcus cracks a self-deprecating smile. "Who knew weddings were so intense?"

Dani laughs, and Marcus wraps an arm around her shoulder. She's already using this weekend for her own benefit. The least she can do is not hurt her friend.

"Let go of whatever you're holding onto. Please?" Marcus asks. "Everything is gonna work out."

"For the groom? Anything."

MAL

THE RENTAL IN AUSTIN, TEXAS
MAY 23, 2024 — AFTER

ALONE IN HER ROOM, MAL UNPACKS. The dresses for the wedding and the rehearsal dinner go first, followed by three identical white T-shirts, a pair of denim shorts, her nicer underwear (she gave up on bras years ago like a true feminist), an XXL Killers T-shirt to sleep in, a bathing suit, heels, and finally, her toiletries case and two queer romance books (the sight of them lightens her spirits; her college-aged, literary-snob self would be horrified to know that her future self not only loves smut but has also started writing a bit of it). Select time-capsule items she brought remain in her bag, and their presence prompts Mal to zip up the bag and stuff it under the bed for safe-ish keeping. Tamar had the decency to stock the rental with fluffy bath towels and a little note welcoming them to the house for the wedding weekend. There's also, to Mal's disdain, a custom robe embroidered with #GroomGang. Still, she grabs both—eschewing the robe for a towel—and pads down the hallway with her toiletry bag in search of the bathroom. Maybe she can sell the robe online. She sold a lot of her stuff already and loved the rush of not just getting rid of her belongings but also seeing her bank account grow by tens of dollars.

She passes a bedroom with two twin beds and spots Dani and Seb's luggage neatly placed on the floor. The room next to it is empty, and then Mal spies Peter sitting on the bed in the last bedroom. His back is to her, but she can see he's fidgeting with something. It reminds her of how Andrew used to play with a lacrosse ball when he got nervous. Mal doesn't linger. She's still trying to regulate her breathing. She needs to be calm and in control for this weekend to benefit her. She's sick and tired of working against her best interests in favor of her principles.

After a long scrub-down, Mal steps out of the shower and immediately tends to her curly hair, dousing it in leave-in conditioner before wrapping the loose spirals around a brush handle. She takes great care with the process before wiping away the remaining condensation left on the mirror to assess her work. The stress of her financial situation, coupled with this last-ditch effort to salvage her career, has left Mal looking gaunt. Purplish circles hang below her hazel eyes, but, as she leans in to study them, a blood-curdling howl lets out from the living room. Mal throws on the robe and sprints downstairs, looking for the source. Instead, she sees Seb waving an envelope like he's at the club.

"Tyra Mail!" Seb shimmies in the living room, where the boys and Dani are hanging out and already dressed for dinner. She almost expects Andrew to jump out from behind the couch and tackle Peter. It all feels so natural, like they've teleported back to college, except Mal's worried that she's going to have a heart attack from Seb's ungodly scream.

"You scared the shit out of me!" Mal sits on the steps and tries to catch her breath.

"You found the robe! How cute are they?" Dani asks.

Of course, she thinks these cheugy robes are cute.

"Okay, Miss Top Model, what does the note say?" Mal asks, ignoring Dani.

Seb holds the envelope close to his chest, a tear shining from the corner of his eye before running dramatically down his smooth cheek. He should have been an actor instead of working for an evil financial corporation.

"My parents gave up everything to send me to America from a little town in Venezuela," Seb says, like he's Tyra giving her speech before she unveils the photo of the model who gets to stay. Always the drama queen.

"Your dad's an oil baron," Mal heckles.

Seb rolls his eyes—Mal knows he thinks it's gauche for her to point that out—and with gusto he opens the envelope. Pulling the card out, Seb reads aloud:

"As the sun sets over Austin, go to the place where the hunting happens often," Seb says like he's doing the candle lighting ceremony for his bar mitzvah.

"A scavenger hunt!" Dani squeals. "Mal, we read the welcome note while you were upstairs."

She hands over a framed note, which reads: *Welcome to Austin, Texas! We're so excited to have you, and for you to explore this great city. Your quest begins now and will end just ahead of the wedding ceremony, though there may even be a final task the day of ;) Keep an eye out for clues. You won't believe where they lead! See you all at the wedding. XOXO*

"So, where are we going?" Dani asks.

"The bridge," Seb rolls his eyes again, like it's the most obvious answer in the world. "Didn't any of you Google Austin before coming here? The bats hunt for food at sunset."

Dani, Mal, and Peter shrug. Marcus takes a long sip from his beer.

"Does anyone want to take a ride with me to H-E-B?" Marcus asks, gesturing to the car in the driveway. "Gotta pick up the meats." He bugs his eyes wide for effect.

"You rented a car?" Mal scoffs.

"I didn't know if we'd need groceries," Peter says with an aw-shucks quality that's suspicious for someone who once nuked a Chipotle burrito with the tinfoil on and nearly burned down Henley Hall, their freshmen dorm.

Dani touches his arm for just a second longer than normal, and Mal narrows her eyes at the two of them. They can't be back on this bullshit again. Plus, Dani's engaged—or last Mal heard she was. Mal perks up at this potentially juicy tidbit but decides to play her part of the group asshole. She never really liked Marcus and Peter to begin, and neither of them would fight back in front of Dani. Peter in particular might even be willing to gossip with her in exchange for her easing off the harassment.

"If Marcus is grilling, we might as well just get Texas barbeque," Mal groans. She thinks of stuffing her face with a brisket sandwich, and her stomach grumbles on cue. All she ate today were free in-flight snacks. Selling old sweatshirts and chipped coasters isn't enough to cover overpriced sandwiches at LAX. "Unless your cooking skills have improved, I'm not in the mood for overcooked brisket."

"Mal's right. We're in the capital of smoked meats," Dani says.

Mal flashes a quick look of gratitude at Dani, though she's surprised Dani's willing to stick up for her. Maybe talking to her will be easier than she anticipated.

"Bet," Marcus says, flashing a smile at Dani like she's his bride. Gross. He grabs his keys. "We'll get some snacks. Anyone need anything?"

"Um, yeah, I'll go," Peter mumbles.

"What, did you forget condoms?" Mal shoots back.

Peter reddens and Mal cackles, though she sees Dani straighten at the confirmation that Peter's single, or at least not in an exclusive relationship.

"All these years later and you're still a pervert," Mal says, shaking her head. "Actually, I guess you're doing the world a service by not populating the earth with little Peters."

"I forgot toothpaste," Dani interjects, grabbing her bag. "I'll take a ride."

The three of them quickly file out of the house. Mal leans back on the couch, pleased that she still knows how to clear a room, and faces Seb.

"Who does Peter think he's fucking?" Mal asks, propping her chin up with her hand. The robe, albeit cringy, is super comfortable.

"Haven't we dealt with enough fucking in this group?" Seb asks, his face trying to find humor even though his tone falls flat.

"We've never talked about what happened," Mal says. "I've tried so many times—"

"I don't see a point," Seb says sharply. "It's in the past, right?"

"Not when it shades every interaction we'll have this weekend," Mal snaps. "Don't you think it'll help everyone by talking about it?"

Seb narrows his eyes. She can hear him grinding his teeth.

"When have you cared about helping people?" he asks.

Mal's breathing catches. Her reputation wasn't the best, but her friends knew that she would have done anything for them. Or at least she thought so.

"Do you really think I don't care?" she asks, her voice cracking. "I've flown out to celebrate your birthday, promotions—"

"You were in the city for work and you needed someone to spend the time with," Seb says, folding his arms. He looks a little scared to confront her, but his voice is unwavering.

"Where is this coming from? You were just dancing and hugging me like what, an hour ago?" Mal asks. "It never occurred to you to say this to me, I don't know, the countless times we've been together since graduation?"

"We just got coffee or drinks," Seb says.

"And dinner," Mal points out. "You could have said something then."

"I didn't want to ruin the short time we spent together," he relents. "And anyway, you never stick around long enough, so it wasn't worth bringing up."

"So you're just attacking me at first sight? I don't live in New York. That's not fair," Mal says. "How do you think I feel that all of you hang out without me? But I still make time for you when I visit. And I came this weekend, didn't I? Even though you're my only friend here."

Seb sighs.

"Babe, we're not really friends anymore," he says, looking at her with guilt. Or maybe it's pity. It's almost enough to make her leave—almost. "And it's not because I don't want to, but you haven't really reciprocated friendship for years. You only want to hang out on your terms, and you never respond to any of my text messages."

"You know how crazy the book and TV stuff was," Mal defends herself. "And the end of our friend group really messed me up. It was a really difficult time, and I think it's worth talking about. We need to address what really happened."

"This weekend isn't the time to do that." Seb's tone is firm, but then he puts a hand on her knee. "But I'd like to try and be real friends again this weekend."

She's furious that Seb is dangling their friendship—or what she mistook as friendship—like a carrot attached to a stick.

Play nice and get rewarded. Her hand jumps onto his, where it rests for a beat. Mal wants so badly for Seb to understand her, to empathize with her, but she'll take this small gesture. He leans back on the couch and immerses himself in his phone.

"What's the Wi-Fi password?" Seb muses, indicating he's over the conversation.

Mal reaches into the coffee table to pull out the host's set of instructions for operating the home devices and hands it over, smiling slightly to cover up the fact that her throat is closing up. She keeps the expression on her face as she ends the voice recording that captured their conversation and then texts Serena, letting her know that the start of the trip is already bearing fruit. Mal needs that LA positivity to survive this weekend.

CHAPTER FOUR

DANI
H-E-B
MAY 23, 2024 — AFTER

"It's like paradise," Dani belts out as the grocery store's doors slide open.

The H-E-B is ginormous, with lots of light and tall ceilings. Dani runs her hand down a row of Baby Foot peels.

"I can only find these at C.O. Bigelow," she says, awestruck.

Peter murmurs about ShopRite being just fine as he turns down the health aisle. Dani freezes. Clearly Mal was right— he's getting condoms.

"Can you believe the wedding weekend is finally here?" Dani asks Marcus, who surveys a pile of charcoal bags. "Does it feel real yet?"

"My bank account has made it feel real for a while," he says, hefting a bag under the crook of his arm. He starts toward the butcher's station.

"T's parents aren't paying?" Dani's aghast. Tamar's parents are richer than hers were.

"Only if it was in Tel Aviv," he says, staring at the cuts. Thick T-bones, juicy filets, and wide sausages fill the display case, glistening under the artificial lights. "But they are covering the venue because Noam needs to do his thing."

Marcus flashes Dani a look.

"I didn't know technology-averse Jews existed," she says before leaning in. "It's because he's in the mafia, right?"

"This place is known for being the only venue in the country that doesn't use any technology," Marcus says, leaning so close his bad breath warms her nostrils. She pulls away, trying to keep her face from showing disgust. "He brought in his own security team, but there's no cameras or phones allowed in or out. You know the photographer and videographer were paid off and probably threatened that if anything leaks they won't live to see their next wedding."

Marcus smirks before putting in their order with the butcher.

"I thought we were eating out," Dani says.

"No, Mal just demanded it," Marcus says. "And I've stopped being in the business of listening to Mal a long time ago."

The butcher smiles at them, pulls out the thick cut from the case and drops it on his cutting board. With the flick of his wrist, the cleaver plunges into the brisket.

"Yo, you guys ready?" Peter emerges with a plastic bag.

"Provisions?" Dani forces a smile, hoping she sounds casual.

"Just some stuff I forgot," Peter mumbles.

Dani eyes the bag suspiciously and then feels her phone vibrate. Alexia.

Dani shoots off a reply, but she's distracted. She wishes she stayed in the house with Mal to talk to her, but she forgot what it's like to be around her: always needing to divert, to protect everyone from each other. She still doesn't know how to let people be themselves and work out their issues. Being a mediator is apparently a lifetime job, like a Supreme Court justice.

"Ruth Bader Ginsburg really fucked us," Dani muses.

The boys look at her with astonishment. Dani never curses.

"You sound like Mal," Marcus says accusingly as he navigates the grocery aisles.

He grabs some snacks and tosses them into the shopping cart, alongside the meat, to avoid making eye contact with her. Peter, meanwhile, shows her the inside of his shopping bag.

"I got eye drops and antacids," he says. "They don't even sell Plan B here."

"So much for a liberal haven," Dani sighs.

The Plan B quip was rhetorical, right?

They pay and exit the grocery store, the gleam already worn off.

"This is why I don't leave New York," Dani grumbles.

As they cross the parking lot, a large black Sedan revs its engine and races toward the trio. The sunshine bounces off the car's windshield, temporarily blinding them. Dani sees the car approach, faster now, and realizes it's not stopping—and that it's racing toward the three of them. She briefly wonders if this is it, and whether that means she'll get to see her parents soon. Then she gets shoved, hard, and drops onto the cement. Her calves are scraped and her knee is bloodied, but otherwise she's okay. She looks up to see Peter standing over her, white as a ghost, and Marcus shaking a few feet away—their chests heaving.

The car has already looped around the parking lot and speeds off toward the highway, gone before any of them dare to breathe.

"Dan, you okay?" Peter asks, kneeling in front of her. His hands are on her shoulders, and his forehead touches hers as he whispers words of comfort. Sweat pours out of her armpits and drips down her back, and the mixture of wetness and panic makes Dani a little woozy. She closes her eyes and sees her parents, smiling and waving, before they fade to black. Peter's face fills her vision when she opens her eyes, his forehead still creased with concern. She can see Marcus behind him, pacing back and forth and muttering. He looks up and makes eye contact with her.

"You can't say anything about this to Tamar," Marcus shouts.

Dani rubs her forehead and tries to get up, but Peter scrambles to help her.

"Babe, I'm okay," she says and then widens her eyes. "Sorry, old habit."

Peter smiles ruefully.

"I said your name during a fight with an old girlfriend," he says. "It didn't go well."

Dani laughs halfheartedly, but she's not in the mood to stroll down memory lane after nearly being flattened.

* * *

Back at the house, Peter's waving his arms wildly as he recounts the story of their near-untimely deaths to Mal and Seb.

"Did you catch the license plate number?" Seb asks. "What did the driver look like?"

"All you can process is an SUV barreling toward you," Dani shakes her head in disbelief, trying to process the chain of events. "It felt intentional."

"Why would anyone want to hurt us?" Marcus asks, before his head snaps at attention toward Dani. "Do you have any political enemies?"

"I mean, a lot of people don't like my politics," Dani muses.

She thinks of her hometown tabloid. Could the *Sentinel* have published another horrendous lie about her since getting to Austin? Dani pulls out her phone to check the Google alerts she set up a long ago for her name. Maybe she should have agreed to let Miguel provide security for her down here.

"She's not AOC," Mal says. "It just sounds like people in Texas are reckless drivers."

Dani spoke to AOC last month. She knows she's not at that level, but she blanches at Mal's lack of sympathy. Marcus and Peter look embarrassed, like they've been chastised for glorifying their experience as if it were *Fast and Furious: Austin*, but Dani feels like Mal thinks she's a fool.

"You don't believe it could happen?" Dani squawks.

"An assassination attempt on a local elected official?"

"It happened to Harvey Milk!"

"Dani, you are not Harvey Milk."

Dani's face gets hot, and she can feel another panic attack come on. They don't understand that this is very much in the realm of possibility, though she can't tell her friends that.

"Well, why else would a massive car barrel toward us?" Dani demands.

"I just think you're shaken up and jumping to conclusions." Mal pushes her chair back, clearly hoping it'll end the conversation. "Should we go eat?"

Marcus' shoulders slump.

"I don't really feel like barbequing," he says, his gaze trained on the ground. Dani wonders if he's upset about giving into Mal rather than processing their big scare.

"That's okay, bud," Peter says, slapping Marcus on the back. "We can grab sandwiches."

He looks to Dani for backup, but she is overwhelmed by the idea of leaving the comforts of their temporary home, where no one can hurt them. Her stomach, however, betrays her and gurgles in agreement. Her team raved about a barbeque spot down by the water, where Carly said there's a secret gluten-free bread offering, after they last visited for a tour of Austin's housing for the homeless program.

"I'll call a car," Dani says, just in case her would-be assassin tracked her whereabouts from Peter's rental. "We're eating well tonight, come hell or high water."

MAL
TERRY BLACK'S BBQ
MAY 23, 2024 — AFTER

THE FIVE OF THEM MAKE THEIR way to the front of the line while loud country music hums from the speakers. All the picnic tables are filled, so they divide and conquer—grab whatever open spot is available and meet out front in an hour to walk to the bridge for sunset. Peter tries to get Dani to partner up with him in the line, but to Mal's surprise Dani hooks her arm around hers and guides them to the counter, leaving the boys to fend for themselves.

"I'm going to go with God and get the sliced brisket sandwich," Dani says to the cute guy behind the counter as she surveys the menu. "I'm gluten-free, and the last time I was here you were so welcoming."

She bats her eyelashes and puts emphasis on certain words to drum up a specific kind of female helplessness. What an incredible way to manipulate a server. The man behind the counter winks at Dani and pulls out the special bag of gluten-free bread. See, this is proof that Dani's posturing at the house was also an act.

"You're such a politician," Mal says, a little jealous she never learned how to charm her way through life. Maybe Dani has a thing or two she can teach her.

Mal and Dani swoop into a two-seater just as an elderly couple vacates the table. They plop their lunch trays down—it almost feels like they're back at Weston—and marvel at the abundance in front of them: brisket sandwiches dripping with juice, green beans and whipped mashed potatoes glistening with butter, and loads of Saran-wrapped baked goods, from corn bread to mini pecan pies.

"So," Dani says, plucking silverware from a cup on the table.

"So," Mal replies, doing the same.

It feels like a low-stakes Western showdown, each woman brandishing her weapons. Mal starts to inventory her list of questions for her old friend, which have grown in the few short hours they've been together, but Dani interjects first.

"Can I be honest with you?" Dani asks, leaning in.

"I didn't realize you weren't," Mal says, though her heart sinks. Dani was always so open with her love and affection and friendship. It never occurred to Mal that there would be a time where Dani wasn't, but here they are. Never mind that Mal herself isn't in Austin for completely honest reasons herself.

"The car," Dani says, knitting her eyebrows together. "My fears are founded, you know. I've been tapped to run for Senate."

"Like the state senate?"

"The DNC wants me to run as the junior senator of New York," Dani says.

She casts her eyes low as she nibbles on the food and drops her left hand in her lap—out of Mal's vision. Mal, in turn, almost spits out her sandwich.

"Plenty of people run for office without getting run over by cars," Mal says, trying to set her expression to suggest she's impressed, or at least intrigued. "Why are you any different?"

"A lot of people think a politician just decides to run, but that's not true. There's a reason all these consultants and strategists exist. They're looking for the next Obama," Dani says.

"And you're that?" Mal can't help the condescension drip from her mouth like drool.

"Probably not, but telling anyone that and declining is essentially giving the Democratic Party the middle finger," Dani says. "First, they approach you. You need to play it cool. In New York, they like having one senator come from upstate and one from the city. The senior senator is retiring next year, so that means the junior senator gets a promotion, and then they want me to fill that empty slot."

"But you need to get elected," Mal says.

"Getting elected is one thing," Dani agrees. "But this is actually the harder part."

"And they think you're the person, rather than some Bernie Sanders kind of white dude?"

"Evidently." Dani sips on her diet Dr Pepper.

"So what do they want from you?" Mal asks.

"They've done some polling. I consistently draw in the women's vote, the left, and young people," Dani says.

"Three concurrent circles." Mal rolls her eyes. This is a longshot campaign, even Mal can figure that out. Dani really has her head up her ass to think she's a target for assassination 1,000 miles away from where she legislates.

"And they think my background will connect with wealthy voters who feel unwelcome in the movement," Dani goes on.

"That's because they want to be given gold stars for being woke without having done any of the work," Mal says with disgust. This is what it always comes back to: Dani's privilege providing clout. "I thought you may have learned something from all this."

"I can make real change, Mal," Dani snaps. "And people know that. Why else would someone try to scare me in a random Texas parking lot?"

"Do you think it was a threat or a real attack?" Mal stabs at the green beans and considers this crazy plot Dani conjured up. Dani seems dead set on Mal believing her, so much so that she's willing to tell her about a top-secret plan. If Mal keeps withholding, Dani might overcompensate and spill more, which means more talking and more fodder for her book. "I really hate to say it, but I think you're being paranoid."

Dani looks up at her with those puppy dog eyes, and Mal feels a tinge of pity followed by the mean voice in her head.

This is how you got entangled in all that bullshit. An echo of Mal's college self emerges from her subconscious. *Don't get involved again. You won't survive it.*

Mal considers it. This time is different, she decides. She's smarter now.

"Okay, who do you think is stalking you?" Mal asks, throwing Dani a bone.

"It could be anyone. People associated with the establishment part of the party, Republican operatives who think I stand a real chance," Dani trails off, listing other potential parties Mal has never heard of before who could be out to get a young no-name politician.

"Those sound like a lot of leads. Maybe try narrowing it down," Mal pauses. "What about Find My Friends? Does the political underworld share that with each other so you can navigate dating in DC?"

Dani eyes a baked good on their trays but doesn't reach for it. Mal picks it up and shoves it at Dani, telling her to eat it. Dani complies.

"I never go to DC," Dani says, breaking off a piece of corn muffin and closing her eyes to luxuriate in what's likely the most butter she's consumed in years. At least she and Dani can appreciate the shared feeling of being hungry for something and then finally getting a taste. "And the only people who are on Find My Friends are Ben and Peter."

"You're joking."

"It's not like I look," Dani protests. "And it feels like a statement to remove him."

"But what if he's looking at you?"

"He and any other person who's interested in local politics can find me pretty easily," she says. "I put out a public schedule."

"I thought that was only for monarchs and presidents," Mal says.

"It only scratches the surface," Dani admits, balling up the empty cling wrap in her hand and throwing it on the tray. "No one really knows what we're up to."

"Shady."

Mal takes a drag from her straw, the coarse Diet Coke bubbles popping on her tongue. When she filled up her cup, she discreetly spiked it with a shooter of rum. The alcohol makes her feel calm and in control. She looks around at the packed restaurant, taking in the kitsch of it all, when she sees a flash of shiny black hair. Mal narrows her eyes, trying to locate the source, but struggles to find the person again. It reminds her of Alexia, but she'd never be in the state of Texas, let alone Austin. And anyway, Mal hasn't seen her since college—though she did hear that Alexia's some fancy-schmancy MIT researcher now. For all of Weston's flaws, their school really did put people on a path for success.

"Do you know if Peter's dating anyone? Bringing a plus-one to the wedding?" Mal asks, thinking back to what she saw in the house. She makes a mental note to add that and any details from this conversation to her notebook the second she can sneak away.

"You in the market?" Peter saunters over from the other side of the restaurant with Seb and Marcus in tow, like he's God's gift to women everywhere, even the bisexual ones.

"I'd rather choke on my own tongue," Mal says.

"You don't want to choke on mine?" Peter asks, sticking his wet tongue in Mal's direction and getting close to her face.

Mal's fist is mere seconds away from contacting cartilage and bone, but then Dani stands up abruptly, prompting Mal and Peter to freeze and look at her.

"We still have a scavenger hunt to do," Dani says, picking up her empty tray. "Let's go solve the first clue."

* * *

As they weave through Butler Park, pink clouds warm up the sky. The small skyline twinkles, reminding Mal of home— just a little. Chicago never really spoke to her; it's trying too hard to compete with New York but doesn't lend itself to driving like LA does. It needs to pick a lane, you know? Austin, though. Austin's pretty nice, even if the humidity is so thick that it casts dark stains under the sleeves of her white T-shirt. Seb points toward the bridge. Hordes of people line both sides of Congress Avenue as the sun sets over the river.

"How do you think we'll find the next clue?" Marcus asks.

"I'm sure it won't be hard," Dani assures him.

As they scale a set of steps to get onto Congress, Mal spots Peter holding Dani's arm out of the corner of her eye. Dani's limping a little bit from getting banged up earlier, but she's clearly fine enough to walk up a flight of stairs. Dani and Peter share a secret smile, like they're in a Jane Austen novel. Mal will corner Peter once he's drunk later and get the details. Dani cheating on her venture capitalist fiancé is nothing but juicy. The group squeezes into an open spot on the bridge and looks down below at the dozen or so boats approaching.

"We should have gone on that," Seb points to a booze cruise where drunk bachelorettes scream-sing about how they're going out tonight and feeling alright.

"Missed opportunity," Marcus grumbles.

As the sun dips below the water, the chatter from the crowd begins to swell. Suddenly, the squeaking noises coming from under the bridge dissipate as the bats flutter out by the dozens. Mal marvels at the volume of the bats, barely visible alone but together a powerful mass. Mal tries to ignore Seb using flash photography to capture the bats heading out for feeding. It feels impossible to capture in an image, anyway. It's more of a feeling.

Once it appears there are no more bats escaping from below, they turn to walk back. But before they can do so, a hoodie-clad person dressed all in black approaches them and hands Mal an envelope before walking away. The movement sends a waft of perfume in their wake, causing every hair on her arms to stand on edge. She hasn't smelled that scent since college.

"Spooky," Seb croons, delighted with the theatrics.

Mal's panicked mind revs to the weight of the envelope in her hands. It's textured and weighty, and looks nearly identical to the ones that changed hers and Dani's lives. Between this, the near accident, and a glimpse of Alexia's ghost, this scavenger hunt is feeling less like a dorky but benign activity and something more sinister entirely.

Mal turns the envelope over in her shaking hands to extract the note. She fumbles with the card while Dani jumps up and down with glee, oblivious to her mounting fear.

"Open it, open it," Dani says.

"The friends are so clever and so bright. We hope you're having fun at the end of the night," Mal reads, taking in the blocky, unfamiliar handwriting. "It's been a long day, so go home and rest. Tomorrow, you'll want to look and feel your best."

Seb starts shaking his hips in Dani's direction, still dancing along to the karaoke from the boats below. Mal feels a sting of rejection. He used to do that kind of stuff with her.

"We're going shopping. We're going shopping," he wiggles his butt into Marcus, who looks up heavenward like he's fighting every urge to push Seb off the bridge. Peter squeezes in between them and wraps his arms around Seb and Marcus.

"You gonna miss men grinding up on you? Giving it all up for your girl, huh?" Peter asks, grinning like an asshole.

"You're still not tired of this?" Marcus asks, shooting Peter a look of resignation. "I still get shit, even on my wedding weekend?"

"Especially on your wedding weekend." Seb dismounts into a twerking position and waves an invisible lasso in the air.

Mal would roll her eyes and make a snarky comment that joking about someone being gay is so boring and unoriginal and dated, except she's too busy scribbling furiously into her notebook. Dani might have been right after all. But it's not a political operative who's tracked them down—it's the very organization they created.

CHAPTER FIVE

DANI
WALNUT HALL, FRESHMAN YEAR
SEPTEMBER 6, 2013 — BEFORE

DANI SAW THE STRAWBERRY-COLORED BALLOONS FIRST,
tied to her door with gold curling string.

When she touched the knob, Dani was surprised that her
door creaked open. Someone had wedged a flash drive of the
same color in the door frame, leaving Dani's room impercep-
tibly unlocked. She pushed the door to reveal an XL
berry-colored tank top that looked like something a sorority
girl would wear and an envelope, again in that bright red
color, neatly placed on her comforter. Dani slid her finger
underneath the fold of the envelope, held together by a gold
wax seal, and loosened it. She pulled out a piece of stiff card
stock that read: *We're Always Watching.*

> *For the first week of classes, wear your tank top every day and
> keep an eye out for your comrades. Don't forget to keep the flash
> drive on you at all times. Remember, women are always
> watching. Tell no one. See you next Thursday.*

Dani's heart started racing, and she did a quick check
around her room for any sort of camera or trace of who might

have been in there. She feared she was being bullied by the sign-off alone, but she didn't anticipate they would leave an article of clothing in her size. Maybe a size smaller to humiliate her, but no one ever paid attention to her, so why would they start now? And who are *they* anyway?

She left her room and then circled back, throwing the tank top under her bed and slipping the flash drive into her jeans pocket, before heading to Sylvia's room.

Dani banged on the door, which flew open immediately. Her R.A., a scraggly girl who seemed to take the job only because it granted her one of the two singles on their floor (Dani had the other), stood in the doorway looking bewildered that anyone needed her.

"Did you let someone into my room?" Dani demanded, uneasy with the realization that she could only tell off someone with less social currency than she had. "Why is my door open?"

"Did you forget to lock it on your way to class?" Sylvia asked, speaking slowly and blinking like an animatronic owl.

"No, there are balloons tied to my door and stuff on my bed," Dani said.

"That's a weird thing to get upset about," she replied.

"Well, did you see anyone? If you didn't let them in?" Dani asked.

She started to panic. What kind of security did this dorm have? How could someone get into her room so easily, one she locked every day? And why did stupid Sylvia think this wasn't a big deal? Didn't the university offer basic training to these people about intruders?

"I've been busy. It's Welcome Week," Sylvia said. "I don't have time to bust your friends. And I don't have keys to any room but my own. The only department that has access is ResLife. Check with them."

And with that, Sylvia shut the door in Dani's face.

For the entire following week, Dani couldn't stop seeing strawberry red. Strawberry-red lipstick. Strawberry-red backpacks. And some very specific strawberry-red tank tops. It was only when she saw Meredith, her former boarding-school classmate, wearing the same color that it clicked. She wasn't the target of some hazing ritual but instead a person tapped for something special. It was Meredith, after all, who had approached Dani during summer orientation and asked about a former Vernon classmate who was expelled. Dani had clammed up but tried to answer as best as she could, which meant she parroted back parcels of gossip from the weeks following the scandal. Meredith, who was three years older, looked frustrated before leaving.

Dani had enrolled at Weston (partially) because it had few Vernon alumni, allowing her to establish herself on her own terms. But the incident with Meredith made her feel more certain that she couldn't outrun her pedigree, no matter how hard she tried. She'd always be known by the conditions of her upbringing, from her alcohol and drug use to whether she knew if Michael Copeland really did corner Shira Schwartz on the school staircase after band practice and made her blow him. But maybe that pedigree was the only reason the older girls allowed Dani into this secret club in the first place, because otherwise it didn't make sense to her how she passed any test. In any event, her lack of knowledge of that one incident indicated she had failed.

While Dani fixated on her inability to be normal around people who kind of knew her, only one person zeroed in on

Dani's outfit choice. Mal, a girl who befriended Dani during freshman orientation, suggested they take political science together. Now, Dani regretted agreeing to such terms, because it gave Mal three days a week to pepper Dani with questions she couldn't answer—prompting Mal to skulk around when it became obvious that she wasn't going to get the results she wanted. Still, Dani found the gesture flattering. It felt kind of nice to be the center of someone's concerns, even if it was rooted in nosiness.

Throughout that week, Dani learned to differentiate the girls like her—wide-eyed and questioning—from the older ones, the members, who acted as if they were wearing any other outfit. There were no winks or secret smiles until Thursday, when a petite girl with matching rows of gold hoop earrings lining her lobes approached Dani and handed her another envelope. Inside, on the same cardstock as before— though with different handwriting, Dani noted later when comparing the two—she was instructed to meet at the administrative building at 10 p.m. and leave her phone behind.

Dani assumed the meeting would take place at Gaskell—a small, seniors-only library that Vernon alumni said was home to a secret society. They had also said graduation from Weston depended on fornicating between the book stacks, so maybe none of this was true at all.

But at 9:58 p.m. on Thursday, Dani arrived at the small, Gothic-looking building on the farthest edge of campus. She waited a few minutes for the berry-wearing older girls to emerge from the woods. At one point she thought she heard leaves crunch.

After nearly 10 minutes, Dani began circling the building, looking for a clue that would dictate what she should do next. Maybe she missed her cue altogether.

Before the panic took hold, Dani checked the doors to see if any of them were open, and then it dawned on her that she already had access. Dani quickly fished in her bag and plucked out her tour guide key, which she had received a few weeks earlier at her weekly training. At the time, Dani thought she was admitted to the most prestigious club on campus—a freshman joining the tour guide group—but could now see it was simply the best of the college-sanctioned ones. This was another beast entirely.

The door opened, just as it did every week, and Dani wondered what she was looking for—and why they wanted her here, of all places. The lobby was empty, as was the waiting room, the offices and the kitchenette. The spiral staircase led up to offices and a dusty crawl space, which Dani doubted she'd need to excavate. The only locked door was the one leading down to the storage room, which she had seen a senior open once. Dani rifled through the building until she found a collection of loose keys to try, one by one. Eventually, the narrow wooden door creaked open to reveal a steep, dark staircase.

Dani couldn't shake the feeling that she was being watched.

For safe return, Dani wedged the flash drive between the old door and the frame, like the girls who snuck into her dorm room had. She never plugged the USB into her computer—her parents' security team had warned her about cyberattacks—and was thankful to have something keeping the door open in case it was another dead end.

As she trekked down the rickety stairs, Dani, in a poor attempt at self-soothing, said aloud that she wished she brought a flashlight. The glow from her new iPhone 5 wasn't enough to illuminate beyond a step at a time as she reached the basement level. Instead of the anticipated storage room, the stairs deposited Dani into a long hallway. A flickering light cast long shadows on the dusty school paraphernalia lining the walls.

She paused in front of framed photos of white men throwing their arms around each other and laughing. Small bronze plaques hammered into the frames indicated the photos were taken during the late 1950s. In more than one photo, the men were naked, showing their pasty butts to the camera or laying down seductively in the campus fountain. Dani wished for that kind of camaraderie, and hoped this group would provide that—if she could ever figure out what they were, or how to find them.

As she wandered down the hallway, Dani hit a dead end with a floor-to-ceiling bookcase. The books looked a lot less dusty than everything else in the basement, so she skimmed her fingers along the hardcover spines. When she reached a Toni Morrison book slightly pulled out, Dani tugged on the novel, thinking it might have a clue inside. Dani heard a click.

The bookcase jutted out, and Dani pulled on the bookcase like a door. Her forehead became damp with the effort, but she was able to open it wide enough to step through the gap. The passage led to an even darker hallway. Uneven cobblestones replaced the wooden floor, and the air grew remarkably colder. Dani hugged herself as she considered whether she wanted to go any farther. The thought of being trapped underground in the woods made her heart jump up into her throat. Before she could decide whether to turn around, the sound of heavy footsteps echoed from behind her. Dani whipped around to face Mal, red-faced and out of breath, as she slipped past the bookcase and barreled toward her friend.

"What are you doing?" Mal hissed, like she was the one who had been snuck up on.

Suddenly, her eyes widened, and her mouth became O-shaped. Dani turned back to stare at human-sized shapes moving in the black abyss, which smelled like pine needles.

"We told you to come alone," a voice intoned.

The person held a small lantern in their hands, and Dani could only make out glistening eyes, full lips and ultra-short dark hair in the dark. As they got closer, the light gave way to a small, displeased person. The girl with the buzzcut glared at Mal.

"Who's she?"

"She didn't make the cut," another voice called out.

The voice belonged to the girl with the small gold hoops. She held two silky scarves in her hands, which twisted like snakes in the breeze.

"The cut for what?" Mal demanded, clearly unabashed to have ruined whatever induction ceremony she had interrupted. "Illegal activities happening in the basement of the administrative building? *The Wrangler* would love to hear about this."

"Charming, an ethics lesson from the woman who stalked one of our recruits," the girl with the earrings said. "And no one reads the student newspaper."

Mal narrowed her eyes.

"Oh, I'm the stalker?" she shot back, her hair whipping around as she cast a glance at Dani, in a can-you-believe-this kind of way. Mal looked like Medusa, but it was Dani who felt that kind of ire. This girl, who she knew for only a few months, was so sure of herself. Indignantly so. Dani had spent her whole life bending for others, making herself feel smaller, and here was Mal feeling entitled to ruin a sacred evening, even if Dani was prepared to leave without a trace.

"Is that why she's been so paranoid? You've been scaring the shit out of her," Mal continued, stepping closer. "Are you hazing her? What the fuck is going on?"

Mal's anger, on full display, seemed to have the opposite effect it was having on Dani. The short-haired girl looked at her with admiration before turning to the one with the earrings.

"I think you've underestimated this one," the girl with the buzzcut said, then she barked at Dani and Mal to face the hallway.

To Dani's surprise, Mal obliged, and then everything went dark.

MAL
WESTON COLLEGE, FRESHMAN YEAR
SEPTEMBER 12, 2013 — BEFORE

MAL HAD DONE SOME RESEARCH INTO her poli-sci class-mate: Dani had gone to a prestigious boarding school in Connecticut, attended galas aimed at collecting checks from the philanthropic one percent, and vacationed in Courchevel. Mal couldn't even point to the French Alps on a map. Dani's lifestyle, frankly, had surprised her; she didn't seem like one of those girls. If anything, Dani seemed like someone who was used to fading into the background, not being noticed, despite the immeasurable wealth that surrounded her. Mal had tried to be that way once, but she found she didn't possess the self-control to mute herself into a more easily consumable shape, someone lovable and easy. Mal tried really fucking hard to be malleable, and her inability to do so empowered her to double down on her worst impulses. The world could take her or leave her. She no longer desired to try and change their minds.

That is, until she realized Dani was being courted for the kind of group that, for generations, men have been a part of. The nucleus of how power worked in the real world started in groups like this, and Mal would be damned if she turned down an Ivy League degree to be excluded from the next best thing at Weston. But being blindfolded and led through the woods in upstate New York was not exactly what she had in mind.

They walked for what felt like an eternity, and Mal worried her captors (allies?) were taking them off university property. She could barely navigate the campus as it was, let alone the greater town. Plus, she was pretty sure the college was in walking distance of a prison. The path under her feet felt rocky, and she breathed in the wet smells of the forest that bordered the campus. She heard Dani's shallow breathing over the sound of twigs snapping as they were directed farther into the woods. For a makeshift blindfold, Mal couldn't see shit. Finally, one of the girls guiding her by the upper arm lightly squeezed it. Mal felt the groove of a ring dig in, putting uncomfortable pressure on her skinny arm. The reconnection with her body followed the memory of her stepmom pleading Mal to eat just a little more dinner so she could get some meat on her bones. Monica didn't take too kindly to being compared to a wicked witch.

"You can take your blindfolds off," a voice boomed.

Mal peeled the fabric off her face and shook out her matted curls. They definitely were in the woods. Mal looked like a black spot among the row of girls in matching red tank tops fanned around a small stone building. Vibrant green vines snaked up the facade, which had a simple wooden door with a padlock attached to it. While Mal stared at the structure, the other girls, in turn, stared at her: an interloper in stakeout clothes.

"For the first time in Newts history, someone who wasn't tapped has joined us," Gold Earrings said, gesturing at Mal. "We're going to let her introduce herself and explain what she knows. Even if she gets it right, we might just expel her for the fun of it."

Mal's heart fluttered as she was put on the spot. This wasn't much different than her middle school bullies' tactics. They wanted her to be nervous.

She turned to face the anointed ones. Mal almost expected fierce faces, angry and pointed, to stare back. Instead, they all looked slightly terrified. They knew less than she did.

"You're a secret society," Mal said slowly, keeping "with a dumb name" to herself. She thought of the conversations she eavesdropped on during orientation, all these older girls asking questions about questionable male behavior. It was why she latched onto Dani in the first place. "You ruin men's lives."

A tither of giggles echoed in the woods, but she noticed Gold Earrings' gaze intensify and her body language jerk to attention. So that's what this was. Mal's confidence surged. She opened her mouth to riff more but got cut off.

"We protect women," Full Metal Jacket snapped, rubbing a hand over her buzzcut.

"That's enough." Gold Earrings held up a hand, and everyone fell quiet. She gestured to Full Metal Jacket, who crossed the crunchy threshold toward the building.

A blonde girl sidled up to Mal and leaned in.

"I'm third gen, and I've never heard that before," she said, looking exhilarated.

Mal smiled tightly and tried to get Dani's attention. She wouldn't meet Mal's eye.

Full Metal Jacket pulled out a strawberry-colored key from the pocket of her skinny jeans. The lock clicked open with ease, and the older girls directed them inside, one by one.

When it came time to let Mal in, Gold Earrings blocked the entrance.

"I know too much," Mal said firmly. "It won't be worth the headache, trust me."

Gold Earrings, who looked barely tall enough to ride a rollercoaster, smirked.

"You want to be an author, right? Turn your novel into a screenplay, or get it made into a TV show?" Her irises flashed black, gleaming like her earrings and long dark hair. "What if

I told you Jennifer St. James—she runs Simon & Schuster—would buy your book? Or that Audrey Zane—head of content at HBO—could make one phone call to get it developed? That's the kind of power this group possesses. I will not let you come in and dismantle this 58-year-old institution because you think you're above it all. We have as much power to help you as we do to destroy you."

"Why are you selling me so hard then?" Mal asked, though the mere suggestion that they could help her achieve her life goal made her more excited than angry. They clearly researched her. For all she knew, this could be part of the hazing routine.

"I'm warning you," Gold Earrings seethed. "My grandmother built this organization, and I won't let some… desperate girl ruin it."

The insult stung, but Mal forged ahead.

"Have you considered that bringing someone in who actually wants it is more important than tapping girls who are just willing to show up?" Mal asked, though she still wasn't sure what the group did in the first place. All this conversation did was make her want it more. "What kind of legacy is that?"

Legacy. That did it. Gold Earrings' expression softened.

"Don't make me regret it," she hissed, stepping aside to let Mal cross into her future.

CHAPTER SIX

DANI
THE RENTAL IN AUSTIN, TEXAS
MAY 23, 2024 — AFTER

Flames lick the firewood and shoot up into the black sky. Dani always loved watching the little sparks shoot out, wondering if they'd ever have enough manpower to fully catch fire. She wonders if she'll be like that in the coming years, a spark growing into a forest fire, and it makes her smile. Dani's happy about how her dinner with Mal went, too, despite being shaken up by the road rage incident. Breaking gluten-free bread together created an opportunity for Dani to use her favorite phrase, "Can I be honest with you? I'm scared." At work, it creates a false sense of vulnerability and intimacy, and instantly softens those bleeding-heart reporters. Like Mal, they see vulnerability as a trait that equates to truth.

If someone wasn't considering taking her out as a political threat, maybe they should. Dani's ready for the big leagues, and she's so close that she can taste it.

She turns her attention to her phone, which has been blowing up all night. All texts from Alexia, asking to talk.

Dani glances around to ensure she's alone before hitting the phone icon. Alexia picks up on the first ring.

"I just wanted to call and say hello," Dani says, and pauses. Rule #4: Always assume you're being recorded. "How's it going?"

"Hi," Alexia nearly sings the word. "Great news! It's ready."

"It's ready," Dani repeats, chewing over the words. "How do you know?"

"Well, I've been trying for months, and I finally got the recipe just right," Alexia says, using their oft-repeated metaphor of baking for whenever they speak about the serum's development. "And everyone who tried it was quick to tell me so. Though it only stuck around for about 10 minutes. Totally gone by then."

"Did anyone get sick?" Dani asks with urgency. The serum's development is just supposed to be for work, but it could radically change her relationship with Mal. She doesn't have to rely on persuasion anymore. She can do what she knows she's meant to do: create real, meaningful change in her personal life and with the Newts, and ultimately in American politics.

"No stomach aches or other side effects to my knowledge," Alexia chirps, her voice gaining a euphoric tone.

It's too soon to celebrate, especially on the phone, but Alexia's invention just might propel the two of them to world domination. The screen door opens, and Dani turns around to see Peter with two beers in hand. He holds them up and grins. Dani congratulates Alexia and asks how quickly she can get the serum down to Texas.

"I can get on the next flight," Alexia says. "Honestly, I could use a weekend to myself. Just need to get the kids' affairs in order—"

"You're going to deliver them yourself?" Dani asks as she smiles at Peter, hoping he can't read lips. "Can't you get someone else to take care of that? We can't risk Mal seeing you."

"I can, but I'll feel better doing it myself," Alexia says, an edge in her voice. "I can give you two vials. I have enough for a third, but I need to keep it for my records."

"Fine, fine. Just get down here with it ASAP," Dani says in a low voice before switching over to a chipper one. "Thanks so much, talk soon!"

Dani ends the call just as Peter sits down beside her. He hands her an ice-cold IPA, and she takes a big swig from it. It's no Dom Pérignon, but Alexia just figured out how to make a goddamn truth serum—Dani is downright giddy with possibility. Think of all the legislation she can pass as a senator if the Republicans start blabbing about anything incriminating. She might even surpass AOC as the first female president that way, and Alexia will get a very nice position as the head of the FDA. Her Manhattan pride swells. The Bronx can suck it.

"It's been a while." Peter's voice is low and gravelly, and Dani's good mood is opening her up to matching her ex-boyfriend's energy. She possesses a level of control no person has ever had, and tonight, she wants to abuse it. "Though I didn't expect a near-death experience to make me feel like no time has passed, either. But I finally got to pull your signature move and be the one to save you this time."

"You were constantly walking into traffic," Dani laughs. "If I didn't yank you back onto the sidewalk, you'd be roadkill a long time ago. I'm glad that didn't happen today, too."

"Seriously, Dan, are you okay?" Peter brushes her knee, and her body screams with wanting. She wants him to keep his hand on her knee, and then move it up her thigh, and then keep going. "You didn't move when the car came. It was like you were welcoming it."

"I saw my parents," she smiles, trying to play it off, but Peter's face drops. He looks at her tenderly, like he's worried she'll break if he says anything. "It would be nice to see them, but I'm not sprinting into traffic normally, if that's what you're asking."

"What if that's your secret kink? Death edging."

"You're so gross," she groans, though she's always found him funny. "That's not a thing."

Sitting with Peter feels just as it did when they were in college, only now they're not raw balls of potential, with hundreds of different roads laid out in front of them. They've been on their own paths for six years now, after Dani made the tough but right decision to separate those roads. She needed to be with someone like her, but also someone who could help her get the Southern vote and offset her "New York values," or whatever euphemism people use nowadays to talk about Jews. Peter doesn't have the business degree or charisma that Ben has, but it wasn't those things her mom pointed out right away. There was something about him Fiona didn't trust.

Dani fought her on it the few times her mom brought it up, mostly because it echoed the same feelings Mal had about him, but neither of them knew him like she did. But without her mom to fight with, the cancerous thought took hold, and she needed to be free from it. She needed to live a life her mom would be proud of, even if it made her miserable— though she didn't know that when she made the decision to sever hers and Peter's relationship. If she knew that then, they'd be married with kids by now. They would have problems, all couples do, but Dani knows in her bones he's the one who got away. And now he's sitting right in front of her, a chance for a do-over. A chance for one weekend of falling back into the pure potential of it all.

"What else have you been up to, if not that?" he asks.

Like he doesn't know. Peter follows all her professional social media accounts as of this morning. Dani confirmed it on the plane ride to Austin.

"I'm chair of the women's health committee in the New York State Assembly." Dani speaks clearly, but the words sound foreign on her tongue. She gets to speak aloud her achievement, and to someone who knew her before she knew what those hopes and dreams looked like. They used to lay in bed and talk about their future, but those fantasies never involved careers. It wasn't because they wouldn't have them, but because there wasn't anything to crystalize. All the literature Dani read during her time with the Newts made her realize that she shouldn't dream of labor.

She, however, was among the few who could afford not to work. The intersection of progressive values and immense wealth felt so oppositional that she felt guilty articulating her concerns, especially to Peter. She had overheard his parents fight about money one time when she spent the holidays with them, and it made her so uncomfortable she avoided spending quality time at their house in the years that followed.

Joy bubbles out of Peter as he tells her how incredible she is, and that he never worried about her because he knew she'd be fine. She cringes at the sentiment. Most days she feels anything but okay, even though her luck appears to be improving.

"What about you?" Dani asks, taking another swig from her beer. She is already feeling buzzed. The perks of being a light weight. Peter shrugs.

"Caddying a bit," he says. "Working a few part-time IT jobs." Dani wonders if he still uses the Miura clubs she bought him for graduation. He was more likely to sell them than hold onto them, but she hoped he was too sentimental to do that. "Nothing serious."

"Does that also apply to your dating life?" The words slip off Dani's tongue. He turns his head ever so slightly toward her but says nothing, just lifting his beer to his mouth. Thick drops of sweat form on his temple, and the short black hairs on his face gleam in the light of the fire.

"I'm seeing someone," he says finally. "It's been going on for a while, but I'm thinking of ending things. Not the right time, you know?"

Dani wants to ask if the person isn't right rather than the time, but she knows that's not fair. Peter drains the rest of his drink to fill the silence, and Dani jumps up to get him another. She doesn't want to think about where this girl touches him, or the fact that maybe he's not interested in Dani at all. The thought makes her stomach swirl. As she approaches the back door, Dani hears hushed voices coming from the kitchen.

"You don't think this is weird?" Mal's voice has a panicked edge to it. "The cards are the same, Seb. Look."

There's an uncomfortable silence before Seb starts talking.

"It's just card stock," Seb says. "And that one is like a decade old."

"You saw how shaken up she was," Mal says. "She's not acting, I can tell."

Dani breath catches. Mal might have played it cool in the restaurant hours earlier, but she knows something is off.

"Mal, why did you come here?" Seb asks. "We know you hate Marcus and most of the people in this house. You didn't come here from the goodness of your heart."

"What's with you and your judgment of my character?" Mal snaps. "Why does everything with me require an ulterior motive, but no one else is held to that same standard?"

"Because that's who you are," Seb hisses. "And it was fine in college because we were all in our early 20s, but you haven't changed at all."

"Why do I have to change? Why do I need to please any of you?"

Dani hears the rustling of papers. She lays flat against the exterior of the house, thankful the bushes block Peter's view of her eavesdropping.

"I told you I didn't want to get into this," Seb says before another voice joins in. Marcus.

"You good?" he asks.

"For sure," Seb says in his normal, happy-go-lucky tone.

"Everything is not okay." Mal's voice goes up an octave. "They're trying to hurt Dani."

"No one is trying to hurt Dani," Marcus chastises Mal. "You need to relax."

"*I* need to relax? You almost became roadkill in a grocery store parking lot. Whoever is putting together the scavenger hunt knows where we are and what we're doing." Mal's voice trails off. The boys start protesting.

"Are you on something? Is that what's going on?" Seb asks, his voice creased with concern and irritation.

"I'm over this," Mal says. "Tomorrow, I want you to call it off."

"It's just fun, Mal," Marcus snipes. "And it's not your place to make that call."

"I'm telling you to do it," she says. "I'm not asking."

"Mal, I'm trying to be a nice guy here," Marcus says.

"Well I can see through your nice-guy bullshit," she replies.

"Yeah, because you have such a great track record with men," Marcus says.

"Fuck you. Rosen tricked all of us. Not just me."

That shuts Marcus up.

"I've known you for a long time, remember?" Marcus finally responds in a voice Dani has never heard before. He sounds knowing, angrier. "You just want to ruin the weekend to get back at us. You're very transparent in your strategy, and I'm telling you once, Mal. Once, you hear me? Knock it off. Be nice to people. I swear it's not hard. Just shut up and smile and try to not make everyone miserable for once in your life."

Marcus slams something down on the table, and Dani can hear Mal's sharp inhale.

"We're doing the scavenger hunt. We're doing everything on the itinerary. And you're going to be excited and enthusiastic, okay? You're no longer welcome to express any concerns to me or Seb or anyone else in this house," Marcus says.

A beat, then footsteps.

"And Mal?" Marcus says. "After Sunday, I hope to never see you again."

Dani holds her breath as she waits for Mal to leave. She can hear Seb and Marcus whispering, so she waits a bit before strolling in, pretending to be tipsier than she is. The boys stop whispering and smile at her.

"What would you like to drink?" Marcus asks, flipping a red Solo cup from a stack and turning to the bar. "Margaritas?"

Dani shakes her head. She needs to stay sober for the evening.

"Just grabbing two more beers for me and Peter," she says, hoping that's tantalizing enough for them to tease her and lighten the mood.

Dani reaches into the fridge to grab the bottles and shuts the door. She turns and jumps as she comes face to face with Marcus and Seb, their faces drawn with concern.

"Listen, I don't think Mal is stable," Marcus says. "I know you wanted her here this weekend, and I only invited her because of that."

Seb nods in agreement. Dani puts down the beers and takes their hands.

"I owe you big time for that," Dani says to Marcus. "I'll keep an eye on her."

"I didn't think she would actually come," Marcus presses.

"Well, she's here, so there's not much more to do about it," Dani says, wanting to get back to Peter. "And she's behaving, for the most part."

"I'm grabbing my stuff early tomorrow and going to the venue," Marcus says. "Please don't let her ruin my wedding."

"Do you really think she will?" Dani asks. She knows Marcus never liked Mal, but she never thought he'd be the kind of guy to hold a grudge.

"I don't trust her," he mutters.

"You never really got to know her." Dani finds she's still arguing the same case long after the jury delivered its verdict and the courthouse emptied out.

"You're a good friend," he says with a finality that means the conversation is over.

She grabs the beers and hurries back outside. Dani wants to forget about all of this drama for just a little longer. She wants to forget that someone may have tried to send her a message or injure her. She wants to forget, even, what tomorrow holds once Alexia arrives with the truth serum. Dani touches Peter's shoulder and settles back down next to him. He thanks her and takes another long swig from the bottle before pointing at a clearing in the backyard.

"Did you notice there's a path back there? Want to see where it leads?" Peter flashes Dani a mischievous smile.

Dani turns back to the house, where Marcus and Seb are engaging in another serious-looking conversation. She assumes Mal took a walk to cool off.

"It probably just connects to the next street over," Dani says, though she fears what lies in the woods. In college, only bad things or lots of sex happened out there. And now she's not sure if she can go through with doing anything with Peter, not after what she just heard.

"Too much of a city slicker now? Central Park is the best you've got?"

"You're really going to make me go back there, now that you've disrespected the grand jewel of my borough?" Dani stands up dramatically, like she's ready to fight Peter.

"A New Yorker through and through, just like me," he says, rising to meet her.

"Well, you know Long Island doesn't count."

Dani stays steady, staring Peter down. The air around them feels charged, and she's acutely aware that if she takes even the smallest step forward, if there's any hint of movement, that she and Peter will fuse together like magnets.

"I'll race you," she says and then takes off toward the clearing, her sandals mowing down the lush grass.

"I'll give you a head start," Peter calls out. "One, two, three…"

Dani moves quickly down the woodchip-dense path, darting past trees until she can no longer hear Peter. A twig snaps beneath her, and she pauses to listen. The full moon shines through the leaves, and even though she got farther than anticipated, she's charmed by the quietness of the path. That, and the fact that she can faintly see the lights of other houses. It's not a spooky kind of quiet, but a peaceful one. She breathes in the clean air and wipes a few beads of sweat from her forehead. She's about to turn back around when a nearby house light bounces off an object just to her left. Someone put together a beautiful wooden bench in the clearing. Dani sits down and closes her eyes, and she can hear the faintest crackle of water running through the woods. Leaves rustle in the distance, and Peter finally emerges.

"You're faster than I remembered." Peter pants slightly. He gestures to the bench, though it's a bit hard to see in the dark. "May I?"

She nods, and then realizes he may not be able to see.

"Of course."

He sits down next to her, making a concerted effort not to touch her, but the bench is too small for the both of them. Their knees slowly move toward each other and when they connect, one of them pulls it back. They sit there in silence, following the same rhythm: knees touch, he pulls away, knees drift back together, she pulls away. Dani's not sure how long this goes on for before Peter admits that he's nervous.

"I am too," she giggles.

She's a laugher in the worst situations.

"I've thought about you every day, you know that, right?" Peter asks, putting his chin in his hands. He doesn't turn to face her. "It's like I'm still holding onto something, and seeing you today, it makes me feel like there's a reason for that."

Now he turns to face her, his expression filled with hope. He takes her bare hands, and Dani realizes that he mistook the weekend, the embrace and the lack of a ring as indicators that this was something else entirely. Something permanent. Dani looks up quickly to correct him, but Peter misreads her reaction. He leans in to kiss her. His lips are soft on hers, and his hand moves up to cup her cheek as he brings her in closer. He still smells of the cologne, and her body is moving faster than her brain. Dani turns to straddle him on the bench, and she can feel him hard underneath her. She shouldn't be doing this. She should stop. Ben will be here on Sunday. Peter doesn't know she's engaged. Or does he? Peter—

Peter slips his hand inside her underwear and Dani loses all thoughts. He flips her over so she's on the bench and he's kneeling on the ground below her, his fingers slowly latching onto her underwear. It's her last means of defense. Once the underwear is off, she's down for the count. Peter slides them off, and Dani curses the high quality of underwear that makes it so easy for him to do so. That should have been a warning on the website: Don't wear if you're worried about who's taking them off. His tongue is rough as it drags through the soft space between her thigh and pubic bone, and she closes her eyes as she falls back into bliss. Here, in the woods, she just gets to be Dani. It could have been two minutes or two hours, Dani's not sure, but there's rustling coming from the direction of the house.

"Is anyone coming?" Dani moans, unsure she has the fortitude to do anything about her friends potentially walking in on her with Peter deep between her legs. He stops to pause.

"Do you need to come again or are you good? I do hear something," he says, pulling away. Dani grabs at his head and pushes him back into her.

"Just a little longer," she whimpers, and just as quickly, her legs shake with relief.

Peter comes up and kisses her again, his face warm. She wants to think she's a bad person for leading him on and cheating on Ben, but how could something so bad feel so good? She's reminded of how good she felt on coke, on molly, on ketamine. Oh man, she really misses ketamine.

"They're probably wondering where we are," Dani starts, and Peter gives her a knowing look but can't hide his smile.

"They know," he assures her. "And you're doing nothing wrong."

Peter looks pointedly at Dani's bare hand, and she puts her hands in between her thighs, feeling all too exposed. He thinks she's single. Single and getting back together with him, apparently, despite whomever he's been dating. Peter will never talk to Dani again once Ben arrives in three days, but she can at least give him what he wants until then.

Seb bounces down the path like Ziti, howling their names. Dani quickly pulls up her underwear and by the time their tattooed friend gets to them, the two are sitting on opposite ends of the bench like prude teens at shul.

"It's barely midnight, and Marcus wants everyone inside for bed," Seb says. "He's being such a bridezilla."

Dani doesn't even look at Peter as she jumps up to chase Seb, leaving Peter following from behind once more.

MAL
THE RENTAL IN AUSTIN, TEXAS
MAY 24, 2024 — AFTER

THE COFFEE POT GURGLES AS MAL gets a super-early morning writing sprint in (she's still on West Coast time). The stress from last night oddly invigorated her, and the act of finally putting pen to paper makes her feel more herself in years. If she's able to take this feeling home with her, the trip will have been worth it. She sends Serena a picture of her notebook and coffee mug, even though she knows her friend won't be up for a few more hours.

The stairs above Mal creak, and her heart starts to race. She's only been up for an hour, and because she does her first drafts in longhand, she's not nearly close to getting all her ideas down on the page. She doesn't want to be disturbed, and certainly isn't ready for another showdown with one of the boys—especially because, with the clarity of morning, Mal thinks she might have overreacted last night. She let her imagination get the best of her. The scavenger hunt couldn't possibly be put on by the Newts. It was just the time she spent with her old college friends resurfacing her anxieties. Still, it's a welcome surprise to see Dani with a Weston baseball cap covering her ponytail. She's decked out in a full Lululemon fit—a brand Dani used to rail against because they weren't size inclusive.

"Is that the next bestseller from Mallory Shepard?" Dani grins and slips into the chair next to Mal to lace her sneakers up.

"Better be." Mal smiles smugly.

Dani looks at Mal's closed notebook and points to the door.

"I was going for a run, but I could settle on a walk," she says. "Wanna come?"

Mal looks down at her pajamas and asks for a few minutes to get changed, but really she just needs to secure her notebook. Within 10 minutes, the two have made their way into the street. Hazy clouds block out the sun for what's expected to be a hot day.

"It smells amazing," Mal marvels, looking at the bright green trees shading the street.

"I think it's jasmine," Dani says softly. "It smells like my mom's perfume."

Mal sets her mouth in a hard line. The news of Dani's parents' deaths prompted Mal to reach out, and their conversation both felt like a major concession and the absolute bare minimum.

"How have you been doing since then?" Mal approaches. She may not like Dani, but it's hard to not care about her, even after all they went through.

"It always stays with you, the grief," Dani says, gesturing with her hands in that New York-way. Mal used to emulate it, but the habit never stuck. "As your life gets bigger, the grief seems smaller in the grand scheme of things. But other days it's all I can think about."

Dani pauses.

"Weirdly, it made the pandemic easier. I could fund food banks and tweet about safety measures without the fear of losing anyone," Dani says, putting a smile on her face to offset the horrendous weight of the statement. "No aging parents or friends who worked at hospitals or grocery stores. My friends were safe in the Hamptons. Ben quarantined at the old barn since I had to lead the city through lockdown."

"You were alone for that?" Mal is horrified. She and Serena hiked nearly every day, commenting on the news footage coming out of New York City. It's the only time in her life that she was thankful to not be there; the photos of the morgue trucks still haunt her.

"It wasn't safe for Ben to stay with me," Dani says, getting defensive. "I was at the epicenter of the worst mass-casualty event in the city's history."

Mal puts her hand on Dani's wrist as they slow their pace, still clinging to the left side of the residential street.

"I'm not judging," Mal says gently. "It sounds like a horrible experience."

"I can't believe there are no sidewalks here," Dani complains, her face red and flustered from Mal's questioning. At least that explains why Dani spent yesterday flirting with Peter; her fiancé clearly is an absent partner. Mal will always choose to be alone than settle, but she only learned that from her college relationship with Adam. Without that experience, she might be in Dani's shoes—desperate to be with someone, anyone, rather than be alone.

"Think that hot take will get you on the front page of the *Sentinel*?" Mal jokes, letting up on Dani. "What? I've seen their coverage. I know what they say about you."

"That they would turn an unassuming comment like 'sidewalks' into a front-page story, probably with a joke about how I'm too fat to even use them?"

"That would be an affront to Big Cement," Mal says. "Anti-union, too."

"I can't win." Dani shakes her head.

They walk in silence for a while, mostly so Mal can figure out how to broach the Peter topic again. Just as she opens her mouth, Dani offloads an emotional bomb.

"Rosen is coming in tomorrow," she says. "Are you really willing to stay in the same house as him?"

Mal extracts her e-cig from the pocket of her shorts and takes a long drag, letting the nicotine calm her frazzled nerves from the mere mention of his name. She breathes out a cloud of smoke and ignores Dani wrinkling her face in disgust. It annoys Mal that Dani doesn't have a vice; for as long as Mal has known her, Dani hasn't abused anything. She saw Dani get drunk only once. If anything, she is an expert in moderation.

"Let me know if I'm overstepping, but I have a proposition for you," Dani says. "I think it'll help you find closure with him."

"Closure doesn't exist," Mal says, quoting a TikTok therapist she watches instead of seeing a trained professional. Hey, at least it's something.

Dani abruptly stops walking.

"What if he told you the truth about that night?" Dani calls out to Mal's back.

Mal turns to face Dani, swatting at the curls blowing in front of her face. Mal knows what happened in college, but her chest is rising and falling more quickly.

"What if you had 10 minutes to ask him anything you wanted to know, and he told you the absolute truth? No bullshit, no lies. An actual, honest conversation," Dani says, reading Mal's puzzled expression perfectly. Now her hands are sweating.

A cloud of darkness descends on Mal. Nothing with Dani is free, ever.

"What do you want in exchange?" Mal asks.

Dani shakes her head.

"Just think about it," she says.

"I can't do that unless I know what you want from me," Mal says. She hates that her voice cracks, that the memory of Andrew still cuts deep. That they all can still hurt her.

"Your spreadsheets," Dani says. "And a consultation."

That's it? The planning documents Mal hasn't looked at since college?

"How do I know you're telling the truth?" Mal asks. "Assuming I'm interested."

"I can show you later," Dani offers. "And then you can make a decision."

Mal thinks back to the first time she met Andrew. How she barged into Adam's room, only to find Andrew sitting on the extra-long twin bed. How he had that smirk on his perfect, symmetrical face when he told Mal he didn't think Adam's girlfriend would be pretty. How he looked at her, and the way he smelled, and the way that he was the first person to point out the obvious: that Adam flirted with every girl he met. How his bicep pulsed when he grabbed the doorframe, and how Mal felt a shot of adrenaline crackle through her body. A chemical imbalance. These *hows* were about how she first fell in love with him. The only *hows* she has left are how he could have done what he did. Dani's proposal might finally answer those questions and prove Mal was never the problem. It would prove how everything was all Andrew's fault.

CHAPTER SEVEN

MAL
WESTON COLLEGE, FRESHMAN YEAR
SEPTEMBER 13, 2013 — BEFORE

MAL BREEZED INTO A SMALL CLASSROOM with large windows overlooking the quad. The space, in both size and location, was an anomaly on campus, where many of the buildings had been gutted and updated without losing the charm of their red-brick-and-white-column exteriors. Patricia Peterson's classroom, however, had stayed the same since the campus was erected, and Mal appreciated the effort to protect its history as one of the most prestigious undergraduate writing programs in the country—and the smallest.

The room could only fit 12 desks, arranged four in a line, so Mal eased into the second row. She was a front-row student only in quality, not temperament. A gorgeous guy with gelled black hair and light brown eyes winked at her from the front row, but she frowned at his greeting. Mal only applied to Weston College because Adam said it was his first choice and that they could keep dating if they were at the same school. She didn't want to give anyone the wrong idea.

Adam's roommate, Andrew, walked in next and immediately slid into the seat next to Mal. She wanted to scowl but found her face muscles couldn't contort that way. He was just so . . . pretty, with those piercing green eyes that made her feel transparent.

"Thanks for saving me a seat," he said, leaning back and stretching his legs out.

Her brain felt like it was wiped clean, with no trace of a good comeback at her disposal.

"Hey man, you're on the lacrosse team, right?" Gelled Hair leaned over his laptop, eager to join the conversation.

Andrew flashed him a toothy grin, likely reveling in being deemed a popular kid so soon after stepping foot onto campus.

"Sebastian," Gelled Hair introduced himself.

"Rosen."

Ugh, a last-namer.

Four other kids—three girls and a guy—sat in their seats, followed by the door slamming shut behind their professor. Patricia Peterson, PhD, led the English department and was one of the most influential professors at the college. This writing program only admitted six freshmen each year, and that cohort would spend four years workshopping each other's pieces. They would also listen to program-wide lectures twice a week, mostly for the networking experiences. That would have excited Mal before she learned about the Newts; this curriculum seemed designed for gen pop, the unfortunate people like last month's version of herself who weren't blessed with connections and prestige.

In Mal's acceptance letter, the admissions department wrote that they flag the top five percent of applicants with writing interests, and those students are asked to apply for the seminar.

She had spent days working on her application. As competitive as the program was, her year turned out to be even stronger: The school admitted seven students instead of six.

Mal looked around the room at her peers, who might go on to win the National Book Award or the Booker Prize in the next decade. Mal pulled her cardigan tight, already giving herself chills. Her whole life she had felt like she was in the wrong place, but all those wrong turns finally brought her here. She wouldn't squander one minute of it.

"Please go around the room and share your name, where you're from, and what you aspire to do after graduating from this program," Professor Peterson said.

There was Julianne Chen of New Jersey, who wanted to be poet laureate, and Atlanta's Darnell Grady, who aspired to write features for the *New York Times Magazine*. Then there was Azza, a San Francisco native whose high school screenplays had won national awards. Mal gulped, feeling proud to be in the room with immense talent but also unsure whether running the high school newspaper at her magnet high school was something she should mention. Was that impressive enough?

"Andrew Rosen, Miami, and I don't know what I want to do."

Everyone's heads snapped to look at the tall athlete without a career path, while Mal whispered: "Aren't you from Fort Lauderdale?"

"Close enough." Andrew smirked.

"And who are you?" Professor Peterson asked, her voice smooth like whiskey but her eyes sharp with interest.

"Um, Mallory. I'm from Chicago. Well, actually the suburbs of Chicago," she stammered.

Andrew snickered when she used her full name, and her shoulders shot up to her ears. He made her misspeak, and she hated nothing more than being inaccurate. She was precise, which is why she never lied about being from Chicago like everyone else did in Highland Park.

"How do you want your education to help you beyond the gates of Weston?" Professor Peterson smiled, and Mal recognized warmth in her eyes. She relaxed a little.

"I want to write literary novels," Mal said, trying to regain her composure as Peterson took aim at her next student.

"Sebastian. Seb. From Venezuela. And I also want to be a poet."

Julianne stuck her tongue out as another screenwriter, Veronica, introduced herself.

"The first thing I tell all my students is to get some thick skin," Peterson said. "To be a writer is to be rejected. But getting comfortable with rejection makes the process a lot easier, and it's important for the psyche. With that in mind, we're going to work on our first assignment: a character study on each other."

Andrew sat up a little straighter.

"I've assigned everyone a student to study. You'll have two weeks to watch them, interview them, do whatever you like—within the bounds of the law," Peterson said as she retreated behind her desk to look at her laptop screen. "Your job is to write something up; it can be as short as a haiku or as long as a profile, but the goal is to get to the essence of the person. We'll then read the works aloud and critique the piece on its face, and then allow the subject to respond. Our classes will always be this way: read and respond in person, and then provide written critique as homework."

Mal's gaze slid to Andrew, and she hoped Peterson wouldn't assign her to him. It would be too weird with Adam if she became intimately close with his roommate. There was already enough chemistry.

"Seb, you're profiling Azza," Peterson said. Seb and one of the blonde girls locked eyes.

"Azza, Darnell. Darnell, Veronica. Veronica, Andrew."

Mal let out a small breath. Good, she wouldn't have to psychoanalyze him. Her brain loved to ruminate, latch onto people she didn't understand, and she didn't have the bandwidth to fixate on him.

"Andrew, Mallory," Peterson said.

Mal barely heard the rest of the assignments. It turned out that Friday the 13th really was worth fearing. She snapped her head toward Andrew, who smiled at her with devilish glee.

"Mallory Shepard, I can't wait to dig in," he said.

* * *

Back at Henley Hall, Mal pleaded for her life.

"You can't talk to him about me," Mal begged Adam.

Adam barely looked up from his economics textbook and told her she was getting worked up about nothing.

"You should be nice to Rosen," Adam said. "He's always in the lounge reading. He's deep, you know, so it'll probably be a good profile."

"He can read?" Mal screeched. "I thought there's a rule against hot people being smart."

That caused Adam to look up.

"It's a class assignment. It's not going in the *New Yorker*. And he knows everything about you anyway," Adam said.

"Everything about me?" Mal shot back. "We barely know each other."

"I told him about why you came to Weston," he said, shutting the shiny hardcover to look at her. "And that you're an incredible writer."

He sauntered over to her, apparently overcome with horniness. Adam pulled Mal close and swayed like they were slow dancing.

"I guess he doesn't know what a good kisser you are," he said. His eyes brimmed.

Mal felt his dick press into her bare leg, and her heart started pounding. Adam reached behind her neck to lift the heavy mass of curls. The coolness of his hand against her skin, warm and sweaty, gave her a jolt, but Adam didn't seem to notice. Instead, he pressed his mouth to hers, his tongue darting in and out. Mal matched his rhythm, though she had better make outs in high school before she even started dating Adam. She thought kissing may never be good. Adam slipped his hand into her cotton underwear. She stiffened, already uncomfortable.

"You're so wet," he breathed into her ear. "Do you think it's time? You feel so good."

Adam started flicking his fingers faster, and Mal's legs began to buckle a little.

"Okay," she said, which prompted Adam to carry her to his extra-long twin bed.

He plopped her on the rock-hard mattress and somehow managed to lock the door and grab a condom from the top shelf of his dresser before she could come up with another excuse.

"You're not putting a sock on the door?" asked Mal, who finally came up with the last thing she could think of when Adam stuck his head under her dress. "What if Andrew walks in?"

"That doesn't happen in real life," Adam said, popping back up to look at Mal with frustration. "Why are you obsessed with him?"

"I'm not," Mal stuttered. "I just want to make sure we're not interrupted. It's . . . special."

Adam paused to consider that and nodded. He grabbed his cell phone to presumably shoot Andrew a text message. After a beat, Adam smiled and declared they were all set before getting up again to turn off the lights. Mal was thankful for the darkness. It allowed her to look apprehensive without Adam noticing. She wanted to lose her virginity and be done with it, already. Then she could finally focus on the things that mattered.

He slowly walked over to Mal and ran his hands up her scrawny legs, which to her dismay hadn't filled out between high school and arriving at college. With one hand in his pants and the other on her breast, Adam climbed on top of her and started gyrating in the least sexy way Mal could have imagined. His unzipped denim jeans rubbed uncomfortably against her bare legs, leaving her feeling sore and overexposed before they even did anything.

"Take your clothes off," she whispered.

"You first," he said.

She complied, pulling off her cotton dress and unclasping her bra. It was a small victory that her boobs reached a B cup before they stopped growing altogether.

"I love seeing you naked," Adam grunted as he ripped at the foil.

He rolled the condom onto his dick and slowly started entering Mal. Pain radiated through her vagina and she gasped. No one ever told her it was going to hurt this much. Tears streamed down her face while Adam looked horrified.

"What's wrong?" Adam asked, panic poisoning his caramel-colored eyes.

"It hurts so much," Mal whispered, with a death grip on his unwashed pillowcase. "Just keep going. Just do it."

Adam pulled out and fell to Mal's side, gently pulling her into his arms.

"I'm not doing that," he said, trying to flatten the coils of hair flying into his face. "It's okay, we'll try again later."

Mal let out a sob. Shame warmed her body.

"What's wrong with me?" she asked. "Why does it hurt so much?"

"Nothing's wrong with you," Adam said. "It's okay. It's okay."

Mal's heart sank. She pictured it tied down to rocks like the way the mafia throws bodies into the river. She hadn't considered losing her virginity would be hard, but now she'd have to go through the same pain all over again. Mal liked anniversaries, dates to mark important moments: her first kiss, her parents' divorce, the day she started working on her novel. Would September 13th count, or was it just the day she was partially penetrated? What a milestone.

She glanced at Andrew's desk, taking in his stationery and notepads neatly lined up on his desk, and stayed in Adam's arms until he decided to take a shower. Once the door clicked, she jumped out of bed to snoop through Andrew's desk, a welcome distraction from her dysfunctional body. Mal flipped through pamphlets for a prison volunteer program and the attached business card, which identified Andrew's buddy: Deandre Downes. She made a mental note to look up what Deandre was imprisoned for. She couldn't imagine the school would partner students with hardened criminals, but she supposed that was the whole purpose of prisons. Innocent people didn't serve time.

Mal turned her attention to Adam's cell phone charging on his desk. She typed in his password—she had watched him pound out the digits of his birthday countless times—and went to Facebook Messenger to search for her name. Mal wanted to know what he was telling their friends from home about college, about her. Maybe it would give her some insight into how she could better perform for him, since she could no longer feign waiting as a reason to not have sex. And dammit, if she was going to have sex, she wanted Adam bragging about it for weeks.

Messages between him and his best friend from home popped up, detailing how it was a mistake Adam had kept dating Mal in college. That there was a girl on his floor that he was interested in. And another girl in his finance class. So many other girls, and he was stuck with Mal, who his friend pointed out had yet to put out after years of dating. Tears pricked Mal's eyes as she exited out of the app and crawled back into her traitorous boyfriend's bed, wishing she had never dared to look in the first place.

DANI
WESTON COLLEGE, FRESHMAN YEAR
SEPTEMBER 20, 2013 — BEFORE

WHEN MAL INVITED DANI TO LAY out on the quad one Friday afternoon, Dani thought about saying no. She didn't appreciate how Mal essentially stalked her and then put in her in a bad position with the Newts. Dani kept her small talk with Mal to a minimum—though Mal didn't seem to notice and yapped away—while she prepared for her hazing period.

The girls had been tasked with reading feminist literature and facing pop quizzes at random hours of the day, a marked difference from her friends who were pledging Greek life at their Big Ten and SEC schools. While they chugged questionable liquor and sat on washing machines while sorority sisters circled fat pockets with Sharpies, Dani ate up the works of bell hooks and Angela Davis. She hoped keeping her head in a book would send Mal a message, but Mal was undeterred—and Dani grew to admire her for it.

The Newts' last words also rang loudly in Dani's ears: Tell no one. Not your boyfriend, not your therapist. And if they ever heard a non-Newt utter their group's name aloud based on something the pledges said, the girls could all but guarantee expulsion, a total erasure.

It still made Dani shudder, realizing her whole life had been just that. She was allowed to be on the campus, so to speak, but she was treated like a ghost. Dani wouldn't risk anything to feel that way again. So, she took a deep breath and forgave Mal. It was better to have Mal on her side, anyway. Dani didn't like the idea of pissing Mal off, which is how she found herself on a tattered picnic blanket and immersed in people watching.

Dani noticed a tall blond guy inching his way toward them. He was fratty, if you were into that kind of thing, and had his eyes lasered in on Mal. Dani elbowed her, possibly a little too sharply, and Mal jumped.

"Do you know him?" Dani whispered, thrusting her chin in the guy's direction.

Mal looked alarmed and then rolled her eyes.

"He's obsessed with me," Mal said. "He's everywhere I go. I can't shake him."

Dani's heart started to palpitate. She had dealt with stalkers before, people angry that her parents had accumulated so much wealth. Dani honestly didn't remember a time they didn't have intense security around 24/7. Her hands shook as she clumsily tried to pull up the number for Jay, the private detective she had grown closest to, and told Mal someone would be here ASAP.

"Woah, I was just kidding," Mal said, holding Dani's shaking hands. "We're working on a project. He's profiling me for class."

Mal looked down at Dani's phone, clearly in shock that her circumstantial new best friend was willing to go to extreme measures for a stranger. Dani wanted to die.

"You weren't joking," Mal said. "Do you have mob connections? Or are you secretly the president's daughter?"

The thought of Dani being Barack Obama's love child sent her into full-body giggles, the nervous energy dissipating with every chuckle as the frat boy approached.

"You ready to go?" the guy's voice hummed, low and satisfying. He flashed a smile at Dani, but his eyes were trained on Mal. "I want to make sure we have enough time for your childhood trauma. You have stories to tell, I can see it."

"You come across as mildly sociopathic. Surely that presented in childhood?" Mal shot back, a dimple punctuating her cheek. "I bet you burned small animals with a magnifying glass. Sid from *Toy Story* was actually inspired by you, but the writers didn't want to terrify children, so he's less sadistic in the film."

"Oh, so you consider *Toy Story* a film. Have you not seen *Annie Hall*?"

"I don't want to support child molesters, even if they did make one of the greatest movies of all time, thank you very much," Mal said. "And *Toy Story* is a crowning achievement in cinema and the history of animation. If your brain cells worked, you'd know that."

Dani watched the two of them volley insults back and forth at each other, feeling like she was watching *Sweet Home Alabama* but with two college freshmen lacking the Southern charm.

"Is this your...boyfriend?" Dani asked, searching for the right word.

"Ew, no," Mal shrieked as the guy smiled down at her.

"This is Andrew. Rosen," she stammered. "My boyfriend's roommate."

"You can just call me Rosen," he said, pulling a flask out from his backpack and taking a sip. He offered it to the girls, who declined.

"Oh, sorry, you two seemed..." Dani flushed, trailing off.

"Intimated, I know," Rosen said.

"Big word," Mal rolled her eyes.

They packed up their belongings and walked back to the dorms. Dani noticed other girls looking at them enviously and guys calling out to Rosen as they strode across campus. Dani wondered what his deal was, probably some sort of athlete.

Maybe Mal's contempt was real, but the more he talked, the less Dani thought anyone could dislike this guy. He had the charisma of people she knew from back home but without any of the pretense that he was better than anyone else around him.

"What are you guys working on?" Dani asked.

"A profile. I'm trying to get inside her. Tear down all her walls." Rosen poked Mal and laughed, clearly amused at her body clenching at his touch. "But she won't let me."

He pouted as they approached Henley Hall.

Mal and Rosen lived in the oldest dorm on campus, a stately building with a reddish-brown façade that reminded Dani of the Upper West Side's Lucerne. It was so unlike her own residential building, which was state-of-the-art and almost felt sterile in its newness. The fact that a bunch of English majors lived at Henley Hall just seemed obvious to Dani—and it thrilled her to get an invitation inside. She wanted to make friends with other people outside the Newts, or at least hang out with Mal in another capacity. When they took the elevator up to the fifth floor, the doors opened to hordes of kids.

"Our R.A. goes to raves all the time, so he lets us be delinquents," Mal yelled to Dani over the music.

Dani didn't even know upstate New York had venues for raves in the first place, unless they were also held by secret societies. She shook her head, feeling woefully underprepared to live in a community where it felt possible to know everyone else's business. In the city, it just wasn't feasible—as long as you left the Upper East Side. A girl with bleach-blonde hair blew past them on roller skates as they maneuvered through the crowd forming in the narrow hallway. Everyone was casually dressed compared to Dani's mini dress, and she suddenly felt attention-seeking and exposed in her outfit.

The trio slipped into an open room, where they were greeted with sloshing red Solo cups of jungle juice—a mid-afternoon treat, Dani supposed.

"Bottoms up," Rosen said, toasting the girls. He drained the cup's contents in one sip before filling it up again. Mal dragged Dani toward a dark-haired boy, forgetting Rosen altogether, and introduced the two.

"I'm assuming you're the boyfriend," Dani said brightly.

Adam chuckled, but his interest in her stopped there. He pulled Mal into a tight embrace and murmured "baby" into Mal's hair like Dani wasn't even there.

"Do you want to take a walk in the courtyard?" Adam asked Mal, the whites of his eyes bloodshot. "I want to show you something."

"Are you okay if we go outside for a little?" Mal asked Dani, her voice strained.

Dani wasn't sure whether Mal wanted permission to go or to intervene. And Mal's eyes—normally animated and conveying urgency—were vacant. No hints allowed.

"Um, I think it's okay," Dani said, still unsure.

Adam pulled Mal out of his room, though Dani clocked Rosen watching the couple from across the room. He draped his arm over another girl's shoulder, his grasp firm, while she twisted a little in her seat to get a better look at him. Rosen then looked at the girl with intensity and bent his head closer to her. The girl scurried out from his grip and left the room, leaving Rosen slumped over on the bed. But within moments his head perked up, catching the eye of another girl smiling at him, and he crossed the room to join her.

Dani awkwardly bopped her head to music and drained the rest of her jungle juice before another dark-haired guy, maybe an inch or two taller than her, approached.

"You look like you need a drink," he said, pointing at her empty cup.

"I'm okay," Dani said. "This isn't the best-tasting thing in the world."

That was an understatement. It tasted like gasoline.

"I have wine. Would you want that? I can get it from my room."

Flattered, Dani smiled, prompting him to sprint out of the room—presumably to retrieve the bottle. She waited for what felt like an excessively long time, one where at least a dozen people looked at her curiously but didn't come up to say hi or introduce themselves, until she couldn't take it anymore. Dani went looking for her mysterious bartender.

She meandered down the hallway, poking her head into each open dorm room. A group of boys in one room sat on the floor and passed around a joint before laughing like a six-headed serpent when they saw her. Dani's face flushed. She hated the person she was on drugs, and even more so that her parents seemed to think it was a rite of passage not worth discussing. The closest she and her dad ever got to talking about it was when he paid off a *Page Six* reporter to kill the story: Out-of-control socialite goes on a bender. Apparently, it was enough to cover the reporter's journalism school student loans, and no one was the wiser. She straightened her shoulders, realizing how pathetic it was to go looking after some guy in the first place. Before she could turn around, though, muffled noises emanated from the second-to-last door on the left.

Dani peeked in and saw him on the ground, blood trickling down his face. Dani suppressed the urge to scream and instead looked around the room for something to soak up the blood. She needed to stay calm. Dani saw the unbroken wine bottle sweating next to him and wrapped it in a towel draped over a desk chair. She pressed the fabric to his forehead, hoping the ice substitute would cut down on the inevitable swelling. He winced, his fists tightened in his lap, though he didn't resist her care.

"What happened?" she asked, surprised that panic clung to her vocal cords and made the words come out higher, unrecognizable to her own ears.

"I slammed my head on the mini fridge," he muttered, his cheeks turning strawberry red—a fact not lost on Dani, who found it ingratiating.

"Do you need help getting into bed?" she asked.

He opened one eye to squint at her and grimaced.

"You must think I'm a loser," he said. "Who injures themselves on a mini fridge?"

"This can't be your worst injury," Dani said, helping him to his feet and easing him onto the mattress. "Do you know your name?"

Dani knew it was a question doctors on TV asked concussed patients, but she also wanted to know the answer.

"Peter," he said, wincing.

She opened the drawers on the nearby dresser looking for pajamas as Peter recalled his worst lacrosse injury: a gnarly toe incident that required a cortisone shot so he could play in the semi-finals. His mom drove him to the doctor and back so he could play in the tournament, despite medical concerns that he could permanently damage his foot. Dani recognized the same kind of passive parenting she grew up with: allowing your child to do whatever they wanted, rather than enforcing boundaries like parents are supposed to. It was the first of many strings Dani would learn connected her to Peter and fortified their bond.

She settled on Islanders-branded fleece sweatpants and a threadbare black T-shirt. Dani sat on the edge of Peter's bed, unbuttoning his shirt and trying to ignore the swirling of desire once she saw his hirsute chest. He half-heartedly persuaded her to let him change himself, but Dani demanded he keep the cold wine bottle to his head. Peter at least made her turn around so he could change out of his jeans and into the pajama pants.

"Okay, I'm done," he called out. "Do I need stitches? My head really hurts."

Dani put her hands over his and directed him to let go. His hand lingered before falling onto his belly, and Dani lifted the bloodied towel to survey the damage.

"I'm not a doctor, but I've watched enough *Grey's Anatomy* to guess that you're fine. Do you have a first aid kit? I want to clean you up so you don't wind up with an infection."

"Under the bed," he said.

Supplies procured, Dani offered him a hand to hold as she cleaned the wound with alcohol. The cut wasn't emergency-room ready, but it wasn't just a scratch, either.

"Are you pre-med?" Peter asked, his eyes steady on her face. "You'd be a great doctor."

"Undecided," she said. "I don't know what I want to be."

He let out a whimper as she wiped him down and dabbed antibiotic cream on his forehead with laser precision.

"There," she said, smoothing on the Band-Aid. "Good as new."

"You're beautiful," Peter said, his hand slipping into the sheet of hair falling toward him.

"You're drunk," she said, smiling.

"Sober enough to know what I'm saying," he shot back with surprising sincerity.

His hand moved to the back of her head, drawing her in. His mouth smelled like nectar.

"Go easy on me," he whispered, his breath hot. "I have a head wound."

Dani tasted the smile on his lips as she sunk further into his bed. His mouth felt urgent on hers, his free hand slowly moving around the curves hidden under her mini dress. Peter pulled away first after what felt like the longest and shortest kiss of Dani's life. She could stay in his bed forever if she was promised just another kiss.

"I want to take you out," he said.

"Will you remember this tomorrow?"

"Aren't you sleeping over? You can remind me then." His devilish grin roiled Dani. He wanted her to stay over? She could scream.

"I sleepwalk. You don't want to share a bed with me when that happens."

"You're hard to get—in more ways than one," he joked.

"Am I hard to get or is your head just gushing blood?" Dani asked. "Maybe I'm just the girl who took pity on you."

"You don't pity me," Peter said, his voice becoming serious. "I barely know you and I already know you're a caring person. It's visible."

"If you can remember that you asked me out by morning, I'll do it," Dani said, expecting nothing but wishing for it to be true. She wasn't sure if it was him or the jungle juice, but her stomach was doing cartwheels.

"Promise?" Peter held out his pinky ring, a thick digit that dwarfed hers.

"Promise."

CHAPTER EIGHT

DANI
SOUTH CONGRESS AVENUE
MAY 24, 2024 — AFTER

After hopscotching from cowboy-boot store to cowboy-boot store on Austin's main drag, the group lands at a trendy thrift shop. Dani pulls out a long denim skirt from the rack and holds it in front of her. Shopping is always a difficult task as a large mid-sized person, but recently she's noticed that thrift stores are more likely to carry clothes that she can at least try on. Not that she normally shops in these kinds of places—she prefers Tanya Taylor and it's gauche to gentrify thrift stores—but it's a nice thing to see, nonetheless. Skirt in hand, Dani plucks a semi-sheer green top to go with it and holds the outfit up in front of Mal.

"Do you think this will go with my new cowboy boots?" Dani asks, propping a foot out so Mal could appreciate the entire look. Dani snagged calfskin cowboy boots at the last store and couldn't wait to put them on. She may never wear them again, but when in Texas. Mal peers up from a small black notebook, pen in hand, before both items disappear into her tote bag.

"Try it on," Mal urges.

"You're not getting anything?" Dani asks.

Mal runs her fingers through a suede fringed jacket and shakes her head. Dani disappears into the curtained dressing room and shimmies out of her athleisure and into her finds.

"I'll show you mine if you show me yours," she calls out to Mal.

"You sound like Peter."

"Peter hasn't talked like that since college. He's reformed." Dani's pleased the shirt has enough stretch and admires her reflection in the mirror. Without her signature blowout and red lips, Dani looks like a cool, 29-year-old woman—not someone who's on the precipice of being nationally recognizable wherever she goes.

"Maybe he's on his best behavior for you."

Dani steps out of the dressing room to argue but sees Mal is wearing the jacket. The fringe swishes around as Mal admires her reflection in the large brass mirror.

"It's giving yeehaw." Dani sidles up to her. "You need to get it."

"This is very Lisa Says Gah." Mal's hand flutters in front of Dani's outfit, though they keep their gazes on their reflections.

"Is that an LA thing?"

"Big LA thing," Mal says.

"Who would have ever thought Mal Shepard would school me on fashion?" Dani smiles.

"I've come a long way from borrowing your going-out wedge heels."

"God bless."

Mal takes the jacket off and gingerly lays it on a chair before slipping her tote bag back on her shoulder. She smiles tightly before wandering off to peruse the racks. Dani flips the tag over: $120. A bargain for a real suede jacket. Dani eyes Mal, wondering why she's leaving it behind. Between the TV writing, the *New York Times* bestselling book, and presumably whatever is in that notebook, money shouldn't be a problem.

Dani's phone buzzes. Alexia.

Should be in this evening, Alexia writes. *Where should I meet you?*

I'll let you know, Dani replies. *Just don't draw attention to yourself*

Me? Never.

Dani slips her phone back into her bag and considers the task at hand: keeping Mal happy until she can show her how the serum works. Dani knows Mal will only consider her offer for so long, and especially because Mal won't believe it until she sees it.

At the checkout counter, the salesgirl clips the tags off Dani's clothes so she can wear them out. Then she takes the suede jacket to remove the security tag hidden inside.

"Dan, c'mon," Mal says as Dani hands over her Amex. "I don't need that."

"Consider it a birthday gift," Dani says.

"My birthday isn't until August," Mal protests.

"Do you want a separate bag for your clothes?" the cashier asks, eyeing the pile of athleisure in Dani's arms.

"Yes," Dani says before turning to Mal. "I know when your birthday is. Your whole personality is classic Leo."

"And I used to be the woo-woo one," Mal says, rolling her eyes, but at least she doesn't argue. The two exit the store, discussing whether Dani should get another hole in her ear at the nearby piercing studio, and walk toward the boys. As they linger outside trying to figure out where to go next, a familiar face catches Dani's attention on the sidewalk. She stares at him puzzlingly, not able to place him, until it clicks.

"Hey, cowgirl," Ben greets her, the corners of his eyes crinkling, as he plants a kiss on her cheek and smooths her hair back.

"What are you doing here?" Dani's voice is leaden, and she sees contempt settle on Peter's face. Seb is puzzled at her reaction, while Mal is downright giddy. Ben, of course, is oblivious to it all.

"I wanted to surprise you and come a little early!" Ben says, looking at her expectantly.

"Sorry, I'm just surprised." Dani embraces him while hiding her bare left ring finger. She turns to face the group, doing her best to look at everyone's faces blindly. She doesn't want to see their judgment. "This is Ben. My fiancé."

She tries to gauge Peter's reaction as her friends welcome him, but he won't look at her. Instead, he and Seb walk ahead to the next store. Ben sidles up beside Dani.

"I've never seen you like this before," he says. "You look so good."

Dani smiles weakly and kisses him, worried whether he can taste Peter on her lips.

MAL
SOUTH CONGRESS AVENUE
MAY 24, 2024 — AFTER

WHAT AN ABSOLUTE DELIGHT. A LOVE triangle right before her very eyes. Mal gleefully approaches Ben and introduces herself. Before he can respond, she's giving him the third degree.

"How long have you been with Dani for?" she asks, trying to remember if she noticed a ring on Dani's hand. It's something she would have noticed, if not to make a judgement on the diamond's cost or the amount of child labor that went into excavating it.

"About five years," he smiles at Dani. "Engaged for three."

"Gotta lock it down, Ben," Mal winks, wondering how anyone could be engaged for that long. "Dani's a hot commodity."

"I've been trying," he laughs.

"And when's the wedding?" Mal asks.

"We're looking at Q3 for the wedding."

Mal's smile stretches wide as Ben continues talking about their upcoming nuptials like it's a board meeting or something else wildly unromantic. Dani shoots Mal a pleading look, but this is why Mal came here, to have fun. Finally.

"Are you staying local? To New York, I mean," Mal asks.

"We're thinking about flying everyone out to Napa," Ben says.

Mal wonders if Dani still has the private plane.

"You hate wine," Peter snorts and turns to face the couple, but he's only speaking to Dani. Ben gives Peter a kind smile, the kind that implies he knows who won the war. Peter's just Dani's butt-hurt ex-boyfriend from college.

"Even if you hate wine, you'll change your tune after going to Napa," he says, pressing his thumb and pointer finger together in a hand gesture. "It's A1."

"A1?" Peter mumbles, squinting in confusion.

Seb, meanwhile, forges ahead. He finally turns into a store selling cowboys hats, boots, and other tchotchkes. They follow him like ants in a line. Ben turns to Mal.

"I've been so excited to meet the famous Mal," Ben says, giving Mal the opportunity to really size him up. He looks like a Lego man, all bulk and square edges. "Dani looks forward to your Sunday calls so much that she insists I leave the house for her one-on-one time with you."

He chuckles as he examines a paper weight the shape of a boot, which is a relief to Mal because her face would immediately give Dani away.

"Our Sunday calls," Mal repeats, knowing for a fact that their only communication since college was one heartfelt message apiece: when Mal sold her book and when Dani's parents died. And that one phone call. But overall, no, there aren't any Sunday calls.

"I hope it hasn't been too invasive." Mal tries to look faux abashed.

"Three hours a Sunday is a small price to pay," he says before holding his hand up in a stage-whisper gesture. "I just watch football at the sports bar near our apartment. But really, I'm impressed you take her call so consistently. Sunday at 10 a.m. is no joke. Dani says it's based around your writing schedule, but I admire your commitment."

Mal wonders how Dani can keep so many secrets, and yet she appears unbothered as she admires a cowboy hat. Ben excuses himself to walk over and try on hats with his fiancée.

Mal flicks the label on a nearby hat and starts coughing when she sees they're $300 apiece. Out of the corner of her eye, Peter is glowering at the couple, who are modeling hats for each other.

"I'm surprised it fits," Ben says good-naturedly, tipping the brim toward Dani.

"Your head is medium sized," the salesman drawls.

He's the first real Texan they've met all day, and Mal saw him guessing people's head sizes since they walked in. Mal pokes Seb, who's eyeing a pair of silver cowboy boots.

"This is like the world's worst carnival barker," Mal says. She's feeling magnanimous today and wants him to make good on his promise of trying to repair their relationship. "Oh, you need those."

Seb winces, saying the price is too high.

"You make half a mil a year," she says. "And you're only in Texas once."

"God willing," he says, inspecting the heel. "I forgot how bad you are for my wallet."

"Better yours than mine," Mal says as Seb slides into the shoes like they were meant for him, his *solemate*. A smile slips on her face as she remembers an essay she wrote for Peterson's class. Seb sashays to the women's section and plucks a pair of pink and brown cowboy boots with cutout hearts up the shaft.

"You have to try these on at least." Seb thrusts the soft leather boots into her hands, raw from the unrelenting heat. Then he leans in and tells Mal the price as she inspects the only pair of cowboy boots she's ever wanted.

"If you're going to make me try on thousand-dollar cowboy boots, you need to be prepared to buy them for me," Mal says, looking at him expectantly.

Seb sulkily puts the cowgirl boots back on the rack. While they can (used to?) goad each other into mostly anything, Mal takes solace in knowing Seb is cheap. Ben pulls out his credit card to buy his and Dani's matching hats, neatly boxed up with the shopping bag handles pulled through, like a travel case for a record player.

"Do y'all want to drop those off at the house?" Seb asks.

"'Y'all?' We've been here for less than 24 hours," Mal mocks.

"We're good," Ben says, taking Dani's box from her hand in exchange for a kiss.

A female customer approaches the sales guy, holding a cowboy boot the color of strawberries—ones so ripe that their juice drips everywhere. The color disorients Mal.

When the sales guy emerges from the back room with the shoe box, he has an envelope in his hand. However, the girl who asked for the boots is gone.

"Dani?" the dude calls out, reading her name off the envelope.

Mal is right. The threat isn't in her head. But what are they barreling toward?

Dani steps forward, oblivious to the danger that might face her, and begins tearing the card open. Mal plucks the envelope out of Dani's hand and unsuccessfully tries to rip it.

"I'm so over this scavenger hunt," Mal says, looking around for a trash can to toss the unopened letter. But before she can do that, Peter takes the envelope from her.

"Don't be a buzzkill, Firefly," Peter says. The words are clunky coming out of his mouth, though Mal stiffens at the use of Andrew's pet name for her.

"Follow your gaze to the east, and let your hips sway to the beat," he reads.

Mal makes a face.

"It doesn't even rhyme," she complains. "Seems like a dumb direction to follow."

"Rainey Street," Seb says declaratively.

"I heard Rainey Street is so cool!" Ben bounces over.

"Guess that's the next stop," Peter says, giving Mal a hard look.

"We're not getting there for a while," Seb points out. "That's a going-out spot."

"I need to go back to the house anyway and check a few emails," Dani rolls her eyes in self-effacing manner, but the whole back and forth heightens Mal's anxiety.

Mal doesn't want to find out where this scavenger hunt ends. It can't be good. Not at all.

DANI
THE RENTAL IN AUSTIN, TEXAS
MAY 24, 2024 — AFTER

DANI CAN'T GET BACK TO THE house fast enough. She wants to lock herself away for a few hours to avoid Peter's red-hot anger at her betrayal. She and Ben do a quick room switcheroo by taking Marcus' vacated room and punting Rosen, once he arrives, to the undesirable position of sharing a room or sleeping on the couch. Dani quickly slips on her engagement ring, which she carelessly tossed in the nightstand drawer, and takes on her soon-to-be wife duties of unpacking for Ben. She unzips the hard shell of his luggage and throws it open with too much force; he's barely packed anything, though his tux is hanging over the door of the en-suite. What he did pack, however, is perfectly folded into little cubes. Just like his clothes, Dani feels neatly slotted into his life, and she scratches at her neck.

"I was only joking earlier. I didn't expect you to unpack for me." Ben cozies up behind her, and when she turns around, his eyes quickly zoom in on her neck.

"Are you having an allergic reaction?" he asks, holding her chin up to inspect the red splotches forming on her neck. "Did you get stung by anything?"

"It's probably pollen," Dani says, shaking him off.

"Do you want to take a shower?" Ben asks politely, though from the looks of it, he's the one who needs a rinse. He looks a bit sweaty and grimy from the flight, though she's surprised he'd look like that after flying business class for a few hours. Unlike Peter, it's not appealing when he's a little rough around the edges. She likes him clean, manageable.

"No, I'm okay," Dani replies. "You can go in."

He nods, takes a towel and a fresh outfit, and walks into the bathroom—clothes and shoes still on. Ben rarely gets undressed in front of her. It's some kind of private act he saves for the bathroom, away from her prying eyes. Dani and her friends used to be naked in front of each other all the time in college. Sure, most of them were hooking up and dating each other, but Ben's behavior, which once seemed quirky, now prompts her to wonder how intimate they can ever be together. Her engagement ring feels heavy on her finger, a foreign entity.

Dani shoots off a few emails and coordinates with Alexia about the handoff when Ben emerges from the bathroom, steam billowing into their bedroom.

"You're going out like that?" Ben asks, his hair perfectly combed and held in place with gel. Dani feels a pang of grief thinking about how Peter used to walk out of the shower naked, rubbing a towel over his head instead of hiding his lower half, before they'd immediately jump back into bed. Dani knows hers and Ben's passion is nonexistent, but being around Peter (and being touched by Peter) makes the truth of it almost unbearable.

"I thought you like what I'm wearing." Dani looks down at her cute outfit, surprised Ben even said anything. She can count on one hand the number of times he's said anything like this to her. Their relationship is mostly compliments and rainbows, but now she sees, with sobering clarity, how plastic it really is. The desire to pick a fight consumes her.

"No, your hair," he says, still not getting that he's rude to even broach these questions. "You're going to leave it curly?"

"Yes," Dani says dismissively. "I don't need to blow it out."

"Who are you and what have you done with my fiancée?" Ben folds his arms, surveying her. "You bought a $600 blow-dryer the last time we traveled—"

"It was a Dyson."

"Because you forgot yours at home," Ben continues. "I barely see you without makeup on, even on the weekends when we don't leave the apartment—"

"We're in Texas. It's too hot."

"Oh yeah, like August in New York doesn't feel like descending into the third circle of hell." Ben moves toward her to tenderly grab her face, his eyes searching like he's unsure who's in front of him. She wants to drop her anger in deference to his confusion. He never curses, either. "Babe, I'm joking, but I'm surprised to see this side of you with your college friends. You know you can be this way at home, right? I don't expect you to look polished every day."

"It's complicated." Dani pulls away, her cheeks burning as if he slapped her. "I'm a politician at home. People are always watching me—"

"I'm not just other people, Dani." Frustration crosses Ben's face. She's seen him look puzzled or frustrated more times today than in the entirety of their relationship. "If you want to have a Dyson for every city, that's fine with me. I've just never seen this side of you, and I'm worried I'm missing out on a key part of who you are. I thought I knew everything about you."

"It's not that deep," Dani says, knowing her words sting. "You're overreacting."

Ben stands up straighter and looks at her, as if really trying to see if someone had replaced her with an alien during the flight, before disappearing downstairs.

Dani throws herself on the bed, wanting to scream, but then realizes that Ben and Peter might be downstairs. Alone. Where Peter might be disgruntled enough to tell Ben what happened before he got here. She flies off the bed and nearly tumbles down the stairs, her legs moving faster than she can control. But instead of a showdown, Mal is helping herself to some chocolates sitting in a bag out on the counter.

"Want some?" Mal holds up a small, bumpy mound. "I love how everything is mushroom-infused these days. There's a place near my apartment that makes these lattes—"

"Can I see the packaging?"

Mal rolls her eyes, presumably thinking Dani wants to count calories, but what Dani really wants is to review the small warning on the bag.

"How many did you eat?"

"Two, why?"

Dani plucks the piece out of Mal's hand and puts it back in the bag. Mal snatches the bag back to read the fine print.

"Because you're going to be high really soon." Dani wonders how Mal has lived in LA for all these years without knowing the difference between plant protein and psychedelics. Worse, it's going to be a lot harder to impress Mal with the serum if she's high. The two of them curse at the same time.

"Why are you mad?" Dani asks.

"Do you have a sense that the vibes are off?" Mal asks.

"And you're not talking as someone who's on shrooms?" Dani asks.

"No, and it hasn't hit yet, anyway," Mal says, her voice trailing off. "I just want to be cautious tonight, that's all."

"Okay, we can do that," Dani agrees, but then Mal narrows her eyes. Always suspicious.

"Why does it matter to you if I'm high?"

"It doesn't, but I thought I'd show you—"

"You already got into the bag?" Peter's voice booms as he enters the kitchen, eyeing Mal with interest.

"Of course these are yours," Mal groans, tossing him the bag. He pops a chocolate bit into his mouth, and then hands the bag off to newly arrived Seb, who does the same.

"Hot potato," Seb throws the bag back to Dani.

Before she can decide if she wants to get in on the fun, despite Alexia's impending arrival, Ben enters the kitchen.

"Whatcha eating?" Ben asks, and then gives a disapproving look at the bag.

"You don't strike me as a shrooms guy." Peter walks over so Dani's in between her current and former partners. He reaches into the bag Dani's still holding to take another bite. "You're more than welcome to participate."

An innocuous statement with the tone of someone daring Ben to go against his morals. Well, maybe not morals. Ben would simply say that's not the way he was raised. A flicker of anger crosses Ben's face as he puts an arm around Dani.

"It's not a priority for us tonight," Ben says with a smile and firm voice.

For us. She can't remember the last time he us-ed someone. Normally Dani is the one doing the us-ing, and it's usually to get out of something incredibly boring.

"Let's get on the road," Dani says, not wanting to give Peter any more ammunition on how she chooses to live her life— one that doesn't involve him in the slightest.

CHAPTER NINE

MAL
WESTON'S CAMPUS GYM, FRESHMAN YEAR
OCTOBER 17, 2013 — BEFORE

"AM I A TERRIBLE PERSON?" DANI asked between breaths.

Their ponytails bounced as she and Mal sweat on neighboring treadmills. Mal pounded at the buttons to speed up, wanting to outrun Dani. Wanting to win.

"Your body told you all you needed to know," Mal huffed, red-faced.

"What if he doesn't want to be friends anymore?" Dani asked after explaining how her tour guide pal Marcus made a move the night before—and that she purposefully hadn't told him about Peter.

Mal could read between the lines: Dani liked how Marcus made her feel like the main character, someone who's worthy of being the center of attention. And she couldn't fault her. Mal did the same thing with Andrew. They had this tug of war-type banter, where someone chased and then the other pulled away, only to come back around and start the process anew. It was intoxicating, and not only because she liked how his presence shifted the power dynamic between Mal and Adam.

Dani looked at Mal expectantly, like she wanted Mal to convince her she did nothing wrong while also waiting for a dressing down. Never one to miss a shot at moral superiority, Mal took a sharp breath to do just that, but then she saw one of the girls in their pledge class (were they pledges? Mal had no idea what to make of their semi-initiation into the Newts) and felt a tug of loyalty toward Dani. She didn't want anyone overhearing what she really thought, especially another girl in the Newts. Not because she cared what they thought of her, but because she didn't want to give anyone an opportunity to see the cracks in her friendship with Dani and use it against her. Dani was puppy-dog loyal, but Mal imagined flesh-eating pitbulls were once that way too. She had a gut feeling Dani could easily be turned against her with the right ammunition.

"He'll get over it. We're just numbers to them," Mal said. "They're used to shooting their shot. Rejection doesn't hit the same for guys."

"You didn't see the look on his face," Dani said. "Maybe there's something wrong with me. Maybe I'm not someone who's capable of being vulnerable."

"Talking to me about this is pretty vulnerable," Mal pointed out.

"With men."

"Well, you're not missing much," Mal said. "Remember how you almost called the FBI when Andrew was shadowing me for that profile? I finally read it. It's terrible."

"Isn't the English program one of the best in the country? How terrible can it be?" Dani upped the incline on her treadmill. Showoff.

"Okay, it wasn't terrible, but it wasn't great," Mal grumbled. "Maybe my expectations were too high, but it just fell flat. It was too complimentary, and Peterson's critique felt so harsh it was almost like she was criticizing me and not the caricature of me that Andrew created."

"We're always caricatures of ourselves," Dani said. "We're always trying to shift to be what people want us to be."

Mal jumped to the sides of the treadmill so the belt whooshed below her, undisturbed. What the hell was Dani talking about? Mal was herself and only herself. She didn't know how to perform her personality.

"It would make my life a lot easier if I knew how to do that," Mal said, giving Dani a funny look, before jumping back on. "At least I think it killed my crush."

"You have a crush?" Dani squealed.

"C'mon you've seen him." It pained Mal to say the words. "I get like this sometimes, fixating on certain people or things."

She paused, unsure if she should tell Dani about it, but her desire to talk about it at all superseded her hesitation.

"You know, that's how I wound up with Adam. I had a crush on him for all of sophomore year and told everyone. He went from avoiding me in the hallways to bam—" she clapped her hands together—"we were dating by the start of junior year."

She glanced at Dani out of the corner of her eye.

"It's hard for me to tell if the chase is because I actually like someone or if I just want to win," she said. "But with Andrew it feels like there's something more real tethering us together."

Dani nodded but didn't seem like she understood.

"I have a great therapist if you need one," Dani offered, confirming Mal's suspicion.

"Nah, I don't really believe in that," Mal scoffed. "Writing's the only thing that works for me. I just thought a practice that's sacred to me would also be sacred to him. It's not a big deal."

She pushed the red stop button, and the machine screeched to a halt. Dani followed suit, eyeing the smoothie station.

"Want to hydrate?" Dani asked, bouncing toward the counter.

"So, what's up with you and Peter?" Mal asked, trudging behind.

"I want to introduce Peter as my boyfriend to my parents when they visit, but we haven't had that conversation yet," Dani said. "Are your parents coming?"

"That was fast," Mal said, trying to avoid Dani's question. She wanted her college and home lives to stay separate. She wasn't sure her parents even knew about Parents' Weekend.

Dani blushed.

"Well, he's slept over almost every night, and I've never dated anyone before—"

"Dating the wrong men is a rite of passage," Mal interrupted and put her hands up like Dani was holding a gun to her head. "I'm doing it, you're doing it."

Mal collected the strawberry smoothie and paused before taking a sip, having not realized what she ordered. She peered at the barista again, making sure she didn't accidentally conjure up Gold Earrings or Full Metal Jacket, otherwise known by their government names as Alexia and Cindy. She might as well have said "Bloody Mary" three times into a mirror.

"If you think Adam isn't right for you but Rosen is, then maybe you should break up with Adam," Dani offered, handing over her student ID to pay for their smoothies.

Mal held up her drink and clinked plastic cups with Dani in a toast as a thank you.

"Hmm, maybe," Mal said distractedly.

Mal had so many things she wanted to accomplish in her life, and the prospect of not adding "find a partner" to that checklist enticed her. She generally liked spending time with Adam and loved him in a way that felt natural, easy. But Mal knew there were things about their relationship that weren't perfect, or even that good, really. Adam was good enough, and frankly, Mal saw what marriages morphed into. Even if she were madly in love, how long could that magic possibly stay with them? Three years? Five? It was better to stick with good enough than to give that up for the fantasy of what if. Mal needed to believe in herself and her work; she couldn't also believe a soulmate might materialize in front of her, too.

"What happened with you guys last weekend by the way?" Dani asked. "You seemed weird in the dining hall the next morning."

Mal thought about lying and saying they just went for a walk. Adam wanted to "show her something" and it just turned out to be his dick in the park behind their dorm. He wanted a blowjob, and then had the nerve to flirt with some girls in their dorm on the way back after she declined. She could have spent the night bantering with Andrew, who flirted with her nonstop, and seemed to take pleasure in her eye rolls and insults in a way Adam never did.

Mal also loved that Andrew knew he needed to walk a fine line with how he treated Mal in Adam's presence. He'd eye Mal and Adam just as he'd done to a lacrosse net last night, when she watched the boys play a game of pickup lacrosse as she worked on her history homework.

Still, part of her worried that his flirting wasn't even about her in the first place. Maybe he's never had to score against a guarded net.

"I looked through Adam's phone when he was in the shower," Mal said, avoiding eye contact with Dani. "He regrets not breaking up with me before we got to college."

"That's terrible," Dani said, then paused. "You guys are having sex, right? Is it bad?"

Mal was horrified. *Is Adam going around telling people that? Did she hear it from Peter? Or worse, Andrew?*

"You'd know if he's not into you," Dani continued, not realizing how her question came across. "But if he's having sex with you and initiates it, he still probably wants to date you."

"I think we're having sex," Mal said, keeping her voice low as they walked out of the gym and back toward the dorms. They needed to be at HQ later for some bonding or whatever. As long as Mal wasn't being forced to make friendship bracelets or do other dumb hazing rituals, she was okay with the time drain. She often spaced out during the more boring parts of their meetings and thought about the plot of her manuscript.

"Wouldn't you know if you were having sex?"

"It's more that every time we try, I have to stop. It hurts too much," Mal said.

"And Adam's okay with it?"

"Why are you asking if he's okay? What about me?" Mal asked, anger bubbling up.

"I don't have to ask because I know," Dani replied. "You don't do anything you're not okay with it."

That snuffed Mal's anger like a firehose aimed at a lit match.

"He's a guy in college. Of course he wants to have sex," Mal said. "I don't think he's thrilled about what a struggle it is, but he does seem enthusiastic about the whole process. I think he hopes all his efforts will eventually pay off."

"What if it's something about him, instead of something about you?" Dani asked.

"His dick seems to work just fine," Mal snapped.

"No, your chemistry." Dani shook her head, presumably because she's had sex in mansions posing as New York City apartments or in cool bars Mal would never be allowed into.

Mal's fake ID was barely good enough to get into Weston bars, let alone ones in New York City. "Your body might be telling you something your brain isn't."

"The health clinic just told me to use lube, as if that'll solve my problem," Mal snorted.

"It's that bad you went to the health clinic?" Dani asked. "They can't even diagnose a cold. Do you want me to call someone to check you out? Maybe something's actually wrong."

Mal waved her off.

"All I'm saying is that he doesn't deserve you," Dani said. "You should find someone who does, and Rosen might be that person for you."

Mal cocked her head and looked at her friend. She was always used to people taking Adam's side. Mal always felt too unlovable for anyone to pick—even if she was right, and especially when she was wrong.

"Do you think Peter deserves you?" Mal wanted to change the subject.

"What's your problem with him?"

"He's…" Mal didn't quite know how to describe it. He constantly told Mal that she should get used to being in threesomes with Adam, which she first thought was him being a buffoon. But then after she saw the text messages, it became crystal clear that Peter knew Adam didn't want to be with her, or at least wanted to date other girls, and that he chose cruelty by mocking her. Peter attended lacrosse camp with Adam and sleepaway camp with Andrew, which is how they all knew each other. She didn't understand why Peter, who should ostensibly be nice to her at a minimum, seemed to hate her guts. She wanted him to like her and hated him because he didn't. And then there he goes, chasing down her best friend at college. Mal didn't believe his intentions were noble. In fact, she believed that his pursuit of Dani was part of a long con, or some kind of extended prank he would pull. She did not trust him one bit.

"He's a pig," Mal managed.

"You should get to know him," Dani said.

"I do know him," Mal reminded her.

"What are you going to do about Adam?" Dani asked, now clearly the one trying to change the subject.

"If I break up with him, he'll go ahead and try to fuck anything that moves." Mal straightened her shoulders, feeling determined. "And I'm not going to let him do that."

"You shouldn't keep dating someone just to hold them hostage," Dani said.

"Men do it all the time," Mal said. "I'll keep him around until I'm ready."

* * *

After saying goodbye to Dani, with promises to go out dancing after their stint at HQ, Mal headed back to the boys' room. Instead of finding Adam, she found Andrew sitting at his desk with a white legal pad in front of him. Paper balls littered the area around him, and his furrowed brow indicated he had yet to find his rhythm. Blue ink filled half the page.

"Is your husband off at war?" Mal asked.

"Just in prison," Andrew grimaced. "It would be easier to text Deandre if phones were allowed, but I like the writing process. You should try it sometime."

"This," Mal gestured to the mess surrounding him, "doesn't look too much like writing. And for the record, all I do is write."

Mal threw her backpack next to Adam's bed and slumped onto the mattress. Dani once screamed at Mal for wearing "outdoor clothes" on her bed, but Mal didn't think Adam would give a shit—nor did she care. She pulled out her laptop, a model that cost a few extra dollars for the bigger screen. She was a writer, and her parents agreed it was a worthy investment, considering the aid package Weston gave her.

"What are you working on?" Andrew swung around in his swivel chair.

Hair crept up his long legs, and his muscular thighs peeked out of his gym shorts. Mal refocused on her screen, which displayed the novel she had started working on since getting to Weston. She wrote every day for at least an hour, usually under one of the large oak trees on the quad. She loved it even more as the weather started to cool and found herself wishing Andrew would finally ask to join her for these writing sessions. He had seen her a handful of times and stopped to say hello, but he never stayed for long. Andrew always insisted she go back to writing, like it was a quirky habit she had instead of a serious passion. Her interest in writing with him wasn't romantic, or at least not totally. She wanted to see his writing process up close, especially after workshopping his middling stories in class. She thought he had more to say and was either facing a blockage or holding back from being vulnerable on the page. Both possibilities intrigued her.

"Just getting some thoughts down," she said, staring at the blank page. "Same as you."

She wanted to fill the blank page with smut about Andrew, the least literary art.

"Read it to me like one of your French girls," Andrew teased, swiveling his chair in her direction. He scooched closer.

Mal slammed the laptop shut. She thought about grabbing his papers, but her flinch gave her away; he went on the defensive and grabbed his writing, holding it in the air.

"Oh no you don't," he said.

"I'm not even interested," Mal sniffed, putting her laptop back in its sleeve—a gift Dani insisted she accept for some reason. "You're so self-important."

"You seem very interested."

"I was just coming here to tell you we're going to Puffs soon, but if you want to keep writing to your prison pen pal then that's fine with me," she said.

"I won't apologize for taking my classwork seriously," he said, holding his hand to his chest in mock insult.

"You're forced to 'volunteer' at a prison for college credit because your athlete mind is not advanced enough for the classwork." Mal tsked. "Some of us have actual talent."

"Allegedly," Andrew said. "I still haven't read your work outside of P-Cubed's class."

"P-Cubed?" Mal wrinkled her nose.

"Professor Patricia Peterson," Andrew explained.

"You're an idiot," Mal said, her lips creeping dangerously up into a smile. She knew she'd only think about their professor that way moving forward.

"Not stupid enough to see you're always writing," Andrew said. "We don't have nearly that much work for class, so it can only be a secret project."

"I'll make you a deal. If Peter becomes exclusive with Dani tonight, I'll show you what I've been working on. But if they don't, you have to read me all your crumbled-up efforts. I'm in the mood to laugh."

"You're on," he said.

* * *

Mal teetered down the steps to Puffs' dance floor, her black bandage dress hugging every bit of her body with little room left to move. She snagged a pair of Dani's going-out shoes, black suede wedges that would have won Most Likely to Break Your Neck for its high school superlative. Mal smiled to herself, realizing she just came up with her short story idea for P-Cubed's class: "Sticky Soles: A Day in the Life of The Going-Out Shoe."

Seb, who would no doubt be her first reader on that assignment, beelined toward her, holding neon blue cocktails in each hand. Peter swayed off-rhythm to the music while Marcus and Andrew bobbed their heads to the beat, not yet drunk enough to loosen up.

"Where's Dani?" Mal asked.

Peter tapped the side of his nose and cocked his head toward the bathrooms.

"Horse-girl-to-ketamine pipeline," quipped Seb, though Mal wasn't sure if he was joking.

She smiled uncomfortably and slurped down her drink. Mal had her first shot during a sleepover with her junior varsity volleyball team. Stealing expensive alcohol from her dad's liquor cabinet was as far as she had gone. *And I guess getting a fake ID*, Mal thought.

Of course Dani did coke in the bathroom; she grew up in Manhattan. Mal read, and then watched, *Gossip Girl*. She had wanted to ask Dani whether her experience was like Constance Billard but thought that would make her sound unsophisticated. Maybe Mal could be someone who did coke in the bathroom, too. The bottoms of her shoes caught ever so slightly on the beer-covered floor. When she made it into the bathroom, Mal was surprised to see Dani with her dress down to her waist.

"I want to rip this off," she said, pulling at the tight fabric gripping her torso.

Mal fished into her purse for a tube of lipstick and stood next to Dani. They stared at their reflections in the mirror.

"You look hot," Dani said.

"Men are stupid and visual," Mal said as she wielded the lipstick. "You put on a tiny dress and their brains explode."

"Maybe for you," Dani grumbled as she twisted her strapless bra around her body, fumbling with the hooks and eyes as she loosened them.

"If you think you're hot, they think you're hot," Mal said. "Capitalism makes us feel bad about ourselves, but men are hardwired to chase anything deemed valuable. Show them you're worth chasing."

"You've been doing your reading," Dani said, and then looked around the bathroom to see if anyone was eavesdropping.

Mal took in the scene for herself. Hordes of girls jammed themselves into stalls, while others reapplied their makeup, yet they all seemed in their own bubbles. And even if they wanted to eavesdrop, no one looked sober enough to do so.

"Do you think it's weird we haven't been tested yet? Everyone is so chipper, but I feel like the shoe's about to drop. I like hanging out at HQ, but that's all we're doing: reading and hanging out," Dani said, keeping her voice low.

"Did you ever get a pop quiz?" Mal asked, her lipstick hovering near her mouth.

She had been waiting for Newts to jump out of the bushes or ambush her during class, demanding her to define "comphet." Mal wasn't sure whether Adrienne Rich's essay on the subject rattled or radicalized her. What she did know was that it spoke to her anger and confusion about trying to figure out who she was—beyond knowing what she thought. People assumed that having opinions meant understanding yourself, but Mal had no idea what she wanted from life. All she knew was what she didn't.

"No, did you?"

Dani's voice drew Mal out of her head, which she shook.

"Whatever, let's not worry about this," Mal said.

"Have you seen Rosen, by the way?" Dani asked.

"Like a few hours ago, why?" Mal's heart quickened. Did Andrew ruin the sanctity of their bet? The thought upset her. Maybe she's imagining their chemistry.

"Him and Peter are in some dumb prank war," Dani said. "Peter swapped his shampoo for black hair dye and now Rosen looks like he should be in My Chemical Romance."

Now Dani's talking. As a punk rock princess herself, Mal was into that.

"Rosen seemed more impressed than angry, honestly," Dani continued. "But then he charmed the girls on your floor and asked them to help him fix it."

"It's amazing what constitutes a good time for men," Mal said. "Can you imagine if a woman did that to another woman?"

"You would assume she hated you. At the very least she'd become your nemesis."

"You would never say, 'Ah yes, that's my best friend,'" Mal said.

"And yet," Dani added.

"And yet."

They paused, but then Mal turned to Dani.

"Does he look sexy?"

"Unfortunately for you, yes."

They walked back to their friends and immediately clocked something was wrong. Marcus was fuming, and Seb had stepped between him and Peter.

"Tell them, Dani," Marcus said. "Tell them we've been seeing each other."

"You told them?" Mal yelled at Andrew, who did, in fact, look hot.

Peter ran his hands through his hair and looked at Dani with a strained smile.

"It's somehow bad timing, but I wanted to know if you'd be my girlfriend," he said as Marcus huffed behind him. Dani barely registered Marcus before she lunged at Peter, and the two started making out aggressively. There was Marcus' answer.

"Sorry, bud," Seb slapped Marcus on the back, who sulked off. Seb turned to Mal and remarked how territorial Marcus had become.

"He's not even in the friend group," Mal muttered, annoyed that Dani brought a straggler into the inner circle. Worse, had she known Marcus had a thing for Dani, Mal could have helped him. This is why it was crucial she knew everything about everyone. How else could she make sure things aligned in her favor?

"You owe me a manuscript, Firefly."

Hot breath misted the back of her neck, and she turned around to face Andrew. His eyes were glassy, like he couldn't totally see Mal, though his voice retained its caustic edge.

"You cheated," Mal said. She wondered if he kept calling her Firefly because it was a play on fire crotch or something equally pedantic. Her cheeks flushed with the embarrassment of not understanding whether she was being made fun of. "I don't owe you anything."

Andrew's gaze flitted over to Dani and Peter still tonguing.

"I've never seen you act that way with Adam," Andrew slurred, his breath smelling dank. "Can't even imagine it."

"I don't need to be all over my boyfriend in public like that," Mal sniffed. The sentiment was empty, but Andrew didn't need to know that.

"You're in the minority," Andrew said as he eyed a girl crossing in front of him, and within moments he swooped into the empty spot beside her. Andrew leaned his head toward the girl, who started rubbing her arm, and handed the bartender his credit card. His glassy eyes and wide smile gave off a leering vibe, rather than the flirty one he deployed so often.

"Why does he look so creepy?" Mal turned to Seb, who gnawed on his straw.

"It's like he turns into another person when he's drunk," Seb replied.

"He needs to get it together," Mal said, sipping her vodka cranberry through a straw. She loved how the alcohol made her feel safe, like she was invincible. She needed the extra boost to say what had been bothering her. Maybe if she spoke the idea into the ether, it would help her make it a reality. "I'm thinking of ending things with Adam. The relationship feels too much like high school."

"Is he really the guy you're going to dump Adam for?" Seb asked, jutting his chin at Andrew, who walked away from the bar with his hand dangerously close to the girl's ass. Mal's cheeks burned with the feeling of being seen by Seb so clearly. "If I were you, I'd know what I was getting into before making a big life decision."

"Who says he's the one I'm into?" Mal asked.

"People are talking," Seb teased, but Mal's smile dropped.

"Whatever," she said, stalking off to find the nearest boy to dance with. Her hips rocked from left to right as she sidled up in front of this guy, who seemed to take her in like he was always waiting for a stranger to rub up against him. He spun her around, assessed her and then spun her back around to keep grinding. Guess she passed the hotness test. Gross.

Mal turned her head to spot Andrew chugging his drink as his hands ran up and down the girl's body, which took on more of a rag-doll posture. He whispered into her ear again and the two headed out of the bar together, the lights flickering as they disappeared into the crowd.

Mal pushed herself off the guy, who barely protested, and rejoined her friends.

"Rosen didn't notice," Seb said, keeping his eyes trained on prospects. His gaze settled on a beefy football player type, who locked eyes with Seb and smiled. "See ya, girlie."

Mal felt a tug in her belly as her friends coupled up, and she trudged out of the bar, content on calling it a night. She made her way through the outdoor patio and almost left when she spotted Marcus smoking a cigarette in the corner. She sat beside him.

"Where did you get the idea that you and Dani were together?" Mal gestured at the cig, which sat between Marcus' lips.

Mal had developed a taste for nicotine because it felt literary to smoke. The only way she could justify it from a health perspective, though, was that it was fine, just as long as she didn't buy the cigarettes herself. He took a long drag and passed it to Mal.

"We had chemistry," he said.

"That," Mal said, trying to keep the cigarette in her mouth while pointing inside, where she imagined Peter and Dani were still devouring each other's faces, "was chemistry."

They were a prime example of why kissing was overrated; it just looked disgusting.

"You two are just friends," Mal continued. "Have you never had female friends before?"

"We spent every week practicing tours together. There were plenty of people who Dani could have done that with. She invited me over to her apartment to hang out, alone!"

"Why does that make you entitled to her?" Mal asked, squinting her eyes.

Marcus shifted in his seat defensively.

"That's not fair. She was giving me signals, and now I'm the misanthrope? Fuck you," he said, taking the cigarette back from Mal. "I'm better for her than that asshole is, anyway."

"That, we can both agree on." Mal nodded. She felt a twang of respect for Marcus. People rarely told her to go fuck herself, though she was confident they thought it often. "Look, if you want to chase after her, it's a noble but losing battle that I'm in full support of."

He perked up at this.

"Want to help me tank their relationship?" Mal asked, a smile stretching over her face.

Marcus slumped back down, unimpressed with her offer, and eyed her suspiciously.

"You're a shitty friend," he said. "I actually like Dani enough not to do that to her."

And with that, he tossed his cigarette on the ground, stomped on it with his neon sneaker, and left Mal and her shitty-friend label on the patio.

DANI
HENLEY HALL, FRESHMAN YEAR
NOVEMBER 8, 2013 — BEFORE

"HEY, BABE?" PETER CALLED OUT FROM the kitchenette in the student lounge.

It had been three weeks since they became official, and Dani still wasn't over how perfectly they fit together. Dani, who thought of herself as a human barometer, was so infatuated with Peter that she temporarily became immune to other people's moods, notably Marcus'. She put her book down and followed him into the kitchenette to assess the situation. Peter held up a mug sloshing with water.

"Can I boil this in the microwave?" he asked.

Dani grew up with a live-in chef and a string of au-pairs, but at least her parents had the decency to make sure they sent her off to college knowing how to feed herself.

"You're trying to make tea?" she asked with uncertainty.

"Noodles," he said, lifting his convenience store purchase.

"Our parents are almost here. We can get food at the game," she said.

"Starving. Won't make it," he replied, turning his attention back to the microwave.

Fiona and Bobby had flown in for Parents' Weekend, and Dani had made them swear up and down that they wouldn't mention the helicopter to Peter's family or else they wouldn't be allowed inside her dorm. Within 20 minutes, both families had arrived and greeted each other warmly, not at all bothered by their children coupling up three months into independent living, like Dani worried they would be. Or at least they had the decency to chalk it up to young love. Regardless, she was thankful everyone was getting along.

"We're paying 60 grand for them to live in this shit hole?" grumbled Peter's dad, Marc.

Her dad, Bobby, slapped him on the back chummily.

"Reminds me of my time at Maryland," Bobby said, running his free hand alongside the beige cinder block walls flanking the linoleum-tiled hallway.

"At least you got what you paid for," Marc said. "I expected more from a private school."

"I'm literally moving to the city the second I turn 18," Sara sneered. "I'd rather be dead than live in rural America."

"It's upstate New York, sweetie," Peter's mom, Miri, chastised her daughter as kindly as she could in polite company. "And it's not so much different up here than on Long Island."

"Weston might as well be Siberia," Sara retorted, then snapped her attention to Peter. "I can't believe you'd choose to come here. Voluntarily!"

"Choosing is the same thing as voluntarily, dumbass," Peter said.

"Peter, don't talk to your sister like that," Miri screeched.

"Why is everyone yelling?" Marc yelled, putting his hands on his balding head.

Fiona caught Dani's eye. Without a word being spoken, they both thought the same thing: This was a taste of what Dani's in-laws were going to be like.

"You two found each other quickly," Fiona said. "Pretty unlikely for freshmen to settle down this fast."

"Mom," Dani said, panic filling her dark brown eyes. So much for an easy meet and greet. "Can you not?"

"Peter told me he found someone special," Miri said, her eyes looking like they might as well be replaced with hearts. Then it was Peter's turn to hush his mom, but it was too late. Dani knew his mom wasn't lying, and that Peter was all in if he told Miri that.

"The game is starting soon," Peter said abruptly. "Let's go."

The two families settled into the bleachers surrounding the football field. Unlike the other schools Dani toured, Weston's football stadium was small. "Stadium" might even be generous; the area on the north part of campus doubled as the school's soccer field. At Maryland and Michigan and USC and UT Austin, there was no question where the football stadiums were. Dani's parents were surprised but supportive when she opted for the picturesque but decidedly not rah-rah school of her choosing. She suspected her parents were relieved that she'd have fewer opportunities to be a fuck up at Weston rather than in the public eye near a major city.

"Wow, up close and personal," Miri said as she clumsily slid onto the metal bench, with her knockoff Louis Vuitton bag in hand (the peeling handle was a telltale sign). "I can smell the sweat already."

Peter rolled his eyes at Sara, who grimaced in commiseration. Dani felt a stab of jealousy watching the two of them move past Peter's mean comment from earlier without so much as a glance at their mother. She longed for that kind of closeness with someone, a connection her parents denied her by having one child in their early 40s. Fiona stashed her Hermès bag on the ground between her feet before asking Bobby to get her a hot dog and a Diet Coke.

"Anyone else want anything?" Bobby stood up, his maroon-and-white Weston T-shirt stretching gently across his paunchy belly. "The boys are treating."

"Can I get a burger and fries and a Coke?" Sara asked. "Ooh and a pretzel or cotton candy or something like that."

Bobby pointed at Miri, who smiled tightly and informed him she doesn't eat fast food.

"Peter, go help Bobby," Marc said. "My back hurts and I'm not getting up again."

"I'll come too," Dani volunteered so she wouldn't be stuck with Peter's family. Fiona shot her a look, clearly unhappy Dani put her in that exact position.

"Be right back," Dani and Peter chimed in unison as they shot out of their seats.

"This is going horribly," Peter whispered into Dani's ear as they trailed Bobby. "Your parents must think mine are nuts. I promise I'm not like them."

"Please, like mine are any better right now," Dani said, jutting her chin at her dad.

Bobby walked around the stadium singing the "Weston Fight Song" and giving a thumbs up to the other dads who passed them.

"Maybe Sara has the right idea," Peter said.

"Disappear," Dani agreed.

As the three of them waited for their food, Bobby peppered Peter with questions. *Heh, peppered Peter,* Dani chuckled to herself about the alliteration. Her dad caught Dani laughing and smiled brightly, resting his hands on her shoulders.

"What are you kids getting into tonight?" Bobby asked, rubbing her shoulders lightly and then planting a kiss on her head.

"Probably going out," Dani said, looking at Peter for approval.

"Some guys in my business class are throwing a party," Peter said before turning to Dani. "Maybe we'll check that out?"

"Oh yeah that sounds good," Dani said, trying to ignore the face her dad was making. It was the face of a man who believed he just met his future son-in-law.

"I'm glad you kids are having a good time. Just make sure to get her home safe," Bobby said to Peter. Dani folded her arms.

"I don't need him," Dani paused for effect, "to make sure I get home. That's so sexist."

"It's not sexist, Danit," Bobby said. "There are lots of crazy guys out there."

"If someone wants to hurt me there's only so much I can prevent," Dani said. "And seriously, who's going to bother me on my walk home? Especially here."

"I always walk her home," Peter said.

Kiss ass.

"Thank you," Bobby said firmly to Peter, their faces solemn as they exchanged some sort of message. Dani hated whatever this was, some sort of transfer of responsibility, of ownership, from father to boyfriend. Bobby was responsible for keeping Dani safe, and now it was Peter's turn. God forbid she was allowed to take care of herself. She kept thinking about it long after the conversation ended and they were back in their seats, watching men tackle each other.

To hell with the kind of world where the only thing between her and violence was the presence of a man who didn't even know how to boil water properly.

Her second thought was that Mal would be proud of her.

MAL
HENLEY HALL, FRESHMAN YEAR
NOVEMBER 15, 2013 — BEFORE

SUNLIGHT STREAMED INTO THE DORM ROOM, casting a glow on Mal's face that awoke her to great annoyance. First, she thought she would murder whoever forgot to shut the blinds before going to sleep. Then she realized she was alone in Adam's bed. She sat up and rubbed her eyes, only to be startled by Andrew, who was the half-naked one this time. While Mal typically had mascara lightly pooling under her eyes and limp hair that made her look like a drowned rat when she came out of the shower, Andrew looked like he had been carved from stone. A light sheen of water glistened on his torso, which was lean and golden brown, and there was no body hair obstructing the view of his very prominent six pack. He rubbed one of those performance towels—the ones that were nearly threadbare and bought by men whose toxic masculinity stopped them from indulging in something as nice as a fluffy towel—over his fresh haircut that made the bad dye job all but a distant memory and grinned at her.

"Morning, sunshine," he said, his gaze lingering just above her eyes. She became acutely aware that her hair was sticking up in a zillion directions, none of which were flattering.

"M'rning," Mal grunted, wishing she had a coffee IV implanted to wake her up. She didn't like that his brain was operating at a higher frequency than hers—and he was at Weston for *sports*.

"Adam and Peter are still in the shower," he said, making no effort to hide his body from her. If anything, he seemed to enjoy flaunting it.

"Together?" Mal's comment stuck to her vocal cords, so it sounded more like a croak than a solid joke.

"We went for an early morning run. Gotta burn off those beer calories."

He patted his belly like he didn't have zero percent body fat and grinned at her with such satisfaction she wanted to get up and slap him, but Mal worried that if she touched Andrew she'd jump his bones. The journey from disgust to crush alarmed her, as did her use of an idiom her mom was lame enough to use. She wondered why she was fighting his magnetic pull.

Do you have any dignity? the mean voice in her head shrieked. *Do you want to be just like all the other girls flinging themselves at him? No.* And then a smaller voice cut through the noise, clear as glass. *He's only flirting with you because you reject him. Once you give in, like you gave into Adam, no one will ever want you.*

"Earth to Mallory." Andrew knelt in front of her, and she could see bits of stubble he missed shaving this morning. He smelled like shaving cream. Mal inhaled quietly, trying to hold onto what she felt might become a core memory. Concern crinkled in the corners of his eyes.

"Are you okay? Do you feel sick?"

His large hand covered her forehead, and his lips twitched.

"No fever," he said, and then tucked a piece of hair behind her ear. A shiver shot through her. "Come on, let's get you some coffee."

Her heart fluttered as she stood up, but then Andrew turned around, smiling wickedly.

"It's no fun when my sparring partner can't hit back," he said.

They held each other's gaze, as if daring the other to make a move. Andrew was the first to flinch, taking a step closer to

her. She leaned in, ready to give in to her romantic urges—
and not because she was trying to win, like she had with Adam.

"Oh, wait. I need to do something," Andrew said, moving
past her to duck under his bed and pull out rolls of cling wrap
and duct tape.

"Why do you have BTK kit under your bed?" Mal rasped,
mortified by her desire.

"Come with me," he said, pulling her arm as he dragged
her into the dorm hallway. They stopped outside the boy's
bathroom before Andrew ducked in and popped back out.

"You need to cover me," he said. "Don't let anyone in here."

Before she could argue, he escaped into the bathroom. She
did as she was told, though it was only because she hadn't fully
woken up yet and truly thought Andrew was ready to declare
unrequited love or something. After having considered the
likelihood of that, Mal realized how she'd look to anyone
passing through the hallway: like a freak. Mal followed
Andrew into the bathroom, where he squatted in front of one
of the stalls. Andrew meticulously wound the clear plastic
wrap around the base of the toilet and then across the bowl,
creating an imperceptible lid.

"Whatcha doing?" Mal asked. She loved a prank, as long as
it wasn't at her expense.

"I spiked Peter's water bottle with eye drops before our
run," Andrew whispered gleefully, though he didn't take his
eyes off the toilet bowl. "I don't think he'll finish his shower
before needing to go."

Andrew pointed at his supplies: printer paper, a Sharpie
and tape.

"Can you write 'out of service' and tape the posters to the
stalls and lock them up? You're small enough to scoot under."

Mal gasped, picturing pee and who knows what else moving up and around toward Peter instead of down. She also went to work being Andrew's co-conspirator. She took such joy in it that she barely minded crawling on the gross bathroom floor.

"He's going to kill you," Mal said when she finished the task.

"You don't mess with a man's hair," Andrew said, and then pointed to a plastic device that looked like a baby monitor, duct taped on the wall.

"It has a camera," he whispered. "I ordered it online so we can watch."

Mal clasped her hand over her mouth to keep from screaming—or to point out that it's illegal to film people while they use the bathroom. Huge pedo energy. The boys' ongoing prank war had always been crass at best, but this prank might be the one to push Peter over the edge. He would either stop talking to Andrew (unlikely), call off their cold war (predictable), or plot an even bigger revenge plot (Mal wasn't sure Peter had the smarts for it, though she anticipated he would try and fail in secret). Someone turned off their water, prompting Mal and Andrew to make a mad dash out of the bathroom.

* * *

The leafy campus had gone from bright green to a dizzying array of umber and orange seemingly overnight. The ongoing temperature drop had inspired Mal to forgo her quarterly haircut, letting her curls become longer and even more unruly. With her dresses, tights and platform Docs, she felt every inch the collegiate writer—and that in turn inspired her to keep writing. She was nearing the end of her novel, a not-so-shitty first draft.

Mal trudged past a Title IX protest to get coffee and was reminded of an off-handed comment Dani made about how she didn't understand why women wanted to make their gender so core to their personhood. Dani had added that "shoving identity down the throats of their male overlords wouldn't make it more palatable," and Mal couldn't shake the thought. It was the kind of self-loathing female energy she didn't know people possessed—and therefore kind of wanted to write a short story inspired by it.

She wanted to talk about it with Andrew ahead of their last P-Cubed class before Thanksgiving break. The prospect of not having the freedom to sit on the quad for hours at a time to write, and instead head home to freezing Chicago, had Mal's spirits in the dumps. She didn't want to leave. But when she reached her friend, his sunny disposition from the morning and his successful prank—they howled when Adam described in remarkable detail what he had witnessed—had disappeared just as her attitude started to improve. Something had shifted, though Mal was unsure of what.

"I'm not ready to go home for the semester," Mal said, trying to draw conversation out of him. "I don't know how I'm supposed to be inspired at home."

"You'll be fine," he said, effectively shutting her down. This was really unlike him. She thought he'd at least bug her about reading her manuscript.

"I won't be," she said, leaning into the dramatic. "You can't write unless you have a life worth writing about. I want to be around inspiring people and exciting things."

"You're always wanting, Firefly."

Andrew nodded his head as he said this, like it was a fact and not a question. Like he understood the ailment that plagued her and didn't think there was anything wrong with it. It felt like such a profound realization that for once it didn't bother Mal that he used the pet name she had grown to hate.

"I'm worried I won't get what I want," Mal said quietly.

He drew his mouth in a hard line as they walked for the rest of the way to class in silence. Gusts of wind blew Mal's hair around as they navigated the winding path to class. She expected him to make a joke about her looking like a witch who summoned evil spirits to fuck with him, or some shit like that.

"Ominous" was all Andrew said.

In their classroom, Andrew fiddled with a lacrosse ball and two folded sheets of paper in his lap. He swapped the items out seamlessly as Seb read his weekly writing assignment. A sheen of sweat glistened near Andrew's hairline, and his perpetually bronzed skin—which was maintained even in November—seemed ashy.

"You have stage fright, princess?" Mal whispered.

Andrew ignored her jab and kept his eyes on Seb, who finished his story and stood in front of their class waiting for the critique to start—the weekly dressing down of their art. One by one, the classmates constructively ripped his story apart. Seb's legs quivered slightly as the critique extended past the typical 20-minute mark. Andrew stayed unusually silent, folding and unfolding the letter in his lap. The rhythm of that action, coupled with juggling the ball in his hands, almost lulled Mal to sleep. To combat the prospect of napping, she zeroed in on Seb and gave him a sharper-than-usual criticism, finding every hole in his story.

The first time Mal offered criticism, she almost expected Seb to start crying. It was the same day Veronica, one of the California girls, dropped the class after a brutal assignment, which was when Mal realized why their class started out with seven students instead of six—to account for the ones who couldn't handle the intensity or criticism. Weaklings.

But during this process, Mal recognized that she had a shrewd eye. It was part of the reason she had few friends growing up. Teenagers don't want the brutal truth, despite their insistence otherwise. But, instead of despising her, Seb met her gaze and gave her a wry smile. He quickly became one of her favorite people at Weston. He saw her for who she was—and actually liked her roughness.

"Mr. Rosen, you're up," P-Cubed said in a voice she reserved only for Andrew.

Despite his intense sports schedule, Andrew never missed class, and Mal knew he did his own assignments (a bunch of athletes paid other students to do their work, which Mal thought was enterprising on the dorks' end). Though she had been disappointed that Andrew's profile of her wasn't executed well, Mal didn't think his writing was disqualifying from being in the program. If anything, someone had to be the weakest in the class.

Mal could also admit that if Andrew could compete with her, she might have liked him even less. It annoyed her that she was attracted to him—to be fair, it seemed like an impossibility that anyone who liked men didn't feel the way she did—and that he was just so smug about it. Like he knew the power he held over women and enjoyed it. There might be worse characteristics to possess, but Mal hated how only a man could be that way. So comfortable in himself and his universal appeal. Any woman who experienced that for even a moment was then torn down, like Taylor Swift.

She glanced at the clock. They only had a few minutes left in class, meaning Andrew wouldn't get a critique. This happened sometimes, and it required the students to leave a written response in Blackboard. Mal wrinkled her nose at the thought of more homework and leaned back, waiting for Andrew to start waxing poetically about the war or some shit. This week's prompt was writing through adversity in first person, with a heavy emphasis on exploring a lived experience very different from your own. Peterson said she'd even excused appropriation because it allowed for an honest first draft and made sure the class spent the time discussing how to research and write authentically. Andrew and Mal were the only white students in their cohort, anyway. Peterson's class was another reason Mal felt less and less hung up on skipping out on Brown. Weston was the place she was destined to be.

The chair squeaked as Andrew pushed it back and went up to the front of the classroom, his hand trembling ever so slightly. He took a deep breath and began to read. It was a suicide note from a man who had been imprisoned for eight years for marijuana possession. Andrew spoke of the prison conditions, the comfort in routine, the fear of returning to a place he no longer recognized and the feeling that freedom would never return to his body. He replaced the first page with the second.

"I am tired of fighting, of feeling like I'm wrong," Andrew read. "That I've been wronged. I'm tired of being angry, tired of apologizing, tired of wishing what my life coulda been had I done something different. That I went home, just went home. I'm now going home."

His voice cracked on the final word, and he lowered his paper down. The class stayed silent for a beat. P-Cubed stood up from her desk.

"That was wonderful," she said. "Thank you for sharing."

He nodded and sat back in his seat. Mal tried to catch his eye, but he stayed focused on the floor and slid back into his seat. When P-Cubed dismissed them, Andrew shot out of the door before Mal could stop to talk to him. She couldn't believe that she had him all wrong.

CHAPTER TEN

DANI
RAINEY STREET
MAY 24, 2024 — AFTER

By the time they pull up, the bungalows dotting Rainey Street seem to pulse with the thumping music. They walk toward the water, looking for their first stop of the night.

"This one does karaoke with a live band," Seb says, pointing to a rickety house.

"Ew," Mal complains, adding that if she's forced to participate in the humiliating task of singing off-key in front of people, it better involve a private room and "hella soju."

"Lethal," Peter whimpers, pained by the suggestion of 20% alcohol content.

Still, they follow Seb onto the balding grass lawn and snag a picnic table. Peter and Seb offer to grab the first round of drinks at the outdoor bar, and quickly return with refreshments in hand; Peter dashes back to the bar to grab the extra one left behind. Women never have that privilege to leave their drink unattended, even for a moment and with the bartender. Dani keeps her eyes trained on the crowd for Alexia, letting the conversation flow around her.

When she does tune back in, she's surprised to see it's between Mal and Ben.

"I like Carson. I want to tell her Eric's being unfaithful," Ben says of his coworkers, or his supervisors? She's heard these names before but can't place who they are exactly.

"It makes me feel better when men acknowledge that other men are being shitty. It's more validating to hear it from men instead of only women, who you know already know the behavior is shitty," Mal says. "But when men say it, it's like, 'Oh shit, this is bad enough for them to recognize it as such.'"

She's belaboring the point, but the men nod.

"We know the playbook," Peter says. "He took the easy way out."

"There's a playbook?" Dani asks, looking at Ben.

"God forbid men see women as people and not a game to be won," Mal grumbles.

Good to know the shrooms haven't tamped down her personality. Dani's phone buzzes.

I'm here, where should I meet you? Alexia's text reads.

Dani gives Alexia strict instructions: Avoid their table, keep her head down, talk to no one, and head straight to the bathroom. Dani will meet Alexia in two minutes to collect the vials. Dani powers down her phone and slips it into her bag. Out of sight, out of mind and off the grid. She drains the last of her drink, keeping her expression neutral as she tries to spot Alexia walking into the bar.

Dani feels nothing as Ben makes small talk, his gaze flitting back to the bartender every few moments as he tries to catch his attention. He's congenial, but it's like he knows he's being watched—although Dani suspects he'd act the same way had he been out in the city, with no watchful eyes. She almost wishes he'd flirt with the girl to get back at her for their fight earlier. Maybe then she'd respect him. Dani turns to Mal.

"Isn't it messed up that women wear engagement rings for months, years even, to show they're taken, while men have that time to still appear unencumbered?" Dani points at Ben and the girl, pleased to have found a topic of conversation that will easily stoke Mal's fury—and her mouth. Mal glances at Dani's five-carat ring: an emerald-cut diamond on a gold band.

"Just take it off again," Mal says simply. "Obviously not here—that could probably buy a house in Texas—but just leave it with armed guards next time you want to flirt with strangers for the thrill of it."

Dani's baffled. She didn't realize Mal clocked that she recently put the ring on. Mal shrugs and tells her there's no harm in having a little fun.

"It is harmful," Peter says without making eye contact. As if she needs a reminder.

"There's always more women to hit on." Mal pats his hand and leans back in her seat against the wooden fence. For the first time this weekend, Mal looks relaxed—to the point that she's comforting Peter of all people.

"All right, Austin. How's it going?" A skinny guy in a barely buttoned shirt takes the mic on the front porch of the bungalow. "First up we got Craig from Boston."

A burst of applause comes from the picnic table at the other end of the lawn, and a curly-haired guy jumps up on the makeshift stage to the swell of "I Want It That Way."

"Tell me why," the group croons dramatically as Peter makes his way to the porch. Dani realizes it's been way longer than two minutes, so she quickly excuses herself to go to the bathroom and bounds up the stairs. But before she can get inside, Peter pulls her arm.

"I signed us up for karaoke," he says hopefully.

"Sorry dude, I'm not in the mood."

"Dude?" Peter seethes. "Dude, really?"

"Can we talk about this later?" Dani pleads. "I really need to use the bathroom."

Peter drops her arm, but she can see his temper flaring on the inside. His eyes look different than she remembers. It's like he's translucent to her—the wheels in his brain turning, unsaid thoughts flashing through his mind—yet she no longer knows him well enough to be privy to them anymore.

"Look, I know, I know. We need to talk," Dani says, backing away. "We will."

Peter mutters a response, but Dani can't hear him. She's already halfway into the bar, looking for the bathroom. Dani pushes her way through the throng of bar goers to get to the back, where signs with "cowboys" and "cowgirls" direct her to the poorly lit, dirty bathroom. Alexia leans against the sink with a Trinity School cap pulled low.

"Howdy," Dani says, and Alexia hands her a leather case a little bigger than Dani's hand. Dani unzips it, revealing two vials of colorless liquid.

They remind her of the mini perfume samples that always get thrown into her online Sephora orders. She always found those samples tacky and wasteful, anyway. She slides one of the vials out and holds it up.

"Nothing that's monumental feels like it at first," Dani muses, wondering why she feels the need to downplay a scientific invention she funded. She envies the men who were able to just see the fruits of their labor and immediately assume greatness.

"I thought about adding dye to the formula to make it look cooler," Alexia admits. "But that seemed self-aggrandizing—and it wouldn't make it so discreet, would it?"

"I'm trying to hold space for this moment, but it's hard," Dani adds, looking around the dingy bathroom. "This is the right thing."

Alexia puts her bony hand on Dani's shoulder.

"I wouldn't have developed it if I didn't trust you," Alexia says, her expression hardening. "I believe in you. I believe in the world you're building."

Instead of excitement or pride or flattery, disgust floods Dani's system. She's not some altruistic angel. What kind of person would lay her professional life on the line for Dani's ambition? Someone who wants to be an equal but really is one of Dani's sheep, led with a smile to the slaughter.

The sound of a toilet flushing jolts Dani out of her self-hatred and sends Alexia on the move. Dani gently slides the vial back into place, hides the case at the bottom of her bag and then scurries back to rejoin her friends. But before she can pass the bar, she's once again stopped—this time by Mal, who drags her toward the pool table. Is this what being a senator is going to be like? Everyone always wanting a piece of her?

"Alexia is here." Mal's voice catches in her throat.

Shoot. She saw her.

Dani doesn't want to panic, but she's panicking. Alexia's involvement with the truth serum is quite actually one of the few reasons Mal wouldn't trust the formula is real. Mal will think that this was an elaborate ploy to embarrass her or make her look foolish. Dani needs to do what she does best.

"Woah, what else are you seeing?" Dani jokes, but then pretends to get serious. "Are you doing okay? You seemed jittery earlier, and I don't know why."

"She knows," Mal insisted, her irises swallowing up. "She knows why I'm here."

"For the wedding?" Dani can't follow, but then again Mal's on drugs, so she shushes Mal and brings her in for a hug.

"Alexia has two kids under the age of three in New York City," Dani says kindly, like she's trying to tell a child there's no monster under the bed. She hopes there's nothing in her voice that indicates the monster is lurking around the corner.

Mal's lips twitch into an outsized frown. It's the expression she makes when she's about to cry, but before either of them can say anything, a fight breaks out next to them.

"Have you, or have you not, gotten a job?" A woman shrieks at the high-top next to them.

"It's in flux, I told you that," her companion drawls, his voice verging on a whine.

"What does that mean 'in flux?'" She uses her fingers to make dramatic air quotes, and in the process, knocks her drink over with her elbow.

As they wipe up the mess, Dani has a brilliant idea. She quickly removes a vial from the case and spikes the man's drink while he runs to the bar for more napkins. Even though Alexia swears up and down that the serum is safe, Dani would rather test it out on strangers in real time before Rosen gets his dose. She's so quick, she's certain Mal didn't see it, but then Mal knits her eyebrows together and leans in.

"What did you do?" Mal whispers.

"Watch."

Dani picks up a pool cue and looks for a piece of chalk to appear busy.

"I can't keep covering rent on my own," the woman complains.

"I don't have any money," the man replies. Once the words come out of his mouth, he clamps his hand over his mouth and looks at his partner wild eyed.

"You told me an hour ago you think something is coming in. That your friend put a good word in—"

"I lied," the man says plainly, sipping more of the spiked drink. "I haven't been looking, I just wanted you off my back. I know you won't kick me out. But if it came down to it, I'd leave and bunk at my brother's."

Dani tries to look nonchalant as she glances their way. Now it's the woman eyes the size of saucers. Mal's expression happens to match. It's working.

"I'm not sure why I told you that," the man says, looking distraught that his brain and his mouth are not in sync.

"Well then." The woman stands up and runs her hands over her dress. "This is the first honest conversation we've had in months."

The man nods and gives her a once over.

"Does that mean you'll let me stay?" he asks.

She looks bewildered, and then eyes her empty glass.

"Do you have enough money to buy me another drink?"

He grins slowly, nods once, and then heads back to the bar.

"Holy shit," Mal says in one long exhale, stretching the words out.

* * *

Dani and Mal don't talk about Alexia or what they witnessed as they rejoin the sullen-looking boys. Panic shoots up Dani's back and into her shoulders as she tries to determine if something happened. The next scavenger hunt clue is sitting on the picnic table, enveloped opened like a table setting at a wedding. Seb is the first to speak.

"Um, I'm really thirsty, but I can't get up," Seb tells the table, his eyes trained on the full moon in the sky.

"I think we're done for the night," Ben says, exhaustion tinging his words.

The others nod, and a mostly sober Ben stuffs the scavenger hunt card into his backpack. Did he always need to carry that thing around?

They close out and call a car. The ride back is uneventful and quiet, even though Seb needs some help getting in. They enter the rental house single file, ready for a good night's sleep. Dani fights the urge to rub her eyes, not wanting to spread mascara all over her face, and then remembers she's not wearing any. She scrubs at her eye sockets, knowing her grand plan is officially in motion. Mal will comply, handing over her planning documents and consulting with Dani, without a fight after what they witnessed. She's sure of it.

All Dani has to do now is keep Ben and Peter away from each other.

Ben calls out that he needs to get some work done in the living room for an hour or so, leaving Dani on her own in their bedroom. She knows he won't be finished until she's long asleep, toiling late into the night. When she and Ben first started dating, Dani joked that she wasn't worried about the other women. The Excel spreadsheets were her main competition.

She changes into her pajamas and slides into bed, the linen sheets crisp and cold on her tanned body. Sleep comes, quick and heavy. That is, until the fog lifts and she's in an unfamiliar room. Her heart thuds heavily against her chest, and she realizes she's sitting on the floor. Sweat drips down her forehead, and she's shaking. Two hands grip her wrists, and she looks around the room manically.

Has she been kidnapped? Where is she?

Dani blinks rapidly and finally notices that she's face to face with Peter, whose thick brows are stitched together with worry.

"In, two, three, four," Peter says, holding a finger in front of her and moving it down slowly. "Out, three, two, one."

She doesn't realize that her breath is following his command. When she sleepwalks, she's awake—but she's not there. Coming out of a sleepwalking episode is like gaining consciousness.

"You're okay, you're safe," Peter says, repeating the phrase over and over, a learned behavior from their years together.

"I haven't done this since college," she whimpers, finally able to speak.

His thumbs keep rubbing her wrists as he holds her, tight and secure. The gesture feels so normal, and her body responds. She throws herself into his sturdy body, one that feels so different from the person she's slept with every night for the past year. Dani breathes him in, smelling the musky nape of his neck and his cologne. Dani wonders if he's still using the same gifted bottle from all those years ago, and the thought warms her. She pulls away to study him.

"You've been so nice to me this weekend, even after what I've done," she says, and he smiles slightly at the understatement. Maybe it's the sleepwalking episode or the fact that she's in his room in the middle of the night, but she knows that they've been falling back in love, or maybe just reigniting the spark that never died inside of her. "I'm sorry I pushed you away."

"You lost your parents," he says. "I thought you needed space. And then he happened."

Peter gestures downstairs, where Ben is getting cozy with his laptop. A lump forms in her throat, and she forces herself to look Peter in the eye.

"I needed to close that chapter of my life," she says. "I lost everything, and being with you…it felt like I had one foot into the happiest time of my life, and one foot out, in my reality."

"I could have made it better. I'd do anything for you," he says. "I still want to."

"It's too late," she says, tearing up.

She's in too deep. She can't leave Ben now. What would the papers say?

"No, it's not," he says firmly.

He gets up and starts digging in the pocket of the shorts he had on earlier to fish out a velvet ring box. His face looks hopeful, and he's no longer holding back from her.

"I've been carrying this around with me for years," he says.

Peter gets down on one knee and pops open the lid.

CHAPTER ELEVEN

DANI
NEWTS HQ, FRESHMAN YEAR
FEBRUARY 12, 2014 — BEFORE

DANI QUICKLY LEARNED HOW EVERYONE IN her pledge class got tapped. Interestingly, the Newts built the experience for the individual, rather than Greek life's emphasis on communally embarrassing pledges. Whitney, a standout on the track team, broke into her coach's home to retrieve a specific trophy. They tasked Kenzie, who came from a family of contractors, with removing commemorative bricks from the garden and replicating them with unblemished ones. Each woman's task seemed not just labor intensive, but also risky enough that expulsion was a real possibility if they were caught. And hearing those stories made Dani realize that was why she and Mal kept waiting for the shoe to drop; they weren't asked to do anything.

That may have been all well and good, except Dani told Kenzie about it. Within hours, it seemed, the entire pledge class turned on Mal and Dani. Some believed Dani was lying. Others accused her and Mal of being an elitist subset of an already exclusive club. A few of the girls cornered Dani about it.

"It's because they don't want you complaining to mommy and daddy about hazing," Nandeeta sneered. "I spent three nights in a row digging up a time capsule in the woods and overslept for an exam. I had to fake a seizure to get my professor to let me take a make-up! It's now in my permanent records that I have epilepsy."

Aisha pointed at Dani, contempt visible on her flawless face, as Nandeeta stood nearby with her arms crossed.

"You have life too easy," Aisha said, her braids swaying as she shook her head in disgust.

Dani knew Aisha was right in the grand scheme of things, but it wasn't her decision. She would have rather been tasked with vandalizing a part of campus than be ostracized by the girls she thought could be her found family. It was all suspect, but not for the reasons Aisha thought.

It seemed like the blowback had died down by the time February rolled around. But when they arrived at HQ, all the tasteful furniture was pushed to the side. A pile of the stolen items greeted the girls instead. Leonora, the Newts' historian, stood in front of them. With a small smile planted on Leonora's freckled face, she gave the impression of a beloved babysitter instead of a scheming pledge master.

"You stole this," Leonora said, her arms flying out. "Official university property. Under the student code of conduct you signed on your first day of Weston, this behavior warrants a suspension at least."

She watched Nandeeta, who had a work-study job and attended Weston on an academic scholarship, turn purple. Suspensions often equated to a loss of financial aid, according to Dani's tour guide spiel for potential new students.

"Who's going to rat about it?" Mal asked, prompting Dani to elbow her to shut up.

"You and Dani actually," Leonora said, her smile carrying a surprising amount of venom. Dani thought Alexia was the scary one, but it turned out all the Newts needed to be watched carefully. "Considering neither of you took anything."

"You didn't ask us to," Mal snapped, but it was useless. A murmur filled the room as the pledges' suspicions were confirmed, dirty glances shot at Dani from all directions. Maybe this was their hazing: separate and conquer.

"It's the first time in the Newts' storied history that this has ever happened," Leonora continued, shooting a pointed glance at Mal. That squashed Dani's hopes that the othering was manufactured. "We've been removing relics of bad men since the beginning of the Newts' existence. Almost all of you should feel a deep sense of pride that you've not only removed traces of these men, but also that when our alumni return to campus, they're not reminded of the bad memories and traumas they experienced on the ground you sleep, eat, learn, and play. It's a service that will never be formally recognized, but know it's an honor to lessen the emotional burden of survivors."

Mal rolled her eyes, clearly above the grandiose sentiment.

"Mallory and Dani, you're going to be tasked with something else to prove to your fellow Newts that you belong," Leonora said.

Mal sat up straighter, suddenly back on board with the mission, while Dani slumped. Couldn't she have just defaced the photographs in the basement of the administrative building?

"You need to save a woman."

Dani's stomach dropped. How the heck were they going to do that?

"What does that even mean?" Mal scoffed.

Alexia strolled into HQ as if on cue.

"You need to uphold our core value of protecting and serving women on this campus," Alexia said. "You seem to have little interest in what we have to say, so we're giving you what you want: control."

Alexia stopped in front of Mal, her gaze sharp. The realization hit Dani like a truck. This was a power struggle between Alexia and Mal, and Dani was simply caught in the middle. Still, if Mal went down, Dani would go down, too.

"If you don't manage to impress us with this mind of yours you're so proud of," Alexia said carefully, "consider your memberships terminated."

* * *

"We're so screwed," Dani said, putting her face in her hands.

They sat at a picnic table outside Henley Hall, waiting for the boys to pick them up for dinner. Rosen had some meetup in Weston proper and firmly insisted that it was not a Valentine's Day dinner, but Dani and Peter didn't believe it. Peter thought he was trying to impress Mal, while Dani thought inviting the only couple in their friend group meant that Rosen thought of Mal as a potential girlfriend. All things pointed to romance, so Dani insisted they get dressed for the occasion. Mal had changed into a slinky dress and slipped on chunky mules, while Dani pulled out several outfits before deciding on a brightly colored tent dress and lace-up ballet flats. Mal's floormates had passed by with great interest as they got ready, considering almost all of them wore pajama pants or workout clothes on a regular basis.

"What if we help every female student get an internship or something for summer?" Mal asked, scrolling on her laptop like it'll save them. "I was looking at the guidebook for Girl Scout badges—"

Dani groaned, deep and guttural.

"These aren't ideas," Dani moaned. "They're setting us up to fail."

Mal looked at Dani aghast, like she had been slapped.

"At least I'm trying," Mal managed. "It's not just going to work out without some effort."

"I just need time to think, Mal," Dani said, rubbing her temples. She didn't want to admit it, but Mal was right. Everything wouldn't fall into place—for Mal. Dani knew she was better liked and better positioned to stay, even if she and Mal failed at Alexia's impossible assignment. And Dani knew herself: She'd have to quit the Newts to stay in Mal's good graces and to keep the friend group they developed over the last few months. She cared more about their weekly movie watching and nights going out dancing than she did about a staid secret society that offered her nothing she didn't already have. But it mattered to Mal, so it mattered to Dani.

She spotted her boyfriend and Rosen coming toward them. "Can we forget about this until tomorrow?"

Mal muttered something under her breath, but it was drowned out by Peter bellowing "double date" from across the parking lot. Dani took Peter, looking sexy in his navy peacoat against the backdrop of bare trees and gray sky. Once he reached her, Peter planted a kiss on Dani. It sent a burst of lightning through her and she kissed back hard. She wanted to rip off his coat and find his warm chest, thankful she could keep her mind off the complications of the Newts with visions of her boyfriend naked.

"At long last," Rosen said, bowing and grabbing Mal's hand dramatically to kiss it.

"Ew, you pervert," Mal said, but she didn't rip her hand

away fast enough. His lips made contact. Mal was rarely flustered, so Dani hoped it meant that she was closer to dumping Adam before the end of their freshman year. Dani was the only one who bet the under on when that relationship would end, with Peter, Seb and Marcus all throwing down cash that it would take at least another semester, maybe two, for Mal and Rosen to hook up. Dani had not-so-subtly tried helping Mal get to that point during their talk at the gym last fall.

It wasn't even to win; Dani genuinely thought it was best for her friend, regardless of the Rosen of it all. They piled into Rosen's car, a black Range Rover with a few dents, and turned the short drive to the nicest Italian restaurant into a karaoke performance, with Mal hitting every wrong note on "Payphone" and Peter a beat behind on the rap part. Dani hummed along, not willing to show off her voice and make it A Thing. She didn't have to worry too much, though. Rosen zipped through town like he didn't fear death, so Dani mostly clung to her seatbelt.

Rosen cut the engine just as Mal was screeching the chorus to "Blurred Lines," sending her off-key echo throughout the car, which was parked askew in the lot. Mal kicked the passenger's seat as Peter let out a gruff cackle. Dani threw herself out of the car with such velocity that she thought about kissing the ground.

"Oh, c'mon, Dani," Rosen said, holding the door open for the girls. "It wasn't that bad."

"How did you even get a license?" Dani muttered. She didn't even have one but felt she could drive better than Rosen.

"I've never gotten a ticket. Clearly, it's not a problem for the police."

"I bet he blows the officers who pull him over," Mal said.

"What's with the oral fixation?" Peter asked, a tad too loud for the white-tableclothed restaurant. "Maybe you and Adam would fare better if you took more interest in it."

"Will you shut up?" Mal swung around, and Dani worried for a second that she was going to give Peter a black eye. He would look kind of hot, like the boxer in a movie where his wife inevitably dies.

Peter threw his hands up in fake surrender, but Mal was no longer paying attention. She inhaled sharply as she surveyed the restaurant. Dani saw her take in the lush, mossy colored couches and well-worn Oriental rugs. Dani followed her gaze to the large photographs dotting the walls, depicting closeups of body parts that made it difficult to decipher where the camera lens was focused on, save for a just-out-of-frame earlobe or nipple. Dani racked her brain for a photographer exhibit she had attended in high school, but the memory was hazy from the coke-fueled frenzy she was in that night. Dani stared at the centerpiece of the bar: a large chandelier from where little crystal fruits hung. A suited man walked over to take their coats. Dani handed over a $5 bill with her jacket in the discreet way her parents always did. She felt embarrassed it wasn't a $20, but assumed the man wasn't expecting a tip from a college student, anyway.

"I can't believe this exists here, of all places," Mal muttered, shaking off her outerwear and handing it to the coat check.

"They just opened their second location here," Rosen said. "The first is in the city."

"Where?" Dani asked, wondering if that was why the restaurant seemed familiar.

"Meatpacking, I think," Rosen said.

Meatpacking. Dani nodded, the memory of that horrible night crystalizing a bit more. The cobblestone streets of the neighborhood and the High Line extension construction. The metallic smell of blood dripping down one leg. Felix's hand firm on the back of her neck.

"My parents are friends with the general manager. They're covering our dinner tonight," Rosen was saying, but Dani stopped listening.

She had gone out clubbing in Meatpacking, when the neighborhood felt perpetually under scaffolding and there were so many alleys to share drugs. Felix had passed a pill to her while they were making out, the drug slipping from his tongue onto hers, before he jammed it down. She remembered trying to leave and not being able to get past his body—a sturdy wall obstructing her. Had Dani been sober, it would have been easy to pass by him, but she was immobilized. After that, all she remembered was the tinkering of his belt buckle and the raw pressure of his extremities on, and then in, her. And then the smell of blood from being pressed under the scaffolding with such force that a piece of metal sticking out from the makeshift chain link fence nicked her leg. It required a tetanus shot later that week.

"Babe, here," Peter said, passing a cocktail to Dani, snapping her out of her head.

Dani grabbed at the Aperol spritz and downed it, hoping the alcohol would send the memory back to the place she kept it—far, far away from her consciousness. If she allowed herself to remember, she didn't think she'd be able to forget.

"To lifelong friends," Rosen said, lifting his glass and winking at Dani, whose glass just held melted ice.

Peter put his arm around her and pulled Dani in close, and she was proud that she didn't let her voice crack as she joined the others in cheers-ing to their bright futures. The conversation quickly turned back to Mal and her novel. She had shown an early draft to her professor without much fanfare.

"What does she know?" Dani slurred.

"She knows a lot," Mal said. "If it's not it, I'll just start a new one."

"Can I read it first?" Rosen asked. "I'm sick of begging."

"I bet you say that to all the girls."

"Mal, you lost the bet. You owe me," Rosen said. "And I might have some ideas before you scrap it entirely."

Mal groaned, asking when he'd have time to read it. "I won't sit around waiting for you."

"Start the new thing," Peter suggested. See, he could be helpful.

"Perfect, then you'll have two books to be neurotic about," Rosen said, smiling warmly at Mal as she playfully hit him.

The twinkle in his eyes matched the sheen from their newly refilled glasses. It was their fourth round, maybe? The piles of pasta and hors d'oeuvres did little to sop up the alcohol coursing through her. Dani's mouth felt gummy as she smiled. She couldn't really keep up with the conversation. Mal leaned forward and smiled at Rosen. Her lips moved, but Dani couldn't make out what she said. Rosen's face drooped slightly, but he gave her a wry smile.

"Is that a yes?" Mal asked, though it wasn't a question. She clinked her glass against his, closing whatever deal they had made. Mal caught Dani's watchful eye.

"How's Marcus?" she teased.

"Still in love with her," Peter said, throwing a protective arm around Dani. She nuzzled into the crook of his arm, happy to be his, and inhaled his scent.

"But has he done anything?" Mal pressed.

Her voice had that cadence, the kind when Mal's mouth ran ahead of her mind.

"Like what?" Dani asked, her eyelids growing heavy.

"He told me he's trying to break you guys up," Mal warned. "Be careful."

Peter made a noise like he was amused. He tipped Dani's chin up so they could look at each other. Staring at him made her melt even more. She was so lucky to have found him, so lucky to be loved this much.

"I love you," she said.

Peter's features—sharply drawn with amusement or annoyance, she couldn't tell—softened, and he kissed her. His mouth tasted like berries. They only pulled apart once the waiter plopped down a dessert platter. Mal and Rosen, meanwhile, were still whispering to each other. It seemed just as intimate, maybe more, than what she and Peter had done. Dani felt the growing, familiar feeling of wanting Mal to be jealous of her for once. To have her approval. Maybe, just maybe, Dani wanted to see a flash of envy in Mal's eye for once. Her shoulders slumped. Peter brushed her hair away from her face, so Dani pushed the negative thoughts away. Peter saw her. Maybe he was enough to satiate her, to fill the gaping void in her chest.

She wanted to feel whole, and despite what all the feminist literature in the world told her, Dani knew she couldn't achieve it on her own.

MAL
LEVIN LIBRARY, FRESHMAN YEAR
MARCH 29, 2014 — BEFORE

MAL DID TWO THINGS AFTER THEIR fancy dinner out in Weston proper.

First, she printed out a copy of her manuscript and discretely hid it on Andrew's desk chair. She couldn't imagine anything more embarrassing than Adam finding it and chastising her for not sharing it with him, even though she had asked him to read her short stories and he'd shown little interest in doing so. Lately, it felt like he only wanted sex, which had steadily improved from their earlier failed attempts. She wasn't sure if that was because she thought of Andrew when they hooked up, or because Adam could feel her grip on him loosening. Either way, her boyfriend was becoming more of an afterthought each passing week. Then she cast aside all thoughts about the boys and her novel to focus on the latest task at hand: figuring out how to save women, as if women needed saving in the first place.

This whole victimhood mentality was why Mal mostly hung out with guys in the first place. She could transcend her gender and just be one the guys, not treated any differently. With women it was always solidarity at the surface and backstabbing below. Mal wished she had the fortitude to walk away, but she didn't want to give into the Newts. It was exactly what Alexia and Cindy and all the rest of the girls wanted from her: to fail. She wouldn't succumb to their pettiness. She'd make hers bigger, stronger, uglier. She'd take them down from within.

Mal watched the latest protest from a window seat near the entrance of the school's library and couldn't believe a few dozen people would rally for a vegan chicken nugget option. Just write a letter to the administration! Another protest—again with the Title IX complaint—marched past her and began occupying the library steps. Weston barely had any sports teams, let alone opportunities for those designated for women. It seemed just dumb enough that Mal, feeling in need of a pick me up, scrambled to her feet to join them. She wanted to press them on why they felt this issue was so important they'd spend a freezing cold day protesting. Mal was in the mood for a fight.

She wrapped her scarf tightly around her neck and yanked her beanie low, an effort that barely contained the coils of hair still springing out, and plodded toward the group. Azza, one of the girls from her writing seminar, waved her down with a bright smile. Mal didn't want to duke it out with someone where there'd be repercussions to her bitchiness.

"Can you believe they won't audit the school?" Azza asked.

"For how much they're spending on sports?" Mal asked, perplexed.

"For how many rapes have occurred on campus," Azza replied, befuddled. "You know Title IX is also about sexual misconduct, right?"

Mal did not know that, but like hell would she admit that.

"There's another Jane Doe case," Azza said, lowering her voice. "You know her."

She didn't know that many people at Weston yet. It was still their first year.

Mal briefly thought about Dani getting hammered at dinner last month and acting a little weird since. Mal reasoned that Dani couldn't possibly be mad about her drunken comment to Marcus. For one, she and Marcus never plotted to break up Peter and Dani, and two, it was just an idea. But maybe the vibe shift Mal felt had nothing to do with her at all and was about something more sinister entirely.

"Do you want a pin?" Seb's voice snapped her out of her spiral.

"You're protesting, too?" Mal had no idea a college protest could be a social event, and yet it seemed like her friends and classmates were dedicating themselves to a cause she knew nothing about. Seb had never even mentioned it to her, and yet he seemed heavily involved.

"It's messed up the school won't audit themselves," Seb said, then brought a handheld megaphone to his mouth. "Not with our tuition dollars."

"Not with our tuition dollars!" The nearly all-women group chanted back.

Seb brought the device to his side and plucked a Take Back the Night pin out of his tote bag to hand to Mal.

"Does she need anything?" Mal asked Azza, hoping this mystery woman might be a woman worth saving.

Azza nodded her head vigorously.

"We're trying to identify him," she said. "Meet us at Dorman Hall tonight."

So not Dani, Mal thought. A small relief. She wanted the help.

"Can I bring a friend?"

* * *

Within five minutes of arriving at Dorman Hall, Mal realized she was an absolute piece of shit. The reason Veronica dropped P-Cubed's class wasn't because she couldn't hack it; it was because Veronica woke up in her bed with no recollection of what happened the night before. Her roommate, Zoe, had taken photos of pink-and-white sheets stained with blood, which Mal and Dani studied.

"The reporting process was horrible," Zoe said quietly, as if she didn't want Veronica to hear. "They asked so many invasive questions and insisted she go to the police for a rape test."

"Being a virgin isn't a defense," Veronica said, smoothing her wavy hair. "And I had too much to drink. They just assumed I'm out of control, or a slut. Probably both."

She smoothed her hair again, and Dani reached out to grab her wrist. Mal glanced at Dani with surprise. It seemed like such an emotional reaction from someone who was normally a bit more buttoned up with new people.

"I would have never brought a stranger back to my room if I were sober," Veronica continued, letting Dani hold her hand in her lap. "It sounds like regret, but it's the truth. I feel taken advantage of."

"And you don't remember anything else about that night?" Mal asked.

"It's hazy," Veronica said as Zoe rubbed her back.

"Think of any sensory details," Mal urged. "Any sounds? Smells?"

Dani inhaled sharply as Veronica simultaneously gagged.

"Soap," she choked. "The smell of soap was overwhelming."

Mal nodded sympathetically as she jotted notes into a little black notebook, but Zoe's reaction to Dani's ashen face made her pause.

"Do you know who she's talking about?" Zoe demanded.

Dani shook her head and excused herself, mumbling that the dining hall food wasn't agreeing with her. She stumbled out of the dorm room.

"I'm sorry about that," Mal said, glancing over her shoulder. "She doesn't have the stomach for hard things."

DANI
WALNUT HALL, FRESHMAN YEAR
MARCH 29, 2014 — BEFORE

DANI'S HANDS MOVED RHYTHMICALLY AS SHE tried to modulate her breathing. Back in high school, she had the same nervous tic as Veronica, where she'd scrape her fingernail against the shaft of her hair so it curled. It was why Dani started getting keratin treatments, so she'd have a reason to stop. Now she was back at it, letting the movement calm her, even if it destroyed her hair. When Mal told her about the Jane Doe case as a solution to their Newts problem, Dani didn't think twice about going over. Had she considered her own experiences, she would have realized she was too sensitive, too raw.

Dani had chalked that night in high school up to a not-so-fun Saturday—a bad experience, not a crime. She had never thought about it as sexual assault until now, and it made her feel incredibly stupid. Not for not knowing, but that she dated that guy. For months. And she cried for about the same amount of time when he dumped Dani for her Mandarin tutor.

When she saw a shadowy figure curving around the side of her building, Dani didn't bother turning her head to confirm it was Mal.

"What was that?" Mal asked. "I looked for you everywhere."

Dani sat on a bench outside Walnut, her dorm. It was the nicest option available to freshmen, at least according to Mal, who had been sure to tell her the first time she came over.

Despite being a loose cannon, Mal was perceptive. Worse, she was persistent. If Dani didn't tell her what was going on, what triggered the panic attack, Mal would likely take matters into her own hands. She wouldn't let it go, like a dog with a bone.

"I think I was raped in high school," Dani said, pinching her thigh.

"You think?" Mal asked, and then seemed to hear how she sounded. She put an arm around Dani and awkwardly rubbed her back, a rare show of affection. Dani wished for a friend like Zoe, who so kindly took care of Veronica during the interview. But somehow, she knew, Mal was the friend she deserved.

"I can handle this if it's going to trigger you," Mal said, a wry smile forming on her face. "It wouldn't be very Fig Newton of me to save one woman at the expense of another."

"That's such a dumb joke," Dani groaned.

"It's not my fault they picked a dumb name," Mal said. "They need a rebrand."

She looked at Dani and leaned in.

"Can I at least tell you what you missed out on?"

Dani felt nauseous but didn't have the stamina to fight, so she just nodded.

"Someone saw Henry Choi leave their floor the night," Mal said.

"That doesn't mean anything," Dani said. She knew Henry; he wasn't a rapist.

"It's a lead," Mal said.

Dog, bone, Dani thought. *At least she'll die on her own sword.*

She manages a smile and is almost alarmed by how natural it feels, like her outside features can so fully detach from her inside feelings. Mal responds to the mask with a big smile and hugs Dani.

"I'm going to catch a rapist," Mal says, with more joy than that phrase should allow.

* * *

April showers brought a list of suspected rapists.

Mal collected 10 names of potential perpetrators who may have harmed Veronica, though she still managed to fixate on poor Henry Choi. Dani, meanwhile, knew he was in the closet and hadn't even kissed anyone, let alone the gender of his desire, so she helped him sort an alibi without tipping him off. She was surprisingly good at damage control and signed up to take a crisis communications class next semester as a reward for her intrinsic talent.

Dani knew Mal would never understand her helping a so-called suspect, but she wanted to keep her from straying and reporting every man to exist on this campus. They needed to narrow down their list, and Dani decided she had done enough waiting.

In the privacy of HQ one rainy night, Dani made a phone call to Jay, her favorite of the private detectives, and sent the list of names. He confirmed one of them, Shawn Harmon, had a record of public nudity and intoxication.

"The Weston Police Department has the rape kit," Dani told him. "Can you find out if it's a match?"

Two days later Shawn Harmon was arrested for the rape of Veronica Pierce.

"I can't believe we didn't find him in time," Mal said, devastated at losing.

But her disappointment didn't last long, Dani made sure of it. News got around campus quick that, despite the university closing Jane Doe's case quietly and with little investigation, Mal's sleuthing led to the police finding Shawn. Dani wasn't exactly sure if that made sense, but it's what she gossiped about on "private calls" in the lounge and in those few minutes when students got settled ahead of class starting.

The women of Weston began inundating Mal with their own stories and proof like text messages, photos, ripped clothing and bloodied sheets: a growing display of evidence that women were not safe at Weston. Most of them, like Veronica, admitted they felt they were to blame—for being too drunk, for going back to a man's apartment in the first place, or for agreeing to sex but then changing their minds and not being able to reverse that decision.

Dani sympathized. She saw the nuance in each instance. How could you blame someone for continuing to have sex if they didn't know their partner was suddenly uninterested?

Mal just became more aggrieved.

"These men are a threat to womankind and need to be stopped," Mal said. "If we don't stop them, who will?"

Dani kept her opinions to herself. Still, she matched Mal's enthusiasm publicly. But that all changed after she ran into Daijanae near the administrative building one afternoon.

Daijanae, a sophomore who would go on to win a Fields Medal, had just reported her rape and was laughed out of the police precinct that covered the college and surrounding town. She went to the police armed with a medical exam, a rape test kit, a bag of ripped and bloodied clothes, and the promise of a witness. Her lab partner had attacked her after a late night of studying at the library, and she took every step to report him. But it didn't matter. She was heading to the administrative building to tenure her withdrawal from the college when she ran smack into Dani.

"I didn't seek out the vigilantes," Daijanae said stone faced after recounting her story, "because I've been exceptional my whole life, so exceptional that systems were forced to take me seriously."

Daijanae's face crumbled.

"They treated me like another Black girl crying rape."

She thrust the documents at Dani and left her there holding the baggage of a crime for which Daijanae would still carry. There was no phone call Dani could make to save her.

CHAPTER TWELVE

MAL
THE RENTAL IN AUSTIN, TEXAS
MAY 25, 2024 — AFTER

THE SOUND OF BIRDS CHIRPING AWAKENS Mal. She stretches in bed—fascia breaks apart and her back cracks—and marvels at how the violence in bodies can feel so good. The cotton is cool against her skin, and she's struck by how well-rested she feels. She should take shrooms more often. But then, two thoughts flood her mind, as if they tucked themselves into her bed with her. To her left: Dani has a secret potion that makes people speak the truth. To her right: Andrew arrives today.

Mal groans and closes her eyes. This is exactly why she came to Texas in the first place. For intrigue, for drama! And yet she feels herself on the precipice of falling back into Dani's trap. She had trusted Dani, who she believed was too kind and open and naïve at times. By comparison, Mal felt like a monster: always angry, always wanting. She was selfish and hated that other people saw it too. And yet, when everything went down junior year, when they could really stand up for their principles, Dani revealed who she truly was—and Mal paid the price.

That couple from last night could have been hired actors, but if anyone wanted to develop a truth serum, Dani has the resources and money to do it.

Then there's the Alexia of it all. In her sobriety, Mal understands that it's impossible for Alexia to know she's writing a tell-all, fictious account about the Newts and their friends' indiscretions. Still, she swears she saw her twice during the trip.

She calls Serena, who picks up on the first ring.

"I literally almost ordered you a smoothie from Erewhon," Serena laughs.

"I miss our weekly treat," Mal replies, smiling. This is how true friendship should feel. "You didn't mention my trip to anyone, right? I feel silly asking but—"

"But you have reason to ask, I'm assuming."

"Unfortunately," Mal says.

"Some chick who came in with one of the regulars asked for you the other day," she says. "I told them you were in Texas working on your next novel."

Mal gulps.

"Did you tell them anything else?" Mal asks.

"I don't think so," Serena says. "Hey, I'm walking into my Pilates studio now. Anything else before I run?"

Mal shakes her head. This isn't what she wants to hear.

"Everything's going to be fine," Serena says, offering support in response to Mal's silence. "I wouldn't bet against you."

They hang up, and Mal feels discomfort wedge itself in between her ribs. It's the sensation that she's forgetting something. Mal leans over to grab the notebook on her nightstand and begins scribbling in it, detailing all the bits she can remember from last night. But then another internal conversation takes over. It's louder and more interesting, and she lets them talk out their problems as her hand tries to keep up. Mal powers through pages and pages of dialogue until she hears Dani and Ben pass her room, speaking quietly to each other.

"I'm happy you're back to your normal self," Ben says. "It was like a body snatchers situation for a bit."

Mal can't hear Dani's response, but her tone doesn't convey any emotion. Mal slides the notebook back in the nightstand. She needs to talk with Dani and get more details on the serum, assuming it's real and the reason Dani may be in danger. That brings Mal to her second horrible thought of the morning, which is how she'll plan to drug Andrew—if she wants to at all.

Mal needs guidance—and doesn't necessarily trust her instincts on this one. Her gut could never reliably parse her feelings about Andrew. But then again, she knows what he did.

Still in her oversized T-shirt splashed with a faded picture of Brandon Flowers, Mal creeps down the stairs. She makes it about halfway when the front door opens—bringing her eye level with those jade eyes and a small, cautious smile.

Fuck, he looks better than she remembered.

She searches his face for a glimmer of regret or atonement. Mal wants him to feel bad for what he's done, for it to shade every interaction, every flutter of his eyelashes. She wants it to have consumed him, a scarlet letter branded on his forehead. He seems nervous to bask in her unrelenting gaze and the intensity radiating off her partially clothed body, but she can't deny the magnetic pull she still feels toward him.

It was a bad idea coming here, Mal thinks.

They stay frozen in place, even as the boys swarm Andrew. Clearly, they've stayed in touch. Ben grabs his backpack, Peter slings an arm around him, and Seb swoops in for a hug. Even though he's smiling and making small talk about the heat wave that just hit Austin, his eyes keep returning to Mal's face.

"This is perfect timing," Ben says, thrusting a curled fist into the air.

The intrusion breaks their connection. Peter glares at Ben's juvenile fist pump, but more interestingly, Dani cringes at her fiancé from the opposite side of the room. Ben pulls out the opened envelope from Rainey Street and shakes the card loose from it.

"We finally have everyone together," he clarifies, and then re-reads the clue. "Never below 70 degrees, this place has everything you need. From food trucks to diving boards, there's a reason the spot is adored. Have a blast, but don't be late. This evening you all have a very important date."

"We're going to the public pool?" Peter grumbles.

"Barton Springs!" Seb brightens, delighted someone else has finally done their due diligence to google the city.

Peter's darkened mood is a distinct change from his behavior the last few days, when he and Dani eye fucked the whole time. Now, they won't look at each other.

"That sounds like an amusement park," Mal says, thinking of trips to Great Wolf Lodge with her parents and their new partners—when everyone was trying to act like a big, happy family, though Mal had ruined it with her own sour mood.

She was even more sour as a teenager, perpetually bullied at school and alone, save for the emo music and her Tumblr friends. The realization hits her hard. She's still unwanted, if Marcus' comment to Dani that first night is to be believed. It dawns on her that the only reason Marcus would have invited her is if Dani asked him too. This whole thing, from start to finish, has been Dani's doing. It would be fucked up if she planned her own near-murder, but Mal wouldn't put it past her. Dani ruthlessly serves herself.

"Is it a water park?" Ben asks. "My favorite ride is the water flume."

"No, babe," Dani says, her tone smooth as honey. Her hand glides up the nape of Ben's neck and gently pulls him toward her so she can plant a kiss on the side of his cheek. He wraps an arm affectionately around her waist, and Peter's gaze settles on Ben's grasp.

"It's this natural spring," Dani says. "It's the place to be."

"We should get our bathing suits on, then," Ben says, guiding Dani up the stairs.

Mal wonders if they're going to have sex while they're up there, and another glance at Peter indicates he's thinking the same thing. Maybe Dani planned this weekend to mind fuck everyone, not just Mal.

"Let me pack a bag," Peter mutters, but he dawdles at the base of the stairs until Dani and Ben have soundly disappeared into their room.

"There's floats in here," Seb calls out from one of the living-room closets, pulling out boxes depicting unicorns and coconuts and other summer-y plastic toys. When Seb notices that only he, Mal, and Andrew are left downstairs, he smiles uncomfortably before bolting.

"Then there were two," Andrew drawls and sits down. "Give me the low down."

"On what?"

"Who puked the most this weekend? Did Marcus accidentally refer to Tamar as Dani? I want the gossip," Andrew says, leaning back on the couch. Mal might almost believe he's relaxed, but his foot is shaking just the tiniest bit. He's nervous. She can work with that.

"Shockingly no one has puked yet, so you still have time to take home the crown," Mal says. "Seb and I got a little too high on shrooms."

Andrew raises an eyebrow but says nothing. Mal wants to hold back on the last thing, she really does, but it's too juicy not to share.

"And I think something's going on with Peter and Dani."

Andrew's eyes light up. Mal can see his muscle flex underneath his T-shirt as he leans forward. Her mind is like a well-trodden path; the thoughts and feelings from before come to her with ease. She just needs to rewire her brain and not let him affect her.

"I can find out if you want," Andrew offers.

No. No favors. No glimpses of what he's lost. She can't give him anything. The rental is starting to feel claustrophobic. She stands up, needing to exit his personal space. It's too much.

"I'm—"

"I'm hoping we can talk, when you're ready for it this weekend," Andrew interrupts. "A lot's changed with me that you might not know."

"Rosen," Mal says sharply, seeing how the sound of her using his last name pierces him like balloon. She forces her mouth to transform into a placid smile, but on the inside, she's boiling. She changed, too, because of him, but that doesn't mean she uses it as an excuse for her own shitty behavior.

Her stomach roils. Mal's her own worst enemy. Her behavior wasn't shitty; it was called for. She's let these assholes dictate her own self-worth. The thought prompts hot, angry tears to percolate. She'd rather drown herself at Barton Springs in front of everyone than let Andrew see her cry one more time.

"Do whatever you want," Mal says. It's a small miracle her voice sounds icy. "It's meaningless."

"I came here for you," Andrew calls out, his voice thick with emotion.

Mal flips him off and heads upstairs. *Always running away*, she thinks.

DANI
BARTON SPRINGS
MAY 25, 2024 — AFTER

UNDER NORMAL CIRCUMSTANCES, BARTON SPRINGS WOULD feel like an oasis. This morning, though, Dani's melting under the pressure—and the horrific heat wave plaguing the city. She figured the public pool would be busy during the summer, but she didn't anticipate what a heat wave would entail: long lines, malfunctioning ticket machines, and spotty service that hinders them from buying tickets on the app.

"We don't have to be here," Mal says, fanning herself.

"You're always looking to leave," Seb points out.

"Who put together this scavenger hunt, anyway?"

A chorus of different names—Tamar, Dani, Marcus—ring out as Mal rolls her eyes.

"What if it's just a trap?" Mal asks, smirking.

"Can you stop touching me?" Dani snaps at Ben, who's rubbing sunscreen unprompted into her back.

"Sorry, you were burning," he says.

"I don't burn," Dani replies. "It's too hot. I don't want to be touched."

They move closer to the entrance, still without being able to buy tickets.

"I just reached checkout," Seb says, jamming a finger at the screen. "And now I'm back to the homepage."

"It's letting me put my address in," Peter says.

They inch closer, and Dani's ready to scream. Mal and Rosen are as far away from each other as they can be, Peter is on the verge of confronting Ben about his proposal, and Dani woke up to a call this morning that they're ready for the background check. It's the last step before she begins to mount her Senate run.

Ben was excited when she told him, of course he was excited. She needs him more than ever now, and she's angry with herself for giving in—just for a brief, beautiful moment—to Peter. She can never be with him, and the faster she lets herself accept that, the better off they'll all be. Her life—her real, adult life—is about to start. It's not what she wanted or expected, but she can't keep running away from her destiny. Look what good it did the last time she tried.

"I got them," Peter shouts. "Six tickets."

They scan in and walk around the pool to a grassy knoll big enough for their party. Mal glances over the chain-link fence separating the main spring from the feral creek section, where dogs splash into the water and people lounge with six packs (the drinking kind—none of these people are remotely attractive).

Dani makes a face at a tangle of limbs on a turquoise towel on the other side of the fence, where a couple looks like they're licking each other. She doesn't understand what Mal sees in the free section. Peter seems just as enthralled, but for all the wrong reasons. This is why she and him aren't together anymore.

"Do you think the spring has healing properties?" Dani asks as they colonize a particularly grassy knoll.

"There's only so much nature can do to the human condition," Mal says.

"You don't think people can change?" Dani asks hopefully.

"The best indicator of future behavior is past behavior," Mal says. "We're all fixed at this point in our lives."

"That's so woo-woo," Seb says.

"No, that's going to therapy," Mal says.

"I thought you were opposed to therapy," Dani says.

"Yeah, when it was dictated by other people," Mal says. "You. My parents. You can't push people to be ready for it."

"Everyone just wanted to help you."

"No, they just wanted to make me more pliable to their own needs," Mal says.

"That's really cynical," Dani says.

"It's not cynical. It's called processing. And I'd rather be someone who processes my feelings and actually feels them, even when they're ugly to other people, than to not feel at all," Mal says, looking at Dani, who feels herself turn an ungodly color of red.

"I process things," Dani says. Ben laughs, and then gets serious once he sees Dani's face. "Are you kidding me?"

"I thought you were joking," he mutters.

Mal's face twists into a grin.

"See? Fixed."

A familiar sound distracts the group. Rosen and Peter, who are ahead of them, start smacking each other around before Peter jogs ahead. Rosen then sprints across the grass and makes a tackling dive toward Peter. His grip is strong enough to pants Peter. In turn, Peter wrestles Rosen until he's in position to graze his balls against his friend's face.

"They're children." Mal throws her hands up. "We're in public."

Seb grimaces.

"Do you think they're going to start pranking each other again?" he asks. "Marcus won't speak to any of us again if they pull something."

"It wouldn't get that far," Dani says. "Tamar would kill him first."

"Maybe Marcus shouldn't get married if he's worried about upsetting her," Mal says.

"Don't start," Seb says.

"Have they spoken since graduation?" Mal asks, jutting her chin at Rosen and Peter.

Seb shrugs while Dani smiles politely. She can't even bring herself to talk about Peter.

"I think this will be a prank-free weekend," Dani says, sliding on her sunglasses.

The pool is packed with young, beautiful people. Men with big back tattoos wait in line to do front flips off the diving board. Women in tiny sarongs and even smaller sunglasses walk past her, their bare feet kicking up tiny bits of dirt under the trampled grass. Dani wants to focus on these people instead of her own problems and revel in her last weeks of anonymity.

A group of boys start splashing each other, while another guy holds a volleyball over his head. They quickly form teams and begin tossing the ball around. It reminds her of something Mal once told her in college.

"That's the thing about boys. Team sports encourage that kind of socialization: vast and shallow," Mal said, then leaning in closer. "Girls only need one another to keep a secret."

CHAPTER THIRTEEN

MAL
WALNUT HALL, FRESHMAN YEAR
APRIL 13, 2014 — BEFORE

WRITING WAS THE THING THAT GAVE Mal purpose. It's
how she processed her feelings and felt less alone and learned
how to articulate what was really bothering her. It was a perfect coping mechanism, until she became wrapped up in
wanting to know what Andrew Rosen thought of it.

As she waited for his feedback, Mal dove headfirst into a
new hobby that brought her a surprising amount of meaning:
listening to women relay the worst nights of their lives. After
every interview with a classmate who spoke about how they
experienced sexual assault, Mal would diligently take notes
and then log the person's name into a spreadsheet. She began
color-coding the accusations, flagging in red when a person's
name came up more than once.

The spreadsheet didn't just include men accused of sexual
assault. Mal had a separate tab for the creeps, too. They
included men like the guy in her stats class who made lewd
comments and the earth sciences professor who allegedly
offered "extra credit" to certain female students. But when

she showed Dani her progress, Mal was disappointed that Dani didn't see the vision.

"'Lewd comments' don't count," Dani said, reviewing Mal's work.

"These are leads," Mal protested. "Where there's smoke, there's fire, etcetera, etcetera."

"This feels like the basis of a lawsuit," Dani said weakly.

"About one in four women are raped on college campuses," Mal replied. "Bad behavior begets worse behavior."

"Okay, but what are you going to do with this? Turn it over to the cops and say, 'Hey, here's a list of men who are rumored to have committed sexual violence?' Shawn Harmon is still graduating next month."

Mal narrowed her eyes at Dani. That was what fueled her to create the spreadsheet in the first place.

"Do you not get it?" Mal asked. "This is what we're presenting next month to Alexia."

"What do you mean? I thought you were just presenting on how you got him arrested."

"I was, but then they came to me," Mal said. "We could make change at scale."

Dani looked at her funny in that moment.

"You know, I thought you were working on your book all this time," Dani said, pointing to the missed movie nights with the gang. While Mal was genuinely busy with the interviews and documentation, her absence was really because she and Andrew were avoiding each other.

At first, she thought it was because he was reading her novel and wanted space from her as a person so he could focus on her writing. Then, she noticed he was muted in classes too, ever since he established himself as the dark horse in

P-Cubed's class at the end of the fall semester. She and her classmates had whispered to each other about the letter assignment in the weeks that followed, surprised that it felt like his writing finesse came out of nowhere. Still, she and her classmates noticed they had all improved in just a semester, so perhaps he was a late bloomer.

For weeks when Mal brought it up, he kept deflecting, and then finally blamed it on seasonal affective disorder and the start to lacrosse season. He hated waking up at 5 a.m. to darkness, and her boyfriend—he said that accusatorially —was going to be a pain in the ass if he made too much noise leaving in the mornings. Mal felt like it was an unreasonable dig at Adam—that man could sleep through an atomic bomb. Then it occurred to her that, out of all their friends, including Dani, who presumably was her best friend, she knew Andrew the best. She understood him. And he understood her in a way she felt no one, not even Adam, did.

Mal also noticed that Andrew's letter writing had stopped. Normally, she'd come to their room to find Andrew bent over a half-filled legal pad, with the soft scratching of pencil hitting paper. Who even used pencils anymore other than crossword puzzlers? People barely used actual pens. Everything was typed nowadays. Since he read that assignment, the legal pads had disappeared from the top of his weirdly organized desk, and his mood had sullied. The dinner in downtown Weston was the last time she saw him act normal.

"Andrew still has it," Mal said, answering Dani after an extended pause. "I should meet up with him, actually."

She shot Adam and Seb quick text messages separately to see if they've seen Andrew.

Library, Adam wrote back. *He's still in a shit mood.*

Before Mal could sprint out of Dani's dorm room, her friend spoke.

"You know, I'm really proud of you," Dani said.

Mal froze. She couldn't remember the last time anyone had said that to her. Her bad attitude usually offset any praise that might have come with it.

"I know I have concerns with the legality of this, but I believe in you and this project," Dani said. "I want you to know that."

Mal didn't know what to say, and Mal always knew what to say. She simply nodded and thanked Dani before jetting off to find out if her intel was right.

Mal found Andrew in one of the no-WiFi rooms at the library, which forced him to focus without distraction. She was ready to be the greatest distraction possible.

"Whatever happened to your pen pal?" Mal asked, barging into his space. Andrew jumped at the intrusion but didn't seem incredibly bothered to see her.

"He's not there anymore," Andrew replied.

"Did he help you with your jail assignment?"

Andrew raised an eyebrow but kept his gaze on his textbook. He stared at that page for a few minutes. Mal tracked it on the clock ticking above them. After waiting for him to offer anything else, or simply look at her, Mal tried again.

"Can I see it again?" Mal pressed.

"Will you stop annoying me if I do, Firefly?"

Mal nodded so enthusiastically that Andrew's face dropped, understanding he had no other option. He sighed and tossed his backpack onto the wooden table to extract the pages. They looked even more worn, the creases softening from wear.

"Andrew, really, this is incredible," Mal said, skimming the papers. "Can I try to get this published? I know the editor of the campus literary magazine. Or have you considered submitting it to the *New Yorker*? I know it's a long shot, but we should start getting into the habit of submitting—"

"Don't," Andrew warned.

Mal startled at his tone. He was angry with her. She opened her mouth, but he cut her off.

"I'm serious, Mal," Andrew said. "I won't show you any of my work again."

"We're in class together," Mal said. "I'm going to see it."

He threw his textbook and notebooks into his backpack and walked out of the room without a word, leaving her holding his papers. She followed him out.

"What's wrong with you?" she shouted at his back.

Other students in the library glared at her, and yet, her missives didn't reach him.

* * *

Weeks passed without them talking, even in P-Cubed's class, and it drove her crazy. He'd slide into his seat just before the bell rang, barely participate, and then slip right back out just as class concluded. Her texts and calls went unanswered, and he stopped telling Adam where he'd be—presumably because Andrew didn't want Mal showing up anymore. The distress caused her to lose 10 pounds, though Mal's face seemed to bloat from the crying she did at night.

"I heard he has a girlfriend," Seb said as they left class one day.

It was the end of April, and the sun shone through the blooming trees. The college was recognized as an arboretum, which meant that half the students couldn't make it across the quad without sneezing in spring. Mal, who felt like it was a personal achievement to not have allergies, dramatically inhaled the warm springtime air. Flowers bloomed around them, and she felt the desire to lay down in the grass. It was the happiest she had been since he disappeared.

"You're full of shit," Mal said, though her stomach flipped with that morsel of gossip. She pointed to a particularly sunny patch of grass. "Want to take a nap?"

"With those pesticides?" Seb asked in mock horror. "Enjoy that cancer in 20 to 40 years."

"You don't want to lay down and gossip?" she teased. "I want to know what kind of sources you have."

"You can just ask him," Seb said.

"I'd rather die."

A pause.

"Do you want my advice?"

"I'm going to get it, aren't I?" Mal grumbled.

"Break up with Adam," Seb said. "That's how you'll get his attention for good."

"All he has to do is ask me out," Mal shrugged, like it was the most casual thing in the world when it absolutely wasn't.

"He's never going to," Seb said. "Not while you're dating his roommate."

"The hurdles actually make it more fun for men," Mal said. "It would never stop them."

"Don't lump me in with them," Seb said, throwing his hands up in mock surrender.

"Mal," a voice called out.

"Speak of the devil," Seb whispered in her ear before ducking away.

"Want to sit?" Andrew asked, pointing to the same spot Mal had identified.

She gave him a once over, like she was merely annoyed with him and not devastated by his act of indifference. She didn't want him to know how much harm he caused.

"Done running away from me?"

He grinned sheepishly and shrugged.

"You were being annoying," he said. "But I want to talk about your book."

Sure enough, a fast-growing rash spread across her ankles as they sat in the grass. Mal fought the urge to scratch and instead stared at the beauty mark just below Andrew's right ear. A slight breeze pushed her hair around, tickling her armpits. It was the longest her hair had ever been, since her mom always insisted on getting it cut just above Mal's shoulders, creating the most unfortunate triangle shape that plagued her childhood. Now that she was in charge of her own hair, she wasn't letting anyone touch it.

She tucked her hair behind her ear as she watched Andrew slip on reading glasses. Leaning against a tree with the stack of printed papers stained with red marks propped in his lap made him look like a J. Crew model. His blond hair had grown out into what Peter referred to as "flow," which meant Andrew kept having to push it out of his face. She didn't understand why he'd have long hair for lacrosse season, when it's more likely to get in the way, but didn't want to get into another argument with him. After all, he was doing her a major favor. Reading a first draft of a first novel was a Herculean task.

"You're going to publish this," he said finally.

"It's not good yet," Mal said, fighting the desire to grab the manuscript from his grasp and cradle it against her chest. It was a mistake showing him, especially if his feedback was only ebullient. If she was looking for a cheerleader, she would have called her mother. "It won't be good for years."

"Why are you underestimating yourself?" Andrew asked, pushing his hair back. His tone was clipped, like he hadn't forgiven her for something. If anything, he was the one who should want her forgiveness. And yet not being around him for what felt like months created a swell of desire. Mal wanted him to understand her. She wanted it so badly.

"I'm not," she said, pausing to be careful with her words. "People overestimate me because they think I'm precocious."

"You're past the age of that, I think," Andrew cracked.

"No, this is the problem. Adults laud my behavior, even if it's ornery for people our age, and that praise has calcified my personality into precocity. There's nothing more to me than that," Mal said.

"You're doing that academic thing again, where you use SAT words to prove your point," he said. "And you're still not making sense."

"You're the one not making sense. You really have nothing critical to say?"

"You're so hard on yourself," Andrew said.

"Am I?" Mal asked. "Or am I just being honest about my abilities?"

"Do you think other people are stupid?"

"Of course not."

"So you think you're pulling a fast one on everyone else around you?" Andrew pointed his finger at her, a gotcha of sorts.

"I don't have the skillset worthy of such praise," Mal said. "I just have the desire, and everyone treats the latter like it's the former."

"Being treated seriously is the only reason you're in a position to get mentorship or noticed. You're in Peterson's class, and I've read your work. It's excellent—"

"I know what's good, and I know my own work isn't meeting that standard," Mal's voice rose with frustration. "I don't know what to tell you. That's not being hard on myself. It's holding myself accountable to what I've created."

"Do you think you're even capable of appreciating your own work? Will there ever be a point where you think something you did is good?"

"You're biased," Mal said. "You're looking at my work and reading it in my voice, assuming the words in my story are saying the thing I intended to say—because you know me—instead of reading what's actually on the page. And what is there is just a bunch of scenes that don't have any higher meaning. There's nothing below the surface."

"Things can be nice-looking and have something below the surface." His green eyes flashed, his irises darkening.

"Andrew, I'm telling you this doesn't," she said, stabbing her manuscript.

"Firefly, you're getting heated."

"Stop calling me that."

He cocked his head at her.

"You know why I call you that, right?"

She glowered at him.

"Because you're so intense. You glow."

Mal's shoulders shot up to her ears. He thought she was someone who radiated anger so intensely that she glowed. It wasn't just that he thought it was a compliment; he was right about her. All this time she thought she could outsmart him, but it turned out he saw through her.

"Anyway, you only say my name when you're mad at me," Andrew said.

"I do not," Mal said indignantly. "I'm not mad at you. I'm frustrated with the situation."

"That you hate yourself so much that you're taking it out on your writing?"

"I don't hate myself," Mal said, biting her lip to keep herself from saying, I don't hate myself, *Andrew*. "Maybe you hate yourself and you're projecting your self-loathing onto me."

"Of course I hate myself," he said, his voice tangling in the back of his throat. "People give me things all the time, and we both know I don't deserve them. They think I'm the one with nothing going on below the surface. Like your writing, apparently. But that would be insulting to you, Mal, because you're so good and so self-obsessed that you can't even see it. It's like you're looking for the trees in the forest. You built this whole forest, but you're obsessed with the tree and how people are going to like one stupid tree. Do you even care about the tree?"

"I don't even know what point you're trying to make," Mal yelled.

"Why are you still with Adam?" Andrew demanded.

"Because I love him," Mal said.

"That's not a good enough reason," Andrew countered. "It's not the real reason, either."

"What do you want me to say? That my life would look radically different if I went to Brown instead of Weston? It probably would be, but I'd have even more student loans and no less certainty on what's next than I do now. I made this choice, and I'm sticking with it."

"You're staying with Adam only because you've already planned to stay with Adam? How does that make any sense?"

He shook his head. "Actually, that makes perfect sense. He's just like everything else in your life. You plan to do something, so you do it. And you don't fail at anything, right?"

"Don't talk to me like that," Mal said, getting in his face. People stared at them as they walked by, but she was too livid to care. "Don't you dare throw my feelings in my face."

"This isn't friendship," Andrew growled, his body bending so he and Mal were nose to nose. "You treat me like your boyfriend. You ask me to do favors for you. You flirt with me. You cuddle with me during the scary parts of a movie. You ask me to walk you home at night. But you never want to sleep with me."

"You're disgusting, you know that?" Mal stood up. "I don't owe you shit. If you were Dani or Sebastian, I would do the same things. Hell, you see me do the same things with them that I do with you."

"You don't do that with Marcus or Peter," Andrew shot back.

"I don't have that kind of relationship with Marcus. And Peter is Dani's boyfriend."

"That proves my whole point," Andrew yelled, his voice cracking. "It wouldn't be appropriate with them, so why do it with me?"

"Because you're my best friend," Mal yelled back.

"No, I'm not," Andrew said.

Mal watched the muscle jump just above the sharp edges of his jaw. The two were at a standstill for what felt like an eternity, until Mal gave in. She yanked her manuscript from him, and tears welled as she processed what she had heard.

"Glad to know I've always just been some sort of conquest to you," Mal said. Her mouth felt wet, but she was too tired to wipe her face.

Let him watch me cry, she thought. *Let him feel bad.*

"I thought we had a real connection, but apparently all you wanted from me was sex."

"I, I don't," Andrew said, his face softening but his eyes darted around Mal's face, looking uncertain. "I don't feel that way. I just want more. More for you. More for us."

"There's no us," Mal said forcefully. "I don't want to hear from you for a while."

Mal turned on her heels and walked away, letting herself cry the real ugly tears. She tried to listen for footsteps coming from behind. It was her turn to dramatically walk away from him. And anyway, this was the part of the movie where Andrew chased after her, grabbed her arm and kissed her. If it felt like fireworks, she'd dump Adam. She wasn't going to give up her future on an unrequited crush or worse, a bad kisser.

Come on Andrew, Mal thought. *It's now or never.*

Mal continued to stomp away, until finally she gave in and looked over her shoulder. Andrew wasn't watching her go; he was gone.

DANI
NEWTS HQ, FRESHMAN YEAR
APRIL 27, 2014 — BEFORE

THE DUE DATE FOR MAL AND Dani's project had arrived. The two girls walked over to HQ with their heads bowed, partly in deference for their presentation, and also to avoid the fine mist that covered their jackets. Dani glanced over at Mal, whose curly hair peeked out from the hood of her rain jacket. Little beads of moisture clung to her hair like ants on a log, and Dani felt a parental urge to wipe them off.

Dani anticipated that the whole organization would be at HQ, but the house was surprisingly empty. Even Leonora, who was perpetually curled up on the couch working on homework or reading a book, was nowhere to be seen. The girls shook off their wet clothes and began setting up for their presentation. Mal connected her laptop to the projector, turning a large blank wall into a movie-theater screen displaying a color-coded spreadsheet. The upper corners of Mal's lips twitched. God, Dani wished she had that kind of self-satisfaction. Dani turned around to see Cindy, Leonora, and Alexia standing near the alcove, their arms folded like they were part of some somber girl group.

"This looks like it'll be good," Alexia said facetiously as the rest of the seniors filed into the room. Dani joined Mal, who straightened her shoulders in anticipation of their final task.

"Not all of these are substantiated," Dani began, her voice shaking just the slightest. "But the colors reflect the likelihood of these claims. You can also sort by accusation."

Mal clicked through the spreadsheet, just as they practiced, demonstrating how someone could search by first name, last name, type of crime, whether alcohol or drugs were involved, if it happened on or off campus and where, as well as several other variables, like if that person had credibly been accused before or whether a university report existed. Dani was particularly proud of that last one, which she was able to access through a computer at the administrative building. She found it irresponsible that every computer in the building connected to the university server. If they were held legally accountable for this spreadsheet, she wanted the university implicated, as well. It could be a useful bargaining chip—if it came down to that.

"There are also notes, with initials indicating which of us conducted the interview."

They continued the presentation for another 10 minutes before opening the floor up to questions. Dani anticipated the older girls would have interrupted them throughout, but instead they took notes—like Mal and Dani were the ones they needed to learn from.

Finally, Cindy, Leonora, and Alexia got up and huddled in a corner. Dani froze up, wondering if they had erred in some horrendous fashion. She and Mal shared a worried look. Cindy broke rank to tell the seniors they could head out. Mal unplugged her laptop, flung herself on the couch and glared at the older girls like a just-disciplined child. The idea of Mal throwing a temper tantrum if the older girls invalidated their research upset Dani. She felt a flash of anger at herself for caring so much about everyone else's emotions above her own. She would also be devastated to leave the Newts. Their short-term endeavor had resulted in Dani reading more feminist texts, which led her to books arguing against capitalism.

Within such a short time, Dani felt like her new education flipped everything she had learned about the world in her 19 years on its head. That life, the one she was born into and assumed was relatively normal, seemed less appealing by the day. Since meeting Peter's family, she longed to be part of that kind of normalcy, including sibling bickering and complaints about wasted money. Dani knew that would never be an issue—she had a trust fund and the kinds of parents who'd never cut her off. If they *had* been that kind of parents, it would have happened already. Money wasn't the thing that would make her happy. If anything, less of it might have improved the relationship with her parents. They would have had to spend time with her, instead of paying other people to do so. Or if they were taxed adequately, that money could support countless other families in the form of universal basic income or better public schools or subsidized childcare. The spreadsheet made Dani feel good about fighting for an equitable society, and that included holding the bad men—rapists, like the ones who harmed Daijanae—accountable. The girls broke from their huddle and turned to face Mal and Dani, who steadied themselves for bad news.

"Your presentation was impressive," Alexia said, as the other two nodded like bobbleheads behind her. "The Newts have an early-warning system for women on campus to avoid bad men, but this is taking that idea and adding jet fuel. We're restructuring our whole system because of your research. This is the future of the Newts. You should be proud."

Leonora and Cindy started talking to Mal as they guided her out of HQ. As Dani moved to follow them, Alexia grabbed Dani's wrist, indicating she should hang back. Once they were alone, Alexia let go.

"You need to be the face of this," Alexia urged. "Mal is a liability."

Dani struggled to figure out what to say. Mal came up with the whole system. And it was Mal who conducted nearly all the interviews and pushed the women to identify others who might talk. Still, she understood Alexia's point. Dani couldn't jeopardize what they built over this minor squabble, but she also knew deep down that she was too cowardly to push back.

"Okay," was all Dani could muster.

Alexia's face broke into a smile, her eyes slightly bugged with excitement.

"Let's set the world on fire."

* * *

The Newts held its annual year-end luau three weeks later, and it was so over the top that even Dani was impressed. The house was decked out in twinkly lights and giant flower leis. Dani touched one of the bright flowers, which reminded her of the luaus she attended with her parents in Maui, and realized the Newts had probably imported them. Impressive.

HQ buzzed with women. The entire organization was there, including girls Dani had never seen before, and, for some reason, everyone seemed to know who she was. For the past year, the other Newts, especially the girls in her pledge class, took a liking to Mal and generally ignored Dani. But today felt different. Girls went out of their way to say hi to her or shoot her a bright smile and wave. It felt exhilarating to be noticed, but Mal seemed preoccupied. Her intensity was muffled, like something was blocking Mal's inner light from shining through.

Dani made her way out to the backyard for the first time, taking in the fire pits and artfully placed outdoor furniture. A pool was the only thing missing, though Dani wouldn't be shocked if the Newts had extra keys to the university pools that were typically overcrowded during the three hours a day they were open. Leonora handed Dani a long skewer and nodded at a picnic table off to the side where Mal tore into a box of graham crackers.

"Everything you need is over there," Leonora said. "And congratulations!"

"We made it," Dani said as she popped three extra-large marshmallows onto her stick, while Mal lunged for a full-sized Hershey bar. They assembled their s'mores with such urgency that they didn't notice Alexia standing over them until she pushed paper in front of their faces.

"I feel like a kindergarten teacher," she complained. "Do I need to separate you two?"

Mal rolled her eyes as Dani accepted the papers on their behalf.

"Has she not had a best friend before?" Dani asked with annoyance.

Mal smirked but kept her eyes glued to the one pager. Red ink swirled across the page in each of their hands. The papers had "The Rules" scrawled at the top, but they were each written by a different person. At that point, Dani could distinguish Cindy and Leonora's handwriting, which matched her previous correspondence with the Newts. She handed Mal one of the papers as they read through the Newts' rules.

> *Rule #1: Always stick to the facts and take painstaking effort to use "allegedly" when appropriate. Always direct the mark to records, including news stories, where your information can be validated.*
>
> *Rule #2: Always smile before speaking, as if to let your warmth indicate you're putting the company/school/brand/etc.'s best interest first in sharing this information.*

Rule #3: Never mention the Newts, indicate bias, or provide personal information, including your reason for calling. When asked, always point to a greater mission. For example, "I believe this information is in the best interest of the students/institution" or "I didn't want this information to tarnish the reputation of the school/institution." Always frame the information of serving a greater good, rather than harming a single individual, to minimize suspicion.

Rule #4: Always assume you're being recorded.

Rule #5: Never answer someone else's phone. This is absolutely crucial, as there can be no suspicion of collaboration among Newts. Note: Always speak from the first-person perspective and never a collective "we."

Rule #6: All correspondence must be documented and saved onto the USB, including names, titles, and phone numbers of the mark, along with a brief description of the conversation and any issues that arose. USBs must be submitted to designated team leads at scheduled dates (available on the flash drive) to keep The List as current as possible.

Rule #7: If service hours are not completed, membership will be revoked. There will be no warnings.

"They took my recommendations, verbatim," Mal said, unable to hide the awe in her voice. Mal looked at Dani, her eyes bright, like she was just learning that she was good at this.

"Welcome, Class of 2017," Alexia roared to great applause from the Newts. The wind seemed to howl its approval alongside them, and Dani rubbed her bare arms. She wished Peter was there to wrap his arms around her.

"You are now ready to begin your service," Alexia continued. "If you know of a sexual assault, you are required to report it to the historians. They will add him to The List, which includes biography information and a job history. The historians will keep the spreadsheet updated. Once they log someone onto The List, you will receive an assignment. Most people get a roster of 20 men by the time they leave Weston, or about six a year. Most Newts come to socialize at HQ and log their hours by calling marks. They can include new girlfriends, internship coordinators, study abroad directors, and grad school admission officers—updates that are tracked by our social media team. All calls must be made on a Newts-issued phone, which you are required to keep on you at all times. The phones should not be used for anything other than calls, and the settings should be reset every year. Do not save any numbers."

"So, we report sexual abusers to anyone who could punish them until we or they die?" Kenzie interrupted. "How is that sustainable?"

"Starting with next year's seniors, Newts will drop their flash drives off at Alumni Weekend each year," Alexia said. "As for the graduating seniors, we will ensure the Newts are taken care of once they graduate by maintaining the alumni network."

"Is there any point that we stop?" Dani asks. "Like if someone goes to prison or if they take responsibility for their actions?"

Mal shot her an accusing look of bringing up something that wasn't part of their plan. Alexia let out a cackle that quickly dampened the back of Dani's linen dress.

"They don't feel remorse," she said. "Without us, they'd be unstoppable."

She crumbled up the rules and threw it into the bonfire. The others followed suit, their papers looking like shooting stars dashing across the night sky before lighting aflame, torched.

CHAPTER FOURTEEN

MAL
BARTON SPRINGS
MAY 25, 2024 — AFTER

Mal breathes in Dani's fancy sunscreen and Seb's familiar sweat. She watches Peter and Andrew chase each other, still carefree at 30, and feels her sense of reality slip away. This is how it should have always been, the five of them forever.

She flops onto her side to face Dani, who's texting furiously under a sun hat the size of Texas. Mal's gaze drifts toward the gaggle of women laid out around them. She eyes their ribs as they stretch out, helping each other put on sunscreen. Mal regrets that she didn't date women in college, let alone make more female friends.

The Newts were always about proving herself and getting ahead—the friendship thing seemed beside the point—and then Mal put all her eggs in the wrong basket with Andrew and company, leaving her incapacitated to make friends as an adult. It stings to have them flaunt their good fortune in front of her. At least she has Serena, who has diligently sent her iterations of "you can do it" text messages every morning since she's been in Austin.

"Can I help you?" Dani asks, still not lifting her gaze from her phone.

"I thought about your offer," Mal replies. Dani's thumbs pause at the comment. "I'm ready to talk about it."

"Maybe you should hang out with Rosen first," Dani says, so low Mal strains to hear her over the squeals emanating from the pool. "It'll be easier to talk with him, you know, when the time comes."

"I can't be alone with him," Mal whispers, even though she wants to explain to Dani that Andrew's undivided attention was what she once craved. He was the person who transformed her life on every single front. No person should have that kind of power. Mal hates him for it, but she also finds the repulsion attractive at some level. Not everyone finds someone who moves them at an atomic level, even if it's for unspeakable reasons.

"I don't trust myself around him," she says instead, unwilling to be vulnerable.

Dani, who looks like a bathing suit model in a shimmery bronze bikini, shifts over to Mal so they're nearly nose to nose.

"You have good instincts," Dani encourages Mal. "You've always had them. And this opportunity is a once-in-a-lifetime one, I don't think I have to tell you that."

"Why aren't you using it for evil, then?"

It's a fair question. Dani could use it however she saw fit. Forcing people to put their foots in their mouths is the only thing wealth and power can't buy.

A wave of hurt washes over Dani.

"It's a gift," Dani says. "I've been trying to make it up to you."

"By bribing me?"

"By giving you your power back," Dani emphasizes. "Between the Newts and Rosen, you lost your autonomy. I know it's my fault on the first thing, but—"

Mal can't listen to Dani defend herself on the second. She loved what they built together with the Newts, but if she could travel back in time, there were so many decisions she would have changed to not end up here, isolated from the people she cared most about in the world. Mal would have dealt with her anger better, would have matched Dani's openness, would have been a better friend. Instead, she had waited for all of them to fuck up, and when they did, no one cared to protect her. So, she needed to protect herself. End of story.

Her gaze floats to a shirtless Andrew tossing a football around with the rest of the guys. His blond hair flops in front of his eyes, and his bicep flexes as he pushes it away from his face. Mal smolders, watching him. She only dates hot women and comedians now; anyone who even looks remotely like Andrew gets a pass on her dating apps. He ruined beefcakes as a genre.

The football flies over Ben's head and bounces in the grass near them. Mal and Dani make no effort to get up. Ben jogs over with a big grin on his face.

"I don't like the looks of this," Ben says, wiggling his fingers at the girls. "You two look like you're in cahoots."

The mere suggestion of plotting prompts Peter and Andrew to look at their respective college allies with feigned or actual concern—Mal can't tell—and then at each other.

"Are you trying to start a prank war?" Peter demands.

"Me? What about you?" Andrew asks. "You threatened me to sleep with one eye open."

"There will be no pranks," Seb says, putting his hands on Andrew and Peter's shoulders to separate them. "You will behave like respectable men."

Mal knows they aren't. She turns to Dani.

"When you invent time travel, let me know," Mal says, standing up. "That's how you can make it up to me."

Still, it seems, she and Andrew have some sort of energetic connection. Mal feels his stare as she slowly makes her way down the hill, alone. She pencil-jumps into the pool, the water rising to greet her. Oddly, it feels like a breath of air, being underwater. She's safe.

As Mal moves to push up toward the surface, she feels something grab her ankle. She tries shaking it off but can't manage. Instead, it seems to tighten. She gulps a bit of water. Even though it's allegedly fresh water, it has the distinct taste of a pool. Or maybe that's just the taste of body fluids flavoring it.

Mal opens her eyes, convinced it's a person literally pulling her leg, but she can't see anything in the murky water. Her heart starts pounding as she flails her arms, trying to escape, or at least draw attention to herself. She's getting lightheaded. She needs to break away.

The pressure of the water thumps in her ear drums. Mal closes her eyes and pulls again. She just has one last tug in her. She can feel her body strain for oxygen. Could her desire for revenge have led to this, her undoing? A scavenger hunt designed for death? No. She'd not leave the world this way.

Like her will to live summoned it, a strong force yanks her up. The second she breaks the surface, Mal gasps for air. Sweet, beautiful air. She lays on a float and opens her mouth. Water and stomach acid dribble out. A hand on her back holds her steady as she's guided to the ladder to exit the pool. She can't look at him as a lifeguard helps her onto dry land.

"You're the eighth save today," the lifeguard says with cheer. "Rest up."

She sits on the cement, gulping air and trying to catch her breath. Andrew crouches in front of her, dripping wet from having jumped in to save her.

"Someone's trying to kill me," she wheezes.

She expects him to pull a Dani and laugh it off, but he's looking at her with an intensity that she hasn't seen in a long time. In fact, he looks more like Mal than himself.

"I didn't see anyone around you when you jumped in," Andrew says. "The lifeguard said you got caught on slippery algae."

"I felt a hand," Mal says, tipping her head back to have the sun warm her up.

"Okay," Andrew says.

"You don't believe me."

"You were underwater for a while. I didn't see anyone come up in your vicinity."

Mal can say a lot of things about Andrew Rosen, truly horrible, terrible, true things about him, but he always believed her. Believed her, believed in her. It's Mal who didn't believe him.

"I think I should head home," Mal says.

"We can go back to the house, no problem," Andrew says, nodding his head. "Can you stay here, and I'll grab everything?"

"No, I mean to LA," Mal says. No plot is worth her life, accidental death or not.

"You're just a little shaken up," Andrew says.

"You have a lot of nerve, you know? Still trying to tell me how to feel."

"How do you manage to still respond to things completely out of proportion?"

"Oh, so you're the decider of how women should feel? That's rich," Mal sneers.

"I just saved your life, but you'll barely make eye contact with me."

Mal's silent. She wants to yell at him and tell him all the things she's thought over the last few years, but she's tired from nearly drowning and the general shame being around the people who knew her in college stirs up. She misses her righteous self, the fearless one. She wants to be that person again.

Andrew rockets up from his squat. He's going to leave her here, Mal assumes. Instead, he offers her his hand.

"The heat," he says. "I can't take it. Will you come into the water with me? I'll make sure no one tries to finish the job."

Mal glances back at the pool. It does look refreshing, despite having nearly killed her.

"Shallow end only," she says.

They walk cautiously near the pool's edge and ease themselves into the water. Mal suspects there's something about their bodies next to each other in the creek that acts as a baptism—wiping clean all their sins until they're back on dry land.

"Before we get into it," Andrew pauses, "I just want to say I told you so."

"That's the first substantial thing you have to say to me after all these years? Not, 'I'm sorry for being a shithead,' but 'I was right?'"

"I've always apologized for being a shithead," he says before holding his nose and submerging himself.

"So, what are you so right about?" Mal asks when he's back up.

"You got a six-figure book deal," he says. "I knew you'd be an author when I read that first draft. But you were so mean to me."

"Even if the book I sold was very different from the ones you read?" Mal asks.

"They had good bones. Your talent was undeniable."

"Tell that to my agent."

"I meant then. I can't speak to now," he says.

She splashes him but keeps her gaze on the sharp planes of his face. Mal feels like Persephone to Andrew's Hades, forever held captive by the god of the underworld. His features soften as he gazes back, like he can read her mind.

"I wanted to come out here with you. Not just to Austin, but to the water. It looked fun, and I miss doing fun things with you," Andrew says softly. Pressure mounts in her ears, and Mal hears the clicking of her jaw and the grinding of her teeth. He pauses. "I've missed you so much, and I'm so happy you're here. I'm thankful for the opportunity to apologize to you."

"Apologize for what?" Mal asks, wanting him to say the words. She longs for her notebook and her phone. She wants to write it all down, every syllable. She doesn't know if she can trust her memory. He breaks eye contact.

"I have a lot of problems," he says before finding the confidence to look at her again. "But I've been working through it. I have a therapist; I talk to my friends and family about it."

"About what?"

"About how I disappointed you."

Mal smirks.

"That's what you're calling it?"

He swallows and looks out at the Austin skyline behind her. She should follow her instincts and go back to the rental. It'll make the rest of her time here easier if she doesn't need to fight everyone all the time. If she's able to give in.

"I've accepted that you hate me, but I'd be remiss if I didn't try to make it right," he says.

"Why does it matter?" Mal asks, her voice cracking. She hates herself for still getting upset about it all these years later and hates the gnawing feeling in her gut that there's something else she hasn't let herself remember.

"I care what you think about me."

"I think you're a predator."

Thankfully her voice comes out clear this time. There's no room for interpretation, no question in her mind and spirit that he did it. No sliver of room for him to weasel his way into and convince her otherwise. And she's thankful for that, because if he could, everything she did—all the friendships she destroyed—would have been for nothing.

"The only thing I can do about that is show you I'm not. I can be your friend again."

She swallows. It's not fair. None of this is fair.

"Let me show you," he pleads. "I'm not the same person I was. You'll see that."

The sun jumps across the water, sending flashes in front of Mal's eyes and making her dizzy. She dips her hand into the water and presses it to her forehead before swimming to the ladder. Just two more days. Two more days until she can leave them all behind.

She trudges up the grass, only to find Seb reading, alone, with another fucking envelope in this hand.

"You're going to like this one." Seb says, fanning himself with the latest scavenger hunt card. "It's our last stop."

Mal plops down next to Dani's bag, hoping she doesn't look suspicious.

"How did you get the card?" she asks.

"Some girlie just walked up to me. Kind of made me want to get my ears pierced."

"She just walked right up to you?" Mal asks, incredulous.

"Yeah, and winked."

Mal pulls Alexia's Instagram account and flashes it at Seb. "This her?"

"Wait," Seb takes the phone to scroll through the photos, pinching one to zoom in. "Yes! She had all those ear piercings."

Mal snatches the card from Seb's hands to read their next directive. Mal looks at Andrew when she announces they're going to Austin's only independent bookstore. Alexia must want to talk if she's willing to reveal herself now. Pride courses through Mal: She was right all along.

"We should get going then," Andrew says, squinting at the sun like he's reading a clock.

"What are you, an explorer?" Mal asks.

She turns to Seb and tells him to corral the others. Mal's thankful he does as he's told. The second he turns his back, Mal throws Dani's bag in her lap and starts digging. Her hand brushes against something velvet-y and hard, and she quickly extracts it. A ring box. She flicks it open and stares at the pear-shaped diamond.

"He can't be that stupid." Andrew shakes his head, watching Mal snoop.

"You said you'd get the inside scoop." Mal snaps the case shut before digging for any other clues that might reside in Dani's purse.

"He proposed last night."

"Did she say yes?"

"The ring's in her bag and the fiancé is still here," he says. "It's inconclusive."

"What good are you?" Mal asks. "He's your best friend."

"We haven't spoken in years," Andrew says, his face scrunched up. "He stopped talking to me when you did."

That makes no sense. Mal saw how they were together all weekend. They acted like nothing was wrong. Nothing seemed wrong. She could, at least, ask him about it in a few hours. Mal keeps rummaging through Dani's bag until she feels a mass inside the lining. She discovers a discreet opening and extracts a small leather case. Inside are two vials: one full and one empty. Jackpot.

* * *

They say everything's bigger in Texas, and Mal guesses that includes indie bookstores. She's a bit disappointed, frankly, that it's not like she imagined. Instead of winding staircases and little nooks to curl up with a book, the store has large white walls and hard edges. It looks more like a big-box retailer than something magical, but Mal supposes anything is magical if it's going up against Daddy Bezos.

When Mal expresses this thought, Dani shoots her a look.

"Different places have different architectural styles," Dani snaps. "Just because it isn't aesthetically pleasing doesn't mean it's not cool."

"That's literally what it means, but whatever," Mal grumbles. She nearly drowned, but Dani, somehow, is the aggrieved one this afternoon.

Mal looks up and spots Andrew flipping through a cookbook, the muscle in his bicep jumping as he leisurely flicks through gorgeous photos of Alison Roman's dishes. Her mind wanders to the last time they were in a bookstore together, before they started dating.

* * *

It was sometime in the fall, and she had that Tumblr dark academia aesthetic:

"Some people go to synagogue in times of stress," Mal said dramatically in their cozy indie bookstore in Weston proper. "I go to bookstores."

"Is this a bit?" Peter asked, who was running an errand for Dani and tagging along.

"Everything's a bit with her," Andrew said. "She can't help herself."

Mal disappeared into the stacks, looking for a specific novel on craft P-Cubed recommended. She felt honored that her professor was giving Mal insight the other students didn't receive. Her time in the woods was starting to feel like the building blocks for her dream life. She turned the corner to go down another row and smacked into Andrew. She hated how clumsy she could be when she was caught up in her thoughts.

"I love seeing you in your element," he said, taking up space so she couldn't pass.

"You're not allowed to flirt with me at a bookstore! You know better," Mal complained.

"What if I want to?" he asked, plucking a book from the top shelf and flipping through it.

"You can't just do whatever you want all the time." Mal folded her arms across her chest in protest. Andrew lifted an eyebrow and bent toward her conspiratorially.

"I can get away with almost anything," he whispered.

* * *

Andrew's 30-year-old face, which has more creases but is still, unfortunately, very symmetrical, takes her out of that memory.

"Do they have your book?" Andrew asks. "Do you want to sign copies?"

A few people in earshot look at Mal excitedly but say nothing. She figures it's something to do while they're here, and the bookseller is more than happy to oblige.

"What are you working on now?" they ask.

Mal sneaks a look at Andrew, whose interest is piqued. Fuck.

"Nothing right now." Mal smiles and takes the stack over to a folding table and chair hidden in the corner, likely for this purpose. Andrew follows her like a dog who caught a scent. He's not going to drop it.

"There's no way you're not working on anything," he says as Mal scribbles her signature on the title page. "You have a compulsion."

"You don't know me anymore," Mal points at him with her Sharpie before scrawling some form of her name in the next book.

"You keep saying that, but you're very predictable," Andrew says.

He holds his hand out, palm down, and moves it from left to right.

"You're consistently erratic, always looking for trouble," he says, hovering his hand in front of her face. Then he jerks it upward. "And then, very occasionally, you throw in a twist, but you're consistent with that too."

Mal shuts the last signed copy and stacks it on top of the others. If he wants erratic, she can surely give him that. Before she releases her poisonous tongue, Ben waves wildly at them.

"This fucking guy," Andrew mutters through a clenched smile.

Ben drags Andrew to another area of the bookstore, saying something about wanting to ask his opinion on teaching Gen Alpha students, when Seb pops out of nowhere. Mal swears and chastises him for sneaking up on her.

"What are you doing?" Seb hisses. "After all this, you and Rosen are just going to go back to normal?"

She never understood why no one ever wanted to be her friend growing up, or why people always assumed she just wanted to talk about her work. No one ever wanted to have fun with her, except for these idiots. It finally dawns on her: Mal's intensity is her problem. It's something so inherent to her, who she is, and no matter how hard she tries, it never goes away. These people are the only ones who ever let her feel like it's okay to be herself. And when they finally, finally made her feel safe, Andrew pulled the rug out. They just took it all away from her.

Mal embraces her full firefly mode and stares at Seb.

"Is Dani going to leave Ben for Peter?" Mal asks.

If Andrew can't get the job done, she'll have to do it herself. This is good interpersonal conflict, the kind of stuff juicy second novels are made of. She and Seb glance over at Peter. He's leaning against a bookcase and flirting with two UT Austin students—of course within earshot of

Dani and Ben in a pathetic attempt to one-up the supposedly happy couple.

"Peter's still a buffoon. Think about how much worse he was in college, and he still managed to pull Dani," Seb says. "I kind of wished it worked out for them, even if Peter's intentions were less than noble in the beginning. But no, Dani's not leaving him."

"What's 'less noble' mean?"

"Peter was originally interested in her because of the money," Seb says, knitting his thick eyebrows together. "He asked Rosen to introduce him to the billionaire's daughter."

"That's not true," Mal says, shaking her head. "I can't stand the guy, but he's always been in love with her."

"I'm surprised you didn't know that," Seb says, taking a step further back to hide from prying eyes and ears. "His parents took out a second mortgage to pay for his school. I don't think they had anything saved for Sara."

A hazy memory of a loudmouthed girl in a purple NYU sweatshirt flashes in Mal's brain, and she makes a mental note to look up Sara later. Maybe her resentment will prove fruitful to the writing process. Plus, the poor girl had to grow up with Peter as a big brother. Mal always wished she had siblings, but, thinking of Sara, Mal has a new appreciation for going at it alone.

"Peter obviously fell for her. I think he would have married Dani for richer or poorer, truly," Seb says, really gabbing. Mal's hit with a twinge of nostalgia for when Seb regularly confided in her this way. She misses it and him, despite the trickles of warmth he doles out to her. "Did you know he used to drive your friends"—another pause for emphasis—"home in the middle of the night?"

"You were all my only friends," Mal says. Then she gets what Seb is saying. "Oh."

"Yeah," Seb raises his eyebrows. "Dani would get drunk calls at 2, 3 in the morning from girls in bad spots and Peter would get into his car and rescue them."

"She went with him?"

"Sometimes? But honestly, I think he went alone most of the time."

Those girls trusted Dani with such blind faith that they went from one strange man to another. The longstanding joke about Peter being the Newts' sweetheart hits differently in this context. Mal always thought it was feminist commentary on the patriarchal structure of Greek life, where women were the ones deemed sweethearts. She flushes, worrying for the second time today whether her memory can be trusted and if her perception of Weston might be wrong.

"I heard that a girl made a move on him once during the pickup. Not from Dani," Seb says quickly. "She tried blowing him."

"Peter loves blowjobs," Mal exclaims, forgetting herself in the name of juicy gossip.

"He shut it down," Seb says. "Immediately."

"Should we give him a medal for being a consent king?"

This time, Mal's serpent tongue strikes, and it's delivered a deadly blow.

Seb smiles tightly as he plucks a postcard from the nearby table, an action that looks to Mal like someone rolling down the blinds after they caught someone peeping: fast and without apology. She isn't getting more from him tonight, that much is clear. Mal brings up her phone, which has been idling in her hand, and discreetly ends the voice memo that recorded their conversation once Seb walks away.

Mal labels the recording before popping in her AirPods, roaming around the front of the bookstore to listen back. If the audio is corrupted, she can grab a notebook from the bookstore and write it all down. Thankfully she doesn't need to; the audio is crystal clear, and she'll make time before the wedding to transcribe whatever reporting she can collect.

Mal glances back at Peter and wonders how much Dani ever told him about the Newts. A wave of stifling heat hits Mal as the doors to the bookstore swish open. A petite person in a sweatshirt walks in, eyes trained on the ground. The hoodie is pulled tight around their head, and they beeline toward the back of the store, where Mal's group has clustered.

Finally, a chance for Mal to take control of this weekend.

She darts toward the person and grabs their waist, dragging them deep into the magazine section—a purgatory for once-relevant media. No one's there. Mal claws at the person's hoodie, trying to take it off.

"Get off me," the person whines, a nasally shriek.

Mal crouches to yank the hood down, ready to reveal her Scooby-Doo villain. She wants Alexia to see her incisors up close. Instead, her jaw unhinges. She may have been onto something, but this wasn't who she had in mind. It's Cindy.

CHAPTER FIFTEEN

DANI
THE BOYS' HOUSE, SOPHOMORE YEAR
DECEMBER 1, 2014 — BEFORE

THE CALLS STARTED TO COME FROM inside the house.
Members of the Newts would go out to parties or spend a cozy
night in the library with a class crush, only for a boy to get
handsy, aggressive or downright hostile. If they were able, the
women would record the interaction and then text Dani for
help. Now a sophomore, she's the first underclassman to serve
as president—a role the society anticipated Dani would keep
until graduation, when the status quo would return to seniors
holding the position. She loved being the exception, but only
because it felt earned. Dani helped create the new iteration of
the Newts, and, to her friend's credit, Mal seemed perfectly
content letting Dani soak up the spotlight.

While Dani handled the people-facing aspect of running a
secret society, which required a deft hand and discretion befit-
ting the child of billionaires, Mal toiled away on a secret
project she claimed would fundamentally change the social
fabric of college campuses. It suited both their skill sets well
and allowed Dani to create strong relationships with the

women she saved. Dani didn't know what her future held, but she did know these women felt indebted to her—and that affinity could be stashed away until Dani needed it.

At first, Dani tried to hide her late-night exploits from Peter. She'd pretend she forgot something at her apartment or that she needed to write a last-minute essay. But there were only so many times she could get away with that, and it reached its boiling point by the end of the semester when he accused her of . . . well, he didn't know. She knew he was suspicious. Dani wracked her brain for a good lie, but if she had been able to come up with one, she wouldn't have been caught in the first place. She decided on a half-truth, hoping she could appease Peter before everyone arrived at his house for the night.

"My friends call me if they're in a bad spot with a guy," Dani relented, picking at a piece of lint on her sweater. "I try to get them out of there before anything worse goes down."

"Dani, that's dangerous," Peter said, the vein in his forehead bulging at the idea she would be putting herself at risk to help her friends. "Are they getting mugged? Why aren't they calling the police instead?"

"You think they're getting mugged?" Dani asked, her eyebrows flying to her hairline.

"Yeah, what else could be happening to them?"

"Rape," Dani said, and felt a tug of affection for her boyfriend when Peter looked ashamed by his immediate and very wrong gut instinct. Rape and murder were the worst things that could happen to a woman—and any woman could tell him that.

"Oh shit," he murmured, running his hands over his cheeks and mouth. He looked up at her. "Next time you go on one of these runs, I want to come with you. I don't want you doing this alone."

Dani looked at him solemnly, and it was the moment she knew she'd marry him. She didn't want to do anything without him ever again.

The doorbell rang, though it was just a courtesy. Mal bounded into the house, followed by its inhabitants.

"Are you guys decent?" Mal yelled out.

"Why do you think we're always having sex?" Dani called back out.

"Because you are," the group said in some semblance of unison.

They plopped onto the couches—yes, count them, three couches—and started tossing around vacation locales for winter break. Cabo, Miami, and Tulum were in the lead.

"*¡Caracas! Podemos quedarnos con mi familia,*" Seb said.

"What does 'quedarnos' mean?" Mal asked, squinting at his mouth as he spoke. She was even taking Spanish this semester, which made her lack of understanding even funnier.

"If we're *staying* with family," Rosen said, "then why don't we go to my parents' house in South Africa? I haven't been in years. This is the time."

"Bro, who has the time or the money for that flight?" Peter asked. Marcus fist bumped him. It embarrassed Dani that she thought Marcus would forever be hung-up on her after she declined his advances freshman year, but he brushed it off with such ease that it made her respect him more, not that he needed it in the first place. She just admired that quality in him.

"We can take the jet," Dani offered.

"Cape Town is dirt cheap," Rosen said. "And let's face it: We're good at doing nothing."

They looked at the greasy pizza boxes and video game controllers spread out from the night before and shrugged. Rosen was right; they could easily chill out for a day.

"I could use a non-Wi-Fi day," Mal added, her head bobbing as she tried to gauge everyone else's interest. She was editing her second book after determining the first one didn't have "emotional depth," or whatever her professor said was wrong with it.

"The jet only seats six," Dani said by way of apology.

"Adam's grandma is sick," Mal said, her fingers flying across the screen of her phone. "I don't think he'd be down to travel halfway around the world in the case he'd need to fly commercial home."

Dani noticed Rosen's flushed cheeks and nervous eyes. Things mostly got back to normal after some weird incident Mal refused to talk about. Dani wasn't sure if Mal and Rosen had hooked up, though she thought she or Peter would have heard if it happened. It was even less likely that Mal would've told Rosen she had feelings for him—which she certainly did, it was that obvious—because they'd be a couple by now. Adam, miraculously, was still around, though Mal was even more certain he was emotionally cheating on her with a girl in his accounting class. Dani knew better than to point out that Mal was doing the same with his former roommate.

"I would let him take the jet back," Dani scoffed, surprised Mal would think she'd let him fly that far in business class.

Mal looked up at her with a confused look on her face, and then seemed to remember what they were talking about.

"It's a moot point," she said, to which Peter began mooing like a cow.

"Moot," Dani repeated, putting emphasis on the t.

"It's ice cream time," he said, grabbing a quart of ice cream from the freezer and throwing it toward the couch. Before it squarely hit Mal in the face, Rosen reached over and intercepted the spinning container.

"If you don't have any money, maybe you should be more worried about throwing a brick of frozen food at my face," Mal snapped. "Do you know how much nose jobs cost?"

"Should have gotten one when you turned 16 like every other girl in your town," he shot back, prompting Dani to look apologetically at Mal. She didn't even stop for air.

"Refer me to your surgeon. I would love to get a nose job as good as your lobotomy."

The boys snickered as Peter emerged from the kitchen with six spoons. He grimaced at Mal and handed her the first spoon, signaling his defeat. She proudly took it.

"Why don't we just go to the Hamptons?" Mal asked, putting her spoon on the ice cream container like a king anointing a knight. "Mother Earth will thank us."

Dani brightened. For months she had suggested everyone stay at the old barn. It was her favorite place in the world. She glanced at Peter, thinking about how special it would be to share it with him, and everyone else too.

"That would make me so happy," Dani says. "I'm in!"

"*Yo también*," Seb added.

"That means 'me too,'" Rosen explained to Mal in a jokingly infantilizing way.

Marcus looked at Dani and raised an eyebrow. They had an agreement: If the group did any travel that was her idea, she'd cover the costs. Dani appreciated that he brought up his concerns to her freshman year when she kept suggesting trips that she didn't realize he couldn't afford. While Mal and Peter both received financial aid, they could call their parents if they were in a financial pinch. Dani knew there was always money to be found. Marcus, on the other hand, did not have that kind of cushion, and he let her know that early on.

It was another thing she respected about him; most people would be intimidated to have this kind of conversation, but he was upfront with her. In retrospect, his choice to share his personal finances may have been an indication he thought they could be more than just friends. Regardless, she obviously had no problem sharing her good fortune. Dani, always the monkey in the middle, squeezed Peter and Marcus' hands.

"Sounds like we're going to Amagansett!"

DANI
AMAGANSETT, NEW YORK, SOPHOMORE YEAR
DECEMBER 30, 2014 — BEFORE

DANI FELT THE HUM OF EXCITEMENT as they cruised down Montauk Highway, spotting her usual landmarks—the balloon store, the windmills, and the rickety sign for the tennis club—to indicate that they were getting closer.

"You want to turn off by the Exxon station," Dani directed Mal as she leaned forward from the backseat to point toward the narrow road often invisible to first-timers. Once they reached the security gate, the car turned onto the crunchy gravel driveway. The sound filled Dani with excitement, not just because she arrived at her favorite place in the world, but also because she was ready to share that experience with her best friends. Dani picked up a little turtle statue from the front steps and flipped it to uncover the lockbox for the spare keys.

"So secret," Mal joked, rolling her eyes as Dani opened the door.

She slipped off her snow boots and lined them up by the door, hoping that her friends would pick up the hint. It was so gross to wear shoes indoors. The group thankfully followed suit and walked deeper inside the house.

"All the bedrooms are down here," Dani said, gesturing to the doors. "Peter and I are taking the master since there's two of us. Everyone else can grab their own space."

She paused.

"Or share. Whatever works," she said, keeping her gaze on anyone but Mal and Rosen.

Mal took off with the exuberance of a child, poking her head inside every room and weighing her options, while Dani and the boys good-naturedly waited for her to decide.

"I'm taking the seashell room," she declared.

"That's my room!" Dani squealed. "Good choice."

After putting their bags down, the group bounded upstairs.

"A lot of homes with lake or beach access out here tend to crowd all the bedrooms on the ground floor, leaving the panoramic views of the water for the kitchen and living room," she said like a real-estate agent. Her house was no exception, but her dad was proud that their kitchen had two islands, which made it easier for the help to prepare meals or cater parties.

"This looks like something on HGTV," Marcus whispered to Peter.

"This is insane," Seb planted his hands on the granite countertop. "We should have a potluck dinner tonight."

"You want us to cook?" Mal screeched. "We're on vacation!"

Dani held up a paper menu.

"I was going to order takeout." She caught Marcus' eye, which had already started to twitch with stress. He wasn't just working as an RA that year. He had also picked up extra shifts at the front desk at the admissions office; although tour guides were not paid, they were prioritized for paid work greeting prospective students and their families. The university instituted a massive tuition hike for the 2015-16 school year without tweaking his financial aid package, and Marcus was trying to make up the difference. She didn't want him to worry about Hamptons-priced Chinese food. "My parents are paying for it, don't worry. We love redistributing the wealth."

"Who knew JAPs were the real comrades?" Rosen cracked.

"You can only say that 'cause you're Jewish," Dani said pointedly. "No one else is allowed to call me a JAP."

Sebastian blanched and Mal burst out laughing.

"It stands for Jewish American Princess," Mal explained. "It's derogatory but we're reclaiming it, you know."

"Miami, New York, and Chicago are top-tier JAPs," Dani said, ticking the cities off with her fingers. "Rosen's the jappiest of us all, though."

"It's true," Mal said. "He told everyone he's from Miami but he's from plain ol' suburban Fort Lauderdale. Embarrassing."

"When did I say that? I never said that."

Rosen leaned toward Mal's face and didn't flinch—even when her hair looked like it was tickling his nose. Dani shook her head, still amazed that they could keep up this sexual tension and not act on it. If anything, it seemed like they cared more about that than any real shot at love.

She glanced at Peter, who smiled warmly back at her, and she felt a tinge of pity for her friends. They were so worried about seeming cool that they were missing out on a true connection, or what could turn into true love. She thought back to chasing Peter down the hall, trying to find him the first night they kissed. If she was a little more sober and a little more insecure, she would have never known that he was the one who'd matter in the end.

"First day of P-Cubed's class, you asshole," Mal shot back.

"You were my roommate's girlfriend. I was trying to impress you," he flirted.

"I thought you were a prick," she said.

"That's too bad, because I liked you immediately," he replied.

"Shut up, I'm trying to order," Dani said, twirling the landline cord with her fingers.

Seb emerged from the walk-in pantry, with two bottles of red wine, as Peter expertly moved through the kitchen to take out six wine glasses and a bottle opener. Everyone settled in nicely, and it filled Dani with pride. This is how she saw the next decades shaping up. Eventually babies would squeal and run the house, and she'd finally feel complete. A real family, not like her very-kind-but-absent parents. She smiled at her chosen family. Seb shot her a weird look.

"What's up with the landline?" Seb asked.

"There's no service out here. You need it," Dani said. "It's kind of retro, though."

Seb filled up the wine glasses and passed them around. The group clinked glasses and made their way out to the deck.

"Ooh it's chilly," Mal said, her eyes set on the horizon. The sun would dip below it, soon.

Peter flipped a set of switches, which turned the heat lamps on. Everyone settled into hefty Adirondack chairs before Dani came out with thick blankets in hand.

"Where do you think we'll be in 10 years?" she asked once everyone was comfortable.

"We'll be in our 30s," Marcus said, blowing out air like he couldn't believe it himself.

"Married," Peter put his arm around Dani's shoulder and squeezed it.

She leaned into him, feeling such a deep sense of comfort, belonging and absolute happiness. It dimmed just a little when she saw Mal make a face. It bothered her more than she let on that even after all these years, Mal still thought Peter was below them. They had all grown. She didn't understand why Mal couldn't see he had too.

"Single in New York," she said. "Writing books and going to literary salons. Dancing until 5 o'clock in the morning and taking the subway home as the sun rises."

"The city will probably be halfway under water by then," Dani said.

"Can I live with you and Peter in your high rise then?" Mal asked.

"Guest room is all yours," Dani told her, trying to find a smile and goodwill deep down. Mal always asked for things and never really reciprocated. She wouldn't even tell Dani about her secret Newts project, and she was the president of the whole thing. "I don't think it'll be seashell themed, though, if you can manage without it."

"My mom had me at 31," Marcus said. "I'd like to have a kid by then."

"Yo, you'd be the best dad," Peter said.

"I'll be doing coke with Mal, and then we'll take the train to Connecticut or wherever you've nested, to be proper for a few days," Seb said.

"It'll be good for us to pretend to be functioning adults once in a while," Mal agreed.

"I don't think I'll make it to 30," Rosen said.

Dani gasped at his admission.

"Don't even say that," Dani chastised him.

"Don't encourage him," Mal said. "He just wants attention."

"C'mon don't you think that the 27 Club is cool?" Rosen said. "Cobain. Winehouse. Hendrix, Joplin, Morrison. I want to roll with the greats."

"You're an idiot." Mal's face buckled under the weight of thoughts obvious enough that even Dani could see them. Yet she turned to face Peter and Dani. "Okay, Mr. and Mrs. Married Losers, where does the proposal happen?"

"In bed," Dani said without a second thought.

"You don't want Peter to get dressed up and surprise you?" Seb asked.

"I want him naked under the quilt in our own little

universe when he pulls a pear-shaped diamond from his bed-side table," Dani said. "I can't think of anything better."

"Is that a thing?" Peter asked. "I thought they only came in circles or rectangles."

"Is that a thing?" Mal mocked him. "What you really mean is 'that sound expensive.'"

Dani shot Mal a look. Let's be real: No one expected Peter to buy the ring himself, unless he took her dad up on his offer to get him a job at any hedge fund in the city. Her parents would be the ones putting their card down for the ring of her dreams.

"Yeah, dummy, pear rings are totally a thing." Seb thank-fully jumped in to defuse Peter's evident embarrassment and Mal's hostility.

"Hope you're taking notes, bro," Rosen said as he used his toe to poke Peter square in his hairy chest. "Mal, how do you want to get proposed to?"

She blushed, her rosy cheeks deepening to a beet-red color. It was Mal's kryptonite, for which Dani was thankful. Without an indicator of how Mal really felt, it would be impossible.

"I don't know. I've never thought too hard about it," she stammered as Seb cackled.

"You're such a liar," Seb said. "You want to be on the beach in Camps Bay or after a safari, all cuddled up in a yurt."

Something must really be off with Mal, because with one look Dani was able to see Mal's mental dialogue: Mal could kill him. She could actually fling herself on his tiny twink body, drag him to the nearby hot tub, and drown him.

It occurred to Dani just then that Mal had thought about wanting to marry Rosen, who had family down there. She never thought Mal would have a dream that extended beyond a career. Worse, Dani realized that Mal was perfectly content keeping all her romantic hopes and dreams to herself—never to be shared.

* * *

They killed about five bottles of wine before everyone dashed off to their rooms to put on bathing suits for the hot tub. Peter waited patiently for Dani outside their room as she contorted her body to fit into an old swimsuit she left at the house. Never again would she force herself into a sad one-piece. Suddenly, there's a thump from the hallway.

"You're like Road Runner," Peter grunted, rubbing his chest.

Mal stumbled back and brought her fingers to her lips. She plucked a piece of his chest hair from her mouth, looked at it, then started wailing. The sound prompted Seb to stick his head out of his bedroom to take in the unfortunate incident.

"Stop licking Peter. You know he doesn't like that," Seb said.

"I thought you didn't like me," Peter said with a sing-songy voice, grinning wickedly at Mal. "But you've actually been in love with me all this time."

Dani was not in the mood for them to get into it. She adjusted her boobs and marched over to Peter to make out with him.

Mal sighed at their wild PDA. Still, Dani leaned toward Peter.

"If you do that in the water you're going to drown," Mal hissed.

"Alright, alright, get upstairs you crazy kids," Seb said, ushering everyone back upstairs and into the hot tub.

Dani high-tailed it to the tub and lowered herself in, breathing in the steam.

"This feels so nice," Seb agreed, his breath visible in the cold air. "I've never done a hot tub in"—he checked his phone to confirm the temperature—"17-degree weather before."

"Finally learned Fahrenheit," Peter joked. "Only took two years."

"Americans are a global laughingstock," Seb shot back. "What kind of developed nation doesn't use the metric system?"

"America," Peter shouted, fist in the air, and then burped.

"You're disgusting," Dani said.

"Oh, I can be filthy," Peter said, moving his hands in between Dani's legs and through her untrimmed pubic hair. Her body buckled at his touch.

"Not in front of us," Marcus yelled.

"Ew," Seb squealed.

Mal and Rosen shook their heads and glared at the couple, though Rosen couldn't stop the corners of his lips from creeping upward.

"I'm not getting whatever disease Peter has," Mal said. "That shit is probably floating around in this water as we speak."

"Lots of spunk," Peter grinned. "We were here over Thanksgiving break."

"That's it, I'm leaving," Mal said as she exited the hot tub.

"I'm coming with you," Rosen said.

They sprinted across the deck, grabbed the blankets to cover themselves and ducked into the house. Dani grinned at her boyfriend and touched his cheek, feeling the texture of his stubble on her soft hands. She wanted to press her lips on every inch of him.

"I love you," Dani said softly as Peter moved in for a passionate kiss.

"Heterosexual culture is disgusting," Seb told Marcus, who reddened.

"You know I'm not gay, right?" Marcus asked.

"This is what I'm saying," Seb declared.

Dani hated when anyone made Marcus feel uncomfortable or unwelcome. Despite him fully immersed in the friend group, Dani knew his presence was contingent on hers. If they ever had a falling out, there wouldn't be bad blood between him and anyone else, but she didn't need to question whose side they'd take. Dani changed the subject.

"Rosen and Mal are absolutely going to hook up tonight, don't you think?"

"Why would you think that?" Peter asked.

"Do you pay attention to anything?" Seb asked.

"I kind of love the idea of them together," Dani admitted.

"You do?" Peter asked. "She may cheat on Adam with Rosen, but there's no way she'll date him once she knows about Peterson."

"What are you talking about? Mal loves that class, even though your professor is being so hard on her," Dani said, turning to Seb. "Did you know that Mal has started on a third book, and nothing she's shown Peterson has passed whatever bar she has. I know she's supposedly brilliant, but who writes three books in three semesters? Plus, isn't your professor constantly dressing Rosen down every class? I'm surprised Mal respects her as much as she does."

"Exactly," Peter said. "Rosen isn't supposed to be in her class."

"It's one of the most prestigious programs in the country. You don't just get in," Seb said, his voice getting a little defensive. Dani didn't realize he was also sensitive about the seminar. She assumed he treated it like everything else on campus: an opportunity for fun.

"Unless your parents are on the board of trustees," Peter said before splashing around in the hot tub to add levity. "Guys, c'mon. It's common knowledge."

"Maybe to you," Dani said, bewildered.

"How many people were in your class freshman year?" Peter asked Seb.

"Seven."

"How many are there normally?"

"Six," Dani answered. Mal spoke about it ad nauseam those first few months of school, citing the difference as an indication that her year was particularly brilliant.

"Rosen's on an athletic scholarship," Peter reminded them. "Don't get me wrong, he's not a dumbass or anything. But Mal is clearly going to be successful. Rosen? He's going to be a high school lacrosse coach who teaches high school English."

"And there's nothing wrong with that!" Peter added after Marcus shot him a dirty look. "My mom's a teacher, too. I'm just saying that it's weird that none of you thought about this. Especially with his parents."

"That they're rich?" Marcus asked.

"That they're on the board of trustees," Peter repeated, annoyed. "His parents fund like half the scholarship kids here. Gaskell is named after his grandfather. The family donated a fuck ton of money, and they have pull."

Everything clicked into place. It made sense how they could casually drink at a restaurant opening in Weston. Underage drinkers in a college town often meant revoked liquor licenses. And although Rosen was good enough at lacrosse and good enough at school, he was like her: a favor that could be called on at any time.

She felt a pit grow in her stomach. Dani didn't know anyone else who had a full ride to Weston other than Marcus, but now she wondered if Mal was also a scholarship kid—which meant Rosen's family paid her bills. Mal had too much pride to let her boyfriend's parents pay for her education, even if it was technically through the school's financial aid office.

Peter was right: Mal would never date Rosen if she knew any of this. But if Mal did know and was ashamed, she'd definitely keep it to herself.

"Does it really matter? We're graduating soon," Peter said, clearly backtracking. "No one outside of college will care about your major. We're getting out of the fishbowl."

"I like the fishbowl. It's safe," Dani muttered. "Can we go back to daydreaming about Rosen and Mal's wedding without you poo-pooing it? I want to be the maid of honor. And you'll escort me down the aisle—"

Dani cut herself off, embarrassed that the first time she mentioned her and Peter walking down the aisle wasn't in the context of their own wedding, for which she had a private Pinterest board filled with ideas. Monogrammed napkins, a chuppah overflowing with lilacs and twinkly lights, and everyone wearing all-black clothing. A wedding that could never go out of style.

"We should rent a house like this the weekend before," Marcus said before hastily noting this was, of course, just a hypothetical situation. He also wanted to move far away from this conversation as possible, and Dani was thankful.

"That would be cool for all our weddings," Peter added, and squeezed Dani's hand. She breathed out a sigh of relief as he fiddled with one of her stacked rings. It was a tacit agreement that they were, and would always be, on the same page.

* * *

Dani awoke later that night with a jolt. Beads of sweat dotted her upper lip, and her long hair was matted to the nape of her neck. She must have had another bad dream. She glanced at Peter, who didn't seem even slightly disturbed by her tossing and turning. He slept on his back, arms folded like a mummy, and looked like he had no worries in the world.

She slipped out of bed and snuck upstairs to get a CWB (cold water bottle). As she reached the top of the stairs, she saw two figures moving gently on the couch. Moonlight shone into the room and reflected off Rosen's back, the muscles tensing and relaxing under its sheen. He was moaning lightly, and Dani was surprised to find herself slightly turned on by what she saw. But the sight of Mal's corkscrew curls sticking out snapped her back into her body. They were finally hooking up. She thought for certain Mal would have dumped Adam before succumbing, but Dani guessed their sexual tension couldn't keep at its current pace. While Dani was happy, she felt like a creep watching them have sex. And doing it on her parents' couch!

Waterless, Dani tiptoed back downstairs to her warm bed and loving boyfriend. She snuggled herself into the crook of his shoulder. He murmured and nuzzled closer to her, his breathing still slow and even. How long after graduation would it take for Peter to propose? The thought lulled Dani asleep, and she dreamed of pear-shaped diamond rings and piles and piles of lilac branches.

MAL
AMAGANSETT, NEW YORK, SOPHOMORE YEAR
DECEMBER 31, 2014 — BEFORE

SOMETHING HARD DUG INTO HER BACK. In a groggy stupor, Mal reached for the blockage and pulled out a 90s-style remote control. Alone on the couch, bathed in sunlight from the wide expanse of windows, Mal propped herself up with her elbows and considered the night before.

After drying off—Andrew insisted he not only blow-dry his hair but Mal's, too—they put on layer after layer to go for a walk outside under a full moon. The grassy expanse of lawn led to a wooden-planked walkway that took them down the dunes to a private stretch of beach. Andrew howled at the moon, which led Mal to do the same. She had a hazy memory of trying to do a cartwheel, but her marshmallow-like stature threw off her center of gravity and she collapsed into the sand. Andrew joined her and they watched the waves crash onto the shore, the salty air making everything about him feel entirely new.

"I've never seen you so happy," he said.

"How could I not be happy?" Mal breathed. She had never been to a place so beautiful with someone so beautiful. It made her heart want to explode. "I'm happy when I'm with you."

Andrew cocked his head to the side.

"Do you really mean that?"

Now it was Mal's turn to tilt her head.

"Isn't it obvious?"

They were so close that Mal was certain she breathed in the air he exhaled. They floated there for a few seconds before Mal made the first move. It was like her body decided for her.

Her mouth met his, and she tasted salt and toothpaste and wine as they consumed each other. Andrew pulled her body toward his, but they could only get so close in their puffy coats. He laughed in her mouth as it hit him, but then his tongue quickly moved back into her mouth and her hands migrated to the back of his neck. She never wanted anything so badly in her life. If there was a way for them to have sex through their puffers, sweatshirts, sweatpants and long under-wear without protection, she'd risk the STDs and pregnancy to do it.

I want to be consumed, Mal tossed the phrase in her mind like the ocean battering a rock until it was shiny and smooth. *I want to be consumed.*

And that's where her memory ended.

Mal heard voices murmur from the kitchen. She padded to the other side of the house, where a pile of glistening lox and freshly sliced tomatoes greeted her. They were stacked high next to tubs of cream cheese and a small mound of bagels nearly toppling out of a wicker basket. It looked like a *Bon Appetit* spread. Her friends, minus Andrew, looked at her with deranged smiles—so much so she worried they were going to eat her. Mal pinched her arm to make sure it wasn't the start to a weird cannibalistic dream.

"He went to the beach," Peter said, smearing cream cheese on a bagel slice.

She nodded and told them she needed a little more time before she was ready for breakfast. Grabbing Dani's puffer and slipping out onto the deck, Mal looked out at the soft waves crashing on the shoreline and the bright blue sky above.

The crispness of the morning felt prescient, like the start of something new was on the horizon.

Andrew sat a few yards ahead in the sand, pieces of wet hair clinging to his neck and cheekbones. Mal sidled up next to him and pulled her legs into Dani's puffy winter coat so it swallowed her whole. He turned to squint at her, like he was expecting someone else. She raised her eyebrows at him to convey the thought.

"Last night meant everything to me," Andrew said, fixing his gaze on the lapping water. White foam clung to the sand, like it was fighting to stay just a while longer, before sinking into the sand. "Did it mean anything to you?"

Mal wondered if this was a test for whether she'd dump Adam. The thought surprised her: Even after addressing their previously unspoken sexual tension, she still thought he was testing her. He looked at her with fearful eyes, but she stayed silent.

Mal felt so unsure, an emotion she had almost never encountered up until that point, and it paralyzed her. Mal took a deep breath and tried to let her face muscles relax. She didn't know why they were clenched so tightly.

"Of course," she said. "I've wanted it for so long, too."

"Will you be my girlfriend?" Andrew asked, and before she had a chance to answer, he leaned in to kiss her.

* * *

Mal and Andrew agreed it'd be best if she broke up with Adam the day they all got back to campus for spring semester. It would have been fine, really, if Mal hadn't experienced guilt-induced insomnia for the first three weeks of 2015. She was like a trapeze artist, moving from one man swinging on a hoop to another—only she didn't want it to appear that way. The safety of landing in a good relationship, one that might possibly be better for her than the one she was in, gave her the confidence to go straight to Adam's apartment to rip the Band-Aid off.

She sat down in his dingy, off-campus apartment that was much less nice than the house the boys lived in. She put her hands together and spread them, palms up, on the table, to display vulnerability and openness—two things she wasn't seriously offering Adam.

"I'm so thankful to have been in this relationship," Mal started, "but I think we've both outgrown it."

Adam sat down in the chair across from her and looked nervously at the closed door behind him, like he was worried about his roommate overhearing.

"Since when?" Adam asked, his neck growing red.

"I got back from out east and felt like we're growing in different directions," Mal said.

"Back from out east?" Adam made air quotes. "You went to a bougie beach town for the first time last month and all of a sudden you think you're better than me?"

"That's not what I'm saying," Mal said, feeling her cheeks warm. "I haven't been happy in this relationship for a while. Neither have you."

"Since when have you not been happy? We just went on a date before break!"

That was true. The date was fine. It was nice. But she wanted better than fine. She wanted a partner, someone who wouldn't just encourage her career goals but actively participate in them. She wanted to be with someone who made her insides quake. She tried explaining that to him.

"I want that for you, too," she said.

That was what did it. Adam stood up and threw a plastic cup across the room. It hit the ground and bounced a few more feet. Mal's gaze shifted to the bedroom door behind Adam. It didn't open. Not that she cared, but she wasn't hoping for an audience.

"First, you've outgrown me. Then you're telling me I don't do it for you."

The tenor of Adam's voice rose, making him sound childlike. Mal recoiled at his high pitch and display of anger. She knew her bouts of anger were frequent, but boy, was it ugly to see it in someone else. Adam's lip curled into something menacing.

"Fine, you're right," Adam said. "I'm breaking up with you."

If Mal were a bigger person, she would have let it go. She was not.

"What do you mean, you're breaking up with me? I already broke up with you! We're broken up!" She gestured at the space separating them.

"You think you're so talented, so destined for greatness," Adam sneered. "But guess what? Rosen showed me your work. You're a hack."

Adam could have slapped her; it would have hurt less. She knew he was saying the nastiest thing he could think of and that it had no meaning, but Mal wondered if his support of her creative ambitions was just a way to get into her pants. She thought back on how every nice thing he said about her talent came just before trying to fuck her.

"Well, you're bad in bed," Mal retorted, thinking this was the only thing that had a similar sting. "Actual medical professionals said that's why the sex is painful. There's something wrong with you."

The look on Adam's face made Mal's body go cold.

"I feel bad for you," he said. "You tell yourself so many lies to get through the day. But if that's what you need to believe, that's fine."

"We're done," Mal said. This wasn't how she wanted it to end. She wanted to have good memories of Adam, or at least have him beg for forgiveness or a second chance, not throw every negative thing he ever thought about her back in her face. "By the way, I'm not breaking up with you because you're bad at sex or a shitty boyfriend. It's because I'm sleeping with Andrew."

Mal thought that bombshell might prompt Adam to hit her. Maybe he'd even leave to find Andrew and beat the shit out of him. Instead, he laughed.

Adam laughed so hard that he started crying, but not in an "I'm dealing with my emotions" kind of way. No, it was a laugh so guttural that made Mal want to pick up and leave so she wouldn't have to hear what he'd say next.

"To be clear, I never thought you were stupid." Adam walked to the front door and held it open for her. "I do now."

I do. I do. I do. The words reverberated through her mind as she walked home. Mal once thought she'd hear Adam say those words when they got married. In her fantasy, though, they'd share their vows over her novel instead of a bible. She'd never been to a wedding before, and for some reason, she got the ceremony and a swearing-in mixed up in her mind. The book was always part of the wedding ritual, because who was she without her work? Who would Adam be marrying, if not a writer?

His last words to her echoed in her mind as she went to search for someone, anyone. She couldn't break down in front of Dani. God, she couldn't go to Andrew and tell him that Adam thinks she stupid to be with him. Mal didn't know where to go, so she lapped the campus in the dark until she felt the tiredness weigh down her limbs. Finally, she ventured into the woods, where she entered HQ and curled up on the couch with her laptop. She opened her password-protected spreadsheet, the one she had worked on for months. It was a list of every school in the country. Mal knew if they could break ground with the Newts, it could be replicated across the country. Women could finally stop being afraid—thanks to her.

DANI
NEWTS HQ, JUNIOR YEAR
OCTOBER 25, 2015 — BEFORE

MIKE BIGGLES WAS THE NEWTS' FIRST success. At least three women had accused him of spiking their drinks and taking advantage of them (to various degrees) at an off-campus party, an important distinction the university was quick to note. Campus officials would not take punitive action, let alone start an investigation, because the allegations took place in non-university-owned property while minors consumed alcohol, according to interviews and documents reviewed by the Newts. The woman who reported Biggles to the university unsuccessfully pointed to various violations of the student code of conduct, but Weston did the administrative equivalent of shrugging. He had since graduated and now worked at a biotech startup in Boston founded by his brother.

"Calling the CEO will be futile, and there's no HR," Mal said after another late night in HQ collecting data on Biggles, which she and Dani were tag-teaming. They were trying to figure out the best way to report Biggles for his crimes, which included at least one count of rape. "This is why none of these damn startups have HR. Big 'boys will be boys' bullshit. This one seems like a lost cause."

"The company just got $15 million in Series A funding," Dani said, her eyes not lifting from her laptop screen. "We could report him to the venture capital firm, which is leading the fundraising round and has a dedicated fund to advancing women in STEM. This would be bad PR for them if Biggles is revealed to have multiple sexual assault allegations against him."

"Does it matter unless we threaten to go to the press?" Mal asked.

They saw *Spotlight* with the boys last month, and it gave Dani and Mal some ideas on how they could find sympathetic allies at news outlets, one like the *Boston Globe* that were used to going up against predators. Why wouldn't they want to report on someone before he reached serial predator status, if Biggles hadn't done so already? Sure, he wasn't a priest, but he was part of a system inherent to attending college in 2015, when all administrators cared about was teaching women how to not to be victimized.

"We could call and imply that we'll go to the press if the VC firm doesn't take action," Dani said. "The public is more likely to get angry at who's funding the startup than the people employed there, because everyone hates money if they don't have it, and no one hates young men whose lives will be altered forever."

She rolled her eyes and offered her best Donald Trump impression.

"It's a witch hunt," she said in his distinct New York accent.

Mal grimaced.

"Let's take this fucker down."

* * *

Historically, most of the calls didn't go well. The Newts struggled to get people on the phone, and when they did, it was rare that their anonymous tips were taken well. In fact, most people (men) screamed at them. It got to the point that Dani worried the promise of what the Newts could offer— accountability—was just a promise, and one they couldn't execute on. Alexia, meanwhile, held up her end of the bargain; the alumni network was thriving. What saved them was the female assistant to the lead investor, who promised to take Mal's tip seriously. The assistant also shared her personal phone number in case Mal needed to follow up.

At their monthly check-in, Dani handed out copies of a small news item about how a local biotech company ousted the chief operating officer over allegations of sexual misconduct at his alma mater, Weston College, at the VC firm's insistence. The story quoted Christa Navins, the investor, who said she was disturbed by the allegation and that the biotech company was no longer aligned with the firm. Whitney popped champagne, and the women celebrated before kicking back to watch *Saturday Night Live* trot out Donald Trump as its guest host.

"This is unwatchable," Mal said as the group of women jeered at Trump. She pointed at the screen. "These are the men we're tracking, and he's, like, the final boss we need to defeat."

Dani felt a coldness settle in as she watched Mal become upset at the TV. Something was deeply, deeply wrong for Mal to show emotion in front of anyone, let alone at HQ.

"He's going to win," Mal said quietly.

Whitney hit the mute button on the remote and asked Mal to repeat herself.

"If we can't make change at a micro level, that should be a big red flag that that man"—Mal pointed a shaky finger at the large white wall projecting the goon's caked-on face and hair-sprayed toupee—"will become the next president."

"There's no way," Nandeeta said, but a hush fell over the Newts.

They intellectually knew Mal was right, but no one wanted to face the truth they knew intimately: A lot of people hated women.

The thought upset Dani so much that she went home to her apartment and cried to Peter. She knew Mal would never approve of this, but wasn't the whole point of the women's movement getting men involved in the first place? They could be the best advocates for women.

"Hold up," Peter said, still holding Dani tight as they cuddled on the couch. "You're doing what?"

Dani held out her pinky, and Peter stared at her for a beat longer than normal before extending his own and wrapping it around hers. She paused before telling him everything.

"Wait, so all those girls are in the secret society with you?" Peter asked. "That's why they call you at all hours of the night to pick them up from bad situations?"

Dani nodded.

"That makes a lot of sense," Peter said. "Am I stupid to have not figured this out?"

"You're not stupid." She kissed him again, but he pulled away and gave her a look she had only seen him shoot Mal. The emotion dissipated the longer he looked at her.

"Isn't it a little unethical what you're doing?" Peter asked gently. "No one has committed a crime."

"What's unethical about holding people accountable for their actions?" Dani asked.

"Alleged actions," Peter said.

"You've picked up girls with me who have scratches and bruises and are sobbing in the car," Dani said, her voice rising.

"And that's valid," Peter said, putting his hands up in self-defense. "I'm just saying that it's possible not everyone has experienced those things or has told the truth. You don't think Mal is above telling some white lies to make men seem like the enemy?"

"That's not what this is." Dani started to freak out, wondering if she made a massive error in telling Peter. She must have conveyed that panic, because Peter immediately took her into his arms, patted her hair and murmured apologies as he pressed his lips to her head.

"That didn't come out right," Peter said. "I'm glad you're doing what you think is right. I don't want you falling into whatever traps Mal is laying."

"She can't find out I told you," Dani pleaded. "Please, you can't say anything."

"I don't want to keep hammering at it, but if you're worried about Mal's reaction, that just proves my point."

Dani sighed and decided to let it go. She knew he was just looking out for her and that he wasn't totally wrong. Everything they investigated occurred on a case-by-case basis, but he wouldn't get the nuances of it unless he participated, too. It gave her an idea. She texted Mal to come over so they could talk.

Within an hour, Mal had taken Peter's place on Dani's couch.

"I have a new idea for the Newts," Dani said excitedly, hoping she could use the skills from her persuasive communication class in real time. A giant smile overtook Mal's face.

"I do too!"

"You first!"

Mal pulled out her laptop, plugged in a password, and handed it to Dani. She scrolled through sheets of accusers' names, though they linked to news articles and lawsuits. It made the original Newts presentation look like child's play.

"These are from different colleges," Dani said.

"Expansion plans," Mal said. "College campuses breed predators who can become monsters with more money and status. We can cut them off at the knees with a network that would effectively make the Newts a national organization. It's the thing we need to survive in Donald Trump's America. I'm ready to become part of the resistance."

Dani couldn't believe her luck. This fit perfectly into her idea.

"You're the most well-connected person I know. I'm sure you know a bunch of people at these colleges, and you can probably make some calls to find the right people at the other schools. I know I don't say this enough, Dani, but I admire how you know everything: how to make friends, how to carry yourself, how to bend to be someone everyone likes."

That last part stung, even though she knew Mal meant it as a compliment. She didn't think she changed herself for other people; she just let certain aspects of her personality shine depending on who she was around. That's adaptability—not a weakness.

"I love it," she enthused, adapting. "The more people we bring in, the more education we can do to prevent it in the first place."

"That's beyond our reach, don't you think?" Mal said. "Sexual assault is only preventable if men saw us as equals. They need to fear us to stop."

"But why not include them?" Dani pushed. "Have them help women who are in trouble so they can see firsthand the harm."

"Dani, if they see what we're doing they'll destroy it," Mal said, shutting her laptop and holding it in her arms, like Dani was a threat to its existence.

"I'm looking at the big picture," Dani said.

"So am I," Mal got up to go. "If you think men are capable of this, you're delusional. They'll burn it all down."

For the rest of the night, Dani could think of only one thing: Peter was right.

CHAPTER SIXTEEN

MAL
VERONICA'S HOUSE, JUNIOR YEAR
DECEMBER 5, 2015 — DURING

AFTER TALKING TO DANI, MAL WAS convinced that the Newts would only last for so long. Her desperate need to make Peter a part of it would be its downfall. Even Alexia agreed with her and told Mal to lay low while she thought about next steps. Alexia insisted she'd talk to Dani—though it wasn't like Mal could say anything. For the first time, Mal did as she was told—and kept her distance from Dani and Peter.

Mal intended to come to Veronica's party to stay sober and make sure the men of Weston behaved. But, after struggling to make small talk without the buffer of a friend group for the last hour or so, Mal turned to jungle juice to ease the social anxiety. Mal sipped her sticky-sweet drink, which tasted like sour cherries and vodka. It was the fourth, or maybe fifth, of the night.

She wedged herself into the corner of Veronica's living room to survey the crowd. One girl squealed and ran toward another, pushing past couples talking or making out. Mal checked her own annoyance. She somehow was the kind of person who wanted to protect women while also being irritated by so many of their existences.

She texted Andrew and told him where she was, in case he arrived late and was out back or somewhere else entirely. She regretted arriving alone.

Her gaze floated from classmate to classmate until she landed on Dani and Peter. She didn't know they were coming. Did they see her by herself and not come over? Mal watched them sway, holding each other's faces and dancing. They both looked like they were on Molly.

But in the glow of some twinkly lights taped to the wall, Dani and Peter looked like the most romantic couple in the world. Mal yearned to just be present and experience life. Instead, she couldn't help but observe and take herself out of the scene entirely. But, if she were capable that, she'd never be a writer. After all, writers are the loneliest people on earth: always on the outside, looking in and taking notes.

A cluster of girls who had been in her general education classes over the years spotted her and waved, but they didn't walk over. Mal hated their mean-girl attitudes and the way they took issue with her ongoing detective work. They took issue with her habit of swearing every time she spoke, especially in class. They took issue with how she paid attention to everyone. They thought she was intense, but not the way Andrew did. To them, it wasn't something to be proud of.

Mal sighed and chugged the rest of her drink. She just wanted to be left alone, which was impossible on a campus of 2,000 kids. She didn't want to be perceived anymore. Mal looked around for Andrew. He should have been here by now. When she stood up, the room immediately started swaying. She stumbled past the crowd and made her way into an open bedroom. Mal had the good sense to lock the door before passing out.

DANI
WESTON PARKING GARAGE, JUNIOR YEAR
DECEMBER 6, 2015 — AFTER

THE NEXT MORNING, DANI SPOTTED VERONICA in the garage as she walked to her car. Dani felt like shit, but it was nothing compared to Peter's state. He had a horrible migraine and was in desperate need of a bacon, egg, and cheese sandwich. Before Dani could wave, Veronica shouted, "We have a big problem."

"With me?" Dani asked. "Did we break something at your house last night?"

She hiked her tote bag higher on her shoulder as two other girls got out of Veronica's metallic blue Benz. Their gazes— bright and unyielding—felt like headlights, leaving Dani feeling dizzy and off-kilter. They were mad at her.

"With all of you," Veronica said, stomping over to Dani. "I'm letting you know as a personal courtesy, but we're about to ruin your friend's life."

"What happened?" Dani said, her eyes darting to the other girls. One girl rubbed the back of her friend and murmured inaudible things. It reminded her of freshman year when Zoe comforted Veronica in that same way. Dani felt like she was going to be sick. "Is she okay?"

"Andrew Rosen assaulted her," Veronica said, straightening her posture to glare at Dani.

Dani gagged.

"We just came from the Title IX office," Veronica said, her voice breaking. "I refuse to let another woman go through what I did freshman year. You'll hear all about it soon enough."

Dani stayed silent, trying to formulate questions to ask, but knew she should stay silent until she spoke to Rosen. She resisted the urge to apologize, because she wanted nothing to be used against her if this went to court. Could it go to court?

"Let's go," one of the girls called to Veronica, who turned around on her heel and left Dani in the garage. She called Peter immediately.

"Rosen's on his way over," he said, miraculously cured of the illness that debilitated him earlier. Peter breathed heavily into the phone. "I think you should go check on Mal."

* * *

Dani didn't know what to say. All she could do was take her phone away, just to make sure she couldn't read the horrible messages coming in directly and through the Newts' WhatsApp. Despite the volume, there was one central message: How could you be so blind?

Dani knew it wouldn't be too long before they started questioning Mal's ability to participate in the Newts, let alone move the organization into its next phase. She called Alexia on her way back to her apartment, but not before making Mal promise not to do anything rash in her absence. Dani didn't think Mal would harm herself, but she knew Mal acted on her emotions.

"I heard," Alexia said.

"Word travels fast. It hasn't even been 24 hours," Dani said.

"We need Mal for the next phase," Alexia said. "But the group comes first. If this doesn't blow over, I trust that you'll know what to do."

"You want me making the decision?" Dani squeaked. She knew her place, and it wasn't the person making tactical decisions. She was everyone's friend, the front-facing person.

"I'm still at the lab," Alexia said, as if that absolved her. Just because she had some prestigious research position at MIT while getting her master's degree didn't mean she could saddle Dani with all this responsibility. "You're the president. You're on campus. And they're your friends. If you're not the most qualified to make these choices, then who is?"

Alexia's right. She needed to step up and be a leader. Dani just didn't want to face would happen after.

She slid into her apartment, hoping for a few seconds to herself before talking to Peter. Instead, she found him at the kitchen table with a bag of frozen peas pressed against his face. He removed it to show Dani his cheekbone, which had already turned a sickly purple.

She sat down next to him and took over holding the peas to his face so he could tell her how it all went down:

"Dude, people are talking," Marcus said once all four of the boys came home. "They're saying you raped her. And that you've done it before. To other women, not just Julianne."

"Why would you cheat on Mal?" Seb asked at the same time.

Rosen's face hardened and he only addressed Seb.

"I didn't mean to," Rosen said. "I was looking for her and I found Julianne instead and she just looked so beautiful. I know that sounds too romantic to be true."

"Romantic?" Seb screamed. "Psychotic. You sound psychotic."

"Why? Because I found a beautiful girl and I kissed her, and she kissed me?"

"Rosen, she was asleep," Marcus said.

"But she woke up!" Rosen's hands flew into his hair. "I hate to be that guy, but she enjoyed it. She came."

"It's not going to matter if it was pleasurable if she couldn't consent," Seb said.

"I didn't rape her. I didn't hold her down and force myself on her," Rosen said.

Seb started googling.

"Penetration without consent is rape—with or without force," Seb read off his phone.

"I would never rape anyone," Rosen said. "I made a bad decision by cheating on Mal, but I was drunk and I was looking for her. I wanted her."

Peter paused, telling Dani he wondered why they were debating this, like any of it mattered. Rosen committed a crime.

"You just need to come clean," Seb said. "Or give some version of the truth. You thought it was your girlfriend. You were drunk and thought it was Mal and you're so sorry for hooking up with Julianne. Bro, write this down. You're so sorry for hooking up with Julianne—you didn't realize it wasn't consensual, and you're deeply sorry about that. It'll be enough to stop her from pressing charges or the school from doing worse than, I don't know, sending you for community service. Bad judgment."

"If you admit that you did it—intentionally or not—you're guilty," Marcus said. "It'll be on your permanent record that you admitted that you sexually assaulted someone. How are you going to get a job? You can't let this ruin your life."

"This is going to affect him either way," Seb snapped. "He needs to be able to live with himself."

"Yo, I need a minute," Rosen said, swatting his friends away like gnats. "I need to think."

"Want to go for a walk?" Peter finally spoke up.

Seb shot Peter a manic look as they left him and Marcus behind, heading to the wooded area at the back of their house. After walking in silence for five minutes, Rosen turned to Peter.

"How bad do you think this is?" Rosen asked.

"Dude, it's bad," he said. "The girls are going to lose it."

"Does Mal know yet?" Rosen asked, his face pale.

"I don't know if Dani told her," Peter said, readjusting his Yankees hat. "But if you're worried about it, you should go talk to her right now. She should hear it from you before she hears it from someone else."

"She can't find out," Rosen said.

"Everyone's already starting to find out," Peter said.

"What do I do?" Rosen moaned. "I'm so fucked."

"I'm not getting involved," Peter said.

"What does that mean?" Rosen stopped. "'You're not getting involved?' This is a crisis."

Peter stopped, and Dani could imagine what came next: Peter breaking his promise and telling Rosen about the Newts. About how Peter had the privilege of being the example of "Not All Men"—the #MeToo rebuttal—and how he knew he wasn't going to throw that away on his friend. And when he did that, Rosen got aggressive. Rosen lunged at Peter with his fists, striking him on his cheekbone. Peter flew back into a tree and collapsed at its base. He held his hand to his face, too stunned to think or say anything. Rosen shook out his red hand and left, leaving Peter alone on the ground.

Or at least that's what Dani imagined happened. But she didn't really want to know. It would force her to pick sides, and nothing, from the Newts to her boyfriend and best friends, would be the same.

"So, you're not helping him?" was all Dani could ask.

Peter held up his pinky.

"I'd do anything for you," he said. The promise wasn't an answer.

MAL
NEWTS HQ, JUNIOR YEAR
DECEMBER 13, 2015 — AFTER

FIRST, THEY SAID HE RAPED HER. Next, they said he ate her out and she passed out halfway through. Finally, they said he was either looking for his girlfriend or cheating on his girlfriend. No one blamed Mal and everyone blamed Mal, for not knowing, for making her boyfriend someone else's problem. It was like Mal's wish had come true: She hadn't wanted to be perceived, and now her classmates went out of their way to do just that.

Mal hated that she was mad at them for it, too. At least Julianne was the victim. She, on the other hand, was Weston College's pariah.

With every step toward the woods, Mal thought about Dani's family house in the Hamptons. Mal had felt not just the weight of Andrew on top of her, but the length in which he stretched over her. The constriction her throat made as saliva dripped down her throat, and her inability to jolt as she awoke under him. The gnawing feeling afterward that something wasn't quite right. Mal knew he did it.

They were convening at HQ in the wake of the investigation. The disciplinary board put out a report, which the Newts managed to get their hands on. The speed of the investigation either meant it was very good or very bad for Julianne, but Mal could sense how it would go. She saw Andrew's parents on campus all week. Julianne Chen didn't stand a chance.

Whitney handed Mal a copy of the report and tried to smile at her, a small kindness that Mal appreciated but couldn't bring herself to accept. Mal's hands shook as she skimmed the report to see if it was what she feared.

"Inconclusive," Kenzie bellowed. "'While Mr. Rosen and Ms. Chen had sexual relations the night of December 5, 2015, the question of consent is inconclusive. A notice of the report will be issued with Mr. Rosen's permanent record, as requested by Ms. Chen, but he will not be penalized for his alleged behavior.' What's indeterminate about this rapist initiating sexual violence while she was asleep?"

Everyone turned to glare at Mal.

"It's not her fault," Dani protested weakly. Some friend.

"We need to act," Nandeeta said.

"What can we do, tar and feather him?" Aisha asked. "All we can do is add him to the list and go through normal procedures."

"Do you have a problem with that?" Kenzie asked Mal, disgust thick in her voice.

"Why would I?" Mal asked, her voice distant, like she wasn't there. She didn't want to be. "He raped her."

"Why would you think they're going to stay together after this?" Whitney shot back. "Mal knows better than to keep seeing a rapist."

"Don't you think every man you've ever known has done something like this?" Mal asked.

Fire returned to Mal's eyes for the first time in days. She finally was able to access the anger that roiled her. She was surrounded by hypocrites.

"Don't you realize that every man in your life will have crossed a line at some point? That without systematic educational changes we are simply another cog in the machine, every effort futile in preventing their bad behavior in the first place? This organization," Mal paused to scoff at the word, "is a shitty Band-Aid that makes you all feel like you're fixing the problem. I'm done with this, and I'm done with all of you. I quit."

She sat there for a beat, like she hadn't processed what she said.

Dani touched Mal's arm and whispered to her.

"What about the plan? You can't leave yet," she said. "You can't give up now."

Mal didn't care about her expansion plans anymore. She was naïve to think she could protect other people. She couldn't even protect herself.

Mal didn't realize she was leaving until she heard someone whisper, seemingly from a distance: "No one has ever quit before."

* * *

For their last class of junior year, P-Cubed sat stoically in the classroom to greet Mal, Seb, Azza, and Darnell. She had almost skipped class, dreading the prying eyes of the people she most admired on campus, but she needed to prove she was courageous, a person of character. Julianne left to go home early, the school agreeing to let her pass her classes without taking final exams. Andrew, unsurprisingly, was absent. Mal knew he had attended his other classes with Seb, Marcus, or Peter by his side to minimize confrontations, yet she had still not heard from him.

"I've been at this university for 25 years," P-Cubed said once the four of them sat in their seats. Her voice carried a hardened edge Mal had never heard. It sounded foreign even to the professor, who carried herself with a kind of determination not usually needed for the work of helping college students write better. "This will be my last one. As of today, I am resigning."

Everyone but Mal gasped or took a sharp intake of breath, but no one spoke. She had read Peterson's resignation letter, another document obtained by the Newts. Peterson had testified against Andrew on behalf of Julianne, who left the party the next morning and called the cops to collect evidence for a rape test kit. Julianne called Peterson shortly after, according to the letter. It was undeniable they had intercourse, and Peterson argued that Julianne's sleeping state automatically made it impossible for her to consent.

Andrew's (winning) argument was that they had flirted all night and that he had "pleasured her"—the evidence supported his claim, he said, and the mostly male board backed him up. It was that fact, coupled with Andrew's parents serving as major benefactors to the college, that the school not only forced her to take him on as a student for coursework he was unqualified for, but that they also ruined a young woman's life to protect their son.

Mal was ashamed of her surprise. She didn't think of Andrew as someone who would have bought his way into their sacred space. He had exuded a sophistication and worldliness that she had lacked, and Mal had felt special under his gaze. She thought her inability to see his talent was her weakness, rather than ignoring the bullshit meter that usually sounded the alarm.

Mal looked around at the falsity of the university, with its prestige and glamour. It was nothing more than a sham, a place to build delusion and ego. She wanted to burn the place to the ground: the university, the Newts, her so-called best friends. She wanted nothing to do with the lie she'd been sold for $60,000 a year. The thing about college is that, when you got there, you learned that the truths you were always told about yourself may not be true anymore, if they were ever true to begin with.

Mal watched herself like she was in a movie. It was different from all the other times she felt outside her environment. This time she was outside her body; her brain was disassociating from her actions—the truest form of being a brain in a jar and bodiless. Mal picked up her bag and walked out, swinging the door open and gliding through—joining the ranks as one of the many ghosts bound to haunt Weston College

CHAPTER SEVENTEEN

MAL
THE FOUR SEASONS
MAY 25, 2024 — AFTER

So much for an intimate event. The rehearsal dinner could be mistaken for a wedding by most people's standards. Cocktail hour is held on a massive property overlooking the river. Big trees with long, cascading branches and lush leaves are drenched in twinkly lights, and, because they had to wait for Shabbat to end, the sky is a bright but fading blue. The tented areas, where they'd later eat dinner, are covered with green vines that swoop from the ceilings and wind downward. The small beams of light cast a slight glow on the wads of wagyu on crispy rice, pistachio-encrusted salmon bites, and pancetta-wrapped scallops circulating. Mal's stomach roars as a waiter passes by with a plate of crispy rice. She makes a mad dash toward the silver tray.

From her perch near the waiter, Mal watches Dani glide from couple to couple, shaking people's hands and smiling that politician's smile. It's impressive, not just because Mal could never, but also because Dani is legitimately good at it. She makes every interaction appear warm and authentic and natural. The hair, the makeup, the blue dress, and sensible wedges comes across as powerful but not overbearing. A true New York politico trying to look casual in Texas with sunglasses perched on her head.

It makes Mal a bit sad, like dropping out of school stunted her adult abilities. She sure as hell can't budget to save her life or hold onto a romantic partner. Then again, at least she's not a loser. Her gaze flits to Andrew, who catches her eye and runs over to her like a child. Mal plucks one of the sliders off his plate and shovels it into her mouth. Wagyu beef. These people are unbelievable.

"Dani's running for Congress," Andrew says.

"I know," Mal replies with food still in her mouth.

"What do you mean you know? No one else knows."

"Besides me."

"And Peter."

"How does Peter know?" Mal asks.

"He overheard Dani on the phone."

That gives Mal pause.

"When did he hear her on the phone?"

"First night in Austin, I think," Andrew says.

"That's all he heard on the phone?"

"What could be more important than that?" he asks.

Andrew points at Dani, whose arm is snaked around Ben.

"They both know she's campaigning," he says. "She's not going to risk a scandal for Peter. And anyway, who we were in college doesn't reflect who we are now."

He shoots her a pleading look, like it can green light the jail sentence he believes he's serving. A thought dawns on her.

"What ever happened to your pen pal?" Mal asks.

"Deandre?" Andrew runs his hands through his hair and lets out a breath. "I haven't thought about him in a long time."

Doesn't seem like too much atonement, Mal muses, if he never even thought about someone who did less harm and faced greater consequences.

"He wrote that letter, didn't he?" Mal asks. "The one you passed off as your own?"

Andrew never once wrote anything as good as that assignment, the one that was sitting in her duffel bag a few miles away, but its presence did enough to change the way their classmates thought of him. It made them respect him.

He looks pained as the affirmative silence hangs in the air.

"He asked me to get it to his family," Andrew says. "It was the last note he sent before he killed himself in prison. I didn't handle it well."

Mal's chest heats. It was so obvious this whole time, and she was willing to ignore what was in front of her. How much did she let him get away with? And would anything have changed if she paid closer attention, if she didn't let him sway her with his short-lived love and affection?

Andrew needs to stop mattering to her. He needs to stop being part of the reason she can't move forward. And anyway, after finding out from Cindy that Dani's the one who organized the entire weekend, scavenger clues and all, Mal is ready to say goodbye to everyone for good. She doesn't understand how Dani could watch her panic these last few days and say nothing; rather, she gaslit Mal into thinking she was paranoid.

"I still want to talk about it," Andrew says. "You never responded to any of our messages or calls. And when I flew out to Chicago—"

"I'm not from Chicago," Mal says.

"When I knocked on your door," Andrew starts.

Mal puts a hand up.

"I appreciate that you've changed, but I haven't," Mal says. "I'm the big bad feminist no one wants to spend time with. It's just made me meaner. You don't want to know me, even if I let you."

"I could never feel that way," Andrew argues. "And you're still so mean to yourself. You are you, and that is correct."

It knocks the wind out of her. This is why she fell in love with him. And when she had him, her worst fears came true. He didn't want her once he had her, and she lost everything because of it. She grabs her purse and goes to find Dani, leaving Andrew confused and alone.

She finally finds Dani exiting the bathroom hut. Mal yanks her arm and pulls her around the building for privacy.

"Why is Alexia here?" Mal demands.

"She's not," Dani says smoothly. "We went over this."

"She handed Seb a clue at Barton Springs. Before I almost died," Mal says, her exhaustion causing her to feel on the brink of hysteria. "I showed him a picture of her. He confirmed it."

Dani screws up her face.

"Mal, I planned the scavenger hunt. I did it for you," she says. "You didn't notice that every place we went to is something you'd enjoy? Well, maybe not the karaoke, but otherwise it's all stuff you like. No country music concerts in some backyard. No two-step dancing or drunk booze cruises. It's been barbeque and bookstores and water excursions."

"Did you fake the car accident too? That's really screwed up, Dani."

"The car accident was not Alexia." Dani claps her hands between every word for emphasis. "I'm sorry I freaked you out, but that's what happened on the first day. It was a weird accident. It has nothing to do with Alexia."

"Then why is she here?" Mal demands.

Dani puts her hands on Mal's shoulders to try and calm her down, but only because people are staring. She's causing a scene.

"She knows about the book, doesn't she?" Mal asks.

"Your book? The one that's published?"

"Stop lying to me," Mal shouts. "You've never trusted me with the truth."

Then it dawns on her.

"Did Alexia have something to do with the serum? Did she make it? Is that why she's here?" Mal asks.

Silence.

Mal starts counting down, waiting for Dani's next lie. One beat. Two beats. Thr—

"Ladies, I don't want you fighting over me," a voice chirps from behind them. "I think we can all walk away happy."

Alexia floats over to them, wearing a simple black dress. She can be anyone, a pretty woman who Tamar and Marcus' families will assume is a cousin or a friend. Someone who looks like she belongs while also fading into the background, undetected. That'll be Mal's undoing, that she can never let herself be that person.

"I've never been happy dealing with you," Mal says, folding her arms over her chest.

"Let's change that," Alexia replies.

"I can hand the spreadsheets over when I'm back home," Mal offers. "They're nearly a decade old, but if you're too lazy to make them yourself, I'm sure they'll suffice."

"They're on the cloud, right?" Alexia asks. "Why don't you just log in on my phone now? I want to confirm that they exist before you use my recipe."

Mal laughs and shakes her head.

"There's no way I'm giving you access to my drive," Mal says.

"Because you're writing about us?" Alexia says.

Mal's gaze falls on Dani, who's doing her best to keep her a neutral impression.

"So, you do know what I'm talking about," Mal says to Dani.

"The Newts keep track of alumni," Dani mumbles. "Just because you quit doesn't mean we stop keeping tabs."

"Vigilante shit sells," Mal tells Alexia and Dani. "I didn't sign an NDA. And it's fiction."

"I will take you to court," Alexia says. "Even if the court rules in your favor, the legal fees alone will bury you. It'll be worse than the hole you're in right now."

"How are you still such an asshole?" Mal snaps, but her insides feel like they're filled with water, making it harder to breathe. She thought she could stay above it all this weekend, but every interaction with her old friends and lovers and enemies has made her more susceptible to drowning—and she already had the good fortune to experience that sensation, too.

"Me? What about you! You're willing to expose the organization that you helped turn into a powerhouse for your own gain," Alexia says. Mal's a bit surprised. She actually seems upset. "We have a real opportunity to help women, and you don't care."

"I don't care? What about her?" Mal points at Dani. "She's the reason I left."

Now it's Dani's turn to act appalled, but instead she holds her hands up.

"Gen Z thinks we're out of touch," Dani says, like she's reading off a script Mal can't see. "Between the Newts being a women-only thing with a focus on men, when women can also commit non-consensual acts of violence—"

"That's some P.C. bullshit," Mal says. "Women are disproportionately affected by sexual violence compared to men—"

"Which is why I'm trying to save it," Alexia points at Mal. "You're the ideas woman."

She turns to Dani.

"We all know Dani's good at packaging and selling an idea."

Mal listens, but she also feels her stomach churn. Even now, Dani gets to be the golden child, the person who got to have her cake and eat it too. It was Dani, not Mal, who got to maintain their friend group and still be perceived as a feminist. Only Mal suffered for her principles, lost everything. She wants to scream in Dani's face and tell her as much. She wants to point out her hypocrisy. But for what? To lose leverage? To lose out on using this for her book?

Suddenly, Mal feels a sense of calm settle over her. It's like her body indicating that from now on, she is no longer willing to self-destruct.

"I have a serum that could be mass produced and distributed to every college campus with a Newts chapter." Alexia is nearing tears. "This isn't some grand evil plan you think it is. This is the start of a revolution."

Mal doesn't know what to think. But before she can say anything else, a blonde spots them and begins waving frenetically.

"Fuck," Dani mutters, but she smiles and waves her over. "She's a donor's wife."

Alexia wipes her tears and excuses herself before disappearing into the crowd.

"Tess," Dani says, pulling her in for a double air kiss.

Tess smiles blandly in Mal's direction but otherwise treats her like someone on the wait staff, or perhaps a decorative shrub. Which, frankly, is fine with Mal.

"How's the wedding planning going? The engagement has been at least a year, yes?" Tess asks Dani like she's consulting her social calendar. "You don't want to wait too long and become an IVF mama."

"We haven't settled on a venue yet." Dani smiles through gritted teeth. "Soon, though."

"Excellent," Tess says.

"And how's your family?" Dani asks.

Tess holds up a photo of her baby, a red-faced squirt. As Dani leans in to look, Mal takes her chance: She spikes Dani's wine glass with the stolen second vial of truth serum.

"Is it Topher?" Dani asks, another trick Mal does not possess: the ability to remember the names of acquaintances' children.

"Tofu, my little one," Tess responds kindly, as if that name makes more sense.

Who has the indecency to name their child after a wet blob that requires being pressed of its liquid? That kid will never make it through life without being deeply, relentlessly bullied. Mal foresees him changing his name, because there was no way that kid could live through life with having to deal with being called fucking Tofu.

"Lovely," Dani coos, linking her arm with Mal's. "You'll have to excuse us."

They move toward the trees and down a trail that leads to a private walking path along the water. She and Dani walk in silence before Dani broaches the subject.

"I didn't know Alexia would be here, I swear," Dani says. "But she dropped off the vials on Friday and I guessed she stayed . . . "

"You made me feel crazy," Mal says slowly. "You made me feel like I was losing my grip on reality by thinking Alexia couldn't possibly be here."

"I appreciate that you were trying to protect me, I really do," Dani starts. "I just wanted you to have fun this weekend—"

"So you could manipulate me?" Mal blurts out.

"No! Because I miss you. My life feels empty without you."

Mal scoffs.

"I find that hard to believe, Dani. You're a politician in one of the most influential cities in the country, let alone the world."

"That's such a Midwestern thing to say."

"This is the first time you've ever accused me of being nice."

"No, that New York is 'one' of the most influential cities. It's the world."

"That's my point. You're at the axis of power. You're beautiful—"

Now Dani's the one to scoff.

"Seriously. You're beautiful and smart and rich and have this hottie of a fiancé." Mal takes in the expression on Dani's face. "Why is there a ring on your finger and ring in your bag?"

"You went through my bag."

"You're not answering my question," Mal presses.

"Peter proposed Friday night."

"What did you tell him?" Mal demands.

"I told him I needed a moment to think, but then Ben came and surprised me. I haven't had time to think about it since."

"You're lying," Mal says, testing the potency and efficacy of this supposed truth serum. "You can't not be thinking about it. I don't understand. You and Ben look like you were born for each other, it's almost obnoxious."

"You said that about me and Peter once," Dani says.

"At the time I had never met a couple that I thought would get married. Even if I wasn't—and I'm still not—Peter's biggest fan. You say nice things to your friend about her boyfriend. That's what people do."

"But you don't do that," Dani says. "You're not the kind of person to say nice things."

"I'm sorry that I'm honest," Mal snaps.

"Then be honest about why you hate Peter. He wasn't that much more obnoxious than all the other boys in college. And frankly, he turned out to be way, way better than most of our friends. Marcus is marrying the first person to give him the time of day, Seb is too old to be in his club era, and Rosen is trying to turn his life around after hitting rock bottom."

Mal cringes. The truth serum is working, because Dani is saying things that only Mal has ever had the balls to say.

"I still don't trust him. I can't explain it, but I just don't. How could he leave you like that, especially when your parents died? I can't believe you even spoke to him after that, or now."

"I'm the one who broke up with him," Dani admits.

Mal pauses. She heard through Seb, back when they were on better terms, that Peter told everyone he initiated the breakup.

"He was trying to protect me," Dani says, understanding Mal's silence.

"From who?" Mal asks.

Dani gives her a look, a slight breeze from the water lifting her hair ever so slightly.

"You and I weren't talking at that point," Mal says. "Why would I care if you broke up?"

"You like making a point," Dani says. "Oftentimes about things you don't care about."

"So you let him protect his fragile ego on my behalf? Dani, even for you, that's rich."

"I just wanted to start fresh."

Turns out the stomach churning was temporary. Mal lifts the empty wine glass in her hand and smashes it on the ground in front of them. Unlike broken glass after a Jewish wedding ceremony, these shards would not bring good luck, Mal decides. She's ready to draw blood.

"You wanted to start fresh?" Mal shrieks. "You did? You got to keep everything."

Dani laughs. It's a deep, guttural laugh that Mal has never heard before, like it's coming from the recesses of her soul. Like she's allowing herself to speak her truth for the first time.

"You love playing the victim, you know that?" Dani says. "You always act like you're above it all, but you're just as full of it as everyone else."

"I'm full of it, huh? How about you lying about talking to Alexia every Sunday or fucking Peter when you have a doting fiancé at your beck and call."

"I just told you he's never going to be Peter," Dani shouts back. "He's never going to make me feel the way Peter did, and still does. He's just not."

"And that's good enough for you?"

"Yes, I don't need everything to be perfect all the time. I'm okay with good enough," Dani defends herself. "You're the one making yourself miserable with things you can't have. And even that's arbitrary. No one has ever stopped you from taking the things you want."

"Sorry I have morals," Mal yells. "Not like you would ever know what that's like."

"No one gives a shit, Mal, about your morals. Everyone has their own stuff to deal with. You could have been with Rosen years before you got together. Nothing was stopping you."

"I was with Adam."

"Barely," Dani scoffs. "He was just an excuse so you didn't have to be vulnerable with anyone. Because, as much as you like talking about everyone else, you can't deal with the fact that nothing is going to make you happy."

"Our friend group made me happy," Mal says. "And you all abandoned me. The boys, fine. Expected. But you used to have principles. After all that you'd still rather associate with him than me?"

"How dare you say that? I'm the only person who talked to him about it." Dani points at Mal, the diamond of her engagement ring gleaming. "You just cut him out of your life. You cut all of us out."

"Because all of you just acted like it never happened," Mal yells.

"That's not true," Dani says. "I asked Rosen what he would have done if someone did that to me, and he said he would have killed them. I told him, 'You did this to another girl. How could you?' I didn't talk to him for years, but when I saw him in New York—because guess what, Mal, he hung out with all our friends, and I wasn't going to isolate myself on his behalf."

"That's exactly what happened to me, but you don't seem to care about that," Mal yells.

"And it seemed like he changed," Dani forges ahead. "He was in grad school, he was making changes to his life to be a better person. You didn't give him a chance to tell you any of this himself. It's like you want him cast out of society instead of letting him learn and grow."

"Why does he get a second chance? I'm the only one who suffered," Mal shouts. "I'm the only one who was isolated, and I didn't rape someone."

The thumping of feet on stone prompts the girls to turn and look up. Marcus, Peter and Seb race down the stairs, with respective looks of anger, alarm and concern on their faces.

"We're having a private conversation," Mal spits out as the boys near. "Fuck off."

"It's not private when my guests can hear shouting," Marcus says, his fists balled up against his body. "Mal, you need to leave. I warned you already."

"I can't wait to get out of here and away from all of you hypocrites and rapist apologists," Mal says, and turns to Dani, ready to throw her next grenade. A small part of her is happy to finally have a stage for the arguments that keep her up at night, and now, an audience. "Rosen used our proximity as a shorthand for safety. Our presence, our friendship, let him operate this way. Women were less safe because of us, and I can't live with myself knowing that."

"Do you hear yourself?" Dani asks. "Everything does not revolve around you, even people's poor decisions."

"You're not the only one who suffered," Marcus says, looking equally ready to explode.

"How did you suffer?" Seb snaps. "It was all your idea."

A hush falls over the group.

Mal watches the color wash out from Marcus' face and seemingly move to Seb's. The sun, now making its way to the water's horizon, casts a glean on their sweating, guilty faces.

"What do you mean, Marcus' idea?" Mal asks slowly.

The boys look at each other, like it's the first time any of them have been asked to answer for Andrew's crime. And it's true: They never have.

"I told Rosen to apologize. To say that he was wasted and was looking for Mal—"

"Is that true?" Mal cuts in, remembering how she passed out at that night. Would Andrew have done to her what he did to Julianne if the door was unlocked? Would it have been her to file the Title IX report? Would she have known it was sexual assault in the first place? Everyone believed Julianne. Would anyone have believed her?

"I told him to say he made a horrible mistake, but Marcus convinced him to deny it. Marcus is the one who told Rosen to call his parents and fight it. He's the one who told Rosen that admitting to the assault would ruin his life," Seb says, tears gathering in his eyes. Mal wonders if it's because he's being forced to confess rather than because of the sheer truth.

Dani gives Marcus a knowing look. She knew they tried protecting Andrew. Everyone knew but Mal. Peter instinctively grabs Dani's hand to comfort her, and she pushes him away to hug herself. The admission pierces Mal like a freshly struck match in a room filled with TNT. But instead of an instantaneous explosion, the match has simply been lit. The flame is making the slow progression upward, almost but not yet ready to annihilate everything in its path.

"If anyone cared to ask, I was asleep in the next room that night. I just had common sense to lock the fucking door. I could have easily been the one who got raped—if your small, ant brains could grasp that if a girl is asleep and he fucks her, it's rape, regardless of relationship status—but all you people ever cared about was protecting Rosen."

"It didn't happen to you," Dani snaps. "It happened to Julianne."

The flame has hit the TNT.

"It did happen to me," Mal screams. It's a scream she's held onto so deeply, she's worried her body will rip in half by finally letting it go. "He assaulted me on your couch."

"When?" Marcus probes. "In the Hamptons?"

"You guys hooked up that night," Peter chimes in, like he's the all-knowing narrator. "That's what Rosen said. That's what you told us too after you decided on the beach that you were together."

Mal sinks to the ground, overcome with tears, and Dani races over to wrap her arms around her. Mal wants to push Dani off her, but she doesn't have the strength. These people and those years killed her, and she's been walking around like a shell of herself. A ghost version of the person she was supposed to be, with a life better and fuller than this one could ever offer. After a few heaving sobs, Mal catches her breath.

"We were getting ready for bed that first night," she chokes out. "We had flirted and made out the whole time on the beach, and I joked that I was ready to bone. Obviously, I was trying to be antagonistic in our way, but I was too drunk and gave in to the impulse. And he chickened out. I didn't even make it to my bed. I fell asleep on the couch and woke up to him on top of me. He was already inside me," Mal trails off.

"But you said you flirted with him all night," Marcus starts.

"I didn't realize it was assault until he did it to Julianne," Mal says, feeling hatred toward him. Real, true hatred for his lack of empathy, his inability to ever give her a chance. "It was weird. It was under weird circumstances. But I wanted to have sex with him, and I continued to hook up with him, but he had inserted himself into me while I was asleep."

"That's assault," Dani confirms.

"And Julianne knew that. She reported it. And to watch all of you—" she turns to Dani— "especially you, take all these efforts to protect his reputation, I saw you would have done the same thing to me."

"That's not what would have happened," Dani cries out. "How can you say that to us? We were your best friends."

"She's right," Marcus says to Dani. "How would it have been any different?"

"Mal was our friend," Seb croaks.

"My advice would have been the same," Marcus admits. "Would yours be any different?"

"No."

"I would have acted differently," Dani protests.

"Do you really think that matters?" Mal asks. "That you single handedly have the power to change things?"

"You can't go through life expecting that you don't matter."

"Plenty of people do."

"Well, I don't."

"Then why didn't you try that for Julianne?" Mal asks, not caring to talk openly about the Newts in front of anyone. They can sue her. She doesn't care anymore.

"We had a process—that you designed," Dani says. "And people did call his employers. Why do you think he couldn't keep a job? Or that he went to some local graduate program instead of anywhere reputable? But you didn't pay attention to any of it. You just left."

"But I came back. I came to you for help," Mal accuses Dani.

"When?"

It was after a particularly rough day at Theo's. Mal had been considering reaching out to Dani for weeks but could never push her pride aside to do it. It was only when Harrison groped a 15-year-old waiter that Mal acted. Dani picked up on the third ring when she was at some loud function.

"Hey, there's this guy at work. He's making my friend's life miserable," Mal trailed off, knowing she didn't have to finish the other part of the sentence, especially if she was calling Dani. "You know I hate favors, but could you get him on their radar?"

"Did he go to Weston?" Dani asked, confused. "I don't know how much buy-in I can get for some stranger—"

"Dani, how is he different from all the other men? He's touched me, he's touched her. He's touched nearly every woman who has worked here. He just grabbed—"

Dani inhaled sharply, and Mal could envision her skimming an invisible version of the rules. Mal has broken them, but for some reason, she's the only one who's ever been punished.

"We don't handle industry problems," Dani said sharply. "Listen, I'm campaigning and can't really talk. I'm sure it'll work itself out."

I'm sure it'll work itself out.

The words rang through Mal's ears like tinnitus as Dani ended the call. The sound continued ringing in her ears as she marched back to the kitchen and only when Creepy Harrison called her "hot lips" did it stop. That was when she gave Harrison Klein a black eye.

"I don't know what you wanted from me," Dani says weakly.

"To give a shit," Mal says. "To help me. After all the times I've helped you."

"I didn't even want to be part of the Newts," Dani says. "It's taken over my life."

"And here you are wanting to save it so badly," Mal says.

"What don't you get? It was an excuse to save our friendship," Dani yells.

"It's never been about that," Mal says. "All this is your pathetic attempts at trying to shore up the life you thought you'd have before Rosen raped someone. You can have your new husband and your new Senate job and be in mine and Alexia's good graces. Everyone says I'm selfish? Well guess what, so are you."

And with that, Mal storms back up to rejoin the party. She's getting her free food and drinks, and then she's getting the fuck out of Texas.

DANI
THE FOUR SEASONS
MAY 25, 2024 — AFTER

DANI LEANS AGAINST THE RAILING ON the path and assesses the situation. She's unsure how she let it get so out of control. Dani closes her eyes to tune out the boys and their watchful gazes on her. She used to love how they'd tend to her when she was upset. They were, and still are, nurturing people. Rosen is also a nurturing person who made bad choices. He's capable of making good ones in the future, and Dani has one last shot at proving to Mal that that's the case. She opens her eyes and smiles plaintively at the boys.

"Go back upstairs and have fun," Dani encourages them. "And leave Mal alone. She needs some time to herself."

Marcus and Seb are the first to go, while Peter lingers.

"Are you okay? That was pretty rough," he says.

"She's right to be angry," Dani says. "I just don't agree with her. Rosen's changed, and I think there needs to be a pathway for people who did something horrible to atone for their crime and move forward in the world. I understand that she doesn't want to be around him, but she can't deny other people if they choose to keep him in their lives. And frankly, look what happens to men if they're canceled. They become so much angrier and that much more dangerous. I don't see a problem if I choose to engage with him about what he alleg-edly did. That's like saying there's only one way to be a feminist or one way to be right. It's more complex than that."

Dani gulps in the air, already out of breath. Peter nods encour-agingly, but Dani shoulders slump at the thought that Peter isn't as engaged with these theories as she is, as Mal always is.

"Can we continue our conversation from Thursday night?" Peter asks hopefully. "Things got sidetracked once he showed up."

"I hope you're not mad at me," Dani says.

"How could I ever be mad at you? We want the same thing."

"That's not true."

"Yes, it is. You wouldn't have done what you did if you didn't want to," Peter argues, a crease forming in his forehead. His hands fly in front of them, becoming more animated as he launches into all the ways in which he's absolutely sure they're on the same page. "And you kept the ring. If you weren't considering it, you would have given it back and sent me packing."

Dani looks up to make sure Ben isn't coming down the stairs at the least opportune moment. She quickly pulls out the ring box from her bag and hands it to Peter. He shakes his head, refusing to accept it.

"I can't, Peter," she says, pushing it into his hands. "I don't regret this weekend with you, but my life is too established. I'm not going to blow it up because I'm nostalgic or because I've always cared about you. I love you, but we don't have a future together."

"I don't want to yell at you after Mal just did, but this is bullshit," Peter says. "You don't love him like you love me."

"Yes, but I chose him. We own an apartment together. We have a dog."

"Those are material things. If you don't love him now, you're not going to love him more later. That usually fades, and the fact that our love still hasn't means that we're supposed to be together," Peter pleads. "Let yourself be happy."

"There are more important things in the world than being happy," Dani snaps. She's sick of everyone telling her how to feel and what to think. She's the only person in charge of her life, not them. "I said no, and that's my final answer. You need to accept that and move on."

"I'm not taking the ring," he says, disgust transforming his voice into something totally unfamiliar. "It doesn't belong to me."

"Who else would it belong to?" Dani throws her hands up. "Because it's not mine."

"I didn't buy it." He gives her a knowing look. "Your dad made a few calls. I've held onto it for a long time now."

Her gaze drifts off toward the water and then back at the ring. Her dad picked it out? She takes the box back from Peter and opens it, pulling the ring out for the first time. It's not as heavy as the ring on her finger, but it has an intense aura to it. Her fingers catch on markings in the ring. Dani flips the ring around to see what's engraved on the inside.

Her eyes water, blurring her vision, and she slips off her engagement ring to replace it with the new one. The pear-shaped diamond feels like instant relief, like she had been wearing itchy clothes and finally slipped into her favorite robe. She wipes the tears away. A ring won't bring her parents back. Being with Peter won't undo the damage. She puts the ring back in the box, snaps it closed and hands it to Peter. She won't make eye contact with him, even as he bores into her with his glare. She absorbs his hatred. She deserves it. Finally, finally, finally, he takes the box from her and stalks away.

When she's finally alone, Dani makes the call.

"Is Cindy still in town?" Dani asks. "And did you really leave the third vial at home?"

MAL
THE FOUR SEASONS
MAY 25, 2024 — AFTER

THE COST FOR A FLIGHT CHANGE is out of the question, so Mal's not leaving Texas early after all. Still, she doesn't need to stick around here. After sweet talking a waiter into making her a doggy bag to take back to the house, Mal on her way out when Alexia chases her down, waving a piece of paper at her.

"I need you to sign this," she says, out of breath.

The paper has the insignia of the pharmaceutical company Alexia works for at the top.

"Do you just walk around with NDAs in your purse?" Mal asks.

"You're really going to write about us?" Alexia asks.

"A fictional version," Mal says.

"I listen to a lot of podcasts," Alexia says. "Every writer insists their book is purely fiction, crafted from the deep recesses of their creative mind."

"Okay, so we're all full of shit. But I still plan on doing a press tour for a novel, not a memoir." Mal narrows her eyes. "Why would you be interested in a novel about the Newts?"

"It would make us more powerful," Alexia says. "Imagine the impact of college students reading your book and then finding out they can be part of something just as powerful. That's how you drum up excitement."

"So you're into it?"

"I just need you to promise that you'll never speak about the serum," Alexia says, and then fills Mal in on its origins:

Alexia led a small team of female researchers who had, for one reason or the other, been banished to Alexia's department, which had been tasked with creating an oral supplement to lessen TMJ symptoms. One declined a date from her colleague. The other filed a complaint with HR when her supervisor told her to smile more often while working on a drug to prevent SIDS, which her infant son had died of years earlier.

When they realized the formula loosened more than just muscles, Alexia and her team agreed to keep it from their male boss. They didn't know what kind of horrors could be deployed using it, including whether their direct supervisor— also a sexist pig—would use it for his own ascent at the company.

Alexia reached out to Dani, unsure if she was making the right decision. It was after Alexia's house call that Dani came up with her grand scheme for the weekend: They could use the serum on men who had been accused of sexual assault and use it as a method for restorative justice. There's only so much that could be done when men fundamentally can't accept a reality in which they are caught committing a crime.

Mal figures Dani can think of other use cases for it, too, but keeps that to herself.

"That's where you come in. Everyone knows what happened with your friend in college. Dani thought it would be a good test subject and make you more susceptible to helping us," Alexia says, and then looks at Mal sympathetically. "Meredith told me about what happened in New York. I know you had a bad taste in your mouth from the Newts, but you didn't have to say what you did to her. It wasn't right."

Mal swallows and feels the shame and anger flood her system. Why hadn't Dani just been straightforward with her? She didn't need to be manipulated into playing along. Plus, Alexia was right about Meredith. Mal took that first meeting with Meredith and used their connection with the Newts as a threat: Buy her book or risk being associated with illegal, vigilante behavior that would surely get her fired from her fancy, well-paying-for-publishing editor job. Mal quickly got a near-seven figure deal, and Meredith earmarked a substantial part of the publisher's budget to marketing. It was a pact of mutual destruction, but Mal almost earned out her advance. It turned out to be worth it for both of them.

"What else could you possibly want?" Alexia's voice cracks, and Mal realizes she mistook her silence for contemplation. Is there anything else she wants from Alexia? Mal's surprised when an answer pops into her brain, like she's been waiting years for someone to finally ask her the question. But as she opens her mouth to answer, Alexia's face darkens.

"You know, don't you?" Alexia asks, and then shakes her head. "I promise, I was never going to hit them."

Mal stays silent, trying to piece together what Alexia's saying.

"I was at H-E-B when Peter spotted me. I guess he remembered me from college; I was flattered. He told me about how much this weekend meant to him and that he was trying to get back together with Dani—apparently they had been emailing?—and he asked me to rough them up just enough so he could comfort her." Alexia brings her hands to her face.

Mal smiles despite herself. She always knew Peter was a real piece of work.

"I don't know what came over me. I was really taken by him, by their love story," Alexia says. "And I thought it was the best for Dani. She's been dragging her feet about marrying Ben. I know you think I'm a horrible person, but I'm really not. I made a bad decision. I'm sorry."

Alexia is crying now. She's doing so softly, but her emotion is real. Mal, once again, is floored to see how human she is, not at all like her memory of bullying, intimidating Alexia.

"It's okay, it's okay. I'll sign the NDA, and I'll never tell Dani. Scout's honor." Mal holds up her hand in an effort to tamp down Alexia's tears. She's never been good with these kinds of things; it's partially why she used to hang around men so much. "On one condition: I never want to see you again."

Alexia solemnly nods and hands the paper to Mal, who signs it triumphantly. Serena was right; no one should ever bet against Mal, let alone herself.

* * *

About 30 minutes later, Mal is back at the rental—out of her dress and into comfy clothes. Basking in the darkness, save for the lantern flickering above her, Mal stretches out on the porch to write. The voices from this morning are back and chattier than ever, and it's the second time today that Mal has a glorious writing session. Finally, the voices in her head on her side, and they want Mal to capture their truth. It's late by the time actual voices pull Mal from her trance, the sky punctured with seemingly thousands of stars. The door to the kitchen slides open, and Dani gingerly sticks her head out.

"The car will be here in 20. Are you all packed?"

Mal says nothing but powers down her laptop so she can pack up. They don't speak as Mal slips past to get everything together for the last leg of the weekend. She's not sure if she's ready to broach the final circle of hell: smiling politely as a college frenemy says, "I do."

The car ride is bucolic, though it would probably be more beautiful in daylight. The vast land unfolds around them in waves, and the stars get brighter the farther they drive from the city. Eventually they turn onto a dirt road with a large cast-iron arch and slow in front of a security booth. The driver rattles off their names, hands the guard a sheet of paper with their faces on it, and then rolls down the windows for inspection. A flash of light shines into the car, causing splotches to temporarily impede Mal's vision.

"They're good," the guard calls out.

The car passes through a heavy iron gate and slowly drives up to what can only loosely be described as a resort.

"You said he was marrying into wealth," Peter tells Andrew. "Not mega-wealth."

It takes everything in Mal to avoid glancing in Dani's direction. As they unload their bags from the car, a team of staff members greets them.

"Welcome to B'reshith," a woman says, gesturing to the behemoth behind her. "Come."

They silently follow the large men hauling their luggage through a winding path that's shaded by trees. Mal looks up and can barely make out the stars through the dense trees. Ben and Dani hold hands in front of her. Mal glances back and sees a sliver of moonlight illuminating a hardened expression on Peter's face. The meathead carrying Mal's luggage stops outside a small bungalow and reaches into his pocket to unlock the door with an old-timey brass key. The lock clicks and the door swings open. Mr. Meathead hands her the key and informs Mal that if she needs anything, she can press the button by her bed.

"The device pouches are on your bed. You'll drop them off tomorrow at breakfast or leave them on the bed for housekeeping, but you will not be able to attend the festivities without surrendering your devices," he says.

When Mal stares blankly at him, the man bows slightly and walks back in the direction they came from. Mal shuts the door, relieved to truly be left alone for the first time since she arrived in Texas, and surveys the pouches, which are adorned with a monogram featuring the bride and groom's initials. There's one for her laptop, one for her phone and other smaller ones that can fit a variety of tech-enabled items. A small card, totally unlike the scavenger hunt cards, informs Mal that the entire property does not use modern technology because of moral obligations against surveillance culture. The card explains this in a much fluffier, polite way, but Mal gets the gist. Still, there's no way she's relinquishing her phone.

There's a knock on the door.

Mal hesitates before getting up to answer it. She's had enough excitement for the year.

"Andrew," she says, surprised.

"Can I come in?" He sounds hopeful at Mal's accidental use of his first name.

Mal steps aside and wonders if she should leave the door open in case she needs to scream. That's silly, she thinks. Andrew only takes advantage of girls when they're drunk. Plus, Mal doesn't feel like a girl anymore. She's weathered.

"Do you want to play a game?"

"Charades?" Mal asks. "Describe a rapist, for ages 18 and up?"

Andrew's face darkens at her fucked-up joke and perches on her bed.

"Twenty questions," he replies. "I want to hear about how your life turned out."

"You can get the whole thing on Google," Mal says. "And select Apple podcasts."

"You sound pretty miserable for someone who achieved everything she wanted."

If this is why Andrew came to her room, she wasn't going to let him have it. Nagging her may have worked in college, but no more.

"I was right," Mal smiles serenely. "You haven't changed."

Andrew groans.

"You always see the worst in me," he says. "You assumed I had bad intentions from the second I got here."

"Andrew," she says, deliberately now, and in the tone that once drove him mad. "I don't think about you at all, anymore."

Mal holds the door open and feels victorious when he leaves without any more pushback. She was right to use the serum on Dani instead of him. He's a lost cause.

CHAPTER EIGHTEEN

MAL
B'RESHITH, TEXAS
MAY 26, 2024 — AFTER

A CROWD FORMS AROUND MARCUS AND his bride with their fists raised in the air. The chorus of "Sweet Caroline" swells, and the dozens of people on the dance floor bellow about how the good times never seemed so good. Mal watches them from where the carpet meets the black-and-white sheet vinyl, her pink lips pinched with disdain as she swivels her whiskey. Mal, clad in a body-skimming mint green dress, feels all the wrong eyes on her. It's not just the older Israeli men checking her out, but also the groomsmen, one of Marcus' uncles, and even a cater waiter. Still, she ignores their oppressive stares and scans the crowd for a familiar face. It would be nice to find someone to kill the last few hours of this trip with.

A strobe light swings across the dance floor and hits a perfect head of slicked-back hair. Mal refocuses her attention to the head it's attached to, her gaze moving down his sharp jawline, flicked with glistening golden stubble, and then to the tiny woman placing a dainty hand in the crook of his arm. He leans down to whisper something in her diamond-studded ear as they make their way to the ballroom exit. There's something about his glassy eyed stare, smile, and the placement of his hands that makes Mal sweat. Adrenaline courses through her veins. If this weekend has proven anything, it's that Mal can trust her instincts.

Mal downs the rest of her drink and cuts across the dance floor to offer up a warning to the woman. She only makes it halfway across the dance floor before a large hand yanks her arm, bringing her to a complete halt.

"Where are you going?" asks Peter, who doesn't immediately drop his grip when Mal winces in pain. "We need to get a photo of the whole gang together."

"Rosen left," Mal says, pushing down the panic in her chest. "Let me grab him."

Peter gives her a curious look, and the hairs on her arm stand at attention.

"Nah, I think we should leave him be," he says. "And we didn't think you'd really want to be in the picture with him anyway."

He holds Mal's gaze, and she takes him in for the first time in the decades of peripherally knowing him. Mal finally sees what Dani saw in him all those years ago, that feeling of being the only person in the room deserving of his intensity and attention. It's not so much tantalizing as it is threatening, and it makes her hate him more. Still, she relents and lets Peter lead her to the photographer and a smiling group of people waving them over.

Seb and Dani sidle up on either side of Mal, wrapping their arms tightly around her waist, as the bride and groom squat in front of the group. Peter throws an arm over Dani, and they all smile for the camera. Mal flashes her brightest

Hollywood smile and hopes that when Marcus' kids ask about this photo he'll shrug and say they were all people he once knew. The camera bulb flashes bright, causing a constellation of shapes to fog Mal's vision.

The lights flicker in the ballroom, and the Kesha song blasting from the speakers skips. Dani and Peter give each other a look.

"Abba knew this would happen," Tamar whines. "B'reshith isn't built for this kind of electricity use."

"At least there are generators," Marcus says, rubbing his wife's bejeweled back. "But don't you think a wedding in the dark would be romantic?"

Tamar hits him in the chest playfully before they spin away to dance together. Mal looks at the group and realizes someone is missing.

"Where's Ben?"

"I think he ate something bad at breakfast," Dani says, looking embarrassed and checking her small Cartier watch—a gauche accessory for a wedding, come to think of it. A proud look flashes across Peter's face. It's barely perceptible, but Mal clocks it.

"Are you sure you want to stay here? I don't think Marcus will mind if you need to tend to him," Mal says, ignoring the dirty look Peter shoots her.

"I don't think there's much I can do," Dani says, checking her watch again.

"Do you have to be somewhere?" Mal jokes, though Peter, not Dani, straightens.

"Sorry, I'm used to having a phone in each hand," she shrugs. "I have that urge to check something, tap a screen."

She checks her watch again.

"You should take a walk," Seb says brightly. "There's research that spending time in nature is the best way to reset your brain."

"That's a great idea. Mal, do you want to come with me?" Dani asks.

Mal glances at Peter. Despite everything that went down with Dani this weekend, Mal realizes this is the last time she'll speak to any of them. This trip gave her closure, albeit at the expense of her mental health. She can suck it up for a few more hours. Plus, if Peter is willing to ask Alexia to almost hit him with her car, he doesn't seem above killing Ben for his own gain. They may need to call 911. Her fingers brush the silk of her bag, where she feels the shape of her phone securely placed inside. Dani looks at her watch a third time and blanches.

"Fine, I'll go by myself," she says and hustles away. Seb shrugs, and returns to the dance floor, leaving Mal and Peter standing face to face.

"Alone at last," Mal says. "Actually, I've been warned to avoid spending time with you."

"By Ben?" he smirks.

"What did you do to him?"

"How do you know I did something?" he asks, narrowing his eyes.

"You can't help yourself," Mal says. She's alarmed by the menace in his eyes. "If you kill him, I'll drag you to the police station myself."

"Relax, Veronica Mars," he says, rolling his eyes. "I put some eye drops in his drink. Fastest way to diarrhea city."

"You had so many chances to win her over," Mal says, relieved that Ben, who she likes well enough, is not dead in a ditch. "And you failed every single time. Move on."

Mal leaves him on the dance floor. She's going to go back to her room, write until she's tired, and then use the last of the money in her bank account to call a car and take her to the airport. But first she's checking on that girl who left with Andrew, a man supposedly reformed.

DANI
B'RESHITH, TEXAS
MAY 26, 2024 — AFTER

DANI SLIPS PAST THE GROUP, CAREFUL not to run or otherwise draw attention to herself. If Cindy timed it right, the serum has only started to hit Rosen's system. The expression on Dani's face is serene—just as it was at her parents' funeral, or when she got screamed at by her Republican constituents when she supported a homeless shelter opening in their neighborhood—as she rushes to his chalet. She tries to focus on mundane things, like whether her flight back to New York will be delayed, as she regulates her breathing. Still, she moves through the winding hallways of the venue until she's outside.

Up ahead, Dani sees a staff member pushing a cart and smiles. The girl. She hears her mother's voice, clear as a bell, ring out in her head. She hasn't heard the tenor of her voice like that in years. Dani wonders if her mom would have become hip in 2024, knowing what's politically correct to say, or if she would have continued using it just among the family. Every day it feels like there are more mysteries that the universe turns over for Dani, questions she didn't know she'd ever have. Dani buries the thought and instead smiles brighter at the woman.

"Howdy!" The cleaning lady says. "Why, you're off in a hurry."

Dani curses in her head as she's forced to slow down.

"There's nowhere here you need to be rushing off," the cleaning lady says, but then her beady eyes widen and begin darting around. "Are you runnin' from someone?"

"No, no, just an upset stomach," Dani says, but something in the woman's eyes is recognizable. The cleaning woman puts a hand on Dani's wrist.

"You know, I came here from the Commodore because we're the first hotel to go totally tech-free," she says. "I don't want nobody tracking me."

Her eyes dart around, like a nervous bird, and that's when Dani recognizes the behavior: The woman looks like someone she'd see at the domestic violence shelter in her district.

"Is anyone tracking you?" Dani asks, her voice a low hum to not upset the woman.

"My ex was," she whispers. "I went fully off the grid. Me and my son live here now."

Dani digs into her bag and pulls out a business card—one that has her cell phone clearly written out on the back.

"Call me if you need anything," Dani says.

The woman squints at the business card, clearly not that impressed with Dani's position of power, and nods politely. As Dani follows the stone path, she imagines how the woman will feel in a few months when she sees Dani's face broadcasted across every news channel. She finally reaches the chalets and looks for the one with the door propped open.

Dani sees it and slips inside, finding Cindy and Alexia standing beside Rosen in the bathroom like the two lions flanking the entrance of the New York Public Library.

"You're late," Alexia says, holding up a stopwatch. Dani has just under nine minutes. She looks at the tape recorder sitting on the counter, which is rolling. "It's old school, I know, but it's the only thing I could sneak in."

"Good, I don't think Mal's making it," Dani says. "But she deserves to hear this."

Rosen clutches his stomach, but otherwise looks pissed off.

"Dani, what's happening?" Rosen asks, sitting on the edge of the porcelain, claw-footed tub. He looks at Cindy. "Are you actually Marcus' high school friend?"

"She's an old friend from Weston," Dani clarifies. "Marcus added her to the guest list when I heard that she was in town. Why were you taking her back to your room?"

"To have sex with her," Rosen says.

"Was she into you?" Dani asks.

"Obviously." Rosen keeps rubbing his stomach, but his tone has a caustic edge to it.

"How do you know that?"

"Because I'm good looking," he says. "Plus, she was giving me indicators."

"Did you ask her?"

"Did I ask her if I'm good looking?"

"No, did you ask her if she wants to have sex?"

"So I could kill the mood? No," he says.

Dani looks at Alexia, who's watching the encounter wide eyed. Alexia said she's tested the serum, but her expression doesn't indicate that in the slightest. Dani's face flushes. This may have been a massive error, but she can't ruminate on it. They only have so much time left.

"Were you happy to see Mal?" Dani asks, forging ahead and trying to ignore the sweat building on Rosen's face and his skin taking on a waxy color.

"Yes, but I was nervous," he says. "I want her to forgive me."

"Forgive you for what?"

Mal's voice calls out from the chalet, and she steps into the bathroom and shuts the door. For a luxury venue, the bathroom is cramped. The five of them can barely fit inside.

"For cheating on you," he says.

"For cheating on me," she repeats back.

"That night, I had too much to drink. I called out your name, looking for you," he says. "Someone told me you were in one of the bedrooms, so I checked all of them until I found someone. I think I just wanted you, but didn't have the where-withal to care that it wasn't."

"What did you do next?" Mal's voice trembles.

"I kissed her," he says, his expression marked with acute sadness. "I thought it was romantic, like a prince waking up a princess."

"Who can't consent," Mal says.

"I didn't know about that," he says.

"Then what happened?" Mal's voice has a strength to it, but also a resignation, like she knows the end of the story but needs to hear it anyway.

"We kissed and did some other things," he says. "She was awake."

"Why can't you admit that it was sexual assault?" Mal explodes. "Why can't you take responsibility for it?"

Rosen stands up.

"I'm not going to ruin my life because other people think I should. Everyone else already did that for me. Do you know I've gotten fired from two high schools because your friends"—he waves a hand at the women surrounding him—"called in with anonymous tips."

He turns to Dani, his body rigid with rage.

"You think Peter didn't tell me what you all do? When I told him what happened, he said you'd all come after me and ruin my life, just because I couldn't keep it in my pants."

Dani's heart thumps wildly. The phrasing is exactly the way

Peter would have said it. She knows it's true, and she feels betrayed. He pinky promised her—and then she feels like a fool for that thought even occurring in the first place.

"He was right," Rosen says. "There was an investigation. They couldn't determine it wasn't consensual—"

"It. Wasn't. Consensual," Mal screams, stepping in front of him. "You're literally incapable of telling a lie, but you still won't admit the truth."

"This is my truth!" Rosen is now toe to toe with his ex-girl-friend. "I was accused of a crime. No one could definitively say it happened the way you all make it out to be, like I'm a monster, and I still suffered consequences you claim I didn't experience. I was blacklisted from parties. Teachers refused to have me in class. I lost a job offer I had. I went to grad school, I went to therapy, I moved home with my parents because I couldn't get an apartment approved."

"Do you want me to feel bad for you?" Mal sneers. "I dropped out of college. Julianne barely graduated. She's traumatized. Her entire life is on a different trajectory because of you."

"She gets to be a survivor," Rosen yells. "I'm just some piece of shit whose life has been blown up for something I did not do."

"I know you did it, because you did the same thing to me," Mal roars.

Rosen looks at her wide-eyed before his breathing becomes labored, and he clutches his stomach again. Then his eyes roll back in his head, and his body starts convulsing. Within seconds, or so it seems, Rosen collapses onto the cold, hard linoleum. On the way down, Dani hears a sickening crack.

His body crumples onto, and then into, the tub.

"Andrew?" Mal's voice is shrill. She climbs into the tub to pull him toward her, but the motion sends a whiff of something damp and metallic straight to Dani's nostrils. Dani's gaze moves from Mal's hands to the floor. There's so much blood. It seeps out from Mal's hands or his head onto the white porcelain tub, dripping down one of the golden legs. Dani follows the trail to avoid taking in the unnatural angles of Rosen's body. A laugh escapes from her mouth.

Cindy's face grows vacant, her mind shutting down. Alexia gawks.

"This isn't supposed to happen." Alexia says, and then hurls herself at the toilet to vomit.

"We need to call 911," Dani says, but she knows it's not a rescue mission.

"Texas has the death penalty," Alexia says, wiping her mouth but still hugging the toilet. "Our DNA is all over this bathroom. I have an NDA connecting both me and Mal to the serum. If we call this in, we all go down for murder."

Alexia isn't lying, and Dani has too much to lose.

"I need to know everything," Dani says. "What went wrong?"

"I used the whole vial like I was told," Cindy says. Her voice sounds like it's coming from far away and she has a dazed expression on her face.

"Was it the same batch from last time?" Dani asks Alexia.

"I've tested how it reacts with recreational drugs, prescription drugs, alcohol. I've never seen this reaction before," Alexia says.

"What will the toxicology report show?" Dani asks weakly.

"The drug is not known to anyone else other than the people in this room and my research team, so it won't come up on any toxicology report," Alexia says.

Dani doesn't really hear her. Even with the toxicology report ruled out, any of them could turn her in. There's so much evidence against Dani: the text messages and phone calls with Alexia over the drug's development and its unauthorized use; her former position as Newts president; the fact that she watched one of her oldest friends drop dead in front of her, with three witnesses to frame her. Two calls—one to the press and one to the police—will have Dani going from being the presumed junior senator from the State of New York to a death-row inmate of some godforsaken Texas prison on trial for the murder of her best friend's ex-boyfriend. Mal's wails punctuate Dani's thoughts.

"Enough." Dani's command stops Mal mid-cry. "You're going to draw unwanted attention. Cindy and Alexia, leave. I'll handle this, but we will never speak of this again."

The two women—looking like typical wedding guests who got extra emotional during the ceremony, with nary a drop of blood on them—nod and follow each other out. Dani grabs Alexia's arm before she passes, digging her nails into her skin. Alexia doesn't even flinch.

"Do I have to worry about this?" Dani asks, making sure to scrape her nails against Alexia as she pulls away.

"No."

Dani sees a slight flicker behind Alexia's checked-out eyes, an acknowledgement that Dani just got a good amount of DNA under her fingernails. They nod and Alexia disappears into the overgrown bushes. Dani stares at Mal cradling Rosen's body, covered in his blood, trying to figure out how to play this. Could he have just slipped on some water? Would any investigator worth their weight think it's murder?

Mal is covered in blood.

"Peter spiked his drink with eye drops. He did the same thing to Ben," Mal whispers over and over as she shakes.

"Mal, I need you to listen to me," Dani says, crouching next to her. "It was an accident."

Mal looks up at Dani.

"An accident?" she asks. "This wasn't an accident."

"It was an accident," Dani repeats. "You know Rosen liked to abuse drugs every once in a while. Maybe he took a Xanax. But whatever he had on him was laced with fentanyl. That causes seizures, you know?"

Mal looks at her, clearly not comprehending. The sound of a door slamming and the thunder of heavy footsteps stops as quickly as it comes.

Peter stands at the threshold, not yet stepping into the bathroom, and takes in the scene. Dani can see the gears in his mind grinding, and that's when she realizes that none of the women will take her down. It'll be Peter.

"It was an accident," Dani repeats to Peter.

"I don't know, Dani," Peter says, keeping his gaze on Mal. "She's made it clear that she's hated him for years. Maybe enough to kill him."

Mal eyes scan the room, though Dani's unsure if she can process what Peter's saying. Dani's not even sure Mal will remember any of this in a few hours, let alone by tomorrow.

"You're bluffing," Dani says, her eyes bugging. His best friend is dead in a bathtub, and yet Peter's more focused on threatening Mal. He points to Mal's purse, which is laying on the ground, and Dani opens it. Her cell phone is inside.

"Location data. It's the only evidence of someone being here at his time of death."

Dani searches his face for a joke, some sort of messed-up reaction to his friend dying, but she sees nothing but malice and certainty.

"Why are you doing this?" Dani asks.

"It's her fault we're not together," Peter booms, causing Mal to whimper. "I did everything for you. Everything. I picked up your friends when they got so blasted they couldn't stand up. I listened to you talk about how you tracked down all these men who did horrible things. So, when Rosen gets accused, I was ready to never speak to him again, because I knew that's what you'd want. But then you change your mind, which, again, I was always fine with, but that pissed her off."

Peter points a meaty finger at Mal.

"And, all of a sudden, her not being in your life makes you miserable. You're second guessing everything we built, everything we dreamed about, because of some brat who hates men. Mal ruined everything," Peter rants. "My life—our life—was supposed to look different than this. And you could easily just choose me and make everything go back to normal, but you won't just because of some guy? I'm the good guy. I'm the one."

Sweat drips off Peter's face. Dani holds still, trying to figure out how to save them all as Peter talks in circles, making little to no sense. Mal isn't the reason she broke up with him. When he finally runs out of steam, he's breathing heavily and still standing just out of reach.

"If I leave Ben, then do you think Rosen slipped and fell?" Dani asks quietly.

Mal's face crumbles, finally soaking in all that's happened, as Peter's softens.

"That sounds possible," Peter nods slowly.

"I need a yes or no, Peter," Dani says.

"Dani, you can't do this," Mal says, slurring her words like she's drunk.

Dani puts her hand on her wrist and shushes her. For the first time in her life, she sees her purpose. This is where all roads lead, no matter the route. No matter who she's saving. Dani faces Peter, who squares his shoulders. She hates how he's looking at her, like she's playing another game and trying to trick him, too. She hates that she would be, if she had a better hand.

"I want us to get married," he says. "Everything I told you this weekend came from the heart. The circumstances may have changed, but my feelings haven't."

Maybe it's the shock taking over, but Dani feels some level of finality, like her body acknowledges this is the final destination. It's the right decision for everyone. The only decision. She'll still get a political career and get to keep her friends. Build a family. And maybe Mal's the one who's been right all along. Rosen was a bad person, a predator. They finally got to accomplish the task they set out on a decade ago: to make the world safer for women. Now they'll be safe. They'll finally be safe.

CHAPTER NINETEEN

DANI
AUSTIN-BERGSTROM INTERNATIONAL AIRPORT
MAY 27, 2024 — AFTER

THEY GOT AWAY WITH IT. DANI repeats the phrase like a prayer. They got away with it.

The process was surprisingly easy. Dani put Mal's phone in a pouch and wedged it near one of the collection stations, so it looked neglected by staff. Since Mal was covered in blood, Dani splashed water on the floor, presumably how Rosen slipped and fell, before pressing the emergency button. It was the cleaning woman who responded first, and Dani did what she needed to do: told her Rosen tried to attack her, and that she pushed him. The push wasn't hard, but he slipped on some water. The cleaning woman, bless her heart, took Dani at her word and agreed to discreetly call an ambulance without alerting the rest of the wedding attendees. Dani wanted to wait as long as possible before they ultimately ruined Marcus and Tamar's wedding.

The EMTs declared him dead on arrival, and the police took their statements. The authorities focused more on Mal's shock than investigating, which turned out to be a beautiful strike of good fortune. Even if any of the law enforcement officials thought about it after the fact, the crime scene was breached. There was no way to collect any good evidence. Dani couldn't let herself give into the guilt. She couldn't sacrifice their lives for a dead man.

The group, minus Marcus and Tamar, decided to go straight to Seb's uncle's house in Miami to wait for the inevitable Fort Lauderdale funeral. Even for secular Jews, the funeral happens as close to a person's death as possible, so it wouldn't make sense to go home before it. Though they are on the same flight, everyone is spread out in the airport lounge, needing their own space to process what has happened—or in most of their cases, what's to come.

"I need to stretch my legs," Mal says to Dani, though it's hard to assess her gaze behind the dark sunglasses shielding her face. Still, Dani gets up to join her. They walk slowly down the dirty, yellowish floor, the din of the airport a welcome distraction. Mal keeps her gaze straight ahead before speaking out of the side of her mouth.

"You can't let him hold you captive," Mal whispers.

"We don't have any other options," Dani says, and then she tries to think of the positives. "And to wind up with Peter . . . it's not the worst thing in the world, is it?"

It's too late for them to turn back now, anyway. They'll have to make peace with it. The girls continue walking in silence before they hear that their gate is starting to board.

"What do we do after this?" Mal asks. "I feel like we're in a different dimension. I don't know what comes next."

"Well, we're best friends. We've always been," Dani says after a pause. "But I think we need to reintroduce ourselves to each other. This is an opportunity to be the people we thought we'd be. The people we want to be. It's like a do-over."

Mal is quiet, and Dani can see she's contemplating this.

"A new start," Mal whispers.

Dani pulls her in for a hug, though she expects to feel Mal strain against her embrace. Instead, she relaxes in Dani's grip, relenting.

"I'll never forget what you did for me," Mal chokes out. "And if the time comes to ever return the favor . . . well, you know where to find me."

A lump swells in Dani's throat, but the acceptance has sunk into her bones. She knows that in a few days, after the funeral, she'll fly home and hand the ring back to Ben, along with the promises of building their life together. She'll give him the apartment—he'll probably sell it, but it's the least she can do—and Ziti. She almost laughs when she thinks about the dog, the one she didn't want and would happily hand off, and then realizes that he'll think that's the most monstrous part. Calling off the wedding is one thing, but abandoning a dog as lovable as Ziti?

"I should have never trusted her. She hated our golden-doodle," Dani imagines he'll tell his friends as he licks his wounds. "What kind of sociopath hates dogs?"

It'll be easy to start over with Peter, someone who will know her for everything she is. The press will be manageable. She can spin a good story about reconnecting with her college sweetheart, and Alexia will help her rally the troops for blind item comments maligning Ben. It can, and will, be done. And anyway, people get into marriages for worse reasons.

EPILOGUE

MAL
SAW MILL RIVER PARKWAY
OCTOBER 17, 2027

T̲ʜᴇ ᴄʀᴏᴡɴ ᴏꜰ Mᴀʟ's ʜᴇᴀᴅ ɪꜱ warm as she barrels down the leafy highway. Her hair, tinged with a few more gray streaks than she's comfortable with, whips around her face. Mal presses her foot to the gas pedal so she can shave off a few more minutes. In the back seat, an oversized gift box rattles next to the aged shoebox covered in Weston wrapping paper as the speedometer's arrow inches toward 80 miles an hour. She can't wait to rid herself of the final abscess of the past decade. It's finally time to say goodbye.

"Babe," Blake says, gently rubbing Mal's thigh. "We'll get there when we get there."

Mal glances over at Blake, pleasure blooming in her chest.

"Good thing you're here to rein me in," Mal jokes over the low hum of classic rock, which is drowned out by the whooshing air.

"I know better than to try," Blake says.

Mal eases off the gas and switches lanes.

"Stronger soldiers before you have tried and failed."

"What makes me so different?" Blake teases, brushing out a knot in Mal's hair.

"I think they all just got me ready for you," Mal says, not even the least bit horrified by a sentiment she would have found cringey just a few years earlier. But after everything happened, Mal finds that she's beginning to crave softness in all aspects of her life. Although they don't live together yet, she and Blake spend their days going on long walks through Brooklyn's tree-lined streets or waiting in line at Ample Hills under the electric blue sky. Her mind's quieter now that she's finally learned to give in. Getting sober, hiring a therapist for in-person appointments, and earning her college degree helped, too.

She quickly takes her gaze off the road to smile at Blake. Even a year in, Mal finds that she's startled every time she stares into those eyes. The mossy green color is just like Andrew's. At first, it was the reason she took her time with Blake. Mal worried those eyes would bring the same kind of trouble Andrew's did. But after a while, it dawned on Mal that maybe, in a very twisted way, Blake is a gift from Andrew—a peace offering sent from another dimension.

When Mal told her theory to the group at their monthly dinner, she expected horror, or at least some pushback. Instead, Dani invited Blake to the baby shower. A new addition to fill the void they all feel—though for all Seb and Marcus know, Mal and Dani's voids are simply grief.

"Do you think they'll have one of those massive cutouts at the party?" Blake asks.

"Of the yet-to-be-birthed baby?" Mal laughs.

"No, of your book," Blake says. "It's not every day that you have a two-time bestselling author twice over at a baby shower."

"That's a good bit. Throwing a baby shower but it's for the book. Next time," Mal says. "But, knowing Dani, I'll probably be one of the least impressive people there."

"Nah, it's New York," Blake says. "Everyone thinks they're unimpressive but that's because the bar is so high."

"So, you're saying I've finally earned my right to be a New Yorker?"

"You need 10 years to get the membership card, or at least you need to live through a major crisis, but you're on your way."

After the wedding and the funeral, Mal called it quits on LA. She never really loved the city—she saw too many men's toes—and began to miss the seasons, especially the fall foliage. She sold and donated what was left in the storage unit and moved in with Dani, just until her advance hit her bank account. Turns out Reese's Book Club loves murderous vigilantes.

It was then that Dani and Peter became official-official again. In a way, it felt like the wedding weekend shook something loose in the three of them, like they had veered too far into the woods. A tragedy—and some blackmail—was the thing that steered them back to their rightful place. That, and seeing more co-ed Newts chapters spring up at universities across the country. Even though she wanted nothing to do with it, the news of it heartened her. College kids still cared about making the world better.

The recipe disappeared, too. Everyone agreed it wasn't worth keeping evidence around, no matter the upsides.

Mal met Blake the week she sold her second novel, though not for nearly as much as what her first one went for. She was lucky Meredith even agreed to meet with her again, but it seemed like Alexia smoothed things over. Seen, but not heard, and Mal appreciated it. Everyone expected it to be the book of summer, and although the news wasn't public yet, her agent already optioned it to a major studio—with Mal attached to write the pilot. The days of skipping meals were long over. It all felt like the universe was finally giving Mal permission to live, to enjoy the life she worked hard for. The one she was entitled to, at long last.

Within 30 minutes, Mal turns up the long driveway to reach Dani and Peter's Westchester home. The couple has been staying in the suburbs during a gut renovation of their West Village townhouse. The *Sentinel* had a field day writing about what an elitist asshole Dani is, as if its primary readership didn't own multiple houses. Mal pulls up to the line of high-end cars parked neatly alongside the half-circle driveway that curls near the front door.

"I'll grab the gift," Blake says as Mal rakes her hands through her hair, trying to look halfway presentable. "Do you want me to take the time capsule, too?"

"I'll grab it."

The usual nerves from seeing the group sweep over Mal as the couple enters the house, but the tension soon dissipates as everyone greets Blake with spectacular warmth. The sounds of Sunday football are muted under the din of chattering guests. Mal barely gets a chance to say hi to Marcus, who's chasing after the toddler-aged twins; each time he grabs one, the other escapes. Dani, donning a blue-and-white maternity dress, waves them over from her cushioned chair.

"I'm sorry, I'm not getting up," Dani says, kissing Mal and Blake each on the cheek.

"You shouldn't have to," Mal says, then catches a glimpse of Dani's unusually bare hands. "What happened to your ring?"

Dani reflexively strokes her ring finger and then points to the necklace around her neck.

"My hands are too swollen for nice things," Dani says dramatically, fanning her truly swollen hands around her face. She grins. "I outgrew the ring—both in size and taste. We used the diamond to make the necklace, and Peter is upgrading my ring to something more my speed now. College Dani wasn't known for her immaculate taste."

"The pear is nice," Blake says, peering at the necklace. "It's unusual."

Dani's tight-lipped smile and flash of discomfort prompts Blake to give Mal a quick panicked look, clearly worried they overstepped in complimenting one of the most powerful women in American politics. Mal grabs their hand and squeezes it to let them know it's all good. Dani said last month that she expects to chair the U.S. Senate Committee on Health, Education, Labor & Pensions, which is basically unheard of for a new senator, especially one who is as divisive as Dani.

"Thanks." Dani's voice is a bit faker than normal, though it's undetectable to Blake. Dani catches Mal's eye and flashes a weary smile before showing a photo of the new diamond.

"We're going with a cushion-cut diamond this time," she smiles exaggeratedly at Mal. "You know how I am. I can't hold onto anything for long."

"Except me," Peter says, slinging an arm over Dani's shoulder.

Again, Mal catches the strain in Dani's smile, which quickly disappears as he starts rubbing her shoulders. Dani puts a hand protectively over her bump, rubbing her thumb back and forth like she always does when she is trying to self-soothe.

"Can you believe we graduated a decade ago?" Seb emerges and absentmindedly starts fiddling with Dani's hair. Dani relaxes immediately under his care.

"We're so old." Marcus walks over, a toddler scooped up in each arm.

"Speak for yourself," Mal says. "I've never felt younger."

"It'll come for you," he jokes. "It comes for all of us."

"I think the key to youth is not having kids," Mal says. "No offense."

"I can't wait to be a dad," Peter says, bouncing a bit. "We should get the cake. I want to find out if I'm getting a lacrosse partner."

"Gender reveals are a little reductive, aren't they?" Mal asks.

"You said you would behave." Seb pinches her. "Let them celebrate Baby Greene-Leibowitz's genitalia however they want."

"The baby is kicking and wants all of you to shut up," Dani snaps.

"The lady needs carbs," Seb says dramatically. "And sugar."

He grabs a waiter to indicate that the expectant parents are ready for their big moment. Within moments, a table is whisked in front of Dani, who is nearly hidden by the towering cake. Seb picks up an errant knife and taps on his Baccarat champagne flute, signaling for attention.

"Thank you so much for coming to celebrate the newest addition to our family," Dani says from her chair. Peter kneels beside her, wielding a gleaming pie knife. "Although it's not typical for Jews to have a baby shower, we chose to have one because the last few years have robbed us of a lot of joy. Welcoming a life into the world feels like a good reason to celebrate."

The attendees whoop and cheer. A photographer snakes around the party guests as Dani and Peter, their hands intertwined, plunge the knife through the frosting. One cut. Then another. Peter takes over to slide the slice out onto a silver platter. The buttercream cake has spongy insides the color of a robin's egg. Dani and Mal lock eyes as blue and silver tinsel rain down and the partygoers shout. The baby kicks hard enough that Dani's face contorts with pain, and her hand flies to her belly.

"It's a boy!"

Mal and Dani share a look, and Mal's lip twitches into a smile. They'll have a new project, soon. Maybe this time they'll be successful, together.

THE END

ACKNOWLEDGMENTS

This book exists because of my community's investment in me and my writing. I'm so privileged to have friends and family that "yes" the hell out of me.

First and foremost, I want to thank my parents, Maria and Gary, who are my biggest cheerleaders. I would never be where I am without them. They also instilled in me a lifelong love of reading—to their detriment. I don't think they want to know how much they've spent on books over the past three decades, be it at the Scholastic Book Fair in elementary school or in Barnes & Noble last week. My sister, Jaime, gave me crucial feedback and support in the early stages of my book, despite only having read three other books in her lifetime. I'm so grateful.

My friends will tell you they deserve to be at the top of this acknowledgement. They're the ones who listen to my long-winded explanations of the editing and querying processes. One even threatened to buy my book from the bargain bin! Obviously, I adore them. There are so many people I'd like to include, but I especially want to thank (alphabetically!): Jonah Allon, who I can always count on to be 15 minutes late to our Brooklyn baklava dates so I can build in some extra writing time; Carly Avezzano, who has loved and supported me as every iteration of myself over the past 20 years; Mel DeCandia, who I've proudly shared a brain cell with over the last few years and is the epitome of a "yes, and" friend; Maris Dyer, who read my first novel and told me, in the kindest way possible, to drop it and work on something new—this book came from that permission, so thank you; Drew Friedman, who is the best college boyfriend and not at all like any of the boys in this book, and has always told me I can accomplish whatever I want; Brian Frosti, who is oftentimes my first call; Alex Green, who cried when I told her she'd be in the acknowledgements and has supported me endlessly; Jackie Levine Parrella, who may have a second coming as a book editor, if she's not too busy unionizing the beta readers; Morgan Lynch, who's one of the most well-read girlies out there and took so much care into helping me get my book ready for querying; Allison Reid, an iconic sharer of batshit stories and one of my top cheerleaders; Jamie Weissman, who will not buy my book full price but will listen to me talk ad nauseum about my publishing anxiety for hours; and Kofie Yeboah, who I'll see at Dromedary (RIP) for karaoke?

To my family—Aunt Joan; Robin, Peter, and Zack Levine (and their many, many dogs); Jill, Seth, Jess, and Jacob Levin; and Anthony, Jackie, Jana, and Dylan Parrella—thank you for always being supportive and encouraging of my writing.

I'm also grateful for my incredible beta readers, including Carmen Catena Lewis, Jenny DeCandia, Erica Grunfeld, Emily Munson, and Hannah Wojszynski, who took so much time and care with my novel. I especially want to thank Katy Stankevitz, who sent me a four-page editorial letter that I clung to for dear life as I made major revisions to my novel (they always say you never forget your first) and has been a steadfast friend throughout this publishing journey.

Lastly, my publishing team: Ashlyn Petro, Julia Diorio, Peter Carlaftes, and Kat Georges. Ashlyn, thank you for being such a bright light during the publishing process and helping get this novel to the finish line. Julia, thank you for getting my book into—and then out of—the slush pile. Peter and Kat, thank you for publishing this book. I'm so lucky.

ABOUT THE AUTHOR

AMANDA EISENBERG IS A WRITER AND adjunct professor based in Manhattan. She's the person her friends call for shoe recommendations or the best new place to eat. Amanda is an award-winning journalist whose writing has been featured in *Politico*, *InStyle* and the *Washington Post*, among other outlets. She's passionate about women's health and has written extensively on health care access and sexual misconduct before recently moving into public relations. Amanda grew up in Bergen County, New Jersey, and is a proud graduate of the University of Maryland's Philip Merrill College of Journalism. She's also an avid sports fan and rides hard for her favorite albeit cursed team, the New York Jets. *People Are Talking* is her debut novel.

RECENT AND FORTHCOMING BOOKS FROM THREE ROOMS PRESS

FICTION

Lucy Jane Bledsoe
No Stopping Us Now

Rishab Borah
The Door to Inferna

Meagan Brothers
Weird Girl and What's His Name

Christopher Chambers
Scavenger
Standalone
StreetWhys

Ebele Chizea
Aquarian Dawn

Ron Dakron
Hello Devilfish!

Ron Dakron
Hello Devilfish!

Robert Duncan
Loudmouth

Amanda Eisenberg
People Are Talking

Michael T. Fournier
Hidden Wheel
Swing State

Kate Gale
Under a Neon Sun

Aaron Hamburger
Nirvana Is Here

William Least Heat-Moon
Celestial Mechanics

Aimee Herman
Everything Grows

Kelly Ann Jacobson
Tink and Wendy
Robin and Her Misfits
Lies of the Toymaker

Jethro K. Lieberman
Everything Is Jake

Eamon Loingsigh
Light of the Diddicoy
Exile on Bridge Street

John Marshall
The Greenfather

Alvin Orloff
Vulgarian Rhapsody

Micki Janae
Of Blood and Lightning

Aram Saroyan
Still Night in L.A.

Robert Silverberg
The Face of the Waters

Stephen Spotte
Animal Wrongs

Richard Vetere
The Writers Afterlife
Champagne and Cocaine

Jessamyn Violet
Secret Rules to Being a Rockstar

Julia Watts
Quiver
Needlework
Lovesick Blossoms

Gina Yates
Narcissus Nobody

MEMOIR & BIOGRAPHY

Nassrine Azimi and Michel Wasserman
Last Boat to Yokohama: The Life and Legacy of Beate Sirota Gordon

William S. Burroughs & Allen Ginsberg
*Don't Hide the Madness:
William S. Burroughs in Conversation with Allen Ginsberg*
edited by Steven Taylor

James Carr
BAD: The Autobiography of James Carr

Judy Gumbo
Yippie Girl: Exploits in Protest and Defeating the FBI

Judith Malina
Full Moon Stages: Personal Notes from 50 Years of The Living Theatre

Phil Marcade
Punk Avenue: Inside the New York City Underground, 1972–1982

Jillian Marshall
Japanthem: Counter-Cultural Experiences; Cross-Cultural Remixes

Alvin Orloff
Disasterama! Adventures in the Queer Underground 1977–1997

Nicca Ray
Ray by Ray: A Daughter's Take on the Legend of Nicholas Ray

Stephen Spotte
*My Watery Self:
Memoirs of a Marine Scientist*

Christina Vo & Nghia M. Vo
My Vietnam, Your Vietnam
Vietnamese translation: *Việt Nam Của Con, Việt Nam Của Cha*

PHOTOGRAPHY-MEMOIR

Mike Watt
On & Off Bass

SHORT STORY ANTHOLOGIES

SINGLE AUTHOR

Alien Archives: Stories
by Robert Silverberg

First-Person Singularities: Stories
by Robert Silverberg

Tales from the Eternal Café: Stories
by Janet Hamill, intro by Patti Smith

*Time and Time Again:
Sixteen Trips in Time*
by Robert Silverberg

*The Unvarnished Gary Phillips:
A Mondo Pulp Collection*
by Gary Phillips

Voyagers: Twelve Journeys in Space and Time
by Robert Silverberg

MULTI-AUTHOR

The Colors of April
edited by Quan Manh Ha & Cab Tran

Crime + Music: Nineteen Stories of Music-Themed Noir
edited by Jim Fusilli

Dark City Lights: New York Stories
edited by Lawrence Block

The Faking of the President: Twenty Stories of White House Noir
edited by Peter Carlaftes

*Florida Happens:
Bouchercon 2018 Anthology*
edited by Greg Herren

*Have a NYC I, II & III:
New York Short Stories;*
edited by Peter Carlaftes
& Kat Georges

No Body, No Crime: Twenty-two Tales of Taylor Swift-Inspired Noir
edited by Alex Segura & Joe Clifford

*Songs of My Selfie:
An Anthology of Millennial Stories*
edited by Constance Renfrow

*The Obama Inheritance:
15 Stories of Conspiracy Noir*
edited by Gary Phillips

*This Way to the End Times:
Classic & New Stories of the Apocalypse*
edited by Robert Silverberg

DADA

Maintenant: A Journal of Contemporary Dada Writing & Art
(annual, since 2008)

MIXED MEDIA

John S. Paul
Sign Language: A Painter's Notebook
(photography, poetry and prose)

HUMOR

Peter Carlaftes
A Year on Facebook

FILM & PLAYS

Israel Horovitz
My Old Lady: Complete Stage Play and Screenplay with an Essay on Adaptation

Peter Carlaftes
Triumph For Rent (3 Plays)
Teatrophy (3 More Plays)

Kat Georges
*Three Somebodies:
Plays about Notorious Dissidents*

TRANSLATIONS

Thomas Bernhard
On Earth and in Hell
(poems of Thomas Bernhard with English translations by Peter Waugh)

Patrizia Gattaceca
Isula d'Anima / Soul Island

César Vallejo | Gerard Malanga
Malanga Chasing Vallejo

George Wallace
EOS: Abductor of Men
(selected poems in Greek & English)

ESSAYS

Richard Katrovas
*Raising Girls in Bohemia:
Meditations of an American Father*

Vanessa Baden Kelly
Far Away From Close to Home

Erin Wildermuth (editor)
Womentality

POETRY COLLECTIONS

Hala Alyan
Atrium

Peter Carlaftes
DrunkYard Dog
I Fold with the Hand I Was Dealt
Life in the Past Lane

Thomas Fucaloro
It Starts from the Belly and Blooms

Kat Georges
Our Lady of the Hunger
Awe and Other Words Like Wow

Robert Gibbons
Close to the Tree

Israel Horovitz
Heaven and Other Poems

David Lawton
Sharp Blue Stream

Jane LeCroy
Signature Play

Philip Meersman
This Is Belgian Chocolate

Jane Ormerod
Recreational Vehicles on Fire
Welcome to the Museum of Cattle

Lisa Panepinto
On This Borrowed Bike

George Wallace
Poppin' Johnny

Three Rooms Press | New York, NY | Current Catalog: www.threeroomspress.com
Three Rooms Press books are distributed by Publishers Group West: www.pgw.com